A

ROARING THUNDER

ROARING THUNDER

A Novel of the Jet Age

WALTER J. BOYNE

FORGE®

A Tom Doherty Associates Book
New York

ROARING THUNDER: A NOVEL OF THE JET AGE

Copyright © 2006 by Walter J. Boyne

This book is printed on acid-free paper.

Design by Jane Adele Regina

A Forge Book
Published by Tom Doherty Associates, LLC
175 Fifth Avenue
New York, NY 10010

www.tor.com

Forge® is a registered trademark of Tom Doherty Associates, LLC.

Library of Congress Cataloging-in-Publication Data

Boyne, Walter J. 1929–
    Roaring thunder : a novel of the jet age / Walter J. Boyne.
       p.   cm.
    ISBN 0-765-30843-6
    EAN 978-0-765-30843-6
    1. Whittle, Frank, Sir, 1907– —Fiction.   2. Johnston, A. M. (Alvin M.)—Fiction.   3. Ohain, Hans von, 1911– —Fiction.   4. Johnson, Clarence L.—Fiction.   5. Aeronautical engineers—Fiction.   6. Aircraft industry—Fiction.   7. Test pilots—Fiction.   8. Jet planes—Fiction.   9. Inventors—Fiction.   I. Title.

    PS3552.O937 R63   2006
    813'.54—dc22

                                                                2005015689

First Edition: January 2006

Printed in the United States of America

0 9 8 7 6 5 4 3 2 1

THIS BOOK IS DEDICATED TO SIR FRANK WHITTLE,
HANS VON OHAIN, ANSELM FRANZ,
AND NATHAN PRICE—ALL GIANTS OF THE JET AGE.

ROARING THUNDER

Germany protests over maltreatment of ethnic Germans in Poland; Great Britain and France pledge to come to Poland's aid in the event of war; Germany and Soviet Union announce non-aggression pact; **The Grapes of Wrath** *published in the United States; Pan Am begins regularly scheduled flights between the United States and Europe; Igor Sikorsky constructs helicopter.*

CHAPTER ONE

August 27, 1939, Marienehe, Germany

The turgid waters of the Warnow River lapped at the stone-covered beach, the gentle gurgling muffled by the dense fog spreading its tendrils deep over the grassy flying field. A thousand yards away five men worked feverishly in the yellow light billowing from the "Special Project" hangar doors, checking the small, almost dainty aircraft they had just rolled out. Cautiously, as if they were handling a live bomb, they wrestled the plane into a 180-degree turn so that the odd circular hole at the end of the fuselage pointed out toward the river.

Fritz Obermyer sat on the edge of the Fiat Toppolino's tiny running board, his 120 kilograms of muscle and fat tipping the car, suppressing its springs, and sending the glow of its headlights at a cockeyed angle. Obermyer drew deeply on the stub of a cigarette, felt its warmth flare beneath his nose, then carefully dropped it beside him, grinding it into the tarmac with his foot.

He nudged his companion and pointed. "Look at him. When he came here three years ago, a little snot-nosed graduate student from Göttingen, I thought he was crazy."

Gerd Müller, short, lean, and wiry, stretched and laughed. "You tried to give him a hard time, Fritz, but he drove you crazy being polite. No matter what you said—or what you wrote on the wall in the latrine—he never lost his temper."

As *Frontsoldaten*, they were accustomed to discomfort and waiting, and the long hours spent at the field meant nothing to them. Obermyer had left the Berlin Institute of Technology to volunteer for the army in August 1914. Now he was nominally a machinist foreman in the new plant building the Heinkel He 111 bomber. A forceful personality, he had used an artful combination of his engineering training and his Nazi Party connections to become accepted as an aide to Ernst Heinkel himself. Heinkel was at first quite resistant to the idea but over time, as Obermyer's talents became obvious, welcomed his assistance.

Heinkel found that he could depend upon Obermyer to know what was happening on the factory floor, in the long rows of drafting tables, and in the local Nazi Party headquarters, usually long before anyone else was aware of it. The information was often invaluable, and within a few months of his employment, Heinkel looked upon Obermyer as an indispensable political divining rod. Müller was an excellent machinist but had been attached to Obermyer—at his insistence—as an assistant.

The arrangement suited the plant management, who saw Obermyer and Müller as agitators. They were glad to have them off the factory floor and worried each time Obermyer came through, acting as if he were the local feudal lord, gathering information and dispensing favors. They, like Heinkel, knew better than to protest. The firm was already at odds with the government, and everyone wanted to avoid any further difficulties with the Nazi Party. When Obermyer suggested that he be attached to the Special Project organization, Heinkel acquiesced—the more sensitive a project was, the more hazardous it was to raise a political issue.

Obermyer could intimidate most people with a glance; stone-cold gray eyes gleamed from his cruelly scarred face, and he walked as he had for four years in the trenches, bent over, moving with a menacing hunched step that made it seem as if he was about to leap on his prey. Yet he was also an able humorist, able to prick egos with the little two-line poems he wrote on the mirrors of the noisome latrines of the Heinkel Aircraft Works factory. He wasn't always malicious but was usually apt, and the workers waited as eagerly for his latest poem as some of them might wait for the latest joke on the Nazi Party. He wrote those occasionally, too, just to see who laughed and to make a note of it. He wielded his party membership just as he had used his role as a quartermaster sergeant in the Roehlk *Freikorps* after the war—to his own advantage. And while most Nazis bragged about their low party membership numbers, confirming their early support for Hitler, Obermyer's reputation was built on the decisive action he had taken in 1934 during the "Night of the Long Knives" when Adolf Hitler had squelched a Brownshirt revolution and executed Ernst Roehm. When one of Roehm's none-too-alert bodyguards had attempted to sound the alarm, Obermyer had cut him down with a single slash of his favorite brawling tool, a razor-sharp trench shovel. From that night on he was an icon in the party, a symbol of action and loyalty to the Führer. But far from being a convinced Nazi, Obermyer was an opportunist, pure and simple, intent on looking out for his own interests at all times.

Müller was an old comrade, a companion in adversity in the trenches, where they had not only saved each other's lives but, more important, saved each other's sanity as well. No matter how desperate things became, no matter how short on food or how bad the morale, they each had the other to rely upon. They were inseparable, with Müller content to follow where Obermyer led, ready always to do what he said. Müller had once made a joking threat to some of the Heinkel workers, saying, "Obermyer is the brains and I'm the muscle." Obermyer heard him and interjected, "I'm the brains and he's the stomach." Both men were correct.

In July 1918, Müller had watched Obermyer save another life, that of a twenty-year-old new recruit in a sappers' battalion. They were in a just conquered French village behind the line of German advance. The young soldier was engaged in loading mortar shells from an abandoned truck into a horse-drawn sled when Obermyer had grabbed him by the neck and tossed him into a shell hole and fallen on him. In the next instant four 105mm artillery shells landed, one detonating the mortar shells and blowing the truck, horse, and sled to atoms.

The old soldier in Obermyer had heard the inbound whistle, judged the accuracy of the artillery, and acted accordingly. The young recruit, Willy Messerschmitt, was profoundly grateful.

By 1937, Obermyer had worked for Heinkel for three years when he contrived a meeting with Messerschmitt, a rising star in German aviation. Obermyer reminded him of their first meeting, suggesting that Messerschmitt might like to have a man inside the Heinkel plant to "keep an eye on things." As grateful as Messerschmitt was to Obermyer for saving his life, he was repelled by the suggestion.

Yet things were difficult for him. The State Secretary for Air, Erhard Milch, hated him, for he had lost a close friend when one of Messerschmitt's Me 20 early passenger transports had crashed because of a manufacturing defect. The feud continued over the years and Milch had repeatedly denied him contracts. At the time of their meeting, Heinkel and Messerschmitt were engaged in a bitter competition to build the Luftwaffe's next fighter, and, given Milch's attitude toward him, Messerschmitt knew that he needed all the help he could get. They made a verbal agreement, never yet breached, that Obermyer would supply important inside information on Heinkel projects directly to Messerschmitt himself, in return for a sizable monthly cash stipend. So far it had worked well, particularly in the fighter competition. Messerschmitt valued Obermyer's carefully collected estimates on the man-hours required to build the Heinkel 112, for these were far higher than Messerschmitt's Bf 109 required. Messerschmitt used the figures with devastating results in his proposal and believed that they had done much to win the competition for him, even though his aircraft was both faster and more maneuverable.

Obermyer had long since found that being disliked in a position of relative power had its advantages. No one ever objected when he proposed that he attend a conference, even those held in other European countries—they were glad to have him away from the factory. Because of his background, he preferred engineering conferences, although an international air show was almost as satisfactory. Two or three times a year, depending upon the business climate, he would travel to conferences where he met representatives of companies in other countries. Almost invariably, he would find among them someone who was willing to pay for information. His latest contact was the firm of Marcel Bloch, which built handsome fighters for France and needed information on the gear retraction system Heinkel had used in the high-speed He 70 "Blitz." He preferred to be paid in English sterling but would accept good information in exchange, as long as he believed he could sell it elsewhere.

Now Müller and Obermyer watched as the twenty-seven-year-old physics specialist von Ohain bounded around the little He 178, peering like a mother hen over the shoulders of the men preparing it for flight. Coatless, Dr. Pabst Hans von Ohain was oblivious to the cold, totally absorbed in the last-minute adjustments to the engine he had created from his imagination and three years of hard work. He had seen his dream move from his ideal of a noiseless, part-less engine to a ferocious whirling combination of heat, sound, and thrust, more than four hundred kilograms of it.

Von Ohain moved like a shadow to Max Hahn, the brilliant mechanic who transformed von Ohain's ideas into the complex assembly of sheet metal and steel castings that formed the primitive jet engine, more than seven meters long, nestling inside the aircraft's fuselage.

"He took my joking well." Obermyer looked at von Ohain's tall, slender figure with approval. "If Warsitz can keep from crashing this crate, young Hans will be a rich man someday."

Müller picked up a stick and began knocking mud from his boots. He and most of the Special Project team had spent the two previous days tramping up and down the field, tamping down high spots and filling in shallow depressions, to make sure there were no problems on takeoff.

"Better save that stick for the birds, Gerd." Obermyer snorted. Yesterday, on an early-morning taxi test, the jet engine had sucked a seagull into the intake, forcing an immediate shutdown. They had to push the airplane all the way back to the hangar, disassemble the engine, pluck out the bits of raw and cooked seagull, then put the engine back together. There was no apparent damage, but it added to the morning's uncertainty and to the intensity of the inspection.

Everything had to be ready for the big moment when Professor Ernst Heinkel himself arrived in his custom-bodied Mercedes. Short, dark, his face dominated by an oversize nose that seemed to overflow his spectacles, Heinkel had been a prime mover in German aviation since the 1914–18 war, designing and building many of the most important aircraft used by the German and Austro-Hungarian air forces. In 1933, he'd been persuaded to build a new factory for three thousand employees in Rostock. Now it employed five times that number and was overflowing into the Marienehe suburb, turning out dozens of twin-engine He 111 bombers every month. The main factory buildings, beautifully aligned, gleaming with acres of windows, were a stark contrast to the ramshackle secret hangar housing von Ohain's creation.

Heinkel was a canny businessman. Recognizing that he was of the wood, wire, and fabric era, he hired the best people he could find as he pushed forward with sleek, all-metal aircraft. He was ambitious and longed to expand his interests to include an engine factory, as Hugo Junkers had done. There was no chance that the Air Ministry would give Heinkel the license and the materials to enter the piston engine market, but this new jet engine of von Ohain's was a different matter. The deferential young physicist, so polite that he seemed more like a choirboy than a genius, had convinced him that turbine-jet engines could be built that would outperform piston engines. More important, von Ohain had convinced him that they could be built more cheaply, using relatively inexpensive conventional equipment, and could be developed far more quickly. This morning would prove whether von Ohain was right or not.

At the edge of the tiny field, Müller shivered. It was cold for late August, and all of them had been there since three o'clock. "Is the movie-star test pilot here yet?"

"No, he's probably kissing some pretty little secretary good-bye. He lives a pretty hectic life." As they spoke, a black Horch drove up and the test pilot, Erich Warsitz, popped out. Even though he was six feet tall, blond, handsome, and talented, Warsitz was still popular with the rough-hewn factory crew because he was so matter-of-fact about risking his life testing the most advanced—and implicitly dangerous—Heinkel planes.

Müller fumbled in his pocket, producing a knife and a sausage wrapped in paper. He sliced two thick pieces of sausage, handed one to Obermyer at the point of his knife, and held the other in his hand; it was a familiar gesture, first practiced twenty years ago, when they were starving teenage soldiers together. Müller had sworn never to go hungry again and ate as much as he could whenever he could, never gaining an ounce of weight.

"I don't blame him—a short life but a merry one. He damn near killed himself just last June, flying the rocket plane. He takes too many chances."

They watched as Warsitz, swinging a good-sized hammer by its handle, joined the group at the hangar.

"Good morning, Dr. von Ohain; are we going to fly this morning?"

"Yes, Herr Warsitz, as soon as Professor Heinkel arrives—and the fog lifts. First, we are going to test run the engine." Smiling, he pointed at the hammer, saying, "I see you have your patented escape equipment in hand."

Warsitz nodded uneasily. He still was not entirely accustomed to aircraft with canopies, preferring open cockpit planes, where if you had trouble you could go over the side in an instant. The hammer was for breaking his way through the canopy if it jammed. Despite his cool test pilot demeanor, he was well aware of the danger. Earlier in the month he had made a short series of taxi tests and actually "hopped" the experimental jet plane off the short runway for brief, straight-ahead flights. He was convinced that the He 178 was the door to the future—but he knew it could easily be his coffin as well, for it embodied so many untested ideas.

Normally companies tested new airframes and new engines separately. They would fly a new engine in an old design to test it or fly an established engine in a new airframe for the same reasons. But the

He 178 was a new airplane and a new engine—and that was doubly dangerous. That morning, for the first time in his test-flying career, Warsitz had left behind a letter to be forwarded to his parents if anything had happened. More telling, he had made a special good-bye to his beloved dachshund, Max.

"I'd like to do some more taxi tests before we fly—I'm still not satisfied with the brakes."

"Of course. We'll do a quick test run, then turn it over to you."

Warsitz and von Ohain companionably walked around the aircraft, looking at it with two widely divergent views. To von Ohain the airplane was just a vessel for his engine, no more important than a packing box. To Warsitz it was, like all airplanes, a thing of beauty that must be courted and also feared. He drew tactile pleasure from running his hand over the surface of the airplane, enjoying its aesthetics, letting its curves speak to him. The plane was simple, with smooth lines, totally functional, exactly what he liked in a design. He dropped down and squatted, letting his eyes look over the entire aircraft, seeking leaking fluids, incipient cracks, loose nuts and bolts, or any other untoward signs that might compromise safety.

"I understand that the bird did not damage the engine?"

"No. We disassembled it, balanced all the parts, and checked for cracks. The only thing we had to do was clean it."

Von Ohain glanced closely at Warsitz's face and went on somewhat anxiously, "It might have been worse in a conventional plane; the bird would have broken a wooden propeller, and perhaps even damaged a metal one."

Warsitz nodded and smiled, patting von Ohain on the back, knowing how proud he was of his engine. "Well, shall we get started?"

Von Ohain nodded to Hahn, and they brought a cylinder of compressed hydrogen over to start the engine. From a distance, Obermyer saw the group scatter, leaving only von Ohain and Hahn at the aircraft. Even as he moved away to stand behind the Fiat he said, "They're scared of the hydrogen. Ever since the *Hindenburg*, everyone expects hydrogen to blow up. It's no more dangerous than acetylene or gasoline, if you know how to handle it."

Hahn could have tested the engine up by himself, but von Ohain stayed with him for moral support. Von Ohain's desire for privacy to think out his engineering problems had evolved an unusual method of dealing with people. Rather than being withdrawn or abstracted, he related to each person as closely as possible on their terms, trying to establish contact on their ground, and by extension removing them from his. He treated everyone with the same consideration and courtesy, whether it was the guard at the gate or Dr. Heinkel himself.

To von Ohain, every run of his engine was as dangerous as the headlong plunges he had taken while skiing in the Harz Mountains and the hydrogen priming was the least of it. Over the course of his three years of testing, he learned that jet engines could explode in many ways, rarely with any warning. The temperatures and the turbine speeds were so high so that anything could go wrong, from an explosion when the gasoline was injected to the turbine blades flying loose. But when it ran sweetly, it was a joy, a smooth, quiet roar of power that von Ohain knew was the sound of a new era in aviation, one he had brought about in just three years with a small team of experts and a few hundred thousand marks of Ernst Heinkel's money.

Hahn was in the cockpit, gently pushing the throttle forward, then retarding it, the Heinkel He S 3 jet engine docilely responding, the spurt of flame and the noise rising and falling in concert. Von Ohain nodded, and Hahn shut the engine down.

"Let's inspect it once more, then let Herr Warsitz do his taxi tests before the Professor arrives."

The early-morning sun sent its welcome warmth from the dark blue sky, slowly dissipating the fog from the hard-surfaced areas of the field first.

Warsitz shoehorned his lanky body into the tiny cockpit and methodically went through the standard control checks before signaling to von Ohain that he was ready for the engine start. The cockpit was stark, with fewer than a third of the instruments of the Heinkel 112 fighter he had flown the day before. They did not need many instruments—all he had to do was get the aircraft airborne, fly it around, and land; that would be enough to prove that the jet engine worked.

Obermyer watched from the sidelines as Warsitz allowed the jet to run forward for one hundred meters. It slowed abruptly and then began drifting to the left, threatening to collapse the gear and end the test—and perhaps the entire jet engine experiment—on the spot. The ground crew was already running toward the airplane when Warsitz regained control and taxied back to the hangar, his concerned expression saying it all.

Hahn and three mechanics swarmed over the He 178, and Warsitz tried it again just as Heinkel's big Mercedes limousine pulled in. The taxi test was satisfactory this time, and Warsitz stayed in the cockpit as the aircraft was refueled. More agile than he looked, Heinkel climbed up the ladder next to the cockpit to shake Warsitz's hand and give him the traditional "break a leg" good-luck wish.

The flight meant much to Heinkel. With the exception of a very few important people such as Ernst Udet, Heinkel was persona non grata with the Nazi Party, in part because he looked so much like the Nazi cartoon stereotypes of Jewish plutocrats, in part because he had fought so hard to retain Jewish workers, particularly engineers, while the government insisted that they be purged. If Warsitz demonstrated that the jet engine actually worked, that this simple, inexpensive power plant could propel a plane through the air, Heinkel could get the backing to buy a factory to manufacture them, and he would build Heinkel aircraft powered by Heinkel engines. If it failed, he was once again at the mercy of the idiots at the Air Ministry, men so foolish that they demanded every bomber, no matter how big, be a dive-bomber.

Von Ohain and Hahn walked cautiously around the airplane for perhaps the twentieth time that day, peering into the air intake, popping open a few panels and inspecting inside, then carefully feeling along the bottom of the aircraft to be sure that no fuel was leaking.

With an impatient nod, Warsitz signaled to start the engine. There was a momentary hesitation, then a sudden blowtorch roar as the engine caught on and advanced to idle speed. Warsitz checked the engine temperature gauge, the fuel pressure, the oil pressure, and finally, satisfied with the readings, waved to von Ohain and motioned for the chocks to be pulled from in front of the wheels.

Warsitz was apprehensive. He had a sense of the plane from the taxi-test hops, but this would be the first real flight in a brand-new airplane, unlike any that he had ever flown before. His big hands held the stick back in his lap and moved the throttle full forward. The tiny jet moved, slowly at first, then more swiftly, and he relaxed back pressure, allowing the tail to come up. Without a propeller, there was none of the customary torque that was so dangerous in piston-engine-powered fighters, and the little He 178 moved over the grass, straight as a die. The noise of the jet was subdued compared to that of the aircraft with powerful piston engines Warsitz had flown recently, so quiet that he wondered if it was producing the necessary power. He passed the tiny white flag that marked the 100-meter point, then felt the plane begin to come alive, moving more lightly on its gear, accelerating as it passed the 200-meter mark, the noise of the engine seeming to decrease, and then, almost instantaneously, at the 300-meter mark the airplane broke ground, transforming into a silent missile being sling-shot upward, hurtling toward the temporary redline speed of 600 kilometers per hour. He tried to raise the landing gear, but nothing happened.

On the ground, von Ohain had stood transfixed as the tiny monoplane rumbled forward, barely accelerating, so that it seemed to take forever before Warsitz pulled it from the ground. A cheer went up as Warsitz climbed steeply to 2,000 feet. Von Ohain whirled to glare at the crowd—the flight would not be a success until Warsitz was back safely on the ground.

Inside the cockpit, perspiring heavily now, Warsitz slowed down and tried again to retract the landing gear, which was operated by compressed air. When the attempt failed, he decided to leave the gear down and land after only one circuit of the airfield. The airplane was nose-heavy, and Warsitz had to maintain back pressure on the stick when he throttled back to hold 600 kilometers per hour on the airspeed indicator, keeping the field in sight, wanting now only to get the airplane down safely to the ground. He turned to the final approach, reduced power, and kept feeding in back pressure until the wheels touched down at the very edge of the field with a gentle thump. He bounced once, recovered, then rolled out smoothly, pushing the canopy back before taxiing in.

Von Ohain joined in the cheering as Heinkel grabbed him by the shoulder, screaming, "Congratulations, Dr. von Ohain. This is the world's first flight in a turbine-powered aircraft! I'm going to make you a very rich man!"

The nose of the little silver He 178 bobbed up and down as it taxied across the rough grass field, to be met by Heinkel and von Ohain leading the entire Special Project team and a pack of excited engineers and maintenance workers.

Warsitz lifted himself out of the cockpit, shook hands with Heinkel and von Ohain, and said just, "Nose-heavy," to Hahn. The fuel was topped off as Hahn and the team of Heinkel mechanics adjusted the stabilizer. Warsitz carefully checked the landing gear system—there was no apparent anomaly, but he decided to have a down lock installed and just leave the gear extended on the next flights.

Calmer now, Warsitz took off again. The trim was now satisfactory and the little airplane flew almost hands off, requiring just a caress on the controls to keep it flying straight and level. He made a half-dozen passes around the field before coming in to refuel.

He talked excitedly to von Ohain and Heinkel, finally persuading them to let him make one last flight, longer than the others, to get a better check on fuel consumption. The takeoff was uneventful and he flew straight to Warenemunde on the Baltic Sea, a fifty-mile flight that he knew ran the little plane close to its range limits.

As his apprehensions subsided, Warsitz felt a growing elation in flying the strangely quiet aircraft, so different from the noisy racket of a conventional fighter. Looking at the altimeter, he realized it was stuck, not moving. He tapped it and it leaped to indicate five hundred meters.

"Ah, no vibration. So quiet the instruments stick!" Recalling the pre-flight briefing, he kept the airspeed just under 600 kilometers per hour. The controls were featherlight, and he rocked the wings back and forth, contemplating rolling the airplane but knowing better than to risk such a move on the first test flight. By now he was comfortable enough to take his eyes off the instrument panel and look out to his right over the whitecapped Baltic to see the local fishing fleet moving toward its station, and then back left to the town of Warnemunde. Defiant, Warsitz flew low over the Arado aircraft plant, in a gross violation of Heinkel's passion for secrecy. Warsitz knew the test pilots there and wanted to give them something to talk about.

Warsitz then banked back toward Marinehe, where von Ohain and Heinkel, acutely aware of the aircraft's limited range, were already feeling a sudden surge of fear that things had gone too well and that trouble was brewing.

Their fears were drowned in the excited buzz that grew as the little jet whistled in from the north, then soared again when they realized Warsitz was too high to land without making another circuit.

Inside the cockpit, sweating profusely again, the test pilot pressed his head against the canopy to keep the field in sight. As he positioned himself to make one high pass over the field, then come in and land, the engine cut out briefly before resuming its song of power. Knowing he was short on fuel and confident in his mastery of the aircraft, Warsitz did not hesitate, side-slipping the new plane to shed altitude swiftly. Heinkel and von Ohain gasped and started forward, their hearts pumping, as the little monoplane slipped steeply earthward, to recover just at the edge of the field, touching down smoothly and rolling in to the jubilant waiting crowd. It was masterly, heart-wrenching flying—few others could have pulled it off.

Heinkel, tears streaming down his face, turned and embraced von Ohain, saying, "You have just given birth to the jet age."

Obermyer and Müller pulled away from the crowd. They had helped set up the celebratory feast that was to follow. There would be plenty of champagne (minus, of course, the case Obermyer had slipped into the back of his car) and both men intended to arrive early.

"Well, Fritz, as you said, von Ohain will probably become a rich man from this. And Heinkel, too."

"They will not be the only ones, Gerd. I believe I can think of ways that will let us profit as well."

"It didn't look like much to me. Just whoosh, up and down—no guns, no bombs, nothing."

"Gerd, let me tell you something. Sometimes an avalanche starts with a single rolling snowball. We just saw the snowball."

THE PASSING SCENE

President Roosevelt elected to third term. Germany scores tremendous victories over Poland, Denmark, Norway, Luxembourg, Belgium, France, but is defeated in the Battle of Britain; U-boats winning Battle of the Atlantic; Japan takes control of French Indochina; Lend-Lease bill signed; Grand Coulee Dam begins operations; Whirlaway wins racing's Triple Crown.

CHAPTER TWO

July 19, 1941, Burbank Airport

Amused, Vance Shannon watched the immaculately groomed chairman of the Lockheed Aircraft Corporation stare fixedly out the big double window, watching the work crews disassemble the grandstand in front of the hangar-style doors of Plant A-1. On that spot the day before, Robert Ellsworth Gross had presided over the ceremonies in which Lord and Lady Halifax accepted delivery of the one thousandth Lockheed Hudson bomber to the Royal Air Force. On the seventeenth, Big Bill Knudsen, Chief of the Office of Production Management, had inspected the P-38 assembly line, where the twin-engine, twin-boom Lightnings were beginning to roll off at a satisfactory rate. Employment had reached thirty thousand, profits were up, new aircraft were in the works, and still Gross was not satisfied. He never was, and that's why Lockheed was doing so well.

Lockheed's leader bit his lip in his characteristic worrywart expression as Shannon contrasted his own rumpled suit, store-bought at Sears, with the Savile Row suits that Gross invariably wore, thinking there might be a lesson there somewhere. Gross's silence and inattention were unusual. Normally he was the soul of courtesy, making every guest welcome, even consultants like Shannon, who were maintained on costly retainers.

At last Gross turned, smiling, and said, "I'm sorry, Vance. Caught up in some GFE problems."

GFE—government-furnished equipment—was almost always a problem, and it usually erased any savings the government got by buying in quantity by creating problems that contractors had to solve. Shannon knew about this one—the GFE carburetors for the P-38's Allison engines were having problems with cold weather. Maybe that's what Gross wanted to talk about. Probably not—too mundane.

Of middle height, Gross was the Adolph Menjou of the aircraft industry, always dapper, friendly, and invariably courteous, even to such chronic pains in the neck as George Putnam, Amelia Earhart's widower. Gross had purchased the original bankrupt Lockheed Company in 1932 and turned it from making the wooden single-engine Vegas to building fast, twin-engine all-metal transports for the smaller airlines. Like other aircraft firms, Lockheed had struggled during the depression, but the European War had saved it. An initial order from Great Britain for 250 Hudsons, the military version of their Model 14 airliner, became a money mill. The Hudson quickly proved itself in combat, and Lockheed was tasked to build as many as it could turn out.

"Are you still doing any test flying, Vance?" There was respect in Gross's voice, for Shannon had been, with Eddie Allen and Bill McCoy, one of the top civilian test pilots in the country. When a new design was coming along, companies would call Shannon in early to get his ideas, then sign him up to be the test pilot. He had made the first flights in hundreds of aircraft, military and civilian, all over the country—and commanded a healthy price for doing so. It always bothered him that he had a reputation for daring, for flying anything with wings. It wasn't so. He calculated the risks on every flight and had refused many when the odds didn't seem right. But when the odds were right, even if just by a hair, he'd fly, and he had always succeeded. Until the last one.

Shannon flushed. "Not since the accident, Bob. I just haven't felt ready." Six months before, Shannon had been testing a new trainer, built of Duramold, the plasticized wood product that the veteran engineer Virginius Clark had developed. A wing had come off in a dive, and Shannon had barely made it over the side, his parachute popping open just fifty feet off the ground. He wouldn't admit it, but he was having trouble getting up the side of an airplane into the cockpit—just too many aches and pains remaining from the jump and the subsequent hard landing on a dirt field.

"It's time you stopped, anyway—you are far too valuable to be jumping out of airplanes." They laughed, somewhat ruefully, and Gross went on. "Vance, you know Nate Price and Kelly Johnson, don't you?"

Shannon nodded; the two men were fantastic engineers, both geniuses, with Nate a little less disciplined and perhaps even more imaginative than Kelly. He knew they had difficulty working together. Kelly was too assertive. As a young man, fresh out of Michigan State and brand-new to Lockheed, he had shaken older, more experienced engineers with his insights and a manner that bordered just on the wrong side of arrogance. The difficulty for the older engineers was that Kelly was always right, and now, at thirty-one, he was the dominant—but not the chief—engineer at Lockheed. Price was more withdrawn but very stubborn, always insistent on doing things his way. As partners, they inevitably had trouble.

"Sure. I worked with them a bit on the multi-seat fighter project—the competition the Bell Airacuda won."

Both men were silent. Gross hated losing any competition, especially this one, where the airplane the Air Corps selected as winner turned out to be a total failure. Shannon was quiet because he had not been able to get along with either Price or Johnson. They were just too bright, too full of themselves, to permit an outsider to horn in.

"Isn't Price one of your protégés?"

Gross winced; he knew he had a reputation for hiring maverick engineers he believed in, then giving them their head, not tasking them with assignments unless they wanted them, and allowing them to work however they wished. It was unusual in the economy-minded aviation industry. He knew that it upset most of the other engineers, who were conventional thinkers for the most part, and it upset all of the accountants, who hated to have a worker without fixed tasks for charging time and overhead.

"Yes, I give Nate a lot of leeway, just as I do Kelly, but it might be paying off." He paused for a moment, then asked, "What do you know about turbine engines for aircraft?"

Shannon stirred in the big green leather chair. This was more like it. His whole body came alive as he leaned forward, broad fingers grasping the arms of the chair, blue eyes bright with interest, a confiding half smile registering. This was wine for his soul, a peek into the future; it was what he lived for, the constant quest to please clients by doing a good job.

But it was dangerous territory. The U.S. Army Air Corps called on his talents, too, and the latest request had come straight from the top, from his old friend Major General Henry H. "Hap" Arnold, who wanted him to oversee the transfer of information on the new British turbine jet engine to the United States. It was top secret, and Shannon could not even talk about it to Gross, a trusted friend.

"Hap" Arnold was big, bluff, hearty, and always smiling in public, but in private he was an irascible boss who often demanded more results than could be delivered and always wanted them yesterday. After long service and some real political brawls, he now commanded Army aviation. Arnold was not much of an engineer himself, but he was nonetheless a visionary, always reaching for the latest technology and finding the top scientists to help him. Arnold found that he could talk in lay terms to Shannon, who could translate them into the appropriate engineering phrases. As a result, Arnold called him in on almost every project, some top secret and incredibly important, others just run-of-the-mill, but of interest to Arnold.

Shannon started slow, feeling his way. He would never willingly betray a confidence, but he knew how intelligent and well-informed Gross was and how quickly he could make the correct inference from the most casual remark. "Well, I've been following the developments in Germany, Italy, and England."

Gross knew what he meant. They all read the technical journals and had foreign reviews, such as *Flugsport*, translated. But the real information came chiefly from the inner circle of military attachés, all of whom carried on as much covert activity as they could. They were always closemouthed about U.S. secrets, of course, but could be depended upon to reveal what they learned about foreign technology.

"I don't have much on what's happening in Germany, outside of the fact that there are two or three companies—Junkers, Heinkel, and maybe BMW—experimenting. You've heard that they flew a turbine jet, a Heinkel, a couple of years ago. I understand Heinkel is building a twin-engine fighter, but there's nothing concrete about it coming in."

"Vance, this is something I need to talk to you about, completely off-the-record. I only do it to because I trust you, and you need to know. Don't tell anyone, not even anyone in the Air Corps, about this, please. It is quite literally a matter of life and death."

Shannon was impressed. Gross was clearly distressed, as if he were about to confess a fearful crime. He was noted in the industry for his integrity—when there had been a problem with his Lodestar airliners, he immediately took all responsibility and had Lockheed pay for all the necessary repairs. To see him in such a state was alarming.

"I'm afraid that what I've done might tarnish Lockheed's name. The fact is that I have a paid informant—spy, that's the only thing you can call it—in Germany. He has kept me informed through our Swiss office about developments in German aviation. I don't know how he does it, but he gets me material from Heinkel and even from Messerschmitt on jet engines and planes that you would not believe."

Vance was stunned. Just knowing this compromised him.

Gross saw his discomfort and went on. "I've done only one thing to protect myself. I went directly to J. Edgar Hoover and told him about it before I began. He is fanatically anti-Nazi, and he encouraged me. But that's my only lifeline. If something would happen to him, I know I could go to jail for employing a foreign national for something like this."

"How did you get in contact with him?"

"That, I cannot tell even you, Vance. He made contact with one of our people during the Volta conference at Rome in 1935. That's all I'll say, except that I know enough now that we had better get started on turbine power, or we'll be hopelessly behind. Now, tell me what you know."

"I guess it's secret-trading time, Bob." He paused, his stomach growling as the clock neared eleven. Shannon was a big eater, and he'd missed breakfast today in his hurry to get to Gross's office. He knew that he had to be careful with the next bit, as it dealt with his Air Corps contract. Shannon took a sip of coffee, wishing that Gross had put out his usual spread of pastries, and went on. "We know that the British Air Ministry published the patent of a jet engine by some RAF serving officer, his name escapes me for the moment, and Italy is flying a primitive jet, the Caproni Campini. I don't think the Italian job worked out; I haven't heard anything on it. It was in all the papers for a while, making a big to-do about flying without a propeller."

Gross nodded. "That's what our man said. We've had some other reports back from Germany, as well. Lindbergh's visits created a lot of contacts with some people not too happy with Hitler, and they've been talking—some for a price. The most important thing about what they say is that they pretty well corroborate our informant." He looked pained and corrected himself. "My informant. I have not told anyone but Hoover and you, not even Courtie."

Courtlandt Sherrington Gross was his brother, his confidant, his adviser. If Bob Gross had not told Courtie, then Shannon knew how heavily the secret weighed on him.

Considering carefully how to phrase what needed to be said, Shannon went on. "As you must know by now, the Germans have flown a rocket plane and a jet, too, both by Heinkel. For some reason, they seem to be on the back burner right now, and I hope they stay there. We dug out the British patent—had to get it translated from *Flugsport*, by the way, couldn't find the British originals—and we know the Royal Air Force flew a jet by Gloster on May 15 of this year. It had what they call the Whittle engine, after the RAF pilot who invented it. General Arnold is very interested in it."

Shannon squirmed inwardly—Arnold was indeed interested. He decided that he would have to at least let Gross know that he had another connection to the subject.

Gross refilled their coffee cups, saying, "Well, we are interested, too. That's why I've asked you here. Nate Price has come up with a design for a jet engine, and he and Kelly have worked out a plane to fly it in. It would be a fighter, and they claim it will fly at six hundred mph."

Shannon whistled. "Pretty sensational if it works."

"I know. It is revolutionary. But I need an outsider's opinion on whether to let them proceed with it or not. Lord knows we have enough to do now, but we have to look ahead. What's your take on jet engines?"

"Well, let me say two things first. One I can only give you a hint about, just a heads-up, and that is that Arnold has filled me in more on the English turbine than I can tell you. Don't ask me any more; I've probably gone too far telling you even that. And then, I must tell you that neither Kelly nor Nate will be very happy about your asking me to evaluate their program. They both think they are smarter than I am, and they're probably right. Besides, we didn't exactly get along on the other project."

"I'm not surprised that Arnold has tapped you for information—you've been in on all the major Air Corps projects for years. By the way, it's not the Air Corps anymore—as of last month, it's the U.S. Army Air Forces."

Shannon nodded. "It'll take some getting used to."

Gross went on, "As for Nate and Kelly, I don't care what they think, Vance; I've known you a long time, and I know you'll give me an objective answer. I'd ask internally, but Kelly is so smart and has such a powerful personality that he has the other engineers intimidated, even Hall Hibbard and Willis Hawkins, and he'd get an automatic thumbs-up. So what do you think?"

"All I know right now is that most people think the jet is impractical—that it requires too much fuel and is too heavy."

Gross nodded. "Yes, but we have problems with piston engines, too. They take forever to develop—the Allison has been in work for more than ten years and still is not fully matured. I've seen studies on many of the big new engines—and there are at least half a dozen of them—and they are becoming much too complex. They have to have intercoolers and turbo superchargers and fuel injectors and everything adds weight and bulk and maintenance hours. Besides that, propellers are already giving us trouble, with their tips going supersonic. We need to find something to replace them."

Shannon was struck by Gross's vehemence; normally he spoke in crisp, short sentences, keeping his tone warm and personal, never emotionally charged. This was clearly an important subject to him, and he was absolutely right in thinking so.

"I'll be glad to work with you on it, Bob, as long as it doesn't put me crosswise with Hap. I'll have to use my best judgment on that. But do you have the space and the equipment to build engines? They are not like airplanes; you can't just rivet sheet metal together and fly them away."

"No, I would go somewhere else, Menasco, maybe, to build the engines, but we could easily build the airframes. The Hudson will probably phase out in a year or two, and we need to have something to follow the P-38."

As he spoke the roar of twin Allison engines split the air and a P-38 came roaring down the runway, fifty feet off the ground, then pulling back in soaring climb that took it out of sight in the bright blue California sky.

Gross shook his head. "Tony LeVier. He thinks he's racing at Cleveland. The CAA is going to get him someday."

"Don't worry about Tony; he has more friends than sense, and if the CAA came over, they'd just want his autograph." Tony was just a "new guy" compared to Shannon, whose flying career went back to the Great War, where he had scored his fifth victory on November 8, 1918, becoming an ace just three days before the war ended. But both Shannon and LeVier had worked with John Nagel at the old Los Angeles East Side airport, and both men knew how to stretch a glide and stretch a dollar.

Grinning in agreement, Gross handed Shannon a briefcase bulging with papers. Some were pushing out the top, their borders cluttered with notes and columns of figures. He recognized the feathery, involved drawing style of Nate Price. Kelly Johnson's drawings were always smaller, almost miniatures, and very precise, done in a spidery style that seemed to say he sought economy in everything, even paper and ink.

"Take this along and study it tonight and tomorrow, and come see me again on Monday, if you can."

"Is this stuff classified? Will I get stopped by the guards?"

"No, it's not classified yet—we've not even shown it to the local government representatives. But it is proprietary, of course. I'll escort you to your car myself, so no one will stop you. And I need to have it all back Monday morning. Don't copy any of it, and try to keep it as much in order as you can."

Shannon understood. Gross had received the material from his two engineers, and he was not going to tell them that he had someone outside the company look at it.

"I get it. Mum's the word. But Bob, my two boys are home at the same time for once. Harry came in Friday. He's ferrying a Curtiss P-40 up to Hamilton Field and has a three-day layover. Luckily, Tom could get the weekend off. He'll be shoving off for Hawaii in a few days. I was planning to spend some time with them."

"Too bad you didn't have a third son, Vance—you could have named him Richard, and had Tom, Dick and Harry all in the family." Surprised, Vance looked at him, and Gross, always the consummate gentleman, was immediately embarrassed—it was unlike him to make any kind of joking remark that might be interpreted as insensitive.

Then Vance grinned, easing the situation. "No, if we had a third son, it would have been Vance Junior. Tom and Harry are named for Margaret's brothers—and they had already heard all the jokes."

Yet as innocent as Gross's remark had been, it triggered the dark, anxious feeling that had enveloped Vance for the last week. He was incredibly proud that both boys had done so well with their military flight training. But he wondered what the odds would be that both would survive the war that he knew was coming. Tom and Harry had always been friendly rivals, but in recent months their flying experience had put a hard edge on their competitiveness. They were not just rivals anymore, they were rival pilots, and Vance knew that led to accidents.

"Spend it with them looking at the jet project. They are both smart boys, and maybe they'll get to fly one someday."

"You mean it? That would be great, if you are serious."

"I'm serious—get them to look at it with you, but tell them to keep their lips buttoned. They are young and might have some insight an old duffer like you wouldn't have. And I know you value their opinions."

It was true. Vance Shannon had brought his sons into the aviation business early, teaching them to fly in his open-cockpit Travel Air biplane in their early teens and later taking them with him on consulting trips in his maroon Beech Staggerwing. They both shared his passion for aviation—they were superb pilots, careful, able to wring the maximum performance from their aircraft. Both had a good grasp of both aeronautical engineering and business, but both were at the dangerous stage of flying, with enough experience to be very proficient but not enough to be cautious.

They shook hands, Gross clasping his arm around Shannon's shoulder as he always did with old friends. They talked about the weather and sports on the way to the car, but Shannon's thoughts were concentrated on the contents of the briefcase and the hope that somehow he could use it to give his sons a little lesson in safety.

July 20, 1941, La Jolla, California

TOM'S RHYTHMIC GRUNTS echoed from the other room as he went through his daily weight-lifting routine, delayed by their perusal of the contents of Gross's briefcase. In the background, Margaret's old Victrola was wound up for the first time in years, as Tom played his latest record, "I Got It Bad and That Ain't Good," for the tenth time.

Still seated at the drafting table, Harry was deeply absorbed in the project books, his fingers stinging from the residual ammonia of the Ozalid process used to duplicate the reports and the fold-out drawings. As new military pilots, they were flattered to be in on the ground floor of what might be the future of aviation and readily pledged to keep the matter secret.

Vance Shannon watched them with his usual combination of affection and apprehension. He loved them both equally and wanted the best for them. As he had done every day since their birth, he worried about how life would treat them. He knew they were going to be successful, if they were cautious enough to stay alive. And, with Margaret gone, he felt doubly responsible.

He realized how contradictory his feelings were. What could he expect from them? They had grown up watching him fly some of the hottest, most dangerous airplanes in the country, even competing in the air races in Cleveland, where he had placed in both the Thompson and the Bendix races. Margaret was always brave and put a good face on things, but she could not have concealed her fears. He'd have to be careful when talking safety to them so that they didn't think he was a complete hypocrite.

The two boys—they would always be that to him, his two boys, no matter how old they were—had always gotten along well, keeping their competitive spirit in hand except when seeking their mother's affection. Margaret had loved them equally, disciplined them fairly, and tried hard—but failed—to conceal her partiality for Harry.

Both boys were perfectly matched physically, just under six feet tall and weighing about 180. Vance Shannon in his youth had sandy hair, but it had darkened over the years. But Margaret was a pure blonde and the boys had inherited her hair and blue eyes. They were well-muscled, built up from swimming most of the year and daily workouts in the stark, functional exercise room Vance had built in the basement against Margaret's protests. Tom had always been more outgoing and popular with the girls, while Harry had been the student, introspective, a little shy. Tom had been the first to walk and Harry the first to talk. In school, Harry was the natural student and Tom the natural athlete, but their competitive routine was so ingrained that each always managed to match and sometimes exceed the other in his specialty. In high school, Tom wound up with a higher grade point average while Harry earned one more letter than Tom.

It seemed to Vance that they had started to change after Margaret's death, just before they had gone off to prepare for their respective service academies. God forbid that they would go to the same school! Vance had to scramble to get them appointments, working his industry connections with a senator and a local congressman. More than one friend had complained about Vance's being greedy, and he knew they were right. But if the boys wanted to go to West Point and Annapolis, he was going to help them, no matter how greedy he seemed.

It was not the money. Vance had always made a good income from his test flying and his consulting, and his and Margaret's only indulgence had been their house in La Jolla. They had not been able to swing beachfront property, but they were only a block away, and as outrageously expensive as it seemed at the time, it had been a good investment. He could have sent the boys to Stanford or even to an Ivy League school and would have sold the house and his soul to do so, but they had been determined to go to a military academy, and then enter flight training.

Tom had whirled through Annapolis, graduating fifth in his class, while Harry had furnished a more gentlemanly thirty-ninth in his West Point class. Both had played football, Tom for three years at halfback and Harry for two as fullback, and as a parent with boys in both schools Vance was relieved when their teams happened to alternate winning in their seasonal match-ups. After graduation, they immediately went to flight school and did so well that they were now flying fighters. Tom had elected to go into the Marines, gladly accepting the basic infantry training as a challenge, and was now flying the Grumman F4F-3 Wildcat. Harry had checked out in the P-40 at Langley and was already on orders to go to work for Vance's old friend Ben Kelsey as a test pilot at the Fighter Division at Wright Field.

It was everything he and Margaret could have dreamed of—as long as they didn't kill themselves.

Harry snapped the last report shut. "Well, Dad, what do you think?"

"You tell me; you're the newest engineer in the family."

"At first I was put off. It didn't make any sense to me at all until I saw these equations. . . ." Harry riffled through the report, pulling out a sheet showing that at 350 mph, a Spitfire with the Rolls-Royce Merlin engine had a thrust of 1,000 pounds. "Take a look at that—it's the first time I've seen thrust calculated that way. And Mr. Price's engine is supposed to have thirty-five hundred pounds of thrust! That's three and one-half Spitfire engines! That's impressive."

Tom came back in the room. "I felt the same way. I'd never seen horsepower expressed as thrust before."

Their father said, "Well, it makes more sense than horsepower anyway—we've been clinging to that antiquated definition for years, even though an aircraft's power varies continually with altitude, air density, and a variety of other factors. Using pounds of thrust certainly makes sense for jet engines."

Vance went on. "You are exactly right, Harry; Price's figures are impressive. I don't know if he can make his engine work, but if he can, he's got a world-beater. Tom, what did you think of the airplane Kelly Johnson has designed for it?"

Gross had put a specially made box with a small model of the proposed fighter in the briefcase—it had a flashy designation, L-133. Tom extracted it and held it up.

"It's like nothing I've ever seen—canard surfaces, the wing and body all blended into one shape. It looks like it's going six hundred mph just sitting in its box."

"And there's the problem, Son. The Army might let a little money loose to develop the engine, but the airframe will disturb them—just too radical. Wait and see. Kelly and Nate will walk this thing through the Pentagon and come back with their tails between their legs."

Harry was pensive. "Can Lockheed develop it on its own?"

It had become a triangular conversation, both boys addressing their father, neither one talking to the other. He tried to change that, asking, "What do you think, Tom?"

"The airplane, sure, it looks different, but it's still an airplane. The papers say it uses lots of stainless steel, and that might be a fabricating problem, but Lockheed could handle it. But the engine! That's something else."

Harry joined in. "The last year at the Point we had a field trip to Pratt & Whitney in Hartford. What a plant. Lockheed doesn't have the room, and probably not the expertise, to get into engine building. It's an entirely different industry, lots of heavy machinery, machinists with years of experience."

Tom responded. "We had a similar deal but went to Curtiss-Wright. Same thing: huge plant, thousands of machine tools, big payroll. They gave us a forecast for the future for their engines, and it didn't look like it was going to be easy. They can only have so many more cylinders, and the big limiting factor is the propellers, which they make a lot of, just like Hamilton Standard does up in Hartford."

Vance swelled with pride listening to them. They were hitting exactly the right arguments, and they were doing it in a controlled fashion. A few years ago, Tom might have taken an extreme position, just to gin up an argument with Harry. Now they spoke like experienced engineers. Flying had done wonders for them.

Vance was silent for a while as the images of the pilots he had known flashed through his mind, reminding him of the depth and range of the people in this demanding business. He'd trained with Jimmy Doolittle, then seen him go on to become the king of race pilots—and an astute businessman. Wiley Post had asked him to work on the pressure suit he used in the *Winnie Mae* for his high-altitude flights. Not as well educated as Jimmy, Post had the same sort of intuitive engineering mind. There were so many more, and too many of them had lost their lives. . . .

Tom interrupted. "What are you thinking about, Dad?"

A little embarrassed to have let his attention wander, he came back with, "You are both right on the ball. Piston engines, even propellers for piston engines, have become way too expensive. If the jet engine works—and it will someday, if not Nate Price's, then someone else's—you're going to see a revolution in the industry. And it won't affect just airplanes, it will knock the propeller people out of business, and there will be a whole raft of old industries that will fold and new industries that will come in. If I had the brains to pick which ones, I'd go out and do a little investing, right now. Get in on the ground floor!"

The boys kidded him for a while on his investments of the past—the molded plywood trainer, the retractable high-heel shoe for women, the Japanese pinball machine—and he had to laugh, too; his investment record was pretty sorry.

Then he said, "Well, a jet engine is way too expensive to manufacture from scratch, and Lockheed is so loaded with military projects now that they wouldn't be able to do more than make a mock-up. They'll continue to work on the engine, though—Bob Gross thinks the world of Price and Kelly. It is so revolutionary that they may be able to get some investors to back it. Or they could form a subsidiary to handle it, or license it to a big engine firm. But the airplane—it is just too weird looking with those canard surfaces and the funny wing/fuselage business. General Arnold will probably have Kelly take it out to Wright Field, but they'll never buy it. They can't take the risk, not now, with the war looming."

As he spoke, he realized that this was something he could use to talk safety to them without them resenting it—he'd wrap his safety lecture in a waving flag.

Harry was obviously intrigued by the L-133 design. "It's weird, all right, straight out of Buck Rogers, but it looks right. It should fly well and be very fast."

"Well, boys, let me make a prediction. Hap Arnold is going to get one of the jet engines from the RAF, and he'll send it back to the United States for some big company to build. And he'll pick some outfit that's getting short on war work to build the plane for it. It won't be Lockheed; they can't do much more than they are doing right now."

Harry was always the more empathetic. "That's pretty tough on Lockheed, eh? And it's tough on Mr. Price and Mr. Johnson, too."

"Well, this is just the first olive out of the bottle. If jet engines work, they will revolutionize flying, and there will be plenty of work to go around. But this is too radical to be the first American jet."

Vance checked the papers as Harry handed them to him, carefully putting them back in and inserting the L-133 model in its case like a sword into a scabbard.

"Look, boys, you know I'm always talking flying safety—"

They groaned, and Tom said, "Lecture number twenty-nine."

"No, no lecture, but you are both at a dangerous time in your careers. How much military flying time do you have, Tom?"

"About four hundred and fifty hours."

"And Harry?"

"Maybe five hundred."

Vance went on. "Well, that's the dangerous time. You are proficient, and you are feeling your oats. That's when most accidents happen. But now, with the war coming on, you've got to really live up to your responsibilities. You can't be fooling around, buzzing, rat racing, doing low-level acrobatics, not when you are going to be needed in combat."

Both boys laughed. They knew exactly what their father was doing and loved him for it.

"Dad, we'll be good. We promise."

July 21, 1941, fifteen miles due west of Marine Base, Naval Air Station, San Diego

CRUISING AT 7,000 feet, Harry Shannon closed the canopy of his P-40, cinched his seat belt and shoulder harness tight, and watched the tiny speck on the horizon hurtle toward him, growing larger by the second until a gorgeous gray Grumman Wildcat pulled up on his wing, flown by his brother, Tom, a big grin on his face.

They flew for a moment, wing to wing, each drinking in the other's airplane; if there had been a way to exchange seats they would have done it in an instant. They had always been competitors, from fighting for positions on the high school football team, to shooting baskets in the backyard, to seeing who could get the fastest times out of their dad's cars. But this was the ultimate competition, each one flying fifty thousand dollars of hot machinery provided by Uncle Sam.

The brothers had briefed each other that morning in the Marine Base flight operations room. Harry could afford to spend only about fifteen minutes out here before cutting up to Hamilton Field. If the winds were good, he'd have no problem—if they were not, he would have some explaining to do.

They planned for about ten minutes of mock dogfighting before breaking off to return to base. Once in the air, they couldn't talk to each other—the frequencies of their radios were not compatible. They wouldn't have done it anyway, because what they were doing was officially forbidden, if unofficially condoned, and someone might pick up their transmissions.

Tom saluted, closed his canopy, and kicked his Grumman into a vertical bank, pulling away for the first encounter. Harry turned in the opposite direction, applying power cautiously to the P-40, letting his speed build slowly. His engine was brand-new and the last thing he wanted was an engine failure fifteen miles off the coast. Yet his airplane had at least a 20 mph speed advantage over his brother's, and Harry intended to use it.

The two fighters roared at each other again, thin black streams of exhaust coming from their engines; as they passed, Tom pulled up sharply, then rolled back down on the P-40's tail. Harry dove steeply and at 300 mph jerked his P-40 into a sharp turn that Tom promptly matched. Harry rolled on his back and dove again.

Horror-stricken, Tom pulled back on his power, leveling off and banking sharply to watch as Harry's P-40 plunged toward the Pacific. Yelling, "Pull out; pull out," he pounded the canopy with his fist.

Inside the P-40, Harry trying desperately to do just that, with the throttle back, his feet on the control panel, both hands pulling back on the stick, the huge blue ocean racing up to engulf him, the altimeter unwinding, he counted the seconds he had to live as the nose slowly began to creep forward toward the horizon. With the g-forces slamming his body back into his seat, Harry struggled, hooking the stick back in the crook of his right arm and rolling in full-up elevator trim. As the nose came toward level, he blacked out, his vision collapsing inward, his hands falling from the stick, the excess speed now working on the elevator trim to hurl the plane skyward.

Above, Tom's scream of rage turned gradually into a prayer of hope as the black triangle of the P-40's tail slowly transformed into a pointed nose, and then the wings and fuselage, flattening out, started a climb. He dove toward the P-40 as Harry's consciousness returned first and then his vision, followed by a sense of overwhelming relief at his sheer good luck. If the dive had lasted another ten seconds, he would have been forty fathoms deep right now.

The two fighters leveled out in loose formation, Harry trying to regain composure. Tom rolled his Wildcat around the P-40 in a loose arc, checking it for damage. They closed again, both opening their canopies. Tom shook his head while a white-faced Harry grinned, happy to be alive and knowing that his brother would never let him live this down. To try a split S in a P-40 at low altitude. It was suicidal.

Tom flew in a shallow bank to a heading that would lead Harry roughly to Hamilton Field, located a few miles north of San Francisco. Harry shook his head, pointed straight back to the coastline; he had had enough of over-ocean flying and would find his way up the coast.

That night, Harry called the bar at the Officers Club at San Diego Naval Air Station, where, as he suspected, Tom was holding forth on his death-defying morning combat. Over the din of the bar, they exchanged some small talk, with Harry signing off. "You know, right now Dad's Lecture twenty-nine makes a lot of sense. You take care of yourself, and don't bust your ass doing something as stupid as I did."

Tom's answer sounded flippant but was sincere: "I won't if you won't."

THE PASSING SCENE

Italians repelled in invasion of Greece; Germany conquers Balkans, Greece, Crete; HMS Hood and Bismarck sunk; Germany invades Soviet Union; back-and-forth fighting in North Africa; Churchill and Roosevelt sign Atlantic Charter; plutonium discovered; Lou Gehrig dies.

CHAPTER THREE

August 3, 1941, Ladywood, United Kingdom

Young Whittle there is very even tempered. Always angry."

It was the wrong thing to say to Stanley Hooker, whose genius with supercharger designs had improved the performance of the Hurricane and the Spitfire to the point that they could win the Battle of Britain. Hooker imperiously drew himself up to his full six-foot, two-inch height, his mouth compressed into a hard slit. Visibly restraining himself, he speared the hapless Ministry of Aircraft Production bureaucrat with eyes crackling fire.

"So might you be if you had seen a stupid government sit on a war-winning invention for almost a decade, then proceed to rob you at gunpoint of the value of your brainchild."

Hooker spun on his heel and strode toward the deep blue Rolls-Royce Phantom II waiting by the hangar doors. Slipping inside the Rolls, still fuming, he waved off the proffered stainless-steel flask of tea and opened the inlaid walnut door to the bar. He raised his eyebrows and pointed to the whiskey in invitation, but his guests all shook their heads.

"Bloody idiots. They have no idea of what they cost the country. If they had given Frank"—he nodded out the window to where the always dapper Squadron Leader Frank Whittle was hectoring a group of workers from Rover—"some support, we would have had squadrons of jet fighters by 1938, and there might never have been a war."

Hooker poured himself a splash of Scotch, waved his glass again in invitation, poured another splash, then downed it.

The three Americans, who had been admiring the utter luxury of the Rolls, waited for him to continue. Hooker had been utterly forthright so far, and they wanted all the information they could get from him.

Hooker waved the empty glass in the air. "We did the same thing to Frank that the French did to the Wright brothers! They ignored all the Wrights had done, called them 'liars, not fliers'—until Wilbur came over to Le Mans in 1908 and showed them what real flying was. Then they jolly well stole their ideas! Blériot would never have flown the Channel in 1909 if he had not seen Wilbur Wright in 1908!" He reached for the whiskey bottle again, shook his head, carefully wiped his glass with an immaculate linen napkin, and closed the door to the bar. "We did the same thing to poor Frank, ignored him; then when it is bloody obvious that he was right, we take his ideas and parcel them out to other companies. It's unforgivable!"

Stunned by the outburst, the three Americans waited cautiously. Then, very tentatively, Colonel Ray Crawford asked, "Can you tell us about it? We'll have our own problems, I'm sure." The other two, William Owen, a plant manager from General Electric, and Vance Shannon, General Arnold's special representative, instinctively leaned forward.

Little need, for Hooker spoke loudly in a crisp but aggrieved tone, as if he felt the pain that Whittle had suffered.

"Frank Whittle invented the turbine-jet engine in the early 1930s. Patented it in 1932, when he was twenty-five years old. Oddly enough, we are the same age." The last sentence was said rather more softly, and Hooker paused for a moment, running his hand over his bulging brow as if astounded by their coincidence in age. Then he went on. "The government ignored him. Industry ignored him. They should not have; Frank Whittle is brilliant, a genius, even if he can be a bit abrasive. If they had the brains to give him even a little funding, we could have had a production version of his jet by 1937, and squadrons of jet fighters by 1938. Hitler would not have dared move against Czechoslovakia, and perhaps some sensible German might have shot him by now, saving us the trouble of this bloody war. And then the government robbed Frank."

Owen asked, "When did he finally get some backing?"

"In dribs and drabs from 1936 on, never more than a few thousand pounds and mostly from private people who believed in him. If you know him, you cannot help believing in him—he's a remarkable man. A trifle sharp, perhaps, doesn't suffer fools gladly, but brilliant in theory and in practice. I thought I knew something about turbines, from my supercharger experience, until I talked to Frank. He is a master of the subject."

Crawford, unlike most Army Air Force colonels, was at fifty a little old for his rank, having spent years with Pratt & Whitney before getting a direct commission in 1940. "You mentioned that they robbed him. Isn't he a serving officer? Wouldn't his invention have belonged to the government, anyway?"

"By no means. He developed the engine on his own time, with private money. He signed all the proper papers, telling him how many hours a week he could work on the project, and giving the government an interest in it. Then the government thanks him by forcing him to give away his ideas to competitors in the industry." He shivered with indignation and spat out, "They even allowed Rover to build his engines." The word "Rover" rolled off his lips as if he'd bitten into a bad oyster.

Owen shot a quick smile to his colleagues. All three men knew that Rolls-Royce regarded the Rover company as a mere tin bender, whose automobiles were not worthy to be on the same road as Rolls-Royces were, and Hooker obviously subscribed to the theory.

Hooker gestured out the window. "It looks like he has a moment free. Let me introduce you to him. You will be doing a lot of work with him in the future."

Shannon, always wishing to know as much as possible before

engaging in a conversation, asked, "How does he feel about shipping his engine to the United States?"

"Whittle is a patriot, first and foremost. He knows that a lot of people who scorned him are going to make a great deal of money from his invention. But he is intent on winning this war. As we all are."

The four men moved across the grass, dry in the unusual August heat, and Hooker made the introductions. Of less than medium height, Whittle had a polite manner that belied the volcanic intensity of his eyes, which pierced each man in turn. His jaw twitched nervously and his movements were abrupt. It was obvious that he was torn between his being put out by being taken from his work and his desire to learn what American intentions were.

"Gentlemen, I hope you'll understand when I say that I'm both surprised and pleased that General Electric is going to manufacture my engine."

Shannon answered, "I can understand your surprise—GE is hardly a household name in aircraft engines. And I'm glad that you are pleased, but may I ask why?"

"Pratt & Whitney and Wright make wonderful reciprocating engines, but their engineers and their management would be threatened by my engine. It's too radical and it goes whistling round and round rather than pounding up and down!" Whittle's arms and hands comically matched his words, flying round and round and then pounding up and down—the little byplay was totally out of character with his previous demeanor.

He nodded his head abruptly and added, "No offense, Colonel Crawford."

Crawford smiled and said, "None taken. Sad but true!"

Whittle went on, with a gesture to Hooker. "No, a 'proper' engine company will never give it the backing it needs, not unless they are as foresighted as Rolls-Royce." He made a short bow to Hooker. "This offers General Electric entrance to a whole new industry. It is a very astute move, and if I had any money at all, and if it were not forbidden, I would be buying General Electric stock at this very moment."

Crawford nodded, and started to speak, but Whittle waved

his hands imperiously and said, "Just a moment. I don't think you realize the implications of what has happened with the introduction of the turbine. General Electric is going to go from being a supplier of superchargers to a mass producer of engines. Rolls-Royce is going to completely change its focus. There is a revolution going on here, gentlemen, and I damn well hope you recognize it and appreciate it."

He glared at them fiercely, daring anyone to deny it.

Hooker tried to smooth things over. "I'm sure General Arnold agrees with you! He made this decision himself, over the advice of a lot of the people around him who think they can beat Germany with thousands of piston engine bombers."

Crawford started to speak again, but Hooker went on, "General Arnold was in England when the Gloster flew with Frank's first airworthy engine, and understood the implications at once. When he found out that the Whittle engine weighed only six hundred and fifty pounds and put out as much thrust as a sixteen-hundred-and-fifty-pound Merlin, he asked us to send copies of the plans back with him, and ship an engine later."

Whittle said, "We'll be sending the W.1X engine in October—along with drawings for the W.2B. That's our latest design!" The sudden slightly bitter emphasis in Whittle's voice did not puzzle the Americans. The engines and the plans were worth tens, perhaps hundreds of millions of dollars of future business—and poor Whittle wouldn't get a dime from them.

Whittle went on, "Is it true that Bell is going to build the airframe?"

There was no mistaking the bitter tone this time. The British had tried the Bell P-39 and dismissed it as a failure—small wonder that Whittle lacked confidence in the choice.

Vance responded, "Yes; Bell has a reputation for the unorthodox, and had some spare production capacity."

"Well, good luck to them, and good luck to you. It has taken me ten hard years to get this far; I hope you Yanks can do better."

Vance smiled. "You'll have to come and help us. Have you been to America yet?"

At this Whittle flashed a warm grin. "No, but I want to come and see if you do things as quickly as everyone claims. I'm sure you'll have a jet flying in a year or two."

Shannon said, "With your help, we'll fly a jet airplane in a year."

Whittle was startled. He had been joking and now he wondered if the Americans were joking back. "If you say so, gentlemen, I'm sure you will!"

There was some more small talk about the proposed trip; then Whittle, obviously now more comfortable with the Americans, saluted and left.

Hooker smiled. "A trifle salty, eh? He's not easy to get along with, but the Ministry has made life hard for him up till now. He had a devil of a time with Rover—their engineers simply wouldn't listen to him, kept introducing their ideas in areas he had already covered. Frank is working well with Rolls-Royce; we respect what he's done and we can help him, as well."

That night, in their tiny shared room in the jumbled Basil Hotel that Lockheed had booked for them, Crawford stopped Shannon as he prepared to leave for a dinner engagement at the Connaught, one where he wanted to arrive early and make sure that everything was perfect.

Crawford gently took Shannon to task. "Vance, I know you are a doer, but don't you think telling Frank that we would fly a jet within the year was a bit thick?"

Stifling his impatience, Shannon ran his hand through the graying stubble of his hair. "You're probably right, Ray, I shouldn't have said it. But I believe we will, and I think Squadron Leader Whittle will be happy that we do. He's given up a fortune to help win the war; we might as well help him win it."

Owen chimed in. "Not so much given up a fortune as had it taken from him. Sounds more like Nazi Germany than Merry Old England."

Crawford frowned and said, "I wonder how they do it in Germany. Can they just grab somebody's idea and run with it?"

Shannon said, "I'm more concerned with what they are doing

with it than how they do it. They've got a couple years' head start on everyone. If their jets are worthwhile, that could make 1943 a mighty interesting year."

With that he bowed to the two men and stepped out the door. They looked at each other and Owen said, "It must be a woman."

And Crawford replied, "Yes; I've seen her and she is a knock-out. Vance has been miserable since his wife died. It's time he found someone."

November 18, 1941, Zuffenhausen, Germany

HANS VON OHAIN walked through the bustling bays of the Heinkel-Hirth engine factory, keeping a discreet two paces behind Ernst Heinkel, who was issuing orders in a loud voice at a rapid rate. His harried assistant, Robert Eissenlohr, was jotting down notes on one of the cheap Luftwaffe tablets Heinkel insisted on using as an economy measure. Arms moving, voice rising, Ernst Heinkel was distinctly unhappy with the factory he had just acquired to build jet engines. Few of the changes he had demanded had been made, and some heads were going to roll.

It was the sort of atmosphere that von Ohain hated, particularly because he hoped that his head would not be one of those to roll. The Heinkel He 280, the world's first jet fighter, had made its first flight the previous April, powered by two of his Heinkel-Hirth 001 engines. After some initial difficulties it was proving itself. Heinkel's engineers had gone all out in the design of the airframe, using a tricycle landing gear, making provisions to pressurize the cabin, and installing a radical new feature, an ejection seat to blow the pilot out of the cockpit in case of a catastrophic in-flight emergency.

Yet apparently the Luftwaffe remained unimpressed, even after a mock dogfight with a Focke-Wulf FW 190, where the He 280 had clearly demonstrated its superiority. Part of the problem was that the war in Russia was going so well. Even the generals who believed it was a mistake to invade the Soviet Union now thought that the war on the Eastern Front might be over by December. Then, after six months to digest the new conquered territories, to build a new fleet of bombers, it would be England's turn at last.

Von Ohain could not understand the Luftwaffe's reluctance to back the He 280. He was his own most severe critic, and he had been pleased with his work up to that point; his engine was now putting out more than 650 kilograms of thrust. The He 280 had flown at just under 850 kilometers per hour—faster than the world's speed record.

But last week, Fritz Schaefer had just taken off in the prototype 280 when a blade broke away from the turbine, sending sheets of flame back for forty yards and ripping the cowling off. The quick-thinking Schaefer made a forced landing with the gear retracted, somehow managing not to do much damage to the airplane. The ill-timed accident caused Ernst Heinkel to combine a long-deferred inspection trip with a conference to announce the fate of von Ohain's engine.

The old Hirth firm conference room was similar to many of those found in successful German factories—long and relatively narrow, brightly lit despite the dark oak paneling of the walls, which were well laden with oil portraits of former leaders. The heavy lighting fixtures had been converted from gas to electric more than twenty years before. A shining mahogany table spanned most of the room, surrounded by heavy wooden chairs amply surfaced with red leather cushions. At the far end of the room wooden doors concealed the only modern touch, a retractable motion picture screen that in turn covered a blackboard.

Heinkel assumed his place at the head of the table, with Eissenlohr, still scribbling furiously, at his left and von Ohain at his right. Egon Scheede, the former Hirth company plant manager, two engineers, and Fritz Obermyer rounded out the group. Obermyer ostentatiously wrote in his own notebook, for the sole purpose of filling his self-appointed role as ranking member of the Nazi Party. To Heinkel's cronies, Obermyer was a gold mine of information, but not to be trusted. To the rest of the Heinkel plant, he was a snitch and a deadly dangerous opponent who should never be crossed. It was a position he enjoyed.

Heinkel opened the meeting with a long list of caustic remarks to Eissenlohr on factory housekeeping, the importance of adequate natural light, and the mandatory requirement to reduce overhead. He droned on and on, listing the goals he had for the plant and the efforts he expected Eissenlohr to make.

Heinkel then assumed his normal managerial persona, nodding agreeably to the group and saying, "Now I want to thank Dr. von Ohain for his continued excellent work. His engine—we call it the 001—is coming along much faster than we could have hoped. Last week's in-flight failure shows that there are some problems, but we all know that is part of any development program.

"The main thing is that we are clearly ahead of Messerschmitt! Their aircraft—it's called the 262—has not even flown yet." He paused, knowing that what he was going to say next would surprise everyone.

"I talked to General Udet last week, and I think he is at last coming around to our point of view."

Generalluftzeugmeister Ernst Udet headed the Technical Directorate of the Air Ministry—and was sorely unsuited for the task. Udet, with sixty victories, was the leading German ace to survive the 1914–18 war. A superb acrobatic pilot but technically uninformed and not a manager, Udet was overwhelmed with the responsibilities that the new *Reichsmarschall*, Hermann Göring, had imposed upon him. Udet had also imposed a reckless decision that had set back German progress all across-the-board. In November 1940, Göring had ordered that any development efforts on weapons that would not be operational within a year be discontinued. The order had fatal effects upon the materials needed for the development of the jet engine.

Heinkel gazed steadily at Obermyer as he said, "I think even General Udet would admit that he doesn't have a wide understanding of the potential of jet aircraft. Contrary to the reports we heard, the successful mock dogfights with the Focke-Wulf helped persuade him. If we can promise him early production of the 280, a year ahead of Messerschmitt, I'm sure he'll give us a contract."

Heinkel glanced at the back of the room and noted that

Obermyer had made a quick gesture as if he were pointing to the ceiling. Annoyed by Obermyer's effrontery but still aware that he had almost omitted a significant part of his talk, Heinkel went on. "Things are going well for the Luftwaffe against Russia. The aircraft we have now will be adequate there. But things are changing in the west. The British have introduced two new aircraft, the Avro Lancaster, a huge four-engine bomber, and the de Havilland Mosquito, a small but very fast twin-engine bomber. Our intelligence reports indicate that these are being built in great numbers, and that by early summer next year, they may be able to put fleets of five hundred to one thousand aircraft over our cities, night after night. Our night fighters will be able to deal with the Avro, as long as it doesn't come in too large a force. But we are currently helpless against the de Havilland. We need jet fighters to catch and destroy it."

Obermyer scanned the room watching the reactions, which ranged from indignation to amusement. One man, Kampfelder, an electrical engineer, was tapping the side of his head as if Heinkel were crazy. His name was quickly written in Obermyer's notebook. One never knew when such information could come in handy.

With some reluctance, yet with a definite change in demeanor, Heinkel turned to von Ohain. "Dr. von Ohain, this is not intended to offend you in any way, but these circumstances have made me decide that we need more time to develop your engine, the 001. As you know, the Junkers Jumo 004 engine is progressing rapidly. If we install the 004 engines on the 280, we can begin producing them at a starting rate of twenty per month in early 1943. General Udet has told me, informally, if we can achieve this, he will order us to start production by January 1942."

Von Ohain's face fell. This was clearly a mortal setback to him and his engine.

Heinkel attempted to reassure him. "This sounds worse than it is, Dr. von Ohain. I want you to continue working on the 001, and to initiate work on a new engine, one capable of fourteen hundred kilograms of thrust. We'll need engines of that size for 1944 and beyond. Only you can do it!"

Innately courteous, von Ohain stood up to reply just as the conference room doors burst open and a clearly distressed aide ran in.

"Forgive me, Dr. Heinkel, but I was ordered to give you this message at once."

Annoyed, Heinkel took the envelope and opened it. As he read it he slumped to his chair. "Gentleman, all that we've just discussed is moot. Yesterday, General Udet was killed testing a new aircraft."

The room was shocked into silence, not as much by the news of Udet's death but by its palpable falsity. Udet's heavy drinking was notorious; those closer to him knew he was taking a variety of narcotics as well. His health was ruined and he had done no test flying for months. He had either committed suicide or been executed.

Von Ohain said, "May God have mercy on his soul."

Puzzled, Obermyer looked up, then scribbled in his notebook. "Professor Heinkel, may I ask a question?"

Distracted, Heinkel whirled on von Ohain, then caught himself. This young man was too valuable, too sensitive, and too nice to be savaged. "Of course."

"Who will take General Udet's place? Will it be General Milch?"

Erhard Milch was a managerial genius who had built *Deutsche Luft Hansa* into one of the best airlines in the world. By brains and force of personality he had become second only to Göring in German aviation.

Heinkel's face darkened. "You are probably right. And that is not good for us. Milch has never liked me. He doesn't like Willy Messerschmitt, either, but he dislikes him less than he dislikes me. We may be in for a very difficult time with the jet engine, Dr. von Ohain."

The meeting ended in disarray, Eissenlohr continuing to follow Heinkel, helping him with his coat, opening the door, scuttling ahead to open the door of the big Mercedes. The others filed out, leaving von Ohain slumped at the table, his head in his hands.

Obermyer paused by his chair. "Dr. von Ohain, do not let this stop you. Things like this always happen in wartime. It may turn out for the best. Udet was not the right man for his job; perhaps Milch will be."

Von Ohain looked up, surprised at the serious sentiments from the normally sardonic Obermyer, wondering if he was sincere or if he was baiting him. Uncertain, he simply nodded and said, "I hope you are correct."

And, unable to resist, Obermyer added, "For the sake of Germany and the Führer."

Von Ohain, clearly overwhelmed by the rapid pace of developments, knew he should say something but did not. As the two men parted, each knew that the other would require watching.

November 18, 1941, Friedrichschafen

MAKING MONEY IN Nazi Germany was difficult; hiding the fact that you made it was even more so, and Fritz Obermyer was grateful for the means provided by a small inheritance from his mother, Lottie, and the cover provided by a substantial working relationship with his uncle Otto Kaufmann. Otto was the black sheep of the Obermyer family. Fritz's mother was the only one who understood Otto and stood up for him after he had avoided service in the Kaiser's army by going to Switzerland in 1910. His father—for whom he was named—had immediately declared Otto an outcast. His brothers never spoke of him again, but Lottie loved him and nurtured him with news and letters, including the doleful news of the loss of two of his three brothers in combat.

Otto was hardworking and smart and circled the post-war economic turmoil in Germany like a vulture, descending from his aerie in Switzerland to buy up good property cheaply even as he expanded his Swiss interests to include an optical firm, extensive real-estate holdings in Geneva and Zurich, and a small bank devoted primarily to international trade.

In 1925, just as the depression and the massive inflation were tearing Germany apart, Obermyer had visited his uncle in Geneva, bringing word of Lottie's death. Otto was impressed by his nephew and offered to bring him into the family business. Obermyer appreciated the offer but refused graciously, suggesting instead that they might someday find a way to work together. Obermyer's concept of work did not coincide with Otto's view that sixteen hours a day, seven days a week, was about right.

Obermyer found a way in 1937, when his combined payments from Heinkel, Messerschmitt, Bloch, and Lockheed became too large to conceal in Germany. Uncle Otto maintained several accounts for him and was happy to send one of his trusted assistants to and from Friedrichshafen to accommodate Obermyer's growing financial situation. In turn, Obermyer looked after Otto's interests in Germany as well as he could without making their relationship too obvious.

Obermyer had booked rooms for himself and Müller in the Bayerischer Hof, a small, comfortable hotel on the promenade bordering Lake Constance. The rooms were plain, clean, the furniture from Bismarck's era, and the quiet employees sophisticated enough to know when to look the other way. Heinkel had booked Obermyer in at the Adlon in Berlin once; it was far more luxurious, but he preferred the simplicity of the Bayerischer Hof, where he could afford to indulge himself in a small suite without exciting comment.

Obermyer liked to walk down to the water's edge after an early breakfast, smoke a cigar, and contemplate his future. Convinced that Germany was going to lose the war, he wanted to make realistic plans. Some of his confidants talked about escaping to Spain or to Argentina when the time came, but that made no sense to Obermyer. Why go somewhere and find the same sort of corrupt Fascist government and the same stagnant economies? It didn't make any sense. He wanted to go only to the United States. It would take an enormous amount of preparation to avoid being caught before he left—or after he arrived. He would need a complete change of papers, a new history, perhaps even some cosmetic surgery, but most of all, he would need plenty of money in the bank in the United States.

He was ready to write off his German holdings right now; they would be worthless after the war. The Swiss interests he could maintain, letting Uncle Otto's firm handle them. In time, Obermyer would just sell everything out and move all his assets to California, which loomed in his mind as a golden land of plenty, filled with big cars, beautiful girls, and great opportunities for his particular brand of crime. It occurred to him that if he was able to save enough money, he might not have to "work" as he had done in the past and instead perhaps just invest in some legitimate business.

During the last war, both zeppelins and aircraft had been constructed in the huge hangars only a few miles from where Obermyer stood, gazing out over the water. The same designer who had created some of the giant seaplanes of the era, Claude Dornier, now operated one of his factories on the same site, turning out bombers and night fighters. The latter were not the object of Obermyer's interest, however. He needed some apparently secret tidbits to keep both Ernst Heinkel and Willy Messerschmitt happy. It was known generally in the industry that Dornier was working on a super-fast twin-engine fighter, a radical airplane with one engine in the nose and another, a pusher, in the tail. The Heinkel firm had been awarded a subcontract to develop new outer wing panels for the airplane, to improve its high-altitude performance, and this provided an adequate reason for Obermyer's visit. Yet he had to come back with something from the Dornier factory floor on a new development, a big problem, a future project, or, even better, a personal scandal that would satisfy his patrons' bottomless thirst for information.

In his first meeting of the morning, Obermyer would talk to Uncle Otto's representative and transfer both cash and documents for deposit in Switzerland, along with instructions for their further transfer to his accounts in the Bank of America in the United States. He smiled at the thought that the only worthwhile thing Italy had done for the Axis was have an emigrant found an American bank for him to use.

Then at eleven, Ernst Staiger, his local contact in the Nazi hierarchy in the Dornier factory, would drop by, expecting to get a sumptuous lunch and his usual payoff. It always surprised Obermyer how cheaply information could be purchased, if the transaction was couched in old comrade terms over a heavy lunch, well lubricated by alcohol, even from men whose lifework was denouncing traitors. Extracting information would be painless this time, given the contractual connection with Heinkel and Staiger's partiality for cognac. Obermyer had brought two bottles, one to drink and one to give him. It would be a very inexpensive exchange.

Exactly at ten there was a knock on the door. Obermyer opened it to find a stunning brunette tipping the uniformed attendant who had escorted her to his room.

Uncharacteristically speechless and mindlessly worrying that Müller, just a door away, would somehow intrude, Obermyer waved her in. She moved easily, walking to the table to deposit a large leather briefcase, then turned to shatter him with a smile. Even in her hat and loden overcoat, she radiated beauty.

"My name is Gertrude, and Uncle Otto told me to wish you a very happy forty-first birthday!" With her right hand she removed her hat, slinging it to the table; with her left, she dropped her overcoat, standing before him stark naked except for her high heels, stockings, and extraordinarily fancy garters. She was breathtaking, holding herself so that her breasts were lifted, smiling as innocently as a choir girl.

Obermyer was stunned; Otto was right, it was his birthday, but what was he thinking of? Their relations had always been perfectly correct; there had never ever before been any suggestion of this sort of earthy good humor. But Gertrude was beautiful and time was precious. He swept her up and carried her to the bed, wishing that he had never made an appointment with Staiger and hoping against hope that Müller would sleep in.

German advance stalls in Russian winter after 750,000 casualties; the United States loans $1 billion to the Soviet Union; National Academy of Sciences recommends immediate construction of an atom bomb; Allied shipping losses continue to rise; German raider Atlantis *sunk; Leningrad under siege.*

CHAPTER FOUR

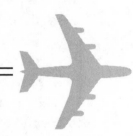

December 8, 1941, La Jolla, California

Vance Shannon sat alone in his library, the radio on, the newspapers discarded on the floor. His usual loneliness and sense of Margaret's passing was gone, submerged in his anger over the news from Pearl Harbor, the anger visible in the reddening of the scar across his forehead, a souvenir of an early crash. Talking to himself, he asked, "How could they have sucker punched us like this? Didn't we have any reconnaissance aircraft? How could they get that close to Pearl Harbor and not be seen?"

As usual, he was thinking about Tom, on his way to the Pacific with his Marine squadron. *He'll be in the thick of it, soon,* he thought. Vance was very familiar with the Grumman Wildcat Tom was flying, and he went to his files to see what he had on the Mitsubishi Zero that had been a major force in the devastating attack on Pearl Harbor.

He pulled out a folder, knowing there would not be much. In an adjacent file, he had six full file folders on the Messerschmitt Bf 109; the Zero's folder had only half a dozen items in it, mostly culled from popular sources. A former Air Corps officer whom he had met on one or two occasions, Claire Chennault, had issued a warning about the capabilities of the Zero, but these had been discounted. Vance himself had not taken them seriously at the time—it was impossible that a carrier-based fighter could outperform land-based fighters, just in the nature of things. Carrier fighters had to be stronger to take the shock of landings, and that meant weight that detracted from performance. Now it looked like he and everyone else were wrong.

Well, some isolationist congressman, a corn-belt isolationist who had voted against Lend-Lease, had said it best; "Now we have to lick the hell out of them." And that was true. Japan would have to be defeated and Germany, too; there was no way out now.

One item in Vance's folder shocked him. It was an American air attaché's report on Japanese selection and training of pilots. If what he said was true—and Vance believed it was; it was written in very thoughtful terms—the Japanese were far more selective about their pilots and far more demanding in their training. Listening to Tom talk about Pensacola or Harry about Randolph Field, Vance would never have believed it. But now the Japanese pilots, and their planes, seemed incredibly formidable.

Still speaking aloud, though there was no one in the house, he said, "We have lots of catching up to do. Let's just hope we do it before something happens to Tom or Harry."

As his anger built over the surprise attack, he was awash in emotions. He thought about calling Hap Arnold and asking for a commission and a combat assignment. For a moment his imagination ran away with him and he was in France again, flying his SPAD XIII in his last dogfight, remembering how he had stitched the fabric with bullet holes, working from the tail right up through the cockpit and into the fuel tank. The enemy Fokker D VII had lurched forward, the pilot dead, the spin intensifying as flames ate away the fabric on the left wings. Then Vance considered the reality: a desk at Wright Field or in the Pentagon, no flying, no combat, no engineering, just endless paperwork. He could do more good by staying out.

July 18, 1942, Leipheim, Germany

A CATALOG OF Messerschmitt products carpeted the undulating, hill-bounded flying field outside the plant, with the preposterous Me 321 gliders looming over everything, their enormous 180-foot wings dwarfing their towplanes, the twin-engine Me 110s. More than one hundred had been built in anticipation of invading Great Britain; now they were assigned the more mundane task of supplying the hard-pressed German Army in Russia. A few of the newer Me 323s were also on the line, really just strengthened Me 321 gliders, each equipped with six captured French Gnome-Rhone engines to help it lumber through the air.

Dotting the field like little black crosses were dozens of the single-engine Bf 108 liaison planes and Bf 109 fighters, parked indiscriminately and surrounded by the usual impedimenta of fire extinguishers, refueling trucks, and toolboxes. As at all airfields, most of the aircraft were sitting idle, some with cowlings off, some on jacks, all awaiting maintenance. A few were being prepared for flight and others had maintenance crews scrambling over them. But for most of the people at the plant, all eyes were fastened on a single airplane, the third prototype of the new jet fighter, the Messerschmitt Me 262 V3. Carrying the factory markings PC + UC and powered by two equally brand-new Junkers jet engines, the aircraft had a pugnacious, shark-like look as it sat on its tail wheel, its nose pointed in the air as if it were sniffing the breeze prior to its first flight.

All across Germany, but nowhere more than in the Luftwaffe and the aviation industry, tension was rife. The effects of the Royal Air Force's unbelievable one-thousand-plane raid on Cologne on May 30/31 were still being felt. Göring had at first refused to believe the reports, telling Hitler that only seventy planes had bombed and that forty of these had been shot down. But Hitler had called Joseph Grohé, the Nazi *Gauleiter* of Cologne, and learned the stupefying truth—474 dead, 5,000 injured, 3,300 homes destroyed. Furious, Hitler had called Göring in for a private audience. The Führer's conversation with Göring was not recorded, but an endless round of stories circulating had it that the *Reichsmarschall* emerged from Hitler's office so shaken that he did not acknowledge any salutes, almost ran to his waiting Mercedes, and was whisked off to his country estate, Carinhall, to recuperate. Some said there were tears in his eyes; others spoke mirthfully of the indignities his enormous behind must have suffered.

Feelings were running high at the Messerschmitt plant as well. Professor Dr. Wilhelm Emil Messerschmitt's management style was unusual in authoritarian Germany. He was a businessman as well as an engineer and knew that performance, quality, production, and profit were all part of one equation. He believed in establishing a joint committee of engineers and manufacturing experts for each project, with less emphasis on who was the boss than on arriving at consensual agreements that made both production and profit sense. Well-known for his ability to delegate authority and responsibility, his project officers prided themselves on being able to make decisions on their own without consulting him. At the same time, he was detail oriented, still reviewing every final drawing personally, one at a time, just as he had done from the early days, when they made small sport planes. From the workers' points of view, Messerschmitt's best characteristic, his saving grace, was his generosity. They knew if they did their work well, if their products were profitable, he would reward them with a sizable bonus, sometimes more than their annual salary. It was a practice that promoted loyalty and efficiency.

Messerschmitt was totally intoxicated with his jet fighter, even though he initially had delayed its introduction, preferring to concentrate on increasing the quantity production of his Bf 109 fighter. The man-hours required to build the 109 had steadily declined, and every order generated extraordinary profits. Yet he knew the 262 was the fighter of tomorrow, the airplane that would give the Luftwaffe ascendancy over its enemies—and Messerschmitt ascendancy within the Luftwaffe.

The forty-four-year-old entrepreneur had followed the 262 from the start, watching as it changed from having its engines buried in the non-swept wings to the current swept-wing version with the two jet engines mounted in pods beneath the wings.

Messerschmitt sat talking with his favorite test pilot, Flight Captain Fritz Wendel. Only three years before, Wendel had set the world's speed record in a specially designed Messerschmitt Bf 209, flying the suicidal little airplane at 755 kilometers per hour. Older, more experienced pilots had refused to fly the Bf 209, on the basis that it was too dangerous with its high wing loading and unusual surface evaporation cooling system. Wendel himself had crashed in the second version of the 209 before setting the record.

Crashes were part of a test pilot's life, and Wendel, a cheerful optimist, already had a close brush with death in the 262 prototype. In April 1941, before any jet engines were ready to be mounted, he had flown the aircraft with a 700-horsepower piston engine in its nose, driving a conventional propeller. The plane was drastically underpowered but flew well enough. Then, this March 25, he had test flown it with the piston engine still operating and two BMW jet engines installed on the wings. Both jet engines had failed just after takeoff, turning from some thrust into pure drag in an instant. Only the pounding piston engine and Wendel's skill kept the airplane in the air long enough for him to fly around the circuit at less than 70 meters altitude to make an emergency landing.

Now they were faced with a new problem. The piston engine had long been removed, replaced by the armament installation, and two of the new Junkers Jumo 004B engines were installed in the under-wing pods. Wendel had attempted to make the first all-jet-powered takeoff in the Me 262 the hour before. The jet had built up its acceleration, but at eight hundred meters down the runway Wendel cut the power and taxied back in to a perplexed Dr. Messerschmitt.

"Sir, there is just no elevator authority. The jet exhaust strikes the ground and blankets the elevator; it never takes effect. I cannot bring the nose down. I could have run it all the way to Poland and it wouldn't have lifted off."

"Well, we knew all along that we should have had a tricycle

landing gear. Heinkel did that in his fighter; we should have accepted the delay and installed it."

Wendel said nothing; both men knew that it had been Messerschmitt himself who had vetoed installation of the tricycle gear in the prototypes, fearing the progress of the Heinkel fighter and not wanting to delay his own program.

"I have a suggestion, sir, but it is risky. It could easily wreck the aircraft."

Messerschmitt nodded impatiently. "Go ahead; tell me."

"If I waited until I had about one hundred and eighty kilometers on the dial, and tapped the brakes, it would tip the nose over, and perhaps let the elevators bite. Once they take hold, the airplane will fly; I know it will."

"If you tap the brakes too hard you'll stand on your nose, and I'll have lost a plane and a good test pilot."

Wendel did not reply. After two minutes of intense concentration, weighing the risks of a crash against the risks of further delays, Messerschmitt said, "Go ahead. But go lightly on the brakes—just the barest tap."

The ground crew, engineers from the plant, and photographers were all ready when Wendel taxied out for the second time, the hot exhaust from the jets burning a trail in the grass, blowing back stones and chunks of the tarmac. Finally he wheeled on the runway, slowly advanced the throttles, and the Me 262 raced ahead.

Crouched in the cockpit, Wendel again noted with pleasure the lack of torque and the relative quiet, compared to a piston engine plane. As the airspeed indicator passed 180, he tapped the brakes lightly. The nose tipped over, he felt the elevators take hold, and seconds later he was airborne, climbing swiftly, delighting in the sheer raw power the jets were delivering, oblivious to the roaring crowd below as the arrow-shaped fighter made a turn to the left.

He flew for twelve tension-filled minutes before dropping the 262 down smoothly on the runway. The cheering onlookers suddenly froze as flames exploded from both engines, trailing the airplane as it slowed down. The flames, apparently just pooled fuel that ignited when the aircraft assumed its normal tail-down position, went out as

Wendel taxied in to accept Messerschmitt's congratulations—and to think about his bonus.

October 15, 1942, Wright Field, Ohio

VANCE SHANNON WAS forty-eight years old today and felt eighty-four. He sat in the end seat of the third row of the tiny briefing room, afraid that the gnawing fear in his stomach might force him to leave during this highly classified briefing, one that Harry was scheduled to give. To walk out on his son, that was unthinkable.

So were Vance's thoughts on his son Tom. The last news had been from Mike Delaroy, his squadron commander, saying that Tom had been shot down just west of Guadalcanal and was missing. There was some hope that he might have survived—several of Delaroy's pilots had made it back after being shot down. In the meantime Delaroy emphasized that Tom had been a first-rate fighter pilot, an ace with six confirmed victories, and that the Navy was still searching the area whenever it was possible to do so.

Now Vance regretted not telling the boys about Madeline. He had met her three years before, in Paris, where she was working for the American embassy. He was in France, negotiating the sale of Baltimore bombers for the Martin Company, and she had acted as a translator in the many endless meetings. She was French, young, Catholic, beautiful, and talented, fluent not only in English but also in Russian and German. It had taken all his courage to ask her out to dinner, where he found out that she was only twenty-eight, that she lived alone, and that she was determined to go to America.

Vance had never been a smooth talker with women. He had the engineer's problem of being factual and direct. He felt awkward in courting a woman, and his compliments were usually delivered with painful obviousness. Yet it was different with Madeline. It was a cliché to say that they communicated without talking, but he soon saw that she focused her attention ferociously on him and seemed to anticipate what he would say. She was far too tactful to finish his sentences or to prompt him, but he felt she understood him as no woman, not even his beloved Margaret, had been able to do. It made decision making easy with Madeline, from which restaurant to choose to which dish to order.

Quite improbably they began an affair, which had now reached the point where Vance felt that they must marry, despite the war and their difference in ages. Madeline had gone to the American embassy in London just before France fell and within weeks was assigned to work with the emerging Free French organization. Vance's work with jet engines brought him to Great Britain many times, and each time they found that the previous separation only enhanced their feelings for each other.

After all his years in the business, Vance had many chits out with friends. Ordinarily he never asked for a favor, feeling it might compromise his business dealings, particularly when he was negotiating for the government. But he wanted Madeline in the United States, and he knew that her language abilities would be invaluable to Consolidated. At first he contemplated going directly to Reuben Fleet, Consolidated's leader, with the request, then thought better of it and simply forwarded her curriculum vitae to the firm's personnel office, with a letter asking that she be considered for a position. Consolidated had replied by return mail, and Madeline had accepted a job as a parts chaser. But within weeks she had been promoted to a job where her language skills counted, working in "The Rock," the seven-story concrete-block building where Consolidated's headquarters was located. Only the top floor had windows, and Madeline often came home complaining of headaches from the fluorescent lights that dominated the drawing rooms. As busy as she was, she went to night school to learn Spanish, adding another language to her repertoire.

All of this—his romance, bringing a woman to the United States, almost asking for a favor from a client—would probably not be approved by his sons, who were only four years younger than their putative stepmother. It was a recipe for trouble, and Vance knew it—and didn't care. Still, until they learned Tom's fate, Vance was going to keep the affair to himself.

The news that Tom was missing had hit Harry hard, for his

concern for his brother's welfare was heightened by the fact that he himself had seen no combat. After a very brief tour in England as a liaison officer with the Eagle Squadron, Harry had been pulled off to lead a mission to the Soviet Union to demonstrate how to use and maintain the Curtiss P-40s supplied by the Lend-Lease program. Then, against his violent protests, he was called back to Wright Field to head the fighter division of the Advanced Projects Branch, working directly under the legendary Ben Kelsey.

Two officers, a brigadier general and a colonel, smiled pleasantly as they eased past Vance, carefully sitting down four seats away to keep their conversation private. They apparently knew who he was, although he didn't recognize them, both very young, neither man much over thirty. Two years ago, Vance knew every senior officer in the Air Corps. Now he was elated if he found a familiar face.

The room was rapidly filling up, and the air was already going bad with cigarette smoke. The building had once housed the Air Corps Museum. He recalled the big, airy structure and calculated that he sat about where the big Fokker C-2 transport the *Bird of Paradise*, the first plane to fly from the West Coast to Hawaii, had been placed. It was gone now, burned in a huge bonfire that destroyed the relics of twenty years, and the building was now cut up into a rabbit warren of tiny offices and conference rooms. Vance closed his eyes, said another prayer for Tom, then returned to searching the smoke-filled room for people he knew. A few old friends came over and spoke to him, and he nodded to others as they filed in to their seats. It was evident that this was a select group, engineers in the main but also the commanders of Wright Field's aircraft and engine divisions.

Harry had told Vance at breakfast what the briefing was to be—a brief survey of the war, followed by a review of what was known of jet engine development around the world. The purpose was to evaluate the situation, determine how critically important a jet fighter was, and decide on how to remedy the disappointing performance of the Bell XP-59. America's first jet had flown on October 1, demonstrating a very modest performance that fell short of that of the latest piston engine fighters. General Arnold was bitterly disappointed, and although he blamed himself for assigning the task to Bell, in typical fashion he ladled his anger out on everyone in the program, demanding a quick fix to match the bad news coming in from Germany.

The Bell aircraft had flown within a year, just as Vance had promised Sidney Hooker, thanks to incredibly diligent work on the engines by General Electric. But somehow, Bell had erred in creating the airfoil for the XP-59A. They had already used the highly successful NACA laminar flow wing on their new—and still untested—P-63 Kingcobra but had elected to use a fat, high-lift/high-drag airfoil on the XP-59A. It was inexplicable, given that the Bell engineers generally tended to the radical side.

As far as Vance was concerned, the failure of the XP-59A created a crisis in the jet industry, both in the United States and in England, and this meeting had better solve it. If it did not, the Germans might well own the air over Europe in 1943.

The implications of an enemy jet fighter force of even five hundred aircraft were staggering. The German jets could simply ignore the Allied fighter escorts and blast the Eighth Air Force bombers out of the sky in wholesale numbers. Far fewer jet night fighters could do the same to the Royal Air Force's efforts. They could even eliminate the previously impervious Mosquitoes. With the bombing threat quelled and with it any possibility of invasion, Germany could turn its full attention to defeating Russia. The Me 262 had the potential of turning Germany's current three-front war into a single Eastern Front conflict.

Vance was bone weary, with the pains from his last bailout—almost two years ago—flaring up with every change in the weather. His life had altered from the inspirational test flying of his youth to a montage of gloomy briefings in dozens of rooms like this, in the Pentagon, here at Wright Field, and at air bases all over the country, the only relief being the brief intervals he spent with Madeline.

There was a stultifying uniformity in the briefing rooms, all painted beige above the chair-rail line and olive drab below. Each one was equipped with a plain four-legged table, a plywood podium, and folding metal chairs. All the meetings were the same as well: crowded, poorly lit, too warm, too smoky, lubricated by quarts of dreadful GI coffee, and attended by anything from ten to a hundred men who were so busy on their jobs that they resented wasting time in meetings.

The lights flashed and Harry stepped to the podium. Vance was proud of him and confident that he wouldn't do what almost every other briefing officer did: start the meeting with a bad dirty joke. Dirty jokes were the inevitable *lingua franca* of briefing officers, and while all were vulgar, few were funny.

Shannon laughed to himself, thinking, *I'm getting to be a prude with jokes at a time when my love life is more exciting than it's ever been.* Madeline was an amazing romantic partner, utterly solicitous of his needs and, most amazing of all, responding so intimately to him that she never failed to climax just as he did. At times he wondered if her responses were genuine, but he knew from the look in her eyes, from the sweet satin sheen of her perspiration, from her breathing, that she felt exactly as he did. Sometimes after an unusually vigorous session she would, eyes still closed, press his hand and murmur, "Hot and sweaty, good, hot, and sweaty." And it was good. And hot. And sweaty. He loved her.

Harry did not disappoint him, opening with a simple, "Good afternoon, gentlemen," and flashing on the overhead projector. The words "Top Secret" appeared on the white screen behind him.

"I'm Major Harry Shannon, representing Brigadier General Oliver Echols, commander, among his many other duties, of the Army Air Force Advanced Projects Branch. I've been asked to give you a very short briefing, passing on the view of Army Air Force headquarters on the world's military situation. I am then going to brief you on what is known of developments in jet aviation. The Advanced Projects Branch has developed several alternate proposals for the development of jet aircraft in the United States, and I'm going to ask for your opinions on which alternative we should adopt. You'll note I said 'alternative.' We really do not have time to look into several 'alternatives.' The results of this meeting will be translated into action immediately."

Vance swelled with pride. Harry was a professional, obviously the master of his material. He was self-confident, without being arrogant, his manner inviting both belief and questions. At breakfast, Vance had chided him about looking so tired and thin, but Harry had laughed it off, saying the work was good for him.

Harry began talking about the European theater, pointing out that the German offensive was continuing to advance in the Soviet Union, where it was now edging toward the oil in the Caucasus. "We frankly don't know what will happen in the Soviet Union. They are trading land for time, and they have stopped losing masses of men to the Germans. They may not have any more to lose: we cannot tell, and they certainly do not tell us anything. But if the Communists can hold out through the winter, it will probably mean that Germany has lost the war.

"In North Africa, the Africa Corps' advance had seemed to run out of steam, and the British had built up heavy defenses at El Alamein. We have to be careful in evaluating this theater—we tend to place too much emphasis on it. After all, the Germans are engaging some two hundred fifty or more Soviet divisions on the Eastern Front; in North Africa they are engaging no more than eight British divisions. It is obvious how they measure its relative importance.

"In the air, the British are continuing their strategy of night bombing of German cities. The Royal Air Force claims that the campaign is effective, but our own estimates indicate that it is not, at least in terms of reducing German production. Our own Eighth Air Force is just getting started. Between October 2 and October 8, we launched twelve hundred bombers at more than a dozen targets, some of them in Germany. We hope to double those efforts by mid-1943. By 'bombing round-the-clock' we plan to cut German war production at least in half."

There was a subdued murmur of approval from the room; despite the fact that every man held an important position, few knew just how large the effort of the Eighth Air Force had become.

Harry followed with some tables showing the size of the forces involved, the number of aircraft available to the Allies and the Axis, and the losses each side had incurred. The most significant element was the relatively stable size of the German Luftwaffe, despite its losses. To Vance, this meant that despite the bombing, the Nazis

were increasing production at a faster rate than had been antici-
pated.

Harry then confirmed Vance's own opinion about the Me 262.

"The greatest danger that we see in the air war is the probable
arrival of the German Messerschmitt Me 262 jet fighter in large
numbers by mid-1943. If that happens, we will have lost air superiority for an indefinite period, until we can get our own jets into action. General Arnold puts the greatest importance on this and is
determined to do everything he can to halt or delay the 262's operational debut. There is no question in his mind that if the Luftwaffe
were equipped with anything like the same number of Me 262 jets as
they currently have in 109s or 190s, the Eighth Air Force would
have to stand down. It could not endure the losses."

No one spoke audibly, but there was a palpable buzz, a combination of indrawn breaths and profane mutters.

Next Harry switched to the Pacific.

"In June we won a fantastic victory at the Battle of Midway—in
the future, it will probably be considered the turning point in the
war. But the Japanese are fighting stubbornly on Guadalcanal. Essentially, we own the air during the day, but they own the seas at
night."

Harry paused for a moment to look directly at his father, Tom
in both their thoughts.

Harry went on. "Despite the hard fighting, the prospects are
good. We should be able to begin pushing the Japanese back by late
fall or early winter. The war in Europe gets priority, as you know,
but by next year we will have built up a big advantage in numbers,
especially in aircraft carriers."

Harry rapidly went through the other theaters of war—the Battle of the Atlantic, the Aleutians, China—and then turned to jet engine development.

"Gentlemen, this entire briefing is top secret, but the most sensitive portion of the briefing is found in the next few slides. Some of
it is pretty raw—crude drawings and long-range aerial photographs.
But I think you'll see enough to help you point the way for the future here.

"Most of you are familiar with how a jet engine operates; for those that are not, let's look at the following three slides. Don't ask me for more information than presented here right now, and let's try to hold our questions to the end of the session."

Harry explained the very simplified diagrams, showing how a jet engine sucked in air, compressed it, injected fuel into the compressed air, ignited the mixture, which expanded explosively to drive a turbine wheel that in turn drove the compressor. The equal and opposite reaction of the jet of hot air passing out the rear of the aircraft propelled it forward.

"Next, I want to show you the jet aircraft that have flown to date."

The first projection was a good drawing of the Heinkel He 178, with the notation that it had flown on August 27, 1939.

"We think this must have been a rush job just to prove the concept of a jet engine, for it is obviously too small to carry any significant weapons. It apparently flew a few times, and is now in the air museum in Berlin. That's where we got this sketch, from a foreign national employed in a cleanup crew there. He dropped it off at the Swedish embassy, and someone was kind enough to provide it to the British. Next, please.

"This is the Italian Caproni Campini—it is not a true jet, for it uses a piston engine to drive the compressor. It made its first flight on August 28, 1940. The report we have says it was very slow, less than two hundred mph. Not much has been heard about it since. Next, please.

"The Heinkel He 178 must have been successful, because Heinkel flew the first twin-engine jet fighter in history sometime in April 1941."

The blurred image of a pretty little twin-engine jet fighter flashed on the screen. "There were Swedish ships in the harbor at Warenemunde. Some Allied sympathizer took this photo and, with some supplementary information, had it passed on to us. Warnemunde, as you know, is where the Arado factory is located. It is just a few miles north of the Heinkel factory at Marienehe. At first this was identified as an Arado, but the lines of the wings and the fuse-lage clearly indicate that it is from Heinkel."

As he spoke, the bulb in the overhead projector burned out. "OK, let's take ten while we get this bulb changed."

Half of the group filed out to go the latrine or grab a breath of fresh air, and Harry came over to where his father was sitting.

"How am I doing, Dad?"

"Great. I'm proud of you, Son. How did you get so inside that you'd be chosen to brief this material?"

"I'm not kidding myself, Dad—being Vance Shannon's son is a big help. That's why I want you to get me back into combat—in the Pacific, if possible."

"I'll try, Harry, because I know you really want it, but the fact is you are probably too important here to let go. I know how their minds work. When a commander latches on to a man like you, he won't give him up, especially to go to combat. That's where he wants to be himself! And I wouldn't blame him."

"Dad, it doesn't even have to be in fighters. I've checked out in everything on the field here, B-17s, B-24s, A-20s, everything. Just get me a slot. I'm trying myself, but I don't think my requests leave the field."

Vance looked at him, realizing Harry had no idea of what he was asking. Vance knew the right people and could—and would—get him transferred. But what if something happened to Harry then? Vance would feel responsible for the rest of his life. It was ir-rational. Harry could be killed tomorrow, flying in a C-47 to a meet-ing. But the feeling was there. Harry would never know what it was—until he had a son of his own.

The lean staff sergeant who'd replaced the bulb in the overhead projector signaled to Harry, and after a check to be sure that every-one was back in the room, Harry went on.

"As I was saying, this is the Heinkel He 280, flown in April 1941 and probably in limited production right now. We estimate a top speed of about five hundred miles per hour, but it is too small to have much range, so it will have to operate as an interceptor. It's one of the first German planes to have a tricycle landing gear, and we understand that it has an ejection seat for the pilot. Next sheet, please.

"Gentlemen, this is the RAF's Gloster jet, using the Whittle jet engine. They call it the Power Jet engine, now, after Whittle's little company. It first flew in May 1941, with an engine that developed eight hundred sixty pounds of thrust. At three hundred miles per hour, that would be about equivalent to the horsepower of one of our old Seversky P-35 fighters. Earlier this year, the prototype crashed, but another version is in the works. Great Britain is going to commit to the jet engine for fighters as soon as possible, with several companies, including de Havilland and Rolls-Royce, also developing engines. Gloster is building a twin-engine fighter prototype that will almost certainly go into production. Next sheet, please.

"Now here is the real worry. This is the Messerschmitt Me 262, which made its first flight in July this year, and insider reports indicate that it is going into mass production as soon as possible. Our engineers here at Wright say that it should do better than five hundred forty mph, and it looks like it carries a heavy armament, four, maybe six 30mm cannon. If the Germans can get this airplane into mass production by this fall, our bombers will have an insolvable problem."

He flashed on two more drawings, one a three-view showing the Me 262s' swept-back wings. The other was a photograph marked "Peenemünde," showing a typical factory and airfield layout, highlighted by a series of scorch marks that the photo interpreter had highlighted with a circle.

"You really cannot see the airplane in this photo, but the scorch marks are clearly the result of running a jet engine up on the tarmac, next to the grass. Incidentally, this was taken from thirty-eight thousand feet."

A collective moan went up when the next photo was flashed on the screen.

"Yes, this is the American jet—the Bell XP-59A. I can tell from your groans that the word has gotten around. It's a nice-flying airplane, but it is too slow. Look at the wings—they are huge! Just too much drag for the two engines, which are General Electric–built versions of the Whittle, putting out about twelve hundred fifty pounds of thrust each."

The overhead projector light was turned off, and Harry went on.

"So this is the situation. The Germans may have two jet fighters in production, and the British have one that is supposed to fly next year. We've got the XP-59A, which looks like it will have to be used as a trainer, since a P-51 or a P-38 can outfly it. Any questions?"

There was a barrage of shouts and it took a minute for Harry to get them quieted down. The first one, from the brigadier general sitting near Vance, was, "What kind of engines does the Messerschmitt jet have, and how much thrust do they produce?"

"We don't know, but our engineers estimate, from the size of the airplane, and the size of the engine intakes, that it has to be in the sixteen-to-eighteen-hundred-pounds-of-thrust range. They could be manufactured by Heinkel, but probably not. More probably they are from BMW or Junkers."

The next question was, "What engines will the new Gloster fighter have?"

"I don't know. They have three to choose from, the Whittle engine, another by de Havilland, and another from Rolls-Royce. Both de Havilland and Rolls-Royce have benefited from Whittle's pioneering, thanks to the British government handing out his information. They'll be in the fifteen-to-seventeen-hundred-pound class, whichever they choose."

A tall colonel stood up in the back of the room. Vance was surprised to see that it was Ray Crawford; he hadn't heard from him in months and had assumed he was off on a special assignment.

"Major Shannon, a couple of years ago, Lockheed was experimenting with a jet engine and a plane. Kelly Johnson and Nate Price worked together on it. Whatever happened to it?"

Harry flushed. Crawford knew damn well what had happened to it.

"Colonel Crawford, I think Wright Field dropped the ball. We didn't see the need for it, and the airframe looked too advanced for the time. Right now we are going to work with developing the Power Jet engine, and perhaps the de Havilland engine. As you all know, General Electric has the responsibility, and they have made phenomenal progress."

Crawford spoke again. "Well, Major, if I were you, I'd be going right back to Kelly and Lockheed and tasking them to come up with a new fighter. I don't believe in taking British hand-me-downs. We went through that when the war started, but we shouldn't be doing it now. It's bad enough that we have to use their engine until we can develop one of our own."

There was general applause; it was clear the group wanted an American fighter, even if it had to use an engine from Great Britain.

Crawford had resumed his seat, but he sat up again. "And somebody better get Pratt & Whitney and Curtiss-Wright in on the act. This is the biggest thing since they put a self-starter on a Cadillac. If General Electric takes as long on this one as they did on the supercharger, the whole goddamn war will be over before we get a jet into combat."

This time the applause was mixed with laughter. Harry fielded a few more questions, then broke the meeting down into four working groups, assigning tasks to each one. He had chosen the groups in the same way that he had sent out invitations to the meeting—on the expertise of the individuals. The first team was to estimate German jet production, the second was to formulate design criteria for a new American fighter, the third was to see what other companies could be brought into jet engine development, and the fourth was to establish a curriculum for training jet pilots, using the Bell P-59 as a trainer. He had put his dad in the second group.

Two hours later, the meeting began to break up as the teams turned in their handwritten reports to Harry for collation. He met with his father later that afternoon in the golf-course bar of the Officers Club. The jukebox was playing "Paper Doll" loud enough to foil any eavesdropper, but Harry looked around carefully, even taking the trouble to check their table for listening devices before whispering the results to his dad. The estimates for German jet production ranged from three hundred to three thousand per month. Either number would be fatal to the Eighth Air Force bombers. The design criteria for a new American fighter specified a top speed of 600 mph, a range of 600 miles, and delivery in a year. Almost everyone agreed that Lockheed should be given the contract. Besides General Electric, they had selected Westinghouse and Allison to begin developing jets. Finally, they estimated that a six-week course in jet aircraft would be adequate for veteran fighter pilots, with ten weeks for cadets coming right out of flying school.

Harry and Vance went on to talk earnestly about Tom for more than an hour, assessing his chances. Both talked optimistically; neither felt that way.

Finally Harry asked, "Well, Dad, did I embarrass you today?"

"No, you know you did well. I was surprised at Crawford, though; he should not have tried to trip you up like that. You didn't have anything to do with rejecting Nate's engine. You probably would have supported it, since you saw the papers on it back home."

"Crawford's angry, Dad, and he has some right to be. He did most of the work on getting the Whittle engine over here, then he didn't get promoted, and he got assigned to some minor jobs back at Pratt & Whitney as a plant representative. I asked him to the meeting because I value his experience. It was probably a mistake."

"Well, the advice he gave you is pretty good, and it coincides with the group's consensus. If you can turn the project over to Lockheed, I think Kelly Johnson and his team can whip up a fighter that will match the Germans'."

"I'm sure they can—but not in time. If the Germans get a few hundred Messerschmitt 262s operational by mid-1943, you can kiss the American bombing campaigns good-bye. There's no way the Fortress or the Liberators could operate against them, even if we get a long-range escort fighter delivered. And they'll figure out a way to make a night fighter out of it, too, to make it tough on the Royal Air Force."

Vance nodded. "You're exactly right. I agree one hundred percent! There's got to be some way to slow them down; bombing the factories might do it, but they are good at dispersal now and getting better. We'll have to come up with something to trump their ace."

They sipped Budweisers together. It was unusual; neither man drank as a rule, and they had not previously drunk together. Vance acknowledged this, saying, "A sign of the times, us drinking beer together. Wish Tom was here to join us."

Unexpectedly, Harry looked up and said, "Anyone else you'd like to have here, Dad?"

Vance choked on his beer. "What the hell do you mean by that?"

Harry looked uncomfortable and said, "Nothing, just making conversation."

Vance wondered if Harry was hinting about Madeline. He toyed with the idea of telling Harry all about it but decided against it. There was time enough for that when Tom came back. When, not if.

October 17, 1942, Guadalcanal

"THINK, DAMMIT; THINK." Lieutenant Tom Shannon, sunburned, dirty, and starving, knew that his time had come. He would either make a break for the beautiful Consolidated PBY streaming in at wave-top level or die trying. Twenty minutes before, he had signaled the Catalina as it passed overhead. The flying boat had returned his signal, but had then, to his bitter disappointment, flown off directly to the north. Now he saw it low on the horizon, hurtling south toward the island to pick him up.

His dogfight seemed like months ago. A flight of three Zeros had thundered out of the sun, nose guns winking furiously, the wing-mounted cannon burping slow but steady. He had turned into the flight and sawed the lead Zero in half with a single burst, but the enemy fire had smashed his oil cooler. Tom had thrown his Wildcat into a dive as waves of oil covered his canopy to run along the fuselage side. The two Zeros followed him down, snap shooting, when his engine froze. The reduction gear exploded and the prop ran away in a fantastic crescendo of noise. One of the Zeros, accepting the victory, pulled away, but the other edged in and blew his wing off with a closely spaced pattern of 20mm shells.

The rugged Wildcat went into an uncontrollable rolling dive

until it broke up at about six thousand feet, throwing Tom out of the cockpit. Shaken but conscious, he delayed opening his parachute until he had fallen to about four hundred feet. The jerk of the parachute opening separated him from his shoes, and he saw that he was dropping straight for a cartoon-like island, a three-hundred-foot-wide circle of sand with a cluster of palm trees in the center. He hit far up the narrow beach, landing without even getting his feet wet.

Tom gathered his parachute and hid in the clutch of palm trees, certain that the fight had been witnessed by the Japanese soldiers in the supply camp three miles away on the southwestern tip of Guadalcanal. He spent the entire day huddled on his parachute canopy before deciding that he must have landed unseen and that the little island held no other interest for the enemy. For the next seven days he had remained almost motionless while it was light, hiding under the trees, surviving on the handful of coconuts he harvested and the few strange shellfish he plucked from the rocky coastline at night. These had tasted terrible the first day, better on the second, and, as they grew scarce, downright delicious by the sixth day.

This was the second Catalina he had signaled with his handheld mirror. Four days before, a PBY had dipped its wings in recognition and set up a pattern to land when it was struck by a gaggle of Zeros en route back to Rabaul. They blew it up in a single pass, arrogantly doing victory rolls as they climbed away from the smoking debris. Tom felt guilty, for the crew never had a chance. The PBY crews were incredible, flying long missions alone in enemy territory and never failing to attempt to pick up a downed American flyer, no matter what the odds. Now another one was coming for him.

Tom moved out to the water's edge, hoping that he'd have the strength to swim to the Catalina when it landed. He watched approvingly as the flying boat touched down smoothly, then turned to taxi at high speed toward him. The artillerymen at the Japanese camp suddenly woke up and artillery shells began to explode, a few around the Catalina but most well over his island, as if the gunners could not depress their guns enough to target the PBY. Lighter guns began firing, hitting the PBY almost immediately.

The PBY taxied past him, then turned to bring him up just off the left waist gun blister, its lower Plexiglas visor already raised. A sailor, dressed only in his skivvies, plunged over the side to help him, while another hung out from the blister to pull him in. The first sailor had just placed his head inside the hatch when the pilot applied full power for takeoff.

After a quick check to see if he was wounded, the gunners moved Tom forward through the narrow door separating them from the bunk compartment and on forward to the navigator's compartment, where they dumped him unceremoniously on a mound of Mae West life preservers before scurrying back to their guns. He lay there, watching the rest of the crew attending to their duties, the tension high as the long, bouncing takeoff continued. The navigator handed Tom a canteen of water and a sandwich—thick slices of Spam between two rough-cut pieces of GI bakery bread—and Tom had never tasted anything so delicious. The radioman tossed him a headset, so he could listen on the intercom.

The PBY, its twin engines mounted high on the parasol wing, seemed to bounce along the water forever, salt spray slashing over the windscreen. The pilot leaned over the control wheel, visibly forcing the overhead throttles forward, the copilot bending low in his seat, as if bullets wouldn't pierce the thin aluminum as easily as the Plexiglas windows. Once the navigator looked over and shot Tom a thumbs-up.

After an eternity in which the bounces turned into long skips and finally a tiny dribbling run that seemed to hold the plane to the water with a gossamer spray, the PBY lifted off, just as a Japanese battery at last got the range, the shrapnel punching holes along the length of the fuselage and into the wings. Fuel began leaking immediately, running back in a fine white spray.

The navigator passed Tom a note, written on a crumpled sheet of paper in big black pencil strokes: "Congratulations; we'll be back at Henderson Field in ten minutes. Drink all the water you want, but slow down on the sandwich—you'll get sick."

Tom nodded and put the headset on to listen to the intercom chatter.

"Nav, this is pilot. Is the passenger wounded?"

"No, they checked him when they hauled him in. He's just hungry as hell."

A gunner broke in: "Here come two Zeros; the first one is shooting!"

The Catalina shook under an initial barrage of 7.7mm machine-gun fire followed by a massive series of blows from the first Zero's 20mm cannon. Ten seconds later, the noises were repeated, this time punctuated by the eerie shriek of a runaway propeller.

The pilot yelled, "Feather number two," and Tom looked up through the copilot's windscreen to see the two Zeros climbing away. He watched his Catalina pilot boot in hard left rudder and bend the left throttle forward, easing the nose down to keep flying speed.

Grunting, sweating, totally concentrated, the pilot flew on at treetop level, desperate to reach Henderson and plant the Catalina firmly on the ground. Tom couldn't see all that was going on, but he knew exactly what was going through the pilot's mind: keep the speed well above the stall, delay putting the gear down until the last minute, don't put in any flaps until he was sure he was in position to land—and pray that the gear either came down all the way or stayed retracted; the worst thing would be a partial extension.

The navigator motioned Tom to a seat belt fastened to the floor next to the aft bulkhead and pointed his hand down. He had barely strapped in when the Catalina slammed down, bounced, then smashed into the pierced steel planking of the runway again, the Catalina's gear screeching and flexing but holding together. When they reached the end of the runway, the pilot kicked the rudder, spun the Catalina off the taxiway into the shrapnel-chewed dirt, shut down the engines, and, reverting to his Navy upbringing, yelled, "Abandon ship!" as he rang the alarm bell.

The crew helped Tom run away from the PBY, stopping when they felt they had enough distance between it and a possible explosion. As soon as the motley set of rescue vehicles rolled up, they pushed Tom into what passed as an ambulance before he had time to say more than thanks. He was in the primitive aide station grandly marked "Hospital" for two hours when his squadron commander showed up, a big grin on his face.

Major Delaroy was carrying a bottle of beer and some more Spam sandwiches, saying, "I knew we couldn't get rid of you! Just three more Wildcats and you'll be a Japanese ace!"

Tom winced—it was the second time he had been shot up by Zeros; the first time he had limped back to the field, but his badly damaged Wildcat never flew again.

"Never again! I'm transferring to bombers, where I can get a little peace."

They talked for another hour, Delaroy filling him in on the victories and losses of the past week.

"We're getting to the point where we can replace some of our people; do you want to go home for a bit and recuperate?"

"Never! I'm ready to go back on operations right now."

Delaroy smiled. "Let me talk to the flight surgeon; I'm sure he'll sign you off in a day or two."

The CO left the room and Tom went back to the details of his fight with the Zero and the flight back from the island in the Catalina. Both times he had been trapped, unable to do anything. If he had not been thrown out of the Wildcat, he would have gone in with it. The same with the Catalina—if the Zeros had come back for one more pass, the airplane would have crashed and he and the whole crew would have been killed.

There had to be a better way to get out of airplanes. Tom decided that if he lived through this campaign, he would find a way to make emergency jumps no matter what the state of the aircraft.

Allies invade North Africa; Germany suffers disastrous defeats at Stalingrad and El Alamein; Allied leaders meet at Casablanca; "round-the-clock" bombing begins; Japan driven from Guadalcanal after months of bloody battle; German submarine victories peak, then decline; U-boat losses go up; first Kaiser "Liberty Ship" launched; Germans surrender in Tunisia; Sicily invaded; Italy invaded; Mussolini deposed.

CHAPTER FIVE

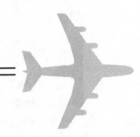

Lechfeld, Germany, May 22, 1943

The Messerschmitt firm was reeling from the backlash of Willy Messerschmitt's angry accusations of incompetence, and no one was more upset than Woldemar Voigt, the lead designer of the new jet fighter.

Voigt mastered his usually powerful personality, stifling his resentment, as he stood in his cluttered office, head bowed, listening to the balding, jut-jawed Messerschmitt rant about his incompetence and stupidity. Abstractly he thought, *'This is so unlike Willy,'* for normally he ran a congenial shop, giving his department heads authority to make major decisions. Now he had lost control and was saying things he would regret later.

Only ten months before, the good Dr. Messerschmitt believed he had won the race to build a production jet fighter with the first flight of the Me 262. On the basis of that success, the Reich Air Ministry had decided not to issue contracts for the rival Heinkel He 280 and instead ordered a pre-production series of the 262s, to set the path for mass production.

Since then there had been a series of diasters that was pushing the program to the brink of cancellation. Last August 11, the veteran test pilot Henrich Beauvais had been unable to master Wendel's takeoff technique. Beauvais had bounded down the field, tail rising, then falling back down, until he plunged off the end of the runway, tore up a cornfield, caught his wingtip on a manure heap, and spun the sole flying prototype into a mass of smoking metal. Fortunately, Beauvais walked away from the crash, but suddenly things were reversed and Heinkel was the only firm with a flyable jet fighter prototype.

Some evil specter seemed to be stalking the program, and only Messerschmitt's eloquence had persuaded the Reich Air Ministry to continue along and even increase the order to thirty pre-production aircraft. This was a double-edged sword, for while it was a godsend to the program, seemingly ensuring its life, it required the acquisition of many more scarce engineers and hard-to-find machine tools. Messerschmitt's forceful efforts to get them caused resentment in the Air Ministry's bureaucracy, and the barely cordial relations created by the 262's success were destroyed.

It wasn't till early in 1943 that they had another flyable 262 prototype. It made one successful flight before it crashed, diving straight into the ground after takeoff, killing Wendel's top assistant, Wilhelm Ostertag.

Messerschmitt's voice, normally low and measured, now seemed to climb an octave as he sputtered, "And now I find out that we do not have a viable test program! We have one prototype flying now, in May 1943! This is impossible! What am I to tell Milch? He'll have Heinkel back under contract in an instant when he learns about this."

Voigt looked up. He had not spoken since Mersserschmitt had burst into his office, interrupting a staff meeting, ordering everyone out of the room. They were all cowering in the hallway now, listening to Messerschmitt scream, ready to disappear if he left the room.

"Dr. Messerschmitt, please let me talk." Voight was always softspoken and deferential in dealing with Messerschmitt, less so when dealing with his own subordinates.

"No, you listen, Dr. Voigt. The Air Ministry is already demanding changes; they want a tricycle landing gear and they want production speeded up! How can I do this if you've allowed all the prototypes to crash?"

It was blatantly unfair, and Fritz Wendel, listening with the others in the hallway, decided to intervene. He eased the door open and walked in uninvited. No one else in the plant would have dared to do so, but he was Messerschmitt's favorite test pilot and had earned the privilege. Wendel came right to the point.

"Dr. Messerschmitt, Dr. Voigt is not to blame on this. You dictated the number of prototypes to build, and you know very well we have to expect losses; we will crash a dozen of these 262s before we begin to get it right, and you know that better than anyone."

Embarrassed, knowing Wendel was right, Messerschmitt sputtered and reached his hand out to Voigt's shoulder.

Wendell went on, "And I can tell you that today is the day that we can get back on track."

Messerschmitt and Voigt looked at him. Wendel was a brilliant test pilot but hardly a production program expert.

"As of today, after a lot of effort on the shop floor, we have two prototypes ready to fly. Last week, I took the initiative to invite General Galland down to fly one. He is here now, in the operations building, getting briefed on the controls and the systems." Wendel knew he was in dangerous waters; he had exceeded his authority, going behind Messerschmitt's back to invite the most admired man in the Luftwaffe down to fly the Me 262.

Messerschmitt literally staggered back to the wall, appalled that Wendel had the temerity to so exceed his authority but realizing at the same instant what an opportunity it was. Adolf Galland was the Luftwaffe's Inspector General for Fighters. He had shot down nearly one hundred enemy aircraft officially and, it was said, many more that he hadn't bothered to confirm. He was barred from combat flying because he was so valuable as an organizer and tactician.

Voigt's heart leaped within him. Wendel had put his career on the line, and everything depended upon Messerschmitt recognizing the value of Galland's approval. They had always planned to have the veteran ace fly the airplane, but not until later in the year.

Messerschmitt's engineering mentality was a runaway train evaluating the pluses and minuses of the situation. The great danger was that Galland might crash and be killed in the 262. If that happened, the program was finished. Milch would cancel it and Göring would approve. Messerschmitt himself would probably go to a concentration camp—he had already been threatened with prison. Ah, but if Galland flew the airplane, he would see its value at once, and his approval would set the program in concrete, assuring mass production. And then there was the morale situation to consider; if Messerschmitt refused to allow Galland to fly, he would have to somehow punish Wendel for his impertinence and Voigt would also have to be censured.

Time slowed in Dalí fashion, but within a minute it had become clear to Messerschmitt that Wendel had thrown him a life preserver. This was in fact the only way out of the shortage-of-prototypes problem—and also the embarrassing personal situation he had created by berating Voigt.

"Fritz, I should fire you, but I won't because this is the only way out. I salute you for your brazen impudence—but don't think you can do it again. Dr. Voigt, I apologize. I was distraught, and I blamed you for things that I am at least equally to blame for. Now let's go see if this *wunderkind* Galland can fly us out of all this trouble."

All three breathing huge sighs of relief, they walked the two hundred yards to the operations building where the dapper major general sat listening to a group of test pilots and mechanics explain the systems of the 262. Of medium height, with a shock of black hair and a mustache that made Hitler's look like an eyebrow, he sat smoking his usual big black cigar. He was the only pilot in the Luftwaffe to have his Bf 109 cockpit fitted with an electric cigar lighter and an ashtray. He smoked continuously while flying, removing his oxygen mask to take a drag on one of the cigars that poured in on him as gifts from admirers all over Germany and even from the occupied territories. His aircraft carried his personal insignia, a pugnacious version of Mickey Mouse smoking a big cigar. Galland was also the definitive ladies' man, with sweethearts at every airfield, many of them so devoted that they followed him from assignment to assignment, creating a tryst-scheduling problem for him.

But he was first and foremost a fighter expert, determined to gain air supremacy for the Luftwaffe, despite its derelict leadership. He had made aviation history during the Battle of Britain when, after a particularly galling speech by Hermann Göring, he was asked by the great man what he wanted in the way of equipment. Galland's response, "A squadron of Spitfires, *Herr Reichsmarschall*," had brought him to within seconds of court-martial, but it also gained him the undying devotion of his comrades.

Galland was a legend who had emerged from the shadow of another hero, his friend and mentor Werner Moelders. They had vied for being the top ace of the Luftwaffe, with Moelders leading by a comfortable margin until he was killed. His death was a total waste, flying back in a Heinkel He 111 to attend the elaborately fraudulent funeral for Ernst Udet. And rumor had it that there was not a crash at all, but that Moelders, a devout Catholic, had been killed because he had protested the brutal Nazi policies used on the Eastern Front, going so far as to refuse to wear his medals.

Moelders's heir, Galland, had seen the Luftwaffe go from dazzling air superiority in Poland and over France to a stymied force over Great Britain. Then, in the vast reaches of Russia, the Luftwaffe became just a fire brigade, sent to where the danger was greatest, unable to achieve air superiority anywhere except by concentrating its forces in a particular area for a short time. Now it was bowing under the great and growing weight of the Allied bombing campaign. Fighters, vitally needed on the Soviet front, were withdrawn to defend the airspace of the Reich.

For three years he had raged against the shortsightedness of Luftwaffe leaders, who had kept German aircraft plants on a one-shift-per-day basis and never bothered to expand production schedules to match the Allied challenge. The same leaders had stifled new developments so that his units were fighting with primarily the same types they had when the war started while the enemy continually reequipped with new and better aircraft. Worst of all, he had to contend with the haphazard strategy of Göring and other leaders, who spread the Luftwaffe around in bits and pieces, instead of allowing Galland to concentrate an enormous force of fighters to oppose the enemy bombers. He knew if he could put up one thousand fighters on a single mission, he could inflict devastating losses on the incoming American and British bomber units and stop the fearsome growing carnage they executed daily in Germany. Anyone else who spoke out as he did, in the forums he chose, would have long since been court-martialed and sent to Dachau. But Galland was beloved by his subordinates and his position was so secure that not even Göring dared move against him—at least not yet.

Galland listened, his dark eyes dancing, interrupting occasionally only to ask a pertinent question. It was obvious that he knew a great deal, that Wendel and others had been briefing him, and it was equally apparent that his enthusiasm was growing as he learned more. No mathematician, he insisted upon going over and over the equations that translated pounds of thrust into horsepower. It seemed impossible that the relatively small, light Junkers engines could produce what the engineers claimed, the equivalent of 900 kilograms of thrust at sea level, an output that would climb with an increase in speed. When told that the estimated speed of the 262 was about 885 kilometers per hour, Galland smiled. That was 225 kph faster than his Messerschmitt Bf 109, and he frankly doubted such a leap forward to be possible.

He sat there, impassive, going over the figures, then finally nodded, for even if the Messerschmitt and Junkers engineers were wildly optimistic, by as much as 50 percent, it was still a fantastic step forward. And if they were accurate—and in his heart he hoped they were; he knew their work—the results would be utterly sensational.

The last Junkers man to speak almost as an aside mentioned that the performance figures would be obtained even if low-quality diesel fuel was used instead of aviation gasoline, and Galland stood up. He had heard this before, but he wanted clarification and got a long exposition on the combustion factors that allowed diesel oil to produce the power they estimated. He stood for a moment, silent. This was a key factor. Even if the performance estimates all were all wrong, it might still be important enough to insist that the jet go into production. Germany was already desperately short of the rotgut eighty-seven-octane fuel that was the standard issue. Moreover, there were larger piston engines being planned, and they would certainly require higher-octane fuels that were going to be virtually impossible to obtain.

At last he slapped his hand down on the desk and said, "Let's go. I'm ready. Roll that Turbo out and let me try it."

A Mercedes staff car drove them to the end of the runway where two beautifully prepared aircraft, the Me 262V3 and V4, waited. Both were washed and polished and Wendel climbed into the first aircraft, which had flown almost twenty times in the last three weeks. Galland had been carefully briefed on the toe-tapping takeoff technique Wendel had developed and watched closely as the Messerschmitt test pilot took off, sending the fighter hurtling down the runway nose high, then at the 800-meter mark tapping the brakes, rotating the nose down, and gathering sufficient speed for flight.

Wendel put on a dazzling eighteen-minute flying show, demonstrating the speed, roll rate, climb, and slow-flight capabilities of the airplane. While Wendel flew, engine technicians emphasized to Galland how important it was to handle the throttles gently—no jamming them forward as was sometimes necessary in piston engine fighters but rather manipulating them evenly and easily, to avoid stalling or overheating the engines.

Wendel landed with the usual spectacular but harmless sheets of trailing flame from fuel pooled in the nacelles. While the airplane was being refueled and inspected, he talked to Galland again about the takeoff technique. It was imperative to bring the engines up to speed slowly and together; if one engine failed at takeoff speed, it would spin the aircraft to one side, careening it off the runway and probably causing a catastrophic crash.

Galland's smoke timing had been perfect; he ground the stump of the big black cigar into the ground, clambered up into the cockpit, and sat, going over the instruments while Wendel talked him through starting the first engine. It seemed to start normally enough, and Wendel leaped down, leaving Galland to start the second. At that moment the first engine burst into flames. Unaware, Galland kept looking at the throttle quadrant, concentrating on a smooth start of the second engine. A mechanic leaped on the wing, pounded Galland on the shoulder, and pointed to the fire. With his long experience in emergencies, it took Galland only seconds to disconnect his seat belt and parachute and dive over the side, hitting the ground in a rolling motion, before being up and running to where the others was waiting. A fire crew swarmed over the burning engine, blanketing the flames with their fire extinguishers.

Galland was unshaken by the incident. He understood how temperamental jet engines were and that over time these would be more reliable and less prone to catching fire. He signaled impatiently to Willy Messerschmitt that he would fly the other aircraft.

Both engines of the Messerschmitt Me 262V4 started uneventfully, and Galland eased it out to the runway, unable to see straight ahead over the long nose, S-turning to make sure he didn't taxi into something. He lined up exactly in the middle of the runway, with his tail wheel resting on the lip of the asphalt. Galland advanced the throttles carefully, steering with the brakes at first, then, as the rudder became effective, with the rudder pedals. As speed gathered he was struck by the comparative silence, the lack of torque, and the slow but rapidly building acceleration. At precisely 180 kph he tapped the brakes, the nose leaned down, the elevators caught the air, and seconds later he was airborne, climbing faster than he ever had before. Galland was not poetic, but he had an instant mental image of a flight of angels pushing airplane in its headlong climb.

He saw at once that the Me 262 was a war-winning weapon, far superior to anything the enemy had, able to take on any Allied fighter. A flight of four 262s could destroy much of a bomber formation in a single pass. As he flew, he tested the airplane's capability, banking it ever more steeply, diving and climbing, carefully adjusting the power, and always keeping his eye on the rapidly declining fuel gauges.

To the west of the field he spotted a larger airplane and immediately headed for it. In less than a minute he discerned that it was one of Messerschmitt's other advanced projects, the four-engine Me 264, the so-called *Amerika Bomber.* The huge aircraft was on a routine test flight near the field, and Galland promptly climbed to carry out a classic fighter attack, moving from high in the rear to below and past the "target."

He flew the same pattern he might have flown in his 109 fighter and found that he whipped by the bomber so swiftly that he wouldn't have had time to fire his guns. He realized that just a few seconds of miscalculation might have seen him fly not by but into the Me 264, thus effectively smashing two important test programs—and himself—in one ill-considered pass.

Sobered by the experience, he flew back to the field, made a conservative pattern, and landed, convinced that in the 262 Germany had found a way to win the air war. Now all he had to do was win a battle with the Air Ministry and convince them to build enough of the 262s.

June 7, 1943, Berlin

FRITZ OBERMYER HAD declined to fly to the meeting in Berlin, though Ernst Heinkel himself had offered him a seat in one of the two comfortably equipped He 111s making the short trip. Obermyer preferred to travel by train, as crowded as they were. Even the uncertain schedules, always subject to delays by bombings, had an advantage, providing him an excuse to come up a day early to be sure he was on time. He had faced his share of dangers on the Western Front during the war and again during the decade of street fighting that had preceded Hitler's accession to power in 1933—he refused to accept the risk of flying when he could. Besides, there was no room on the plane for Müller, and where Obermyer went, Müller followed.

Although there were continual calls from the party and the government to reduce the number of conferences during wartime, they continued to proliferate, and this one, a review board for jet engines and aircraft, was probably more legitimate than most. It had been called by his old *Friekorps* commander, Erhard Milch, who never wasted anyone's time. He had made *Deutsche Luft Hansa* a financial success and then became one of the top leaders of the Luftwaffe. An organizational genius, he was succeeding exactly where Udet had failed, rationalizing the industry, concentrating on fewer types, and insisting that production be increased. Göring was jealous of how well Milch performed and would gladly have gotten rid of him if he had dared. But Milch had Hitler's confidence, and that meant Göring could not do as he usually did, hammer down anyone who he felt threatened his position. Milch was cordially disliked by many of the top Luftwaffe generals, men who spent long years in the lower ranks after the Versailles Treaty had destroyed the German armed forces. They regarded him as a civilian and resented his meteoric progress. He had been a captain in 1918, entered the Luftwaffe with the rank of major general in 1934, and by July 1940 had been promoted to field marshal.

Yet as rapid as his advance had been, Milch was terribly vulnerable in the poisonous Nazi climate where every leader but one—Hitler—was fair game for any other. Milch's father, whom he scarcely knew, was a Jew, so he was half-Jewish and therefore automatically precluded from furthering his career. Yet it developed that his mother, whom he adored, had been forced into marriage by her parents with Anton Milch. She resisted the arrangement, saying yes only when her prospective husband agreed not to have conjugal relations with her and to let her bear children by another man. That man was an Aryan. Göring had once grandly declared that he decided who was a Jew and who was not but had insisted on carrying out an elaborate procedure in which Milch's mother signed a sworn affidavit that he was not the son of her husband but rather of her Aryan lover. Milch was relieved by the agreement, which meant he kept his power and his perks. But he could never consider the issue at rest. Göring could make Milch a Jew tomorrow, and he would disappear the same day, to the applause of many.

Obermyer maintained a small apartment in Berlin, less than a mile from the grandiose Air Ministry building. It was one of his perks as an old Nazi. The apartment had formerly belonged to a Jewish doctor and his wife. When they were sent to Theresienstadt, the "model" concentration camp maintained for propaganda purposes, an old comrade in party headquarters alerted Obermyer, and he promptly purchased it. Half of the absurdly small amount went into party coffers and half into his friend's pocket. Obermyer knew that owning it was risky. People were already suspicious of his standard of living, and he was forced to pretend that he had family business interests and also made large sums gambling. It was ironic, because he tried never to gamble. Sure things were his forte.

One sure thing was Müller's loyalty. Obermyer watched tolerantly as his old comrade snored in the big leather chair in the living room, his head down on his chest and his legs sprawled out on the floor, a half-eaten sandwich and an empty stein of beer on the table beside him. No intellectual, Müller was a good man to have at one's back in a bar fight. Even better, he had good common sense and an uncanny ability to size people up and know how to handle them. But best of all, he was loyal—to Obermyer. No foolish nonsense about loyalty to the Führer or to the party or to anyone else. Müller was Obermyer's man, and that was it. In return he received his salary from Heinkel and a considerable stipend from Obermyer. If Müller had a fault, it was his tendency to complain about everything; periodically Obermyer spoke to him sharply about this, but for the most part he accepted his querulous nature as part of the overhead of having a loyal servant.

Reaching down, Obermyer shook Müller's shoulder. "Wake up, Gerd; it's time we went to the conference."

Müller was instantly wide awake, checking his pocket watch and saying, "I'll get the car."

Obermyer shook his head. "No, it's too conspicuous. We'll take the underground."

Müller, who loved the sleek BMW that Obermyer had obtained with the apartment, complained about not driving all the way to the Leipziegerstrasse, where Göring's grandiose four-hundred-thousand-square-foot Air Ministry building dominated the scene. The massive block-square twenty-eight-hundred-room structure was Göring's attempt to outdo Albert Speer, the architect who had created the magnificent Chancellery for Adolf Hitler in a single year. But while Speer's building had been applauded—it was for the Führer, after all—Göring's building evoked a negative reaction. The public thought it too elegant for a nation brought up on short rations—and for a Luftwaffe that apparently could not stop the bombing raids.

Göring was above such criticism. He wanted the best for the Luftwaffe, and the building was simply a demonstration of that desire. Besides, the building soon possessed his prize tool, the greatest power lever that any German leader possessed, surpassing that of even Hitler and Heinrich Himmler. Within high-security areas in the building was the "Research Office," where faceless civil servants worked twenty-four hours a day, seven days a week, managing a vast system of telephone and cable taps, recording conversations and messages. Hollerith punch-card computers were used to consolidate the information, and information considered worthy of passing up was provided to Göring daily on what were called the Brown Sheets. No one was immune, from Catholic priests suspected of a dalliance to the highest-ranking officers. It was the single most effective espionage system in the Third Reich, and it was controlled by Göring alone.

Air Ministry employees were generally aware that Erhard Milch was gradually taking control of the Luftwaffe. Göring had begun to distance himself from day-to-day matters, concentrating more on building up his art collection than on building up "his" air force. To Milch, work was life, for he knew his position depended upon his performance, and he approached the Luftwaffe as he had *Deutsche Luft Hansa*, as an instrument to perfect.

The difficulty was that the Luftwaffe, unlike the airline, was not a for-profit industry, and the cost-conscious Milch reacted adversely to many pleas for research and development. Further, Milch saw conspiracies everywhere, and just as he had done at *Deutsche Luft Hansa*, he sought to quell these by personnel transfers. In looking over the turmoil of the jet industry, he had concluded that there was not enough cooperation between the Air Ministry and the manufacturers and far too little among the competing companies. To remedy this he had made a series of reassignments that had plunged the jet industry into chaos.

The manufacturers had protested as forcefully as they dared, and Milch had responded by calling this conference, to get the complaints out into the open. Unlike Göring, he could take some criticism, if it was couched in courteous terms and if he felt it was fair. The manufacturers knew that, but they also knew they could not press him too far without repercussions.

The only positive thing that could be said about his extensive personnel reassignments was that they were damaging to all parties and most of all to the still infant German jet engine development. For reasons known only to himself, Milch had acted on the advice of two of his deputies in the Air Ministry, Hans Mauch and Helmut Schelp. The two men believed that they were rationalizing the jet engine industry by assigning jet engines of certain types and sizes to certain companies. In the mature airframe industry this had made sense and worked quite well. In the engine industry it was absurd, because there was not yet a sufficient body of knowledge on jet engines to make such a decision. Further, all of German industry, but particularly the more technologically advanced sectors, suffered enormously from the sweeping security restrictions that limited the spread of information on a rigorous "need to know" basis. The result was that the same mistakes would be made in many different factories, when a free exchange of information would have accelerated progress.

Milch ordered that Professor Herbert Wagner, Max Müller, and their development group at Junkers be transferred to the Heinkel factory, where they were placed under the nominal direction of von Ohain. The so-called Prussian group, under von Ohain, was immediately at odds with the "Swabian" group under Wagner, and there was a steep decline in research results and general productivity. Von Ohain's men were considered by Wagner's group to be theorists, academics unwilling or unable to get their hands dirty. In turn, von Ohain's people believed the Wagner faction to be mechanics, unable to get their nails clean and totally incapable of seeing the larger goals to be sought.

Milch's conference was to be held in one of the lavishly equipped conference rooms in the Air Ministry. Göring extended his openhanded style to the lowly workers in the building, ensuring that the polished marble halls were well supplied with seats, tables, telephones, and, on special occasions like this, refreshments.

Hans von Ohain waited nervously outside the doors of the conference room. Always conscious of his youth, he felt it even more keenly in these polished halls where a continuous flow of Luftwaffe airmen in their smart new uniforms hurried past, all seeming to say, "We are pilots and you are not." He stood ramrod straight, but his eyes searched for a man he knew only by reputation but whose position was almost as untenable as his own—Dr. Anselm Franz. With the reassignment of Wagner's group, the primary responsibility for jet engine work at Junkers had been transferred to Franz. Because of his previous experience with superchargers, he had been working quietly on jet engine development since 1939. Von Ohain wanted to talk to him, to gain some insight into working with Wagner and his team, and to offer any help that he could, in spite of the galling "need to know" security restrictions that operated in Hitler's Germany.

Franz walked in alone, spotted von Ohain, and came briskly down the hallway to meet him. Slightly shorter than von Ohain but of a much more athletic build, Franz was about ten years older, with a square, open face, a shock of blond hair already turning silver, and a flashing smile.

"Dr. von Ohain, it is a great honor to meet you. I greatly admire your work."

Von Ohain flushed with pleasure. Franz was well-known in the industry, and von Ohain was pleased with the deference he extended. They talked of mutual friends for a moment until von Ohain, glancing at his watch, suggested that they move down the hallway to a point where they could speak privately.

Franz laughed. "Talk privately in Göring's building? Impossible; there probably is a microphone in every potted plant." The two men felt an instant empathy. Both had been tasked with crushing assignments and were harassed by both their employers and the Air Ministry to do the impossible with minimal resources.

Von Ohain came right to the point. "I'm having difficulty with Dr. Wagner and his group. They seem determined to go their own way, without regard to my instructions. Is there any way I can control them short of going to Dr. Heinkel and demanding that he do something?"

Franz shook his head. "The Air Ministry did me a great favor, and you a great disservice. Wagner and his group are simply too bright, and they are spoiled. They had their own way at Junkers for so long that they won't be inclined to let someone—particularly an academic such as you—control them. I advise you to do as I did—let them go their own way, give them whatever help you can, but work on your own. If you try to control them, they will fight you every step of the way, and no one will make any progress. If you let them alone, they may surprise you and come up with something workable—they are really quite clever. But certainly do not expect them to help you. They just do not know how to cooperate."

"How did you work in parallel? Did Junkers have so many engineers that it could afford two entirely separate development lines?"

"No. I let them go on their own, and I'm not even certain what they have done. For myself, I worked with a tiny group and set modest aims. I had never seen a jet engine of course, and decided to build one first, to see how they operate, and only then attempt to design an airworthy engine. So I didn't worry about weight or using strategic materials; I just used the best information I could gather—including all I could learn about your engine, I might add—and cobbled together a jet engine to see if it would run. It is axial flow, as you no doubt know, and it taught me a great deal. I also learned that I could not trust the Air Ministry."

He laughed again and von Ohain leaned forward, intent.

"You see, they took my test engine, the Jumo 004A, and ordered me to put it in production! It didn't make sense, I told them I had only made a model of an engine, but the Air Ministry did not care! So we are building a modified version of my test engine, calling it the Jumo 004B1. The first production engine came off the line this January. We are still having problems, of course, particularly in engine life—if we get ten hours we are fortunate, twenty-five and we are ecstatic. Quite frankly, it is a miracle that it turned out as well as it did. A miracle."

Von Ohain was stunned. Franz's progress had been remarkable, from start to production engines in four years! Von Ohain was still a year or more away from mass production of his own design.

Two of Milch's aides began circulating through the group, asking them to enter the conference room. Von Ohain and Franz shook hands, von Ohain saying, "I wish we could work together. I'm sure we would both benefit."

Franz sighed. "Certainly that would be the best. We desperately need help to stop cracks and vibration in our turbine blades. But you can be certain that the Air Ministry will forbid us to do so."

As was his invariable custom, Obermyer waited until almost everyone had gone in, then slid into a seat in the last row. One of his legacies from the previous war was an obsession for cleanliness; he bathed almost every day and had a supply of colognes that Müller had once remarked upon in a joking manner. He did it only once, for Obermyer had responded savagely. Now Obermyer's nose wrinkled—the wartime shortages of soap and hot water became very evident in a closed room like this.

Müller, who had aggressively worked the refreshment table, continued grousing. "I don't see why we have to be here. They never ask us our opinion; we never tell them anything."

"Shut your face, Gerd. That's enough. We're here because I say we should be here."

Obermyer knew the meeting was important for more reasons than one. The ever-increasing bombing raids had at last convinced the Air Ministry that it had made a mistake in neglecting the development of jet engine technology, particularly in metallurgical research. Now it was in a sudden frenzy to redress the balance and at the same time offset the problems caused by the haphazard reassignment of personnel that had set the entire industry on its ear.

The doors sprang open and Field Marshal Milch strode in, followed by his usual entourage, much smaller than Göring's, of course, but still suited to his rank.

"Gentlemen, let me begin by saying that I have had enough of your complaints and not enough of your successes!"

He went on to catalog the latest American and British bombing raids, naming cities, casualties, the number of bombers employed, and the number shot down.

"The people are saying that thanks to the Luftwaffe, we are losing the war! And they are very close to being correct. The aircraft industry has not delivered the quantity or the quality of the airplanes that it should have."

He went on to voice his dissatisfaction with all of the elements of the jet engine industry, giving equal weight to shortcomings at Heinkel, Junkers, and BMW.

"This is unsatisfactory. The *Reichsmarschall* has informed me that the Führer is placing great emphasis on the jet aircraft to offset the enemy's numerical superiority. The Führer's appreciation of the situation is, as usual, quite correct. Moreover, it is supported by operational personnel. I have in my hands a wire from General Galland. He says, and I quote, 'The Me 262 is a major success which guarantees us an operational advance of unimaginable proportions, assuming the enemy continues to fly piston-powered aircraft. From a flying standpoint, the airframe makes quite a good impression. Its engine is quite satisfying, except on takeoff and landing. This aircraft opens up completely new tactical possibilities for us.' "

Galland's report created a low rumble in the room. Grunts of pleasure came from the Messerschmitt people, while a suppressed groan of dismay came from the Heinkel faction. Anselm Franz looked understandably pleased, glanced at von Ohain, but then quickly looked away, for the statement was obviously damaging to the young engineer's aspirations.

Müller nudged Obermyer in the ribs. "It looks like we may be backing the wrong horse." Obermyer gave him his steel-eyed death stare and Müller lapsed into silence.

Milch went on. "General Galland provided this opinion directly to *Reichsmarschall* Göring. The general also advised me to stop production of the Messerschmitt Bf 109 in favor of the 262, and continue only the Focke-Wulf FW 190 as a piston engine fighter."

There was dead silence. Such a decision would be a short-term catastrophe for Messerschmitt from which it could probably never recover financially. The 109 was its milk cow of money.

Now Milch seemed momentarily to lose control of his anger; his voice cracked and his face contorted. "However, thanks to your lack of progress we are faced with the same problem we faced with the Messerschmitt 210. For those of you who don't know the hard facts, that miserable design cost the Reich at least six hundred aircraft and many millions of *Reichsmarks.*"

This time the Messerschmitt people looked down at the floor or stared fixedly at the ceiling, for the Me 210 had been a financial disaster, a net loss of 30 million *Reichsmarks*. Intended to supplant the workhorse Bf 110, the Me 210 had been rushed into mass production, only to develop into an operational nightmare as a wide variety of problems caused fatal crash after fatal crash. The 210 was eventually pulled from production, with some finished aircraft being sent to be salvaged before they ever flew. Some said that the 210 was the straw that broke Udet's back, driving him to suicide.

Relentless, Milch went on. "Nonetheless, we must press on with jet aircraft. If Dr. Messerschmitt had his way, we would devote all our resources to the 262. But we cannot. A failure would be a disaster; it would lose the war for us. Therefore I've decided that only twenty percent of our resources for fighter aircraft production will be allocated to the 262 program. The rest will continue to be applied to the Bf 109 and Focke-Wulf 190 programs."

His voice again took on a sharp edge. "But I want to warn you gentlemen that we must have more jet fighters and jet bombers by 1944, or we will have lost the air war forever. So I do not want to hear any more complaints from you about who works where and who does what. What I want to hear is that you are meeting your program guidelines, and that the Reich will have new jet engines in mass production this year—not 1945, not next year, but this year."

Milch slammed his fist down so hard on the podium that he knocked his field marshal's baton to the floor. Few in the room were superstitious, but even Milch recognized this instantly as an extraordinarily bad omen. He grabbed the baton, saluted with it to the appalled group scrambling to its collective feet, and, fuming, marched out of the room.

Obermyer looked at an obviously shaken von Ohain, who was staring at the door through which Milch had departed. Then von Ohain turned, caught Obermyer's eye, and said, "Is this how business is conducted at the top?"

It was a dangerous, inflammatory statement, especially when made to a man like Obermyer. But instead of quailing at Obermyer's narrow-eyed look, von Ohain came up to him and said, "How do you expect to win a war with leaders like this? Udet commits suicide; this man Milch threatens everyone. Is this the Nazi way of doing business?"

Obermyer took a step back. Perhaps he had underestimated this young man. He had guts as a well as brains.

June 14, 1943, Wright Field, Ohio

Brigadier General Franklin O. Carroll was slim, of average height, and totally unaware that his thinning black hair and graying mustache gave him the appearance of an aging Adolf Hitler. A long-time veteran of Wright Field, Carroll had an infectious grin and a tittering laugh that unnerved those who did not know him well, for when combined with his habit of eagerly rocking back and forth in his seat it seemed to place him one step short of the loony bin. But his nervous mannerisms masked a managerial genius that had overseen the expansion of Wright Field's engineering capability from its relatively small size in 1939 to its current gigantic status. In the past, Carroll's amazing faculty for deciding where the Air Corps research efforts should be directed had achieved great things with a tiny budget. Now, with a virtually unlimited budget, Carroll still sought to get the maximum for the Army.

Carroll's office, like everything about him, was simple and efficient. The walls were a varnished yellow pine, his desk the simplest government-issue oak—but highly polished. He sat in his swivel chair, listening to what he fondly called the father-and-son team brief him on his next scheduled meeting. Lieutenant Colonel Harry Shannon and his father, Vance, had been working with the industry, implementing the suggestions that Harry had derived from their conference the previous October.

"General, I have Kelly Johnson and Hall Hibbard waiting down the hall. They have a proposal I think will be of interest to you."

Carroll looked pained. "It's not that project that Kelly and Nate Price were pushing a few months ago, is it?"

"No, sir, this one is intended to use the de Havilland Halford engine. It is putting out three thousand pounds of thrust, and looks like the ticket for our next fighter."

The de Havilland engine had been designed by a veteran of piston engine construction, Frank Halford, using data on Whittle's engine furnished by the British government. In peacetime it would have been a blatant violation of copyright; in war it was simple expediency.

Carroll spoke again. "Vance, I know that you, Kelly, and Hall are old friends, and let me tell you that no one appreciates Kelly more than I do. You've heard the old statement that Tony Fokker designed good airplanes because he could 'see the air'; well, Kelly sees more than the air—he sees the heat, the strength, the fatigue, even the shape of projects almost as soon as you define the requirements. But he is a stubborn man! He wants to tell you what you need rather than listen to what you want. You've got to control that. I'm not giving Lockheed a contract for an airplane to find out that Kelly has improved it to the point that it won't get produced!"

Vance Shannon nodded. Carroll was right on the money. Johnson was a genius and he reigned supreme at Lockheed, barely held in check by Hall Hibbard, who acted as a go-between for Robert Gross. Gross admired Kelly immensely but found him too loud and too strong willed to work with in person. Hibbard now saw himself as a middleman, able to calm and direct Kelly as no one else could and thus do more for Lockheed than anyone else.

Vance knew he was not a good closer—he respected the opinions and feelings of other people too much to impose his will on them just to make a deal. But this was an exception. He had to sell this to Carroll, because there was no real alternative. Summoning up his brightest smile, slapping Harry on the back, Vance leaned forward and said, "He'll produce your airplane, sir, and it will on schedule and under budget—but the Army has to let him do it his way. If we try to ride herd on him through plant representatives, meetings, and the usual things we do, he'll rebel. And that we cannot afford," Vance said.

Carroll signaled to his aide, and Hibbard and Johnson came in, carrying two briefcases filled with drawings. Shannon had briefed Johnson on his demeanor, and Hibbard had reinforced it; all three men knew what was at stake. Johnson went through the drawings quickly, quietly, answering all the questions Carroll asked that he could. The questions he could not answer he noted down in his daily logbook, writing with such uniform precision that the words looked as if they were typed.

Hibbard was beginning to relax as the meeting wore on; Kelly had evidently taken Shannon's words to heart and was behaving beautifully.

After a final survey of the drawings, Carroll nodded and said, "When can you give me a definite proposal?"

Johnson consulted briefly with Hibbard and answered, "June 1, sir."

Carroll replied, "I'll handle the paperwork on this end myself, and I'll get you a response in two weeks or less. How long will it take you to build the prototype?"

Johnson spoke. "If we do it the Army way, General Carroll, twelve months, minimum. If we do it my way, I'll roll your prototype out in one hundred and eighty days from the date you issue the contract."

Hibbard started to speak, but Carroll raised his hand. "And what is your way, Mr. Johnson?"

"My way is to make this a special project; I'll pull together a small team of the best engineers and workers Lockheed has. I'll contract with Vance, here, to come in with us. We'll sequester the project and work night and day. The Army can have one officer on hand for inspection. No one, not even you, gets in without my approval. No visiting dignitaries. No change proposals. Just leave us alone and we'll deliver you a first-class jet fighter in one hundred and eighty days—or less."

Hibbard shrank back and Carroll began his tittering laugh, rocking back and forth in his chair. Vance and Harry were appalled. Kelly had blown the deal with his outrageous requirements.

Finally Carroll spoke: "OK, Mr. Johnson, have it your way. But if you don't fulfill your promises, Lockheed will never get another contract from the Army. You can bet on it." And he began laughing again.

November 26, 1943, Insterburg, Germany

THE MESSERSCHMITT ME 262 program had become a monster, devouring man-hours, materials, and resources on an ever-increasing basis—and still only a few of the jets were flying. One of them, the first pre-production aircraft, Me 262V6, was vastly improved, with more streamlined nacelles and the badly needed tricycle undercarriage. Adolf Hitler continued to prod *Reichsmarschall* Göring about 262 production, and he in turn nudged Milch, who tried to galvanize the industry. Committees were formed, meetings were held, but nothing could change two cold hard facts. The first was that the ill-fated American bombing raid on Regensburg on August 17 had destroyed the fuselage jigs for the 262 and set back airframe production by months. The second was that shortages of nickel and chrome were holding up the production of turbine blades for the Junkers Jumo 004B engines.

Now a scowling Hitler was walking down the flight line, lips pursed. He had been to other displays of Luftwaffe aircraft in years past. They had shown him aircraft like the Heinkel He 177 four-engine bomber and the Messerschmitt Me 210, which were going to win the war. Both were colossal failures and none of the other airplanes, not one, had delivered on their promises. Göring, subdued as he always was in Hitler's company, walked behind him to the flight line. There the veteran test pilot Gerd Lindner was already seated in the cockpit of the Messerschmitt V6, marked VI + AA. It had the new tricycle undercarriage and many other improvements.

Hitler nodded impatiently and Lindner went through the engine start, with everyone familiar with the aircraft praying that there was no fire. Lindner taxied out, took off, and put the 262 through a dazzling display that showed the aircraft to its full advantage, combining its blinding speed with a remarkable maneuverability.

Lindner had just touched down when Hitler turned and signaled for his car. He left the field without comment, leaving Göring, Willy Messerschmitt, and others dumbfounded.

"What does it mean, *Herr Reichsmarschall?* Did the Führer approve? What are we to do?"

Göring shook his head. He was in an impossible situation, his lack of authority evident to all. Finally, as his own Mercedes drove up, he said, "I will talk to the Führer this evening. And I will have someone call you with the results."

Gerd Lindner walked up as Messerschmitt stood watching as the second Mercedes sped off. "Dr. Messerschmitt, how was the demonstration?"

Messerschmitt turned to the young pilot. "Herr Lindner, if our leaders were as competent leading as you are flying, we would have won the war a year ago."

The next day Messerschmitt received a personal call from Albert Speer, the Minister of Armaments. The Me 262 was to receive top production priority, and the Führer was to receive bimonthly reports on the production of the aircraft as a fighter-bomber.

January 8, 1944, Muroc Army Air Base, California

VANCE SHANNON HAD worked hard before, but never for so long or so unremittingly as he had since the $515,018.40 contract for the XP-80 had been signed. When they started the new program in Burbank, Kelly Johnson had relented on the seven-day workweek. Instead he worked his team ten hours a day six days a week, and they were still on the point of exhaustion.

Happily, Vance had another drain on his energy—Madeline. When she visited him in Burbank their already tempestuous sex life reached new heights. His appearance became so wan that Kelly had pulled him aside and insisted that he see a doctor to treat his exhaustion. He couldn't believe it himself, but occasionally he had actually resorted to telling Madeline that he had a headache, to get a little respite.

He missed her now, though. When Vance went with the XP-80 to Muroc, he knew that he would have no time to spare, not even on weekends, and she decided she would not try to commute from her job with Consolidated in San Diego. It turned out to be a good thing, for Harry had been sent out as General Carroll's personal representative. At Madeline's request, Vance still had not told his boys about his intention to marry her. Having her drop in for the Sunday day off at Muroc would have been awkward.

The XP-80 program had been arduous, but Kelly had kept all his promises. He had chosen well from the Lockheed workforce, assembling a team of 128 specialists. In Burbank, they had worked in a closely guarded scrap-wood and canvas temporary shack located next to the main factory building. The work had proceeded smoothly, and the XP-80 was delivered exactly 178 days after the contract had been signed. On the day it rolled out, Kelly picked up Vance in a bear hug and said, "What did I tell Carroll? One hundred and eighty days! We beat that by two days! And what do you say to that, Mr. Shannon?" Shannon, his lungs compressed and his ribs aching, couldn't say anything, but he gave Kelly the thumbs-up and scurried out of his way.

There had been problems all along, but Kelly's team had leaped upon each one and solved it in hours, not days or weeks, as had always been Vance's experience in the past. The key was Kelly's insistence on dropping all unnecessary paperwork and getting the engineers and the workmen to bump elbows together, with neither Lockheed management nor the Army interfering. When a solution was reached it was documented, and for that reason the first drawing was often the final one.

The worst crisis came late in the program. The Halford engine was run up to 8,800 revolutions per minute on a static test when both air ducts leading to the engine collapsed with an explosive roar, the debris cracking the engine's compressor. After seventy-two hours of uninterrupted work, Shannon directing the effort, the ducts were redesigned and rebuilt. There was a delay until the replacement engine arrived for installation, but Johnson and the Skonk Works, as they called his group, stayed ahead of schedule. The Skonk Works name came from a mythical factory in Al Capp's famous *Li'l Abner* comic strip.

Aesthetically, the XP-80—the workers named it "Lulu Belle"— was a masterpiece. Where the XP-59 looked bloated with its huge wing and engine combination, the Lockheed fighter had a slim, rapier-like appearance. Its low-aspect ratio laminar flow wing eased out from where the wing-root engine inlets were carefully faired into the narrow fuselage. The pilot sat forward of the wings, under a streamlined bubble canopy. The long, tapering nose housed six .50-caliber machine guns, radios, and navigation equipment, all easily accessed by large swing-out panels. Vance noticed that everyone caressed the airplane as they worked around it, running their hands along its flanks as if it were a Thoroughbred racehorse.

Lockheed's chief test pilot, Milo Burcham, was scheduled to make the first flight. Burcham was more than ready, having shepherded the P-38 through its long and arduous test programs. To get jet experience, he had flown the Bell XP-59A, coming away with a thorough understanding of the jet engine's slow acceleration characteristics and of the need to handle the throttles with care.

Shannon watched Burcham and laughed to himself, for Milo was so unlike the Hollywood image of test pilots. In an MGM film titled, fittingly enough, *Test Pilot*, Clark Gable played the title role, portraying a brash, bullheaded outsider who defied regulations and trusted to guts and luck when testing airplanes. Oddly enough, Milo slightly resembled Gable, with his quiet smile and tiny mustache, but he was far more cerebral in his approach to test flying and indeed to life. Burcham was very bright, holding patents on a number of devices, including a burglar alarm that he invented while in high school and sold to pay for his first flying lessons. But he was very cautious, not allowing any of the eighty-plus test pilots who worked for him to take any risks that were not precisely calculated.

Top Lockheed management, including Bob Gross, turned out for the test flight, watching Kelly Johnson fuss around the XP-80 like a mother around a new baby. Wearing a dark overcoat against the desert cold, Johnson went over the airplane inch by inch, doing everything from checking each of the fasteners to clambering up the ladder to the cockpit and polishing out a tiny spot on the canopy with his handkerchief.

Burcham, dressed in a natty two-color sports jacket, his dark hair slicked back, took off at exactly 9:10, climbing to pattern altitude before radioing that he could not get the gear to retract. Six minutes later he landed, to the applause of the crowd. Mechanics swarmed over the gear, quickly found a malfunctioning switch, and repaired it. The fuel tanks were topped off (Bob Gross kidded Kelly by saying, "We're going to need more range if you have to refuel this often") and Burcham flew again, a twenty-minute flight that showed both the speed and the maneuverability of the XP-80.

No one felt more relief than the Shannons, father and son. Vance had dozens of high-priority projects that he had deferred to be with Kelly on the XP-80. He needed to get to work on them. And General Carroll had been very fair, telling Harry that when the XP-80 flew he would see that he got an operational assignment, in fighters if possible, in bombers if not.

It was more than time. Tom had returned from the Pacific with nine victories and a smug smile. It had been almost intolerable for Harry, even though Tom only bragged when they were alone together, when they both knew he was teasing. But teasing or not, it was difficult to suffer.

Tom's combat status had gained him a plum assignment. He was sent to Eglin Army Air Force Base on exchange duty, test flying captured enemy fighters—a fighter pilot's heaven. Harry had some catching up to do, and it looked like the war was running out.

THE PASSING SCENE

U.S. planes bomb Berlin for the first time; Soviet armies continue their advance; Monte Cassino bombed; Germany occupies Hungary; Wake Island recaptured; Rome captured; first raid by B-29s; D day, June 6 invasion of Europe; Battle of the Philippine Sea destroys remnants of Japanese Navy; assassination attempt on Hitler's life; **The Glass Menagerie** *a big hit; V-1, V-2 vengeance weapon attacks begin; huge Soviet victory on Eastern Front; MacArthur returns to Philippines; Roosevelt reelected to fourth term; Battle of the Bulge.*

CHAPTER SIX

March 1, 1944, La Jolla, California

An almost palpable fog blocked the ocean view from their long porch, and to Vance Shannon that seemed perfectly appropriate, right in line with his current run of luck. He had made two important decisions after listening to his inner voice for the pros and cons of each of them and apparently had been totally wrong both times.

If I performed like this for my clients, I'd be in the county poorhouse, he thought, cupping the mug of black coffee in his hands, and wondered what to do next. From the kitchen there came the rattle of dishes as Madeline began preparing their usual breakfast of rolls, butter, jelly, cheese, and coffee. He could have had his favorite ham and eggs if he had asked, but things were a little delicate at the moment. Madeline had opposed the two choices he had made. He had overruled her, and she had been correct on each one.

The first was the question of her coming to live in this house. She was against it from the start, saying that Tom and Harry would regard it as an intrusion. They had grown up here with their mother, and Madeline felt her presence would jar them, perhaps even be insulting. She wanted to stay in the little apartment she had rented near the Consolidated plant when she first came to San Diego. Vance had insisted that she move to his far more comfortable home in La Jolla. To his utter surprise, both Tom and Harry had objected. Tom made a long and bitter phone call from Eglin Army Air Base. He was hurt that his father had not told him about Madeline before and very upset that she was staying in the house where his mother had raised them. The conversation ended abruptly when Tom hung up, saying, "I'll call you later." "Later" turned out to be almost sixty days afterward.

Harry's letter did not arrive until two weeks after the conversation with Tom. He wrote from RAF Deenthorpe, his base in Great Britain, where he was flying a B-17 in the Eighth Air Force. The letter was long, well reasoned, temperate, but still laden with resentment for the way his father had handled things. One clue was in an offhand attempt to be facetious; Harry noted that as both his mother and Madeline had names beginning with *M*, there would be no need to change the monograms on the bath towels. The feeble attempt at humor hurt Vance more than the more thoughtful arguments.

Both boys said that they knew he was seeing someone and neither admitted to a concern about the age difference. It seemed to him that her presence in the house was the problem, and that was totally imponderable. Madeline insisted that they were dissembling.

"Darling, as clever as you are, you miss the point entirely. Age is the problem. I am supposed to become their stepmother, and I'm not much older than they are. They resent it."

After Harry's letter, Madeline came straight to the point, as she always did. It was a quality that Vance had loved but was beginning to fear.

"They probably assume that I'll take advantage of you for a few years and then leave you for a younger man. That's what anyone would think." If Vance and Madeline were on better terms she would probably have made a joke about it, saying, "That's what I think, too," or something similar. But things were too serious.

His second error was the question of marriage. Madeline pleaded that they should not marry until after the war and not even then until she and his sons had had a chance to become acquainted. On that she had said, "Why rush things? Your sons are at war, in a dangerous profession. Let's not add to their worries. I don't think they mind if you have a girlfriend—they know you are a vigorous, healthy man. They'll probably boast to their comrades about you—as long as I'm not your wife and their stepmother."

Vance also worried about a younger man attracting her, but it was not the time to admit it. Still, he was too wildly jealous to contemplate delay. He had never been more than mildly jealous of Margaret, who in her youth used to flirt harmlessly at parties just to see his color rise. It never occurred to either of them that they would ever part. Then he remembered that one time he had reacted jealously—a young wise guy named Bill Lear had patted Margaret on the bottom at a party. Vance saw red and belted him, to everyone's acute embarrassment.

But with Madeline, he was sharply aware of their twenty-year age difference. It galled him every time he looked into a mirror, especially when he noted the incipient paunch. He was certain that sooner or later she would meet someone younger, better looking, and, though he hated to admit it, more potent than he and that this new young love would sweep her off her feet. Every time he left on a trip, he was miserable, certain that someone would steal her away. He had insisted on setting a date, and she had at last agreed, asking only that they wait until December. Since then the very word "marriage" triggered an argument.

He wondered why he had challenged her. She had so much common sense and worked so hard. At Consolidated she had swiftly risen from a runner chasing parts on the factory floor to an employee in Reuben Fleet's office, where her language ability was put to full use. Her English was flawless and she picked up the American idiom at once. Most of her work now dealt with foreign sales. Consolidated PBYs were being used by many other countries and were even built under license in the Soviet Union. Her fluent Russian had proved to be especially effective in dealing with the dour Soviet representatives.

Vance had become so profoundly convinced of her intelligence that he often discussed things with her that he would never have broached with Margaret. Madeline was not mechanically inclined, but she was able to pick up on the thread of his technical problems and discuss them objectively. She was a godsend in preparing his reports, correcting his grammar and spelling as she went.

There was no argument yet this morning. On awakening, they had made love as usual, not ardently but conjugally, familiarly, and at length. It had been wonderfully satisfying, but even now he was stirred as she emerged from the double doors to the kitchen, almost totally enveloped in the old pink-checked bathrobe that she invariably wore in the morning. Sated as he was, he was moved by the thought of her naked body beneath the robe, still warm and wet from the shower, and made an unkind but inevitable mental comparison. Margaret had in time grown a little heavy. Madeline was petite, just under five feet, four inches tall and weighing 110 pounds. Her figure was perfect, with small but perfectly formed breasts, a flat stomach, and a tight, flat bottom that he reflexively caressed whenever she was within reach. And as practical and hardworking as she was, she never forgot that she was a woman, always being carefully made up, whether in the morning or late at night. Even as she approached now, he noted that the bathrobe was open at the top just enough so that he could catch the curve of her bosom. It was no accident.

Slipping her arm around his neck, she kissed him on the cheek. "Shall we eat out here, or do you want to come into the kitchen? I have a fire going in the fireplace."

He nodded toward the kitchen, dropped his arm around her body, and pressed her to him as they moved side by side to the double doors, as happily as if they didn't have an argument brewing.

They ate quietly for a while, her bare foot reaching under the table to rest on his ankle. After he had refused a third cup of coffee, she began the fight as formally as a matador entering the bullring, a question serving as her cape. He responded with his formulaic answers, knowing he would lose, hoping only that she didn't demand his ear at the end.

"Have you decided what you are going to tell your sons?"

"They will be your sons, too. I'm going to tell them that we will be married in December, and that you will live here until then. It is crazy to maintain two places, and unpatriotic, too; there are lots of people who would love to have your apartment. This is wartime, we are adults, and to hell with what people think, even my own sons."

She nodded, growing silent. He and Margaret had rarely argued, but when they did, it was at the top of their respective voices. Madeline withdrew into a quiet, impassive, and totally unnerving reserve, remaining icily courteous, never raising her voice, and somehow creating an air of menace that frightened him, not of physical harm but of the possibility that she would suddenly leave him forever.

It was a winning psychology, and he had already decided to surrender. They sat silently for a quarter of an hour. He pretended to read a magazine. She stared out the window, motionless. He hated this familiar pattern, his own private series of Munichs, but the thought of her leaving sapped his will.

With a sigh, Vance moved to her side, raised her chin in his hands, and said, "You win. Keep the apartment. I'll deed this place over to the boys, and find somewhere else for us to stay. And if you don't want to get married in December, we'll wait."

She moved slightly, slipping her robe from her shoulder. Abundantly grateful, Vance reacted as a teenager might, throwing off his robe, gathering her to him, easing her out of her chair. He would be totally unaware of the cold tile floor until his rubbed-raw knees began to ache much later in the day.

August 4, 1944, RAF Manston

LAUGHING LIKE TRUANT schoolboys, Stanley Hooker and Frank Whittle tumbled out the back door of the stately Rolls-Royce.

Whittle stopped to catch his breath. The fresh air was intoxicating. He had just spent six long months in the hospital, confined with exhaustion and a crippling eczema, trying to recover from overwork and the grinding pain of seeing the British government seize his invention, his company, and his patent. He had labored to create the jet engine for more than a decade, and when he had succeeded beyond all doubt, his firm had been nationalized. The government had offered him the option of accepting a token payment of one hundred thousand pounds for his life's work or seeing the firm simply shut down. He accepted the money reluctantly, conscious of his shareholders but bitter that all he had done should be given so little regard. Most of all he was fearful of what engine companies, unfamiliar with turbines, would do to his masterpiece. He had already seen the Rover company muck about, ruining what he had done.

Despite the fact that his firm, Rolls-Royce, had benefited from Whittle's research and the government's decision, Hooker was totally sympathetic. He knew that Whittle was a genius who had succeeded where everyone else had failed, that his engines had given impetus to the development of new engines at several firms in Great Britain and the United States. They had forced creation of totally new jet aircraft types at Gloster, de Havilland, Bell, Lockheed, and elsewhere. Yet there was nothing Hooker could do now but attempt to sustain Whittle in his time of need. He had arranged this carefully planned trip so that the now almost fragile officer might see the first combat fruits of his endeavors.

The ride to the field with Hooker and the anticipation of seeing his engines in action against the enemy had buoyed Whittle's spirits for the first time in months. Hooker kept them up with a constant stream of anecdotes about the antics of the leftist Minister of Aircraft Production, Sir Stafford Cripps, which were all the more amusing because they were true.

Manston was home to No. 616 Squadron, the first to be equipped with Gloster Meteor F.1 twin-jet fighters, powered by Rolls-Royce Welland engines, the production versions of Whittle's W.2B jet. Wing Commander Henry Wilson greeted them and took them for an immediate tour of the flight line, where seven Meteors stood wingtip to wingtip, supplementing the squadron's standard-issue Spitfires.

The Meteors had entered combat on July 27 but were still waiting to draw their first blood against the flood of German buzz bombs that flowed from Occupied Europe. Winston Churchill and the few top Allied leaders who had access to the Enigma reports had immediately recognized the gravity of the threat, for Hitler had authorized a program that would fire eight thousand of the flying bombs against England every month, beginning in January 1944. The Germans had not reached this goal because a mammoth bombing campaign—sometimes as much as 40 percent of all Allied effort—was directed against factories known to manufacture the components of the weapon and the "no ball" sites from which they were launched. These sites were long, narrow concrete ramps, surrounded by a few buildings and a compass rose, all pointing like malignant fingers to the heart of London. The buzz bombs were catapulted along the track until they reached a speed that would sustain their pulse-jet engines as they headed for Great Britain.

The extensive bombing had delayed the first combat launches until the night of June 14 and vastly reduced the number of weapons and of launch sites available for use. Great Britain had become spoiled, accustomed for the last three years to dishing out punishment to Germany, not receiving it. Now it seemed as if the blitz bombing of 1940 and 1941 had returned, and the unexpected loss of civilian lives to German air attack in mid-1944 was bad for British morale.

While Whittle was in the hospital, his doctors had tried to sequester him as much as possible, keeping all bad news from him, and letting him learn of big events, such as the D-day invasion, only after their success had been confirmed. He was especially eager to learn about the new weapon because it was jet-propelled.

Wilson brought them into an austere office on the flight line and showed them a provisional drawing of the buzz bomb.

"The Germans call it the V-1 for 'vengeance weapon number 1.'

They have another one, the V-2, but it is a rocket-powered ballistic missile. They haven't fired it yet, and when they do, I don't see how we will stop it. But we can stop the V-1."

Whittle studied the drawing. No more than a thousand-kilogram bomb with simple wings and tail, it was equipped with a pulse-jet engine. He knew the theory—it was jet power simplified to the extreme. Instead of a complicated compressor and turbine system, as in his engine, a panel of shutters at the front of a long tube was sucked open to admit air. Fuel was injected into the incoming air and ignited. The resulting explosion blew the shutters closed, the flames and heat were exhausted out the rear of the jet tube, propelling the aircraft forward, and the cycle was rapidly repeated. Despite its apparent simplicity, Whittle knew that it must have taken an enormous amount of work to make it effective.

Hooker asked, "What kind of speed and altitude do they fly?"

Wilson replied, "It varies, but usually no more than three hundred or three hundred and fifty mph. Some have been clocked at four hundred, but that may be an error. They come over somewhere between fifteen hundred and three thousand feet. They are not controlled in flight; they just fly a pre-set course, using a gyro stabilizer. They have a simple air-log timer that cuts off the fuel at a predetermined point, and shuts down the engine. That's why they are not dangerous as long as you can hear their engine running—they'll keep on going. But if the engine quits—look out below."

Whittle had flown fighters long enough to know that even at 300 mph, the buzz bombs would be difficult to intercept in a tail chase. If you were not positioned to make a quartering attack from above, they would be an elusive target. If the first attack missed, it would be almost impossible to catch them before their timing mechanism sent them on their fatal plunge.

"The Jerries are methodical, you know, like to keep regular hours and all that. We expect to see a salvo in about an hour. Let me have one of my pilots run you out to a likely spot where you might see them come in—and see us go after them."

Wilson introduced him to a smiling young blond pilot officer, Richard May, who slid into the front seat of the Rolls to direct the chauffeur, while in the back Hooker and Whittle discussed the pros and cons of the buzz bomb.

"It's damn ingenious. What else can the fellow do? He cannot put a bomber over England without it being shot down. The bloody things must be cheap to manufacture, a few hundred man-hours at most. I understand that the Germans were planning to fire eight thousand a month at London! Even as inaccurate as they are, that would be devastating."

Whittle was still working out the engineering details. "I don't see how they can keep the blasted things together! The vibration must be incredible. The pulse engine is just a tube, a pipe, containing a series of explosions, *bang, bang, bang*!"

They were still talking when the Rolls slowed down to turn in a freshly made gravel road for half a shaded mile, then came to a stop. They were led to a clearing, not two hundred yards from one of the hundreds of anti-aircraft batteries that had been redeployed from the defense of London to positions on a line that ran along the coast from Beachy Head to Dover, smack across the V-1 routes. A second line of defense was allocated to fighters, and just on the outskirts of London was a third line—a huge balloon barrage. It was an old-fashioned defense, reaching back to World War I, but it was still effective against a low-flying aircraft that charged blindly ahead without deviating from its course.

May told them, "It will be pretty noisy here, sir, but when it quiets down, you'll know that an RAF fighter is moving up from behind to attack."

Hooker signaled to the chauffeur, who retrieved a basket from the Rolls's trunk. Whittle looked on without much pleasure as sandwiches were laid out, a fruit bowl provided, and a bottle of champagne uncorked. He felt as if he had not eaten well for years, and he was ashamed that his once sturdy body had become so frail. Yet the champagne was going down uncommonly well until he dropped the glass when the anti-aircraft battery let loose a wild barrage.

No one had heard the incoming V-1. It passed serenely through the seemingly impassable barrier of anti-aircraft shell bursts and went on; when the battery ceased firing, they then picked up its odd popping sound, as if an old Austin were backfiring continuously. The flying bomb continued on its course until the buzz died away. May handed them binoculars. "Keep a watch to the west, sir. That's where the fighters will be."

Hooker yelled, "Frank, here comes another one now."

They turned to look to the east, and in the distance, still not audible, they saw a tiny cross advancing, a black stream of exhaust trailing it. Whittle glanced over to the anti-aircraft battery and was surprised to see them standing around, staring as he was. Then he saw why. A Gloster Meteor—it had to be from 616 Squadron—was diving down in a curving approach. They heard the first engine noises as the Meteor settled down, some three hundred yards behind the V-1, to fire.

Nothing happened and the anti-aircraft crew ran to their stations. The Meteor's four 20mm Hispano cannon must have jammed, and the gunners were going to take over when the Meteor pulled away and the buzz bomb continued on its course.

But both the V-1 and the Meteor continued straight forward, the fighter gaining position, then sliding into formation with its target. With infinite care, the Meteor pilot slipped his right wing under the V-1's left wing and with a short movement tipped the V-1 up and over. It rolled into a screaming full-power dive to explode not four hundred yards from where Whittle and Hooker now lay facedown, their heads covered, their champagne spilled.

Then they were on their feet, screaming with the same excitement as the gun crew, for the Meteor now appeared low on the horizon, boiling straight for them, so low that it disappeared beneath the distant hedges, reappearing ever closer until it roared right at them, dust curling up behind its headlong rush. They fell to the ground again, and the Meteor pulled away almost vertically up into the sky, rolling as it went.

May was on his feet dusting himself off and saying, "That would be Pilot Officer Dean, sir. He's very keen about flying very low."

Whittle turned over on his back, watching the Meteor disappear, concentrating on the circles of flame held so tightly within the jet orifices, outlining the black streams of exhaust pouring from the engines that he had brought into being. Tears poured from his eyes as he looked up and said, "Hooker, I don't care if they did steal my damn engine! Seeing that V-1 go down made it all worthwhile."

Hooker reached in his sleeve, handed Whittle a handkerchief, then moved to block the view of May and the chauffeur. They did not need to see the man who had started a new age in aviation cry like a child.

October 20, 1944, Burbank, California

VANCE SHANNON SAT in Bob Gross's expanded and far more luxurious reception area, remembering how austere the offices had been only ten years before. He sipped a cup of coffee as he read an internal Lockheed bulletin that summarized the world events of the previous weeks. For the most part, the news was good. The Allies had long since broken out from their invasion beaches. The Germans had suffered catastrophic losses, with fifty divisions being destroyed on the Eastern Front and another twenty-eight on the Western Front.

Shannon shook his head. How could they keep fighting with such losses? Only fanatics would continue when the war was so obviously lost. The Bulgarian and Rumainian forces—for whatever they were worth—had defected to the Soviet side. The Allied advance was continuing in the Pacific, with the Caroline Islands operations moving forward as well. The only bad news was in China, where the Japanese had unexpectedly mounted a big eleven-division offensive intended to capture U.S. Fourteenth Air Force bases at Kwelin and Liuchow.

In the air, the news was much better than it had been a year before, when the Luftwaffe had wrested control of the air from the Eighth Air Force. Now the long-range North American P-51s were able to escort bombers all the way to their targets and back, and he was grateful, for it made Harry's job safer. The German jets and rocket planes had begun to appear, but in much smaller numbers than expected. The Allies tried to minimize their threat by maintaining combat air patrols over their airfields, so they could catch them landing and taking off.

Vance was a little put out. He'd received a call personally from Bob Gross, asking him to come in as soon as he possibly could. Vance had made an appointment for nine o'clock, it was now eleven, and he was still waiting. The last thing he needed was idle time to think—for thinking meant worries about Madeline, about Tom, and about Harry. The "two boys" were grown men now, warriors, and he still felt for them as he did from the time they were born, wanting to make things go well for them and, most of all, keep them safe from harm.

The delay was very unlike Gross—something very important must have come up. He hoped Gross was not ill—like everyone else, he had been working long hours and was not really taking care of himself as he should.

The door opened and Gross flew in, ashen faced, his coat off and sweat beading on his brow. "Forgive me, Vance, a terrible accident. Milo Burcham just crashed in the gravel pit off the end of the runway. He was in a P-80 and it flamed out. Didn't have a chance. Poor Milo! He was a wonderful man."

Shannon tried to express his sympathy. It was a major loss. Burcham was a top test pilot and a magnificent asset for Lockheed. "Bob, would it be better for you if I came back? I can arrange another appointment with your secretary."

Gross shook his head. "No, just give me about ten minutes alone, to pull myself together. I'm going to go out and see Peggy." Vance knew her well. She and her two sons would be devastated. Once again it occurred to him that jet aircraft were going to take a toll of many pilots before they were perfected. Jets were clearly the coming thing—they were even talking about jet airliners now—but lots of lives would be lost in perfecting them. Including, perhaps, one of his sons'. It was a horrible thought.

A few minutes later Gross poked his head out of his office and signaled Shannon to come in.

"I never get used to this, Vance, and I always blame myself."

"I know the feeling, Bob. My two boys are flying now, and if something happens to them, I'll never forgive myself for inoculating them with the flying bug."

Gross pulled a crystal decanter from his desk and poured a minute amount of brandy into two glasses. They clicked glasses and Gross said, "To Milo."

After carefully storing the decanter—it was the first time Shannon had ever seen Gross take a drink, even at parties—the Lockheed executive pulled out a leather folder and handed it over.

"Vance, you'll remember that I had some contacts that I wasn't too proud of in Germany?"

Shannon nodded.

"Well, this is the latest thing he has sent me. All the translations are paper clipped to the original documents. It is pretty disturbing, for it shows the blasted Germans are somehow increasing their jet aircraft production despite all the bombing we've done. He has the full dope on the new Arado jet bomber, and gives the specifications for both the V-1 and the V-2." He was quiet, thinking of Milo again. He shook his head and resumed. "More than a year ago, I told Hap Arnold about my sources of information, and after he chewed me out at the top of his lungs, he calmed down and told me to keep doing it."

Shannon riffled through the papers. The Arado was a beautiful airplane, judging by the drawing, and its performance was sensational, almost as good as that of the Messerschmitt jet fighter. He knew quite a bit about the V-1, but the V-2 was fascinating, and this was the first official information he had seen.

Gross tossed over one more paper, obviously from the same batch. "This is the most distressing part. It is sick." As Shannon read it, his heart sank. At a huge underground plant, the Germans were using slave labor to build the V-2, killing thousands of people in the process. There were even a few photographs attached, obviously taken covertly and smuggled out of the camp. They showed ragged skeleton-like creatures working on assembly lines.

"This is grotesque. How can they be so cruel?"

"It is monstrous. Hap called me on a secure phone and said he planned to lay on bombing raids on the rail lines to the camp—

Nordhausen, they call it—but he's afraid to bomb the camps themselves because it would kill so many of the prisoners."

"Bob, this is fascinating, but what is it you'd like me to do?"

Gross walked to the window. "The war in Europe will end pretty soon. Perhaps even by the first of the year. I know that Hap intends to send a flying squad of top officers and scientists into Germany to scavenge all the information and the equipment they can, before the Germans destroy it, or the Russians get their hands on it. I told Hap that you should be on the team. Do you want to go?"

Shannon did not hesitate for a second. "Absolutely, Bob. Put me down. And put Harry down, too! He'll be finished with his tour, for sure, and he would be a big help to me."

Gross smiled for the first time that day. "I cannot promise that, Vance, but I'll try. They'll probably be using C-47s or C-54s to make the trip in; maybe he can go along as a copilot or something."

Shannon rose to go and said, "Bob, it is none of my business, but what is going to happen to your informant when the war is over?"

Gross flushed, angry with himself, angry with a war that forced him to soil his hands working with people like this unnamed informant. "With the amount of money we've paid him, he can go to Argentina and live for the rest of his life. I sent word to him that our arrangement was terminated. He's on his own now."

November 8, 1944, Achmer, outside Osnabrück, Germany

ADOLF GALLAND TOOK off well before dawn in his special Messerschmitt Bf 109, so that he could land at Achmer at sunrise, too early for the ever-present American fighter-bombers that dominated the air over Germany. It was his first flight as a lieutenant general. At thirty-two, he was by far the youngest man of that elevated rank in the German armed services. He was probably also the most severely fatigued, from his overloaded combination of work and romances.

Two airfields, Achmer and Hespe, were the home of Kommando Nowotny, a service test squadron. It had been established early in October, equipped with no fewer than forty Messerschmitt Me 262s. The airfields were positioned perfectly to oppose the almost daily flights of Eighth Air Force bombers. The arrangement would have been ideal if swarming British and American fighters did not orbit the area, waiting for the jets to take off and land. Some measure of relief was afforded by a four-mile-long corridor of anti-aircraft guns set up off the ends of the runway. They were designed to put up an umbrella of flak, creating a safe corridor for arriving and departing jets. In addition, the very effective Focke-Wulf 190D aircraft of Jagdgeschwader 54 flew protective patrols, fighting off the enemy while allowing the Me 262s to gain speed after takeoff, when they became virtually invulnerable to piston fighter attack. The 190s performed the same service when the jets returned, low on fuel and forced to give up their great speed advantage to slow down for a landing approach.

Major Walter Nowotny had scored 256 victories before being appointed commander of the unit that bore his name. In one month of operation, his pilots had shot down twenty-two enemy aircraft—but lost twenty-seven of their precious jets, most of them in accidents. Galland's mission was to find out what was wrong with the operation, but to do it in a way that did not destroy what remained of the pilots' morale.

In the primitive operations shack, Nowotny introduced Galland to his senior people, then took him into his office, where a surprisingly sumptuous breakfast had been prepared by the Russian cook Nowotny had brought back from the Eastern Front.

Nowotny did not hesitate. "I know you must be disappointed with our results. So am I. I thought that we could do far more damage than we have. And we've lost so many good people."

Galland shifted his cigar and bowed his head. "The Luftwaffe has lost almost ninety percent of its experienced pilots since January. And the sad thing is that it did not need to happen."

Relieved at the slight turn the conversation had taken, Nowotny piled plum preserves on a piece of bread and looked inquiring.

"That pig Göring started it all, as far back as November 1940. He thought the war was won, and stupidly ordered that all new weapons that could not be put into battle within a year be canceled. That ripped the guts out of jet engine development." Galland pawed at his flying suit, looking for his lighter. Nowotny handed him his own, and Galland relit his cigar. "If we had only pressed on with research just in the metallurgy needed to withstand the high temperatures in jet engines, everything would have been fine. We could have had a thousand 262s by late 1942, with plenty of time and fuel to train the pilots. But no, that all had to be left until two years later. And, if that were not enough, we had all the changes, and all the experimental models. It didn't help that Milch and the Air Ministry were suspicious of Messerschmitt, and would not give him the people or the resources he needed."

"Afraid of another 210 fiasco!"

"Exactly, and blind to what they had in the 262. If everyone had reacted properly, we would have stopped the bomber offensive, day and night. There would have been no invasion, believe me. And we might even have held our ground in Russia. We have had less than five hundred fighters on the Eastern Front for the last two years; we put thousands of our 88mm guns to use in flak batteries when they should have been used to knock out Soviet tanks. They even frittered away our conventional fighters, wasting them."

Galland had long begged to be allowed to build up a huge reserve of day fighters and hit the incoming American formations with a massive attack, using a thousand 109s and 190s in a single Great Blow, as he called it. But every time he had the airplanes gathered, Göring would order them out on some useless task. When the invasion came, the *Reichsmarschall* had wasted aircraft in such a profligate manner that only two airplanes were available to strafe the invasion beaches on June 6. Now he was going to use Galland's carefully husbanded resources for a big attack on the Western Front in December. Galland started to mention this, then caught himself; it was so top secret that he could not even tell Nowotny, a loyal hero of the Reich if ever there was one.

"What about this making the 262 a bomber?" Nowotny asked. "I hear people blame the Führer for the decision; they say he insisted that it be produced only as a bomber, not a fighter, that pilots couldn't endure the g-forces at high speed."

Galland nodded. "That's only partly true. He did ask to have bombs fitted, and saw the airplane as a fast bomber, but he knew that it would be a fighter, too. On balance his support helped the program more than his ideas about making it a blitz bomber hurt it. But the real problem was engines. We did not begin to get production engines until June of this year, all because we did not do the necessary research. The irony is that when the research was finally started, they quickly found a way to solve the problem. Instead of rare metals, they formed hollow turbine blades that could be cooled by passing air through them. Ingenious."

He reached over and placed a huge slice of ham on his plate. "Where on earth do you get ham like this? And this coffee—it is real!"

Nowotny smiled for the first time. "Your fans send you cigars; mine send me food. This came from a firm in Westphalia; they manage to get one to me every month."

There was a pause as Galland chewed; then in a low, kindly voice, he asked, "And what is happening here, Nowotny? We've got the airplanes we wanted at last. Why are they not working as they should?"

Nowotny flushed, accidentally banging his coffee mug down on the table, spilling it. He apologized as he mopped it up, then said, "You know the answers as well as I do. First of all, the pilots don't have sufficient training in the airplane. It's far different from flying a 109 or the 190. It doesn't turn as tightly, it's slow to accelerate, and the engines are very tricky, have to be handled with extreme care, or they will flame out. You know all that. But all of these shortcomings wouldn't really matter if I could get them to fly the airplane correctly, using its speed and climb to fight. Yet, despite all I tell them, despite what the manuals say, when a fight starts, they forget everything and try to maneuver with the Mustangs. Fatal! We stress over and over that they have to use their speed to engage and disengage when it is to their advantage, but when the guns start shooting, almost all of them start turning! Crazy."

Galland shook his head. The British and the Americans trained their pilots in perfect safety, some of them thousands of miles from combat. They had all the oil and gas they wanted, so they could give a pilot three hundred hours' flying time and more before sending him into combat. German cadets could get shot down on their first solo flight, and there was so little fuel that they were sending green pilots, with fewer than one hundred hours' flying time to frontline fighter units.

It was only a little different with the *Experten*, the veteran pilots who had survived years of battle and could fly anything. They might get from one to twenty hours' instruction in the 262 before being sent into combat, but there was no time to teach tactics, gunnery, or even formation flying. It was a murder mill, pure and simple.

"Any ideas on what you can do to improve things? We've got to start killing hundreds of the Allied bombers—to hell with their fighters, we've got to stop the bombers. They are burning up what's left of the Reich."

Nodding, Nowotny was walking toward a blackboard on which he had written half a dozen ideas for improving the situation when air-raid sirens blared. Nowotny said, "Sorry," grabbed his helmet, and ran toward his aircraft, parked at the side of the runway. Nowotny and three other pilots took off, their Messerschmitt jets leaving a trail of smoke as they disappeared through the low overcast.

Galland returned to the operations shack, where a radio was tuned to the frequency Nowotny was using. The Americans were apparently in force over Lake Dummer, and within minutes Nowotny calmly called that he was starting his attack on the bomber formation. A minute passed, and he reported that he had blown up a Liberator, and then moments later, a P-51.

Galland smiled. The 262s' armament package was lethal; the four 30mm Mk 108 cannon chewed up everything before them. And better things were coming, R4M rockets that could take out a formation of B-17s in a single pass.

An excited young pilot turned to Galland and slapped him on the back, saying, "That's numbers two fifty-seven and two fifty-eight," before realizing what he had done. Galland smiled, shook his head, and listened intently.

Nowotny's voice came back on the air. "Right turbine has failed; I'm returning to base."

Moments later, his emotions now not under control, he screamed, radioing, "Over the field. Right engine on fire. Mustang attacking."

Galland burst through the doorway of the shack and ran the hundred yards to the runway. Through the clouds he heard machine-gun fire, identifying it immediately as 50-caliber. The Mustang was shooting and Galland knew that Nowotny was a sitting duck. Then, through the low clouds scudding across the field, Nowotny's jet came plunging straight down, impacting the ground a little over a kilometer away, the raging smoke reaching up to the cloud cover.

Galland turned and trudged slowly toward his own aircraft. Nowotny was dead, and so was Kommando Nowotny. Someone else would have to create the tactics for the jet fighter. As if it made any difference now.

January 2, 1945, Eglin Army Airfield, Florida

LIEUTENANT COLONEL TOM Shannon almost never drank and absolutely never drank to excess. But there had been a wild party at the Officers Club on New Year's Eve, where he met Ginny, an agreeable, attractive secretary at Base Headquarters. She had been standing at the club door as if waiting for someone; when Tom walked in, she grabbed him by the arm and said, "Let's go have some fun," by way of introduction. Ginny was blond, with a great sense of mildly ribald humor, if not a great mind, and she tossed off the dreadful club drinks as if they were water, which they mostly were. Best of all, she was definitely romantically inclined, pressing close to him on the dance floor when they played "Sentimental Journey," kissing his neck and responding to his clumsy comments as if he were Errol Flynn.

He made one mistake—matching her drink for drink. Things progressed nicely, especially on the dance floor, where, never much of a dancer, he was pleasantly surprised to find that he was able to jitterbug so well that a circle of admiring, clapping friends had gathered around them. The festive mood was dampened when he suddenly began projectile vomiting all over his partner and the dance floor. The clapping ceased as the laughter began.

Mortified, legs wobbly, unable to attend to Ginny, and deeply humiliated in front of his military colleagues, Tom excused himself, realizing that he had forfeited the Marine Corps reputation for holding its liquor forever. He stumbled to his quarters, showered, and spent the next day miserable in bed. A half-dozen fellow pilots dropped by, each with his own special form of humor, which ranged from bringing a plate of pork chops for his absentee appetite to advising him that once she was cleaned up, Ginny turned out to be wonderful in bed.

The rest restored him and when duty called the following morning he reported to the operations building for a twenty-four-hour stint as Aerodrome Officer. The not too arduous duties included checking the quality of meals at the enlisted mess halls and meeting each inbound aircraft to make sure that it was properly serviced. For Tom there was a big dividend. The Aerodrome Officer was allowed to visit headquarters and go through the intelligence bulletins as they came in. If there was anything of particular importance, he was to alert the Base Commander.

The big news was a massive Luftwaffe attack on Allied airfields in France and Belgium on January 1. As many as four hundred Allied airplanes had been destroyed, most of them on the ground, while it was estimated that three hundred Luftwaffe planes were shot down. His thoughts immediately went to Harry, who had finished his tour in B-17s and had applied to fly another tour in either the B-26 or the P-51. Tom wondered how many jets the Germans had used.

Then his mind drifted back to his father. Tom knew he should call him, but it was difficult nowadays, for he was never certain who would answer and he did not wish to speak to Madeline. He was still debating this when Lieutenant Colonel Bert Swofford, the deputy Base Commander, came in for his own reading of the intelligence reports.

Tom and Swofford had flown against each other often in serious engineering trials of performance and in the inevitable mock dog-fights that followed them. They took turns, one flying a captured enemy aircraft one day, the other flying an American counterpart, then exchanging roles the following day. Tom had developed a particular affinity for the German fighters, a Messerschmitt Bf 109F and a Focke-Wulf FW 190A. Both required careful maintenance to keep them in top shape, but each had special characteristics that in the hands of a good pilot made it a deadly adversary. They flew Japanese aircraft as well, and while the Zero was delightful to fly, it was clearly obsolete by current standards. The other Japanese aircraft, a Tony and a George, were more modern but almost impossible to keep in flying condition because of parts shortages and their general lack of manufacturing quality control.

Tom took the bull by the horns. "Bert, I want to apologize for my exhibition the other night. I drank way more than I ever did in my life, and I paid for it, believe me."

Swofford nodded. "No problem with me, Tom, but I'll let you in on something I shouldn't pass on to you. Somewhere along the line here, you've made some enemies." He paused contemplatively, saying, "I don't know why—you are the easiest guy to get along with in the business. But the incident at the club has been reported by Captain McGuire on up the line to your boss back in Washington. He's recommending some sort of formal action be taken. The report came over my desk; I noted that I did not concur, but, obviously, I couldn't stop it."

Tom flushed. He knew exactly what the problem was. McGuire was the senior Navy officer on base. He had gone through the Academy four years before Tom attended—but had washed out in his first six weeks in Pensacola. He envied all flyers, and had taken a particular dislike to Tom, a Marine ace, in a plum assignment flying enemy fighters.

Although he didn't plan on making a career of the Marines after the war, Tom hated to have his record sullied by something so stupid. Swofford tossed him a packet of papers. "Take a look at this. They are calling for volunteers for a special project to go into Germany and fly some of their new fighters back for analysis. A friend of mine, Hal Watson, is heading the team. I'll call him if you want to go. If he takes you, you'll be sent up to Wright Field, and then overseas. Sounds like a natural to me."

Tom flushed with gratitude. "Bert, I'll owe you plenty if you can pull this off. Get me on this; it's a great way out, and it sounds like a hell of a lot of fun."

April 10, 1945, over Germany

LIEUTENANT COLONEL HARRY Shannon considered for the hundredth time the total stupidity of being there, in the left seat of a B-17, on his sixty-first mission over Germany, headed for Rechlin, where German jets were supposed to be stationed. He was stretching his luck and he knew it, but orders were orders. He was just glad that his friend Joe Mizrahi had come down with a cold. If he had not, Joe would be in flying the airplane and Harry would be stuck between the seats, observing, the most useless feeling in the world of combat. As it was, he had to be very careful of his manner. Crews hated to fly with a strange crew member and detested flying with a strange pilot in command.

Still, Shannon was proud to be leading more than twelve hundred bombers to targets deep in Germany. He wondered how it must look to the battered civilians on the ground, the impeccable boxes of Boeing B-17s and Consolidated B-24s, contrails streaming bright behind them, moving inexorably toward their targets and surrounded by a swarm of more than eight hundred fighters, mostly P-51s, their young pilots thirsting for a fight.

There had been little aerial opposition predicted and none encountered. Flak had been moderate, for the planners had arranged their route to avoid the major concentrations.

The bare minimum of intercom chatter indicated that the crew of his aircraft, *Bouncing Betsy*, was recovering from his displacing Mizrahi. There had been a long delay for takeoff. Fog had socked almost all of England in and they had waited impatiently for four hours for it to clear off. The worst part was, no one had thought to prepare an extra meal or even coffee for the waiting crews, and most of the muttered intercom remarks were references to food.

Harry was not there on some quixotic whim. An additional order had come down from Eighth Air Force, specifically directing him to fly because intelligence had reported that they could expect opposition from a new German unit commanded by the German ace Adolf Galland. The message contained two daunting speculations. The first was that Galland's new outfit was manned almost entirely by the remaining top Luftwaffe aces. The second was that they were armed with a new weapon, an unguided rocket that was capable of knocking down a bomber with a single hit. Shannon's task was to observe and evaluate the rocket fire.

Sixty miles away, Adolf Galland was quietly orbiting as his small group of Me 262s formed up. There were at least another twenty-four 262s in the air, from JG 7 and JG 54. They would attack the long bomber stream farther to the rear. The Me 262s needed a lot of room to operate, to speed past the defending fighters and to line up on the bombers, but the endless parade of B-17s and B-24s and the blue German sky provided more than enough space. The sad thing for Galland was that the sky could have been crowded with Me 262s, if the right research had been done, and then the 262s would have emptied the sky of bombers.

Flying the Me 262 in this fashion, with no one shooting at them yet, was sheer pleasure; the 262 was so responsive, so fast, and so quiet that it somehow made the world seem peaceful. And indeed, the ground below, a patchwork of fallow fields, green hills, and tiny villages, looked as peaceful as it had in 1939. The reason was simple. On the ground, the war was over. The Russians and the Americans had met on the Elbe, and there was precious little fighting still to be done. In Berlin, buried in the ruins of the Chancellery, Adolf Hitler and his dwindling coterie of Nazi leaders continued to exist. They were not resisting, just staying alive beneath the barrage of Soviet artillery shells. Their deaths and the final surrender had to come within days.

But in the air it was different. The 262, the Turbo, as the pilots called it, reigned supreme. It had almost matured as a warplane, and its speed and firepower made it easily the best fighter of the war. The engines were getting more reliable, and some would run for as long as twenty-five hours before needing replacement. The four 30mm cannon had been supplemented by a battery of twenty-four R4M rockets. Fired at the right spot, the rockets arced out ahead to fill a section of the sky almost thirty meters by twenty meters. Nine such salvos covered a huge area and could easily break up an entire enemy bomber formation. Then, when the surviving bombers scattered, the 262s could pick them off with cannon fire.

Adolf Galland, summarily dismissed at last by Göring from his role as the Inspector General for Fighters, was ending the war as he had started it, commanding a small unit. This was Jagdverband 44, the final distillation of the Luftwaffe's top aces and the war's best fighter. Galland had called for the best pilots to come to JV 44, and they came gladly, Barkhorn, Krupinski, Steinhoff, Spate, and more. They knew they could not affect the course of the war, but they sought to fight, and die if necessary, with the dignity that only the 262 could confer.

As expert as his pilots were, they were not familiar with the fabulous Me 262 that they were flying. Galland was going to talk them through one mock attack, then lead them westward, where he could already see the first wave of Ami bombers.

Earlier that morning he had drawn out the tactics on a chalkboard. The 262s were so fast that the long-proved tactics gained in four years of air warfare were now obsolete. Today JV 44 could put nine aircraft in the air. The 262s' engines were still so sensitive to throttle movement that in executing turns they held formation by overshooting or undercutting the turn, rather than reducing or increasing throttle. So, to reduce the time and area covered in turns, they now had to fly in elements of three, instead of the classic "finger four" formation that had been developed in Spain. They flew about fifty meters apart, with about one hundred meters separating the elements.

Galland planned to fly in a wide, high circle and attack the lead group of American bombers from the rear, slicing down from about two thousand meters above the bombers to pull up about fifteen hundred meters behind them, with as much speed as possible, at least 900 kph. When the wingspan of a B-17 filled the special marker on the Revi 16B gun sight, the range was about two hundred meters and the twenty-four R4M rockets each plane carried would be fired. When the B-17s scattered, each of the veteran pilots would seize upon a victim and shoot it down with cannon fire. Then they would climb away before the enemy fighters came, to return to base.

Shannon had just spotted the nine swift dots on the horizon when a P-51 pilot called, "Big Friends, looks like about a dozen jets coming in to attack from the east; we'll try to cut them off, but I don't think we can get there from here."

As he swung high and to the north of the bombers, moving out of range of any of the escorting fighters, Galland watched the seemingly endless flights of American bombers and remembered another of Göring's famous gaffes. When warned about the American four-engine bombers, Göring had remarked that he was glad they were coming, for while the Americans could make good razor blades, they couldn't make good airplanes, and the larger they were the easier they would be to shoot down. Grinning with the thought of Göring's enormous bulk being squashed in the tight seat of the 262, Galland signaled the attack.

On the intercom, Shannon called quietly, "OK, my friends, let's look alive; they'll make a tail attack, so call them off as they come in. Randy, you'll probably be looking right down their throats, so keep telling me what they are doing."

Randy was a nineteen-year-old tail gunner from Tyler, Texas; he looked like a saint, swore like a devil, and held the highest gunnery scores of any man in his squadron. Randy called back, "Roger that, sir."

"Pilot from bombardier."

"Go ahead."

"We are about ten seconds from our initial point. We've got the wind drift killed, so keep on this same heading for at least thirty seconds. Then I'll take it."

"Roger." No word from the crew. Shannon thought how perfect the jets' timing was, making their attack at the one moment when they would be straight and level.

The Me 262s' long turn now changed into a trail formation, three elements of three jets positioned to cover the maximum area of the formation.

Randy's voice, cool as a Texas spring, called out, "They're coming in behind the formation, sir, about fifteen hundred feet low, but climbing. They've got something under their wings, looks like little bombs."

Shannon replied: "Keep your eye on them, and tell me if they fire them off. I think they are rockets, but I'm not sure."

In the lead Me 262, Galland saw the B-17's wing grow to fill the marker on his gun sight and fired his rockets. At his side, almost at the same second, the other two aircraft in his element fired theirs.

"They're rockets all right, sir; they just fired them. They are filling up the sky with smoke and flames; they're blocking out the whole formation behind us."

Randy came back on, his voice an octave higher. "Oh my God, they've blown up four airplanes already. There goes another one!"

Shannon had seen a large number of the rockets streak ahead of him and blow up; somehow his airplane had made it through. After an interminable wait, the bombardier called, "Bombs Away," and Shannon began a fifteen-degree bank to the left. As he turned he saw huge explosions in his own formation and in the formations behind him—the jets had hit at least ten, perhaps twelve or more, B-17s with their rockets and now were curving around, their 30mm cannon ready to fire.

Galland had grimaced with satisfaction as his R4Ms took out a B-17, and he swept through the rest of the formation firing, his 30mm cannon shells literally sawing the nose off of another B-17, sending it into an endless spin to the earth. Pulling the Turbo into a tight turn, he fixed his sights on the lead B-17, its bomb bay empty now, turning and running for home. He pressed the trigger and all four guns gave a short burst before going silent.

Harry felt the 30mm cannon shells ripping through his fuselage and wing, hammering the cockpit and wounding Mason, his copilot, and killing Kennedy, the bombardier, men he had met just this morning. The B-17 lurched to the left, its number one and two engines shot up and burning. Fighting the airplane, he reached up and feathered the two engines. The fires diminished, but he would have to keep an eye on them. The intercom was dead. Nagel, the radio operator, came forward and moved the copilot out of his seat and put pressure bandages on his wounds. Then Nagel leaned over Shannon and said, "Fuel leaking from the left wing."

Shannon nodded and said, "Go back and see what's happened to the rest of the crew. I'm going to try to make a field in Belgium or France."

Like vultures scattering from their carrion prey, all nine of the sleek gray-green Me 262s suddenly left the formation, climbing to rejoin for the flight back to their base outside Munich. Shannon's B-17 continued its gradual descent, wisps of smoke trailing with a shaken Harry Shannon trying to remember the exact sequence of events. The rockets had done the most damage—thank God the Germans did not have them or the jets a year ago. If they had, the war would have taken a very different turn.

THE PASSING SCENE

The United Nations formed; Japan surrenders; Joe Louis defends crown; Nuremberg trial of Nazi war criminals; Churchill proclaims "Iron Curtain" in Eastern Europe; **Best Years of Our Lives** *plays; Marshall Plan called for; India and Pakistan made independent; Juan Peron becomes President of Argentina; "flying saucers" reported; Jackie Robinson joins major league.*

CHAPTER SEVEN

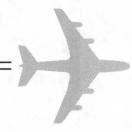

May 26, 1945, Aachen, Germany

The contrast was incredible. Below, the little German towns were strung like pearls on the string of the river, the jumbled houses lining curving cobblestone streets, the irregular fields glowing green with the spring. He had crossed Germany many times before in a B-17 with a cargo of destruction. Now he was flying a cargo of genius, not at a frigid 25,000 feet or higher, but at a comfortable 5,000 feet, with the earth-scented breeze filling the comfortable cabin of the Douglas C-47. Sitting in the back of the aircraft was his father, Vance Shannon, surrounded by some of the most eminent engineers in the United States.

Flying with his father was not a novelty. Harry and his brother, Tom, had learned to fly on cross-country trips with their dad. But never had they flown with so many important people, almost all members of General Arnold's Scientific Advisory Group. They were the top scientists and engineers in the United States, commissioned by Arnold to go to Germany and round up all the advanced scientific data on jet engines, rockets, German nuclear experiments, and more. Harry knew that his dad had special reverence for two of them—the

famous Dr. Theodore von Kármán and Boeing's leading aerodynamicist, George Schairer. Now all of them, regardless of their learning,
were doing exactly the same thing, pressing their foreheads against
the Plexiglas windows like excited kids, drinking in the sad fate that
Hitler had brought to Germany and all of Europe. The pleasant
breeze was soon tainted with a rank odor, and Harry knew that a major city was coming up, charging the crisp tang of early May with the
smell of dust and wet ash. As the C-47 edged closer to a city, the
scent grew more pronounced, too often tinged with the death smell
of bodies still concealed beneath the rubble.

The navigator passed a note with their position indicated, but
Harry Shannon had flown too long not to keep his own map at his
side. The route southeast from Hannover had carried them across
devastated city after another, Dortmund, Düsseldorf, Cologne. In
each one, the gutted buildings stood like tombstones, swaying without
roof or windows, obscuring the life that stirred below in cellars and
makeshift hovels, as families tried to survive in the bitter aftermath of
defeat. Aachen was the next major city. He looked back and signaled
to his relief pilot, Captain Ron Clendenning. It was his turn to make a
landing, and Harry wanted to go back and visit with his father a bit.

"Ron, make a couple of circuits of the city, please, before you
land. They will want to get a good look before we set down. Some of
them went to school, or even taught here."

He glanced out the windows as he walked back to his father's
seat. Most German cities had a familiar pattern of destruction; from
a distance, they looked like a burst egg, oval and burned black on the
western approaches because Allied bombers had a tendency to walk
their bombs back from the aiming points, increasing the tonnage
dropped on the western sides of cities. Aachen looked different,
somehow, the destruction more evenly arrayed, blackened all around
but a gray-brown jumble inside. Then he remembered that Aachen
had twice been pummeled by artillery fire—first by the Americans
when they seized the city in October, then by the Germans when
they tried to take it back in January.

He was talking with his father, thanking him again for getting him
this plum assignment, when a hand reached up and grabbed his sleeve.

"Come here, please, both of you. I want to show you something." Theodore von Kármán's rich Hungarian accent was choked with emotion. "Down there, that's my city. Look what we have done to my university, my wind tunnel. Gone. All gone." He made no attempt to wipe the tears coursing down his face. "What of the people? What will we find of the people?"

Both men felt sorry for him, but not for the people he sought. Kármán had seen what was coming and left. Those who stayed behind and worked for Nazi Germany deserved what they got. Harry's mind flashed back to his last raid on Germany, just over a month ago, when the swift, predatory Messerschmitt 262 jet fighters had slashed through his formation, firing their rockets first, then closing to hammer the B-17s with 30mm cannon. He still remembered the black smoke boiling from their jet engines and how their arrow-like gray-green swept wings looked like arrows hurtling by. The German jets had destroyed four of his squadron in a single pass, shooting up his own airplane so badly that he had to make an emergency wheels-up landing at a tiny fighter strip in France. As he pulled his wounded copilot from the smoking wreckage he swore that in the next war he was going to be in fighters doing the shooting and not in a bomber being shot at. The jet engines and swept wings of those Messerschmitts had come from the geniuses resident in places such as Aachen and Göttingen.

His father patted Kármán on the back. Vance idolized the man who had taken him under his wing when he was doing contract work for the Air Corps at Cal Tech. There, in beautiful Pasadena, Kármán had taught him many things, from aerodynamics and the potential of rocket power to the pleasure of sipping big tumblers of Jack Daniel's bourbon as a way to cut the richness of the paprika dishes that flowed from his kitchen. But Vance could feel no sympathy for Kármán's former German colleagues or for the destruction meted out to German cities.

George Schairer from Boeing joined them, and Kármán repeated his query. Schairer shrugged. There was no answer to Kármán's question. The devastation was dreadful, but it could have been stopped at any moment if Germany had done the inevitable and surrendered. Somehow a relatively small clique of desperate men had used fear to control the German people until the very end. Then, when surrender finally occurred on May 8, the entire Nazi apparatus had seemed to wither and die like a punctured balloon, all the swagger and hatred replaced by groveling pleas for American understanding of the need to follow orders.

Their visit in Aachen was uneventful. Kármán toured them around in the lead jeep, showing them where he had lived and taught. But the feeling of animosity was intensified two days later when they visited Nordhausen, the hellhole the SS had created in the Harz Mountains, some fifty miles south of Braunschweig. Nordhausen was a huge underground factory carved out of the region's soft limestone where the Nazis had used slave labor to build jet engines and V-2 rockets. Quite by chance, Kármán had run into one of his many former students, a Frenchman, Charles Sadron, at Nordhausen.

Vance sensed Kármán's embarrassment. At Cal Tech, Sadron had weighed more than two hundred pounds; now he was down to half of that.

"Dear Charles, how good to see you." Kármán handed him a Hershey bar and looked away as Sadron wolfed it down. In the thin sun that bathed the outbuildings of Nordhausen, the two old friends sat down on an abandoned packing crate, Kármán with his arm around Sadron's frail shoulders. Vance listened carefully. Out of courtesy to him, the two men spoke in a fractured English when both would have been more comfortable speaking French. The words tumbled out. Shannon knew he was missing much but could not interrupt.

"We built rockets here; you called them V-2s. We were all slave labor."

Kármán nodded, listening intently.

"It was a work camp and a death camp. You came in, they assigned you so many months to live, based on how fat you were."

"You were heavy at Cal Tech, I remember—about one hundred kilos?"

"Yes, not when I got here, of course, I was down to about eighty kilos, but that was enough for them to give me six months to live.

Others got less; if they were thin, maybe they'd schedule them only for three months' work, or even less, two months, one month . . . it all depended on how much fat you were carrying. The more fat, the longer they thought they could work you."

Kármán shook his head. "What did they do at the end of your schedule? Put you in the gas chamber?"

Sadron laughed and Vance winced; it was painful to watch Sadron's poor thin body shake. "No, that was the beauty of it. SS efficiency. When your date expired, they cut your rations until you starved to death. I had just a few days to go before the Americans came."

Kármán's face was white with shock and rage. Sadron turned his head and vomited. Kármán, his arm still around Sadron's shoulder, offered a handkerchief. Sadron looked at it in amazement—the simple clean white cotton cloth was a luxury beyond his imagination. "Sorry. The chocolate was too rich—and I ate too much of it. What a waste."

Shannon caught Kármán's glance and understood; he left to make arrangements with the local commander for Sadron to be hospitalized. They didn't speak again until they were airborne, on their way to the next stop on their itinerary, Göttingen. The ancient university town was the very birthplace of German aerodynamics. Here Ludwig Prandtl, the most famous name in aerodynamics, lived and worked. Prandtl had been Kármán's professor, then his somewhat grudging mentor, and later his rival, the rivalry tinged with Prandtl's contempt for Kármán's Jewish origins. Not by accident, the U.S. military governor had assigned Kármán the university office that Prandtl once occupied as professor.

"Now Vance, you and your son just stand there and listen. How's your German?"

"Doctor, you know I can barely understand you when you speak English, so I don't expect to understand your German." Kármán smiled, the first time he had done so since leaving Sadron's side at Nordhausen. It seemed to promise that he would make short work of Prandtl.

When Prandtl came in he was nervous, bowing obsequiously to Kármán, who was dressed in the uniform of a major general, his simulated rank for the mission. Prandtl looked nervously at the other men in the room, then seemed to bristle.

"You are sitting at my desk!"

Kármán merely nodded, then got briskly down to business, pinning Prandtl down on details of advanced German engineering. To the Shannons' surprise, they could follow the conversation closely, realizing that Prandtl was spilling his guts on all he knew on jet engines, swept wings, and rocket technology. He wasn't just giving engineering details; he was doing more, telling who the primary engineers were, where they were located, who could be trusted. Kármán's hand flew across the tablet, noting in his cramped handwriting everything Prandtl said, occasionally glancing up at them to see if they understood the import of what was happening.

Harry Shannon understood all too well; he had seen the Messerschmitt 262s' swept wings in the sky, and now he was going to get the engineering details straight from the source. At the end, as if exhausted from talking, Prandtl said, "Now you must go to Volkenrode, near Braunschweig. Most of the papers relating to high-speed aerodynamics are there—or were there."

Vance Shannon looked at Kármán. No one had mentioned Volkenrode as a scientific source before.

Prandtl, seeing their confusion, said, "It was a completely secret organization, hidden in the woods; I've visited there myself only once. But as the enemy . . ." He paused, realizing that he had perhaps insulted them and identified himself as a patriotic German, the last thing he wished to do today. Then he continued, ". . . as the Americans advanced in the south of Germany, much was transferred there. I'll give you the name of a man you can rely on to take you to the site."

Vance conferred with Harry. Their C-47 was being refueled and having a tire changed. Braunschweig was only sixty miles away. Harry Shannon asked Kármán and Schairer if they were up to the hazards of a road trip, cautioning them on the possibility of renegade troops holding out and the probable conditions of the road. Both men agreed to go immediately. Shannon arranged to borrow three jeeps from an American armored unit to make the trip, one with three soldiers armed to the teeth for security.

The ride up was a revelation, for while larger towns like Paderborn showed significant damage, there were intervals where entire villages had been spared the bombing—but not the refugees who crowded everywhere, in barns, schools, and open fields. Shannon was struck by the look of passive indifference on most faces. Here and there he would see a flash of resentment, usually by someone still wearing the remnants of an officer's uniform. Most of them seemed stoically preoccupied with enduring for yet another day.

Prandtl's directions had been good, although the quality of the road declined as they approached the forest where the institute was hidden. It appeared at last, a collection of almost sixty buildings, all shaded by enormous trees to be invisible not only from the air but from one another. A few had been built to resemble farmhouses; others were the typical bunkers that studded Germany. A cleverly camouflaged runway ran the length of the facility. Some buildings were destroyed, not by bombs but apparently by local people salvaging material to repair their shattered homes.

Only a few Germans were present. Kármán sought out the first one and gave him the name of an old assistant, Rudolph Kochel, whom he had known at Aachen. The man nodded and led Kármán's group to a building that had been perfectly concealed by being partially buried in the ground, then having trees planted directly onto its roof.

Inside, Kochel was working at a desk. When Kármán entered he stood up and said, "Ah, Professor. It is so good to see you," as if they had parted just weeks before. Kármán immediately began questioning him about the high-speed wind tunnel and swept wing research. Kochel was nervous; switching alternately from German to quite good English, he pretended that he knew nothing about the experiments, insisting that all of the engineering information had been carried off by the Luftwaffe personnel, weeks before.

Harry Shannon walked to a bookcase, where there was a tiny metal model, no more than three inches in span, of the Me 262. He whirled on Kochel and said, "One of these nearly killed me. I demand that you show me its drawings."

Vance Shannon was almost as frightened as Kochel was by

Harry's rough tone. The German slumped in his chair behind the desk, waved his hand weakly, then said, "Come; I will show you."

Kochel led them through the back of the building, unlocking a series of doors as they progressed. Each room was filled with filing cabinets, and the Americans longed to stop each time and examine them. The last door opened to a courtyard, where there was a covered well. Kochel said nothing, just pointed to it.

Harry grabbed an ancient rusted mattock and pried the wooden top off. He looked in at an endless heap of reports, documents, and plans that filled the well to its very top. Reaching in, he pulled out several, passing them to his American companions.

Schairer spoke. "This is the mother lode. These confirm their experiments with the swept wing."

Harry arranged with his soldiers to guard the site, promising them relief by morning. On the ride back to Göttingen, the men were absorbed in the documents they were able to bring with them, scarcely speaking except to erupt with howls of joy at some newly discovered insight. Once Kármán reached forward and shook Schairer's shoulder, yelling, "This vindicates Bob Jones." Schairer nodded back. Robert T. Jones had advocated the swept wing to the National Advisory Committee for Aeronautics, but his argument had been rejected as unsound.

The group was under no restrictions about the dissemination of information they discovered to U.S. industry. That night two of the group wrote letters home. George Schairer advised Boeing to drop the currently proposed straight wing configuration for their new multi-jet bomber and adopt a thirty-five-degree swept wing. Vance Shannon, under contract to North American, gave the same advice for their new jet fighter.

March 31, 1947, Wright Field, Ohio

TWO ATOMIC BOMBS had brought the war to a close in the Pacific, a mere four months after Germany's surrender in Europe. The surprisingly rapid end to the war stunned the United States just as it was gearing up for a long campaign culminating in the invasion of Japan. The September 2 surrender found Tom Shannon en route to join his Corsair squadron in San Diego, Harry Shannon learning to fly a B-29 at Randolph Field, and their father contemplating which job he wanted to take from among the four that were currently offered him. The first two were from the Army, with one calling for him to tour the scientific facilities in Japan, as he had done in Germany. The second Army offer would take him to Wright Field, where he would work with the German scientists and equipment that had been picked up in the closing months of the war in what became known as Operation Paperclip.

The civilian offers were more attractive financially. George Schairer had prodded Boeing to invite Vance to work in Seattle, where he would serve directly under Ed Wells on two new secret programs, one a bomber and one a civilian transport. The other was from Vance's old friend Bob Gross, who asked that he come to Lockheed and, as Gross put it, "ride shotgun on Kelly Johnson" as they developed their line of jet fighters.

Vance paused to consider how fortunate he had been to have his engineering career coincide with an almost continuous series of advances in aviation. And how privileged he was to have been able to work with men like Johnson at Lockheed, Schairer at Boeing, and Laddon at Consolidated. If Vance had worked at just one of the big companies, he would have been overshadowed by the geniuses who presided over their engineering departments. But as a consultant, he got to rub elbows with all of them and, perhaps most important, do some engineering cross-fertilization, bringing ideas and outlooks from one company to another, without violating any confidences.

The welcome Japanese surrender had immediately affected everyone, and the ensuing two years saw a complete collapse of the greatest, strongest, most effective armed forces the world had ever seen. Vance Shannon had watched in disbelief as the Army Air Forces declined in just eighteen months from a highly trained force operating more than seventy thousand aircraft manned by more than 2 million personnel to a skeleton force of three hundred thousand people with fewer than ten thousand operational aircraft. The

Army and the Navy went through a similar convulsion, laying down arms indiscriminately in the laudable but laughable headlong rush to get the troops back home.

As welcome as peace was, it disrupted the American economy. The aviation industry had been producing aircraft at the rate of one hundred thousand per year in 1944. In 1946, fewer than seven hundred aircraft were purchased by the Army.

For the Shannon family, peace brought a thousand blessings. Neither Harry nor Tom would have to fly combat again, and both were going to be released from service soon. Tom had contemplated making a career of the Marines but had been disillusioned by the rapid demobilization. For his part, Vance was nearly exhausted by the continuous traveling that had carried him almost continually from one theater to another. Now, at last, he would be able to stay at home with Madeline.

The peace did have a downside and the first was Madeline's continuing to refuse to marry him, despite her wartime promises. He understood her reasons well enough—the age difference was there and would always be there, growing worse in the next years as she moved toward a sexual peak. He was already well beyond his, and Madeline was an intensely passionate woman. And then there were the boys, young men now, accomplished war heroes, and still not willing to accept his relationship with Madeline. It wasn't that they wanted him to marry her, far from it. Neither boy was a prude, and as unconventional as it was, they accepted that he was living with a woman who was not his wife. It was simply that they had disliked Madeline from the start and their few meetings had not changed things.

Nor did the coming of peace help things on the financial side. Three of Vance's job prospects had dried up and the fourth, working at Wright Field with the German scientists, was now clearly a temporary position.

In many ways this was a relief. Vance had always enjoyed being a freelance contractor, working the entire industry as a busy bee might work a field of flowers, going from one tempting job to the next. The industry was bound to recover, for jets had revolutionized aviation, and there would soon be competition for new generations of jet fighters and bombers and even, if his contacts in Boeing were correct, jet airliners. He saw jet aviation at being at about the same point automobiles were when Henry Ford introduced the Model T. There would be no shortage of work in the future, once the production lines got rolling. Or so he hoped.

Vance glanced at the standard government wall clock, found in almost every room in every government building and rarely displaying the correct time. In fifteen minutes he was going to meet with the newest arrival from Germany, Dr. von Ohain, the man who had invented the jet engine in Germany almost simultaneously as Frank Whittle had invented it in Great Britain. Vance wasn't looking forward to the interview. The last two men he had interviewed, scientists from Peenemünde, had complained continuously about the poor food, inadequate pay, and drafty quarters. He wondered how much thought they had given to the quarters they had made drafty in England as a result of their work on the V-1 and V-2.

Yet he knew they had a point. They were not paid their salaries directly. Instead the money was paid into an account in Germany, so that their families could benefit. They did receive six dollars a day per diem, which more than covered the twenty-three hundred calories of mess-hall food allocated to them. Most saved enough from their per diem to send packages of food and clothing back to Germany. Their quarters were austere, just the standard two-story barracks that some 16 million American GIs had endured, cold in winter, hot in summer, with open bathrooms and no privacy. But even so, Vance did not take kindly to their complaints. They were living better by far than the families they had left behind in Germany, many of whom still camped in bombed-out ruins. He hoped von Ohain might be different.

Shannon knew his days at Dayton were numbered, and as he waited behind his battered oak desk, he experimented with names for the new company he was forming. His first choice was still "Aviation Consultants, Incorporated," but Madeline was insisting that he should take advantage of his reputation by naming the company after him. He jotted down a series of names, including "Vance Shannon and Sons, Aviation Consultants," "The Shannon Group," and "Vance Shannon Aviation," but all of them struck him as pushy. The right people would soon know who was behind "Aviation Consultants, Incorporated," and for the rest it didn't matter.

What did matter was somehow getting his sons to accept Madeline. They were still resistant, and he hoped forming the new company might help, with himself as president, Tom and Harry as vice presidents, and Madeline as secretary-treasurer. She had been such a source of strength for the past two years, enduring his long absences and following him to the cramped apartment in Dayton with never a complaint. As helpful as ever, Madeline worked at home for him and was far more efficient than any secretary he had ever employed. She had an amazing ability to help him decide who to turn to for help on a contract. Never much on filing, and a terrible typist, Vance relished the way Madeline turned out his work, professionally, with never a mistake. And nothing was ever lost—if he needed a paper, a contract, she could pull it out for him in an instant. Once or twice she tried to instruct him in her methods, but it was too intricate. He preferred just to give things to her, confident that when he needed something she would have it. They could discuss any problem, and she was showing a greater grasp of technical matters than many of the engineers he worked with. Usually she would quickly understand the problem, going right to the heart of the matter with a point that he might have overlooked or felt was not sufficiently pertinent. How she put up with him he didn't know, but she remained as loving as ever, more tolerant of his weakening desires than he might have expected, given the ardor of their early years.

Classified material was different, of course. He kept everything at work in the standard filing cabinets, with their bar locks, and only took things home to work on when something had to be ready the following day.

Tom and Harry had never seen this side of Madeline, her competence, her dedication. Their meetings had always been almost formal, at dinners or at company receptions. Once they got to know her, when they were actively working together in the company,

Vance hoped they would understand—at least in part—her fascination for him. Then they would come to accept her. Or so he dreamed.

Precisely at three o'clock there was a knock and he hastened to open the door to his office. A slender man, impossibly young to have invented the jet engine, stood in the hallway, smiling diffidently, his hands nervously twirling his fedora.

"Come in, Dr. von Ohain. I'm very pleased to meet you."

Von Ohain extended his hand, then withdrew it as if afraid that Shannon would refuse to shake it. Shannon reached forward, seized his hand, and pumped it. Von Ohain's first words were, "My English is not yet good."

And Shannon smilingly replied, "And neither is mine. We will get along well."

They spent the next hour talking about engineering matters, with von Ohain detailing, step-by-step, the progress that in just three years had led him from an idea to the first jet flight in the world. It took him longer to explain the ensuing years, when changes of programs, and unexpected technical problems, had delayed completion of his larger, more sophisticated engines.

The German scientist was excited to learn that Shannon had known Frank Whittle and had participated in the transfer of Whittle's engine technology to the United States. When Shannon mentioned that Whittle had not received backing from the British government, von Ohain was quick to understand. He shook his head, saying, "What a shame. If his people had backed him as Dr. Heinkel had backed me, there might never have been a war! England could have had jet planes in 1938, and we might have been able to get rid of Hitler."

Von Ohain paused for a minute. It was obvious that his comment about Hitler was spontaneous, but it was equally obvious that he did not wish to appear to be currying favor. After a moment he went on.

"Dr. Heinkel was not always the easiest man to work for—he wanted results in a hurry. He had to have them, or all the work would have gone to Messerschmitt. The engine that we made for the first jet flight was no more than a working model. Then he wanted me to develop a larger engine than the Junkers 004, so we had the usual development problems." Then, proudly, he added, "But jet engines are still more easily developed than piston engines."

It suddenly struck Shannon that neither of the men who had invented the jet engine independently but almost simultaneously, von Ohain and Whittle, had reaped any substantial rewards for having done so.

"This may seem personal, Dr. von Ohain, but I'd like to ask you how you were compensated for work. Do you mind?"

"No, not at all; it is all history now, anyway. When I started working for Dr. Heinkel he paid me a relatively low stipend, about what you would expect to pay a graduate student; it was three hundred Reichsmarks per month." Shannon did a quick calculation—at the official exchange rate that was about $720 annually. Von Ohain went on. "After about a year, he raised the salary to five hundred Reichmarks a month. It was enough for a young unmarried man—I was working seven days a week, and had little time to spend money, anyway. Then he promised me a royalty on my engines as they were produced."

Unashamed and having no need to know, Shannon pressed on, simply curious. "Was this significant?"

Von Ohain seemed genuinely amused. "It was significant but meaningless! After the war, in July 1945, he sent me a check for four hundred thousand Reichsmarks, which were, of course, by that time worth exactly nothing." He laughed so spontaneously that Vance joined in, thinking, *The damn German bureaucrats treated him just like the English bureaucrats treated Whittle!* Then he decided that perhaps he could make von Ohain feel more at ease and perhaps comfort him a bit. They were going to be working together; they needed to be on good terms.

"You might be interested to know that your counterpart, Air Commodore Whittle, did little better. He received his pay as a serving officer, of course, and was given an award of one hundred thousand pounds. And that was it."

He watched von Ohain's reaction closely and was pleased to see a combination of concern and genuine sympathy in his face.

"That is so unfair! His engine has been used by everyone, by Roll-Royce, by de Havilland, even by your General Electric!" He made a sort of clucking sound and repeated, "That is so unfair!"

It was obvious to Shannon that von Ohain was not dissembling. He obviously felt genuine indignation that Whittle should have been treated so shabbily. It was also obvious that von Ohain had been keeping up on developments after the war. *And*, Shannon thought, *who would know better than von Ohain how much effort Whittle must have expended, how many difficulties had been put in his way?* The two men would have to meet at some point in the future—and when they did, Vance wanted to be there.

Vance probed again. "And not only those companies. The British government saw fit to sell fifty-five engines, thirty Rolls-Royce Nenes and twenty-five Rolls-Royce Derwents, to the Soviet Union. You can be sure that they will copy them down to the last safety wire."

Von Ohain turned pale. "But that is not possible. How could anyone be so foolish? Do they not know what the Russians plan? They have great engineers of their own, but to give them Whittle's engines is just impossible."

Vance knew that unless von Ohain was the greatest actor in the world, he was anti-Soviet. Most Germans were, and with reason. Von Ohain's reaction had another element to it, however—he was concerned about the injustice to Whittle as much as the effect on Western security.

There was a brief pause, each man lost in his own chain of thought, but Shannon soon got back to business, saying, "You did work for the U.S. Navy. I understand that engines you created for it were excellent, much more powerful than anything we have now."

"Yes, that was my He S 011. Four years of development went into it. But I'm glad that it never went into a Nazi warplane."

This time he spoke more decisively. It was clear that he was sincere.

They chatted on and on and when Shannon glanced up at the

clock he realized that they had talked for almost two hours and he had not written down a single note. Von Ohain was not just fascinating as an inventor, a brilliant physicist who had become an on-the-job trained engineer. He was also an innately charming human being to whom one immediately warmed. Shannon thought about inviting him to dinner, knowing Madeline would be delighted to meet him.

"I'm sorry, Dr. von Ohain, I know that you have other appointments in the building, and I've delayed you. Just one more thing, there is another gentleman arriving tomorrow, someone you undoubtedly know, Dr. Anselm Franz."

Von Ohain's face brightened. "Oh, good. He is a great man, a great engineer. Can you—"

Obviously unwilling to ask a favor on such short acquaintance, he caught himself.

"Go ahead, please; what is it?"

"If it is possible, can you place Dr. Franz in my barracks? I can help show him how things operate."

"I'll see to it."

Smiling, bowing, von Ohain left for his next appointment.

Shannon sat back at his desk, his pencil tapping its surface, his mind racing. With people like von Ohain, Franz, and this rocket chap, von Braun, all coming to the United States, the prospects for aviation were looking up. The next few years would be decisive in terms of getting a new generation of jet aircraft built.

He looked at the paper in front of him and carefully lined out all but one name. "Aviation Consultants, Incorporated." He'd just have to put his foot down with Madeline on this one; the Lord knew she won almost every other argument they had.

July 18, 1947, San Diego, California

IT HAD STARTED three months before as an affectionate joke by Madeline, an attempt to ingratiate herself with Tom and Harry, to break somehow through their reserve.

In her years at Convair, Madeline had made many friends, and one of the best of them was Luigi "Lou" Capestro, an engineer who served as Issac "Mac" Laddon's right arm in designing a long line of Consolidated aircraft. Capestro, a big, jovial man with a contagious laugh, was responsible for the signature retractable floats on the Catalina and had been a major advocate for including the Davis wing in the B-24 design. Lou, for all his good humor, was rigidly proper and vainly tried to mask the warm spot in his heart he felt for Madeline, a disguise she and everyone else saw through at once. His feelings were in part simple physical attraction—Madeline was lovely; there was no denying it. He admired her also for her ability at work, having used her time and again to explain contract details to the surly Russians who regarded everyone at the plant with suspicion—everyone but Madeline, who simply charmed them. But she had done more. When his wife, Catherine, became ill in 1945, Madeline had spent hours with her, helping her through an illness that was largely due to her anxiety over her four sons, all in the service. Even though Madeline worked long hours at the plant, she managed to come by to cheer Catherine, sometimes going to Mass with her and the identical twin girls, Marie and Anna. Born on March 15, 1926, the two girls were stunning brunettes, petite but with a wild, ribald sense of humor that they tried to conceal from their parents and their brothers. Extremely close, the girls never went on single dates, always insisting that they had to be together. No suitor for one ever had a problem finding a friend for the other.

Madeline learned that Tom and Harry were going to meet in La Jolla in April to make arrangements for the sale of the Paseo del Ocaso Street house their father had deeded over to them. It was easy to persuade Lou Capestro to throw a party for two sons of Vance Shannon, who had many friends throughout the firm. For a kicker, she arranged with Lou for Marie and Anna to be their blind dates, thinking that the contrast of the tall, blond Shannon boys and the tiny, brunette girls would be a pleasant joke for all, even though nothing could possibly come of it. The Shannons were totally preoccupied with aviation, and despite being Lou Capestro's daughters, the girls were more than indifferent to flying and flyers; they were actively hostile, having been pursued relentlessly from the age of sixteen by naval aviators. There was a religious problem, too. Vance Shannon had been Catholic, but Margaret was an Episcopalian and the boys had been brought up in her faith. The Capestros were devout leading members of the Our Lady of the Rosary Church, which the Barnabite Fathers ran with an iron fist in a steel glove.

Lou never did things by halves, and he invited more than a hundred people from Convair for the evening at his big house on Guy Street in the Mission Hills. It overlooked the ever-growing Convair plant and had a nice view of the Point Loma peninsula.

Madeline wandered out on the porch, and to her left the sun was setting into San Diego. She found Vance sitting in a chair, watching the evening activity on the water. She joined him quietly, slipping her arm in his, and pointed to the hundreds of little boats, skiffs, barges, and motorboats that crisscrossed the bay like pedestrians on Fifth Avenue at noon.

"What do you think?"

Vance smiled and squeezed her arm with his. "What do I think? I think how in the hell do you always do everything right? I would never have thought that you could pull a party for the boys out of the hat like this, even from Lou. This is fantastic."

"We'd better go inside. You can't chance looking standoffish at an Italian party."

Vance went in and was soon engaged with Lou in a heated discussion over baseball, both men being ardent fans. Madeline circulated, as always, leaving smiles behind her as she went. Lou had not spared any expense. There were two bands, an enormous buffet catered personally by Mama Ghio of Anthony's Seafood Grotto, and three strategically placed bars. One of these was dedicated to serving the currently popular "Atomic Depth Charge," a potent combination of rum, gin, orange juice, and ginger ale. One was pleasant, two were dangerous to driving, and three were fatal to sexual inhibitions.

Madeline's harmless joke had backfired at the introduction, where it was obvious that the Shannon boys were bowled over by the spectacular beauty of the twins, dressed alike in low-cut peach dresses. Maria and Anne were only a little harder to convince. By the end of their first dance, Tom was enchanted while Marie felt only that things were going better than she had believed they would. Anna was smitten by Harry, who, typically, was more reserved. None of it mattered. By the end of the second dance and the first Atomic Depth Charge, all the reservations were gone, along with many of the inhibitions. Before the evening was over, both couples believed themselves to be in love, and from that point on they were inseparable.

This posed a problem, as the Capestro sisters were well chaperoned by the Capestro brothers, all back from service in the Marines. The four brothers—Jasper, Augie, Sal, and Ross—were both openly menacing and ever-present until Tom and Harry proved their good intentions by buying engagement rings a month to the day after they met the twins.

The news rocked both families, especially the insistence of the young couples on marrying immediately, threatening to go to Mexico if an early date was not approved. To Vance Shannon's astonishment and Madeline's delight, both boys agreed to convert to Catholicism. They immediately began taking instructions and going to Mass. Lou Capestro assigned the conversion job as if it were a wartime rush order for armament to his old friend and drinking buddy Father William Trombley. Harry and Tom treated the instruction as if it were an aircraft manual and were ready for baptism by July 17.

The wedding had gone well. Tom's and Harry's reservations about Madeline evaporated in the light of the genuine affection in which she was held by the Capestro twins and by the inescapable fact that she had somehow engineered the whole happy transaction.

As the wedding reception drew to a close, Madeline was called on for a toast, and she responded with one she had been preparing since the two sets of twins had fallen mutually in love. A little unsteady from too much champagne, she rose and said:

"Here is to Anna, who has found her Marie in Harry;
Here is to Marie, who has found her Anna in Tom;
Here is to Tom, who has found his Harry in Marie . . ."

A wave of raucous laughter swept around the table with Lou yelling, "He'd better not find Harry in Marie!"

When the laughter and the cascade of increasingly ribald remarks had subsided, Tom and Harry spoke briefly together, and Harry stood up.

"It's our turn now, Madeline."

Tom and Harry filled their glasses and said in unison, "Here's to Vance and Madeline; may the next wedding be yours."

Smiling, Vance pulled Madeline to him. She backed away for an instant before kissing him. No one noticed her initial reticence but Vance. It troubled him. Something was wrong. Another man?

August 1, 1947, Wichita, Kansas

SWEATING FROM HIS climb up the hangar stairs, Vance Shannon called his sons into the second-story office that the Massey Company had provided them at its factory building at its privately owned airport on the outskirts of Wichita. A whisper of wind blew the ninety-eight-degree heat through the open window, rearranging the dust on the ancient desks.

"Boys, I'm proud of you! Just married and you get the first—and only—contract that we have. But I've looked the airplane over, and I say that we back out. I don't want you flying it."

Tom raised his eyebrows at Harry. They had predicted as much. Their father had been concerned with their safety from the time they learned to ride two-wheel bicycles, and nothing would ever change him.

"Come on, Dad; we've been all over this. You are just spooked because we're going to be making the first test flight, which strikes us as funny, because that's how you supported us all your life."

Harry chimed in. "You know yourself that Massey makes good aircraft—you used to fly us around the country in one."

Vance shook his head. "That was then, and they were building conventional steel tube, wood, and fabric biplanes. This is now and this thing is a monstrosity."

He went up to them; they were taller than he was now. He put his arms around them and guided them to the window that over-looked the factory floor. Below, ready to be rolled out for the test flight, was the Massey Double Quad airliner. Workers were still scrambling over it, checking to be sure that every panel was closed, every screw tight, and nothing was leaking.

The unusual name for the twenty-passenger airliner came from its engines. Four 350-horsepower Lycoming engines were installed, two in pairs on each side, and buried in the high wing to reduce drag. The engines were coupled, and each pair drove a single pro-peller through a complex gearbox. Vance knew this was an interim arrangement. Massey planned to install a turboprop engine as soon as they were commercially available. Then he might have some-thing. Vance knew intuitively that the gearbox would be trouble; they almost always were, no matter how good the engineering.

Worse, the rest of the airplane just did not look right. Massey advertised that the portly fuselage was strong enough to resist a wheels-up landing. Vance considered this to be a stupid claim, a hangover from the early 1930s when a retractable landing gear was news. But, he reflected, Massey might know something, for the gear was unusually tall and slender looking, almost like the legs of a pray-ing mantis. It looked inherently weak, susceptible to collapse in a crosswind. Maybe the bottom of the fuselage needed to be strong. Then there was the final anomaly. Instead of a conventional hori-zontal and vertical stabilizer setup, the Double Quad used a large V-tail that combined rudder and elevator functions like the Beech Bonanza. It probably saved a little weight, but it looked unusual, and Shannon had test flown the Beech Bonanza enough to know that it would impart unusual flying characteristics.

"Did you boys ever see a Heinkel 177?"

"Dad, we don't have time for history lessons. The airplane is scheduled to take off in ninety minutes, and we are going to be in the cockpit. If we walk out on this one, we'll never get another con-tract."

Vance went on. "Heinkel put exactly this sort of arrangement in the He 177. Sure, it cuts down on drag, but it's not reliable. The

German Air Force lost so many of them on practice flights that they called it the 'Luftwaffe Cigarette Lighter.' They never did get it to work."

Tom was stubborn. "Dad, that was a lot bigger aircraft, with much bigger twelve-cylinder engines. Massey has spent four years developing this; they have run these itty-bitty engines in test rigs forever. We've run them ourselves in the airplane, on taxi tests. They are as sweet as can be."

Vance acted as if he didn't hear his son. "And you see that V-tail? That looks good, it cuts down on drag and weight, too, but I tell you that the airplane is going to hunt, it will oscillate back and forth, and it will make flying instruments tough. I don't know what it will do if you lose an engine, 'cause you're not losing one engine at a time; you're losing two."

Bill Stephens stuck his head in the door. "Ready, boys? We're going to roll it out in five minutes. You want to make the run-up?"

Tom and Harry moved to the door. Vance knew he was beaten.

It was a scene he had dreaded all his life. During the war there had never been a day that he had not felt guilty about inoculating his boys with the fever to fly. It had all been so perfectly natural, a part of raising them. Wartime was somehow different—they would have been in danger as infantry officers. But here his responsibility was obvious. He knew that today was just the first of many times that he would wish he'd encouraged them to choose another career. And if it was not this airplane, it would be another.

"All right. But from now on, you both never fly the same airplane on a test flight. I cannot stand the thought of losing one of you; losing two of you at one time would be . . ." He couldn't finish.

Harry chimed in. "Dad, you're not losing anybody! We'll take this around the pattern a few times, and then check out a Massey pilot in it. The rest of the flights we'll alternate." They clapped him on the back and walked out to the field. He went to the window overlooking the runway to watch.

The two young pilots, so remarkably alike in appearance, walked briskly around the aircraft with the chief mechanic and Stephens, the project engineer. They had studied the plane for weeks, run the taxi tests, and knew it as well as anyone in the Massey firm. Its president, Gerald Massey, had already offered them jobs as company pilots, even though he knew they would not accept.

Inside the aircraft, as the entrance to the small flight deck, they flipped a coin to see who would be pilot-in-command for the flight. Harry won, said, "OK, I'll be Orville and you be Wilbur," and slipped into the left seat. Stephens sat in the temporary flight engineer's station—when the aircraft entered airline service, there would be no engineer, and, the Massey brochures bragged, the airplane could be flown safely with just one pilot, a major saving in the cost of operation.

They took their time going through the now-familiar checklist. Every cent that Gerry Massey had was poured into the project, along with some significant loans from the Wichita banks that had grown rich and powerful backing aviation projects. Tom and Harry were not going to make a mistake that killed the project.

After a long and careful run-up, Tom called for permission to enter the six-thousand-foot-long Wichita runway. The temperature was ninety-eight degrees; the pressure altitude was just what they had predicted. The two pilots had done their takeoff calculations independently, and they agreed to the mile and to the foot.

On the intercom, Tom said, "I'll call, 'Abort,' if we don't have seventy mph by the fifteen-hundred-foot marker. We'll lift off at about one hundred fifteen mph, shouldn't take more than thirty-five hundred feet. We'll use twenty degrees of flaps for the takeoff."

Harry double-clicked his mike button, the equivalent of "Roger."

"You ready, Bill?"

"All the gauges look OK, I'm ready."

"Massey Tower, Double Quad 001 is rolling."

The aircraft moved forward smoothly, Harry feeding in right rudder to keep it lined up, and at the 1,500-foot marker Tom said, "Seventy-two." At 115 mph, the aircraft broke ground.

Harry called, "Gear up," and Tom flipped the gear lever to the up position. The nosewheel and the left gear indicated up with a green light, but the right gear indicator was red.

Tom slid his window back and peered at the gear. "Right gear is partially up; it looks like it's half-turned."

"Massey Tower, this is Double Quad; we are going to level off at a thousand feet. We've got a gear problem; right gear has not retracted."

"Roger, Double Quad. We can see that. I'll get the emergency equipment out. Keep us posted."

"Thanks, I'm going to company frequency now; maybe they can talk us through the problem."

Bill Stephens came on the intercom. "They better be quick, Harry; the number one gearbox oil temperature is way too high. Can you cut the power back to a minimum to stay airborne? We need to get the airspeed down to work on the gear anyway."

Fear grabbing him by the throat, Vance Shannon hurtled out of his office and down the steps the instant he saw the right gear fail to retract. He made his way into the Massey operations office, where the entire engineering section was huddled behind Gerald Massey, who was on the radio with Harry and Bill.

An engineer at the rear of the group saw Vance come in, motioned him forward, and slid him into position next to Massey, who looked at him, grimaced, and went back to his conversation with Harry.

"What's the gearbox oil temperature now, Bill?"

"It's past the redline, over two hundred seventy degrees. We better shut it down. I don't want it to freeze and maybe tear the propeller off."

"Harry, what do you say?"

"I'll ease it back to minimum power and advance number two far enough to maintain about one hundred knots. That's about twenty above the stall; we should be safe there."

Massey's fingers drummed the desk as they waited.

Harry came back on, his voice a little strained. "I can keep it airborne at one hundred knots all right, but with number one shut down, there's not enough rudder authority to keep the airplane straight and level—it keeps turning to the left, even with full right rudder and aileron in."

Vance thought but didn't say, "Goddamn V-tail bullshit." If a big enough rudder had been hung on the airplane, there'd be no problem.

Massey looked at him as if he knew what he was thinking, then asked, "Bill, how is the number two gearbox oil temperature? Holding steady?"

"No, it's climbing. Looks to me like we've got about ten minutes, maybe twenty, before it's redlined, too."

Massey's voice became very quiet and controlled. "Harry, we're running out of time. Can you get a little more altitude and bail out?"

"Stand by one. Go to intercom, Tom, Bill."

Harry knew his father would be standing by in the operations office and he did not want him in on this discussion.

"What do you think, Bill?"

"If you put climb power on number two, it will heat up before we get another thousand feet of altitude."

"That decides it. Tom, you and Bill bail out. I'll see if I can follow; if not I'll make a crash landing."

Tom spoke up for the first time. "You'd never make it back to the door, Harry, even if you shut both engines down and killed the turning. I say that Bill bails out, and we land it, one wheel down."

Bill spoke up. "Land the son of a bitch; I ain't jumping out of no airplanes, not at my age."

Harry switched back to company frequency. "Massey Ops, we've talked it over. I'm going to pass over the field at about one thousand feet, and then do a three-sixty-degree left turn and put the airplane down into the wind at the south end of the field. I'll put the rest of the gear down late in final approach; if the wheels come down, I'll try to land on the left gear and keep the right wing up for as long as I can. If the left gear doesn't come down, I'll land on the right gear, and trust that the fuselage will hold up when it gives way."

Vance shook Massey by the shoulder. "Gerry, that's the best plan they'll get. Tell them you concur."

Massey picked up the microphone again. "Roger, Harry, we'll have all the equipment in place."

Harry passed over the field, pulled both throttles back, and began a thirty-degree bank to the left, descending at about three hundred feet per minute. As he entered what would be his base leg, he added a little power, sustaining his altitude in the bank until he turned final.

"Everybody cinched up?" Two quick "Rogers" came back. Harry reached up, wiped the sweat off his brow, and said, "Call off my airspeed, Tom."

"Roger, you have one hundred ten mph and I'd say you were a little high."

"Roger, gear down, full flaps."

There was a rumble and two green lights came on, the nose gear and the left gear had extended, the right showed a red light, and the flaps were full down.

"Eighty-five."

"Roger." Harry maintained 85 mph until he was over the end of the field, banking the airplane into the good gear, crabbing to keep a straight line. He touched down lightly on the left wheel, the aircraft rolling forward another thousand feet before the right wing began to drop. About halfway through the turn, the right gear contacted the ground and ripped away; the right wing dug in and spun the airplane to a halt. The aft door opened and all three men erupted from the Double Quad just as the fire trucks arrived, Vance Shannon riding the running board of the first one.

There was no fire. Gerry Massey shook their hands, saying that they had saved the airplane and that saved the company.

On the ride back, Vance did not even try to control himself, letting all the years of his parental anxiety spill out in an unbroken flow. "What did I tell you? What did I say about gearboxes? And V-tails? Huh, you won't listen to your old man, will you? No, you guys had to go prove something. Thank God you didn't bust your asses. If you had I would really have been ticked with you."

Tom and Harry, glad to be alive, glad to have such a father, let him rant for a bit, but finally Harry couldn't resist.

"Dad, you have to admit, the strengthened fuselage held up real well."

The Last Days of Hitler *published; Gandhi assassinated; Princess Elizabeth marries Duke of Edinburgh; Communists take over Czechoslovakia; Israel comes into existence; Soviet Union blockades Berlin.*

CHAPTER EIGHT

January 10, 1948, Inglewood, California

The only reason Vance hated to work on Saturdays was because it distressed Madeline, who liked him to be at home, doing the endless puttering required of their new house in the Malaga Cove section of Palos Verdes. She was amazingly inconsistent, behaving exactly like a wife in every way but the second-most fundamental: she would not get married. She stoutly refused to have her name on the mortgage papers, as if it were some sort of American stigma to be formally designated as a home owner. Vance had long since given up trying to understand her, knowing that he was lucky to have her and hoping to hold on to her for a few years more.

Normally he wouldn't have gone in, but the problems with the North American XP-86 were severe and the first two orders for P-86As were due to start being delivered to the eager young pilots in the Air Force during the summer. The biggest trouble was the General Electric J47 engine, which was not putting out its required thrust and was failing at faster intervals than specified. Then the three-thousand-pound-per-square-inch hydraulic system was giving trouble—the nose gear would just fold up on the ramp without any warning, and there were also problems with the aileron system. Vance knew he was getting old because he distrusted a powered aileron instinctively, even as a backup, although intellectually he knew it was the only solution at jet aircraft speeds.

He had done his bit for the XP-86 three years before, sending word from Germany to use a thirty-five-degree swept wing. North American had acted on his input and changed the fairly sedate straight wing design they were working on into a tiger of an airplane. Then he had kept his hand in from time to time on special projects after its first flight on October 1, 1947, with George "Wheaties" Welch at the controls.

Welch, who had gotten a Curtiss P-40 off the ground when the Japanese attacked Pearl Harbor, was rumored to have taken the XP-86 supersonic soon after the first flight. The story was that the Air Force suppressed the news because it wanted the honor of breaking the sound barrier go to its expensive new experimental rocket plane, the Bell XS-1. Chuck Yeager had duly exceeded Mach 1 on October 14, and although the flight was classified, industry insiders were aware of it. Welch, a good and trusted friend, never told Shannon personally that he broke the sound barrier, so Shannon was inclined to discount the rumors.

Now Dutch Kindelberger, North American's president, impatient with the progress at General Electric, had tasked him and a special so-called tiger team to come up with a solution to the engine problems. He excused himself with the task of increasing the thrust—he felt this would be solved with the later version of the engine that was due off the production line shortly. But he did think he could help with the reliability problem. To him an engine was an engine and it didn't matter whether there were pistons or turbine wheels; they all rotated and they all depended upon adequate lubrication. He was convinced that somewhere in the GE engine's system there was a weak link in the lubrication that was causing the early shutdowns. Then, too, he hated the fact that electronics had become such an integral part of engine design. He didn't mind the old-fashioned temperature gauges, but now the engine thermocouples, whose purpose was to sense heat and register its degree on an instrument, were exposed to such extreme heat that they were almost certain to malfunction.

The difficulty was that post-shutdown analysis reports were all over the waterfront, with blame being pinned on everything from turbine blade design to the shape of the engine inlet. He realized that it could be construed as arrogance on his part to believe that he could compete with General Electric, with all its tremendous talent, but he felt he knew intuitively where the problem must lie.

The huge North American hangar was almost vacant except for a company B-25, used as an executive transport, and a visiting Lockheed P-80 from Edwards Air Force Base. In the center of the hangar, a J47 engine was suspended on a carriage, and two GE engineers, Walter Baker and Steve Shaddock, were on hand to help him. On a table, bathed in the blaze of the hangar's overhead lights, were stacks of drawings and manuals.

Vance knew both engineers from the days when he had helped bring Whittle's prototype over and felt that they were comfortable with him, even though the meeting was an implicit criticism of General Electric. It was important not to appear to be one of the infamous "experts from out of town" who soured so many industry relationships.

"Well, boys, let's begin tearing this beauty down."

The three men worked silently together, carefully disassembling the engine, with Vance's eyes searching each part as it was removed.

Four careful hours later, the J47 parts were laid out on the hangar floor in the same relative position in which they were mounted in the engine. Vance walked among the parts, stopping occasionally to stare, to scratch his head, to pick up a piece, examine it closely, then move on. After an hour he called, "Walter, Steve— come take a look at this."

They looked at a short length of stainless-steel tubing, about three-eighths of an inch in diameter. "Vance, that's the oil supply line. What about it?"

"I say it's too large in diameter. At high altitudes, with the temperatures up, the oil is almost certainly foaming, at least a little, and this line probably doesn't allow enough oil to get through to lube the bearings."

Both men shook their heads. "That's hardly likely, Vance. Jet engines don't use oil like a piston engine does; you can run them practically dry of oil and they'll keep on turning."

"I'm sure you are right. But I feel in my bones that when the oil foams, it blocks the line, and the bearing temperatures go way up, way beyond anything you'd see in a piston engine. And we don't have any sensors to tell us. I'm proposing that we put a temperature sensor on a J47's oil line and see how hot it gets when it's flown at high altitudes at a high Mach number. That's what happens in combat, for sure, and probably in a lot of the training."

Shaddock and Baker looked dubious, but Vance went on.

"If it has a sustained high temperature for most of a flight, almost no oil will be getting through, and it will be tearing the heart out of the bearings. That would explain a lot of failures."

Steve stopped shaking his head long enough to say, "Well, putting a sensor in is no big deal. We can go back out to Muroc tonight, put the sensor in tomorrow morning, and do a test flight tomorrow afternoon. But I think you are wrong, Vance. Maybe we ought to have a little side bet on this. Tell you what. If it runs hot enough tomorrow to indicate a problem, I'll buy dinner for all of us at Pancho Barnes's place. If it doesn't—you buy."

Pancho's place, the Happy Bottom Riding Club, was a home away from home for the test pilots and the longtime regulars at Muroc.

"I hate to take your money, Steve, but a bet is a bet. You're on! But that's not the only thing." Vance pointed to the wiring leading to a thermocouple used to monitor engine temperatures. "What would it take to get a bulletin out to the field having the thermocouples on the fleet checked for accuracy?"

Vance knew the North American system of communicating with its field representatives was first-rate. Every tech rep would have a bulletin in his mailbox in the morning. They would run the tests the same day, and the results would be fed back in that night to North American for analysis and distribution.

"I can write it up this afternoon. What do you want me to say?"

"Just ask them to recalibrate all the thermocouples as soon as possible, and then recalibrate them after the next flight. I've got an idea that they are malfunctioning, and not registering the actual heat being produced. That would account in part for the reports on rotor blade erosion."

"Can do, but it will take a few days; they cannot get the results back faster than they fly the airplanes."

"Sure, of course, but tell them to send the results as they get them, not to wait until the test is complete."

Shaddock agreed willingly. He trusted Vance's instincts.

The following afternoon they were installing the sensor on the fourth prototype XP-86 when there was a yell of, "Stand clear," as the nose gear collapsed without warning. The aircraft's nose came down with a bang that had people running from all over the field to see what happened, while the tail flew up into the air, tossing workmen aside like dolls. The stabilizer was ripped where it had lifted up through one of the maintenance stands, and the gear doors were smashed. Fortunately, no one was hurt.

Shaddock shook his head. "Before we do anything else, let's get an adequate hydraulic system installed here. We can pull one off a B-25 and modify it so that it will work better than this. What do you think, Vance?"

"Man, with three thousand pounds of pressure, I can't believe that it's the hydraulic system. Let's take a look at it." Within an hour the F-86 was put on jacks, and they had the damaged nose gear doors removed.

Shannon asked, "Where is the ground safety pin?" A red-flagged pin was designed to go through the gear scissors to prevent a collapse. "The pin's not in. Who is the crew chief?"

A crestfallen staff sergeant named Jensen moved forward. "I'm crew chief on this airplane, sir. I guess I forgot to put it in. We don't usually use them." Jensen reflexively touched the stripes on his sleeve, obviously worried that he might lose them if the accident was blamed on him.

Shannon slapped him on the back and said, "We all make mistakes, Sergeant Jensen. How about helping me find out what caused this one?" He nodded to Shaddock and Baker, signaling that they were to let him and Jensen work it out.

There was only room for one of them to get inside the narrow nose gear aperture, and they alternated, one moving in and one moving out. Shannon spotted the problem early but didn't identify it—he wanted Jensen to find it. Finally Jensen said, "Sir, it looks like this drag brace is what's wrong." They knelt together on the ramp, peering upward. Jensen put his hand on the slim steel billet that was designed to go over-center when the gear was extended and keep the gear locked down. "Look, it's rigged wrong—it's not going down over-center."

"You're right, Jensen; congratulations, you've solved it. When this happens, the only thing that will keep the gear from collapsing is the safety pin. We need them to redesign the part so that it has to go over-center every time." Jensen grinned in relief, a little more confident about keeping his stripes.

Two days later, the XP-86 was ready to fly. Steve had carefully placed two sensors on the oil line connecting them to two instruments he had attached in the only space available, crowded on the left side of the cockpit.

Shannon talked to the test pilot, George Welch. "Georgie, my boy, you don't have to do anything fancy. Just fly a normal intercept profile—rapid climb to altitude; cruise at high Mach for thirty minutes; make a high-speed descent and landing. Keep your eye on the two gauges, and note what they do temperature-wise. Don't put any excessive g's on the airplane—and don't go supersonic."

Welch didn't even acknowledge Vance's jest, just nodded and climbed into the airplane.

Forty-five minutes later Welch landed. "Both gauges went off the clock, Vance! I don't know how hot they got, but they were pegged ten minutes into the climb and they stayed that way. Made me nervous! I don't like it when the needles are bent into the side of the case."

Shaddock and Baker were convinced—despite all the nonsense about jet engines running forever without oil, it was evident that the bearings in the J47 were being starved for lubrication at high altitudes and airspeeds. Best of all, it was a fairly cheap fix—existing engines could be retrofitted inexpensively, and the newer engines coming down the line could be fixed at virtually no cost. Then they checked the thermocouples, and Vance was right again. They needed to be recalibrated. When the reports began to come in from the field, they confirmed the problem. To get the correct engine power and to cut down on overheating, the thermocouples had to be recalibrated after every flight. It was tedious, but it would save engines.

Baker put his arm around Shannon's shoulder. "Vance, I guess this means that we are buying you dinner at Pancho's. They are going to love you at North American and hate you at GE. The last thing they want is for the airframe manufacturer to be changing their engine design, even when they need it."

"Well, Walter, what's the problem? You and Steve fixed it; you are GE reps—you ought to get a bonus out of this. You write up the reports, I'll sign them for North American, and you'll be the most popular guys at GE headquarters."

Shaddock shook his head. "I don't know, Vance; that doesn't seem right—I don't want to cash in on your insight. You saw the problem; you should get the credit."

"No, Steve, let's do this my way. I'll tell Dutch what happened, he'll be happy with me, I'll be happy with GE, and GE will be happy with you. It's the government that benefits in the long run, so what difference does it make to any outsider who gets the credit inside GE? None, that's what."

They shook hands, but as they started to leave, Vance said, "Tell you what, though—give me and Sergeant Jensen credit for pointing out the gear problem. That's out of your bailiwick and right in mine, and it's the sort of thing Dutch loves, finding problems in the field."

Vance was especially intent on keeping in Dutch's good graces, because he had to tell him he was leaving Inglewood for at least four months, maybe more, to go to Seattle. This was one of the hazards of being an independent consultant. Tom and Harry were great for test work and were beginning to learn the maintenance and engineering end of the business, but Aviation Consultants, Incorporated, remained a one-man operation in the eyes of the major aircraft companies. When they had a problem, they wanted Vance, not one of his sons.

At Boeing, his old friend George Schairer had put in a special plea for him to come up and check into the beautiful but trouble-prone XB-47, which had flown for the first time on December 17, 1947. It was a revolutionary airplane, with six jets and thirty-five degrees of sweep in the wing, but there were myriad problems. There had to be in such a radical step forward, but there was constant pressure from the Strategic Air Command to get the airplanes fixed and into operation. The B-47s were a weapon the Soviets could not counter, and the Air Force wanted them to be ready on twenty-four hours' notice to attack with nuclear weapons.

Vance knew Schairer well enough to insist that he needed Tom on the project. After the usual corporate bureaucratic hand-wringing, Schairer got approval, but only after negotiating a cut in their combined rate. The truth was, he did need Tom's insight, and he also had to help him get away from home. Marie had turned almost overnight from a charming girl, outgoing, even flirtatious, into a religious fanatic. Although he did not say so directly, Tom implied that their sex life had started badly and dropped off to zero within weeks of their marriage. They had been to see a priest, but he had only cautioned Marie to fulfill her marital vows, while telling Tom that he had to stop being so demanding.

Shannon hated to leave California, but he, too, needed to get away. For the first time since they had been together, Madeline had become cold and distant. Instead of the lingering feeling of sexual inadequacy that had haunted him for most of their time together, he now wanted her far more often than she wanted him. Their lovemaking had long since gone from the torrid to the routine, but she had always remained responsive. Where before he had but to extend his hand to have her roll over to him, now she would often turn away. She had even used the classic, "I have a headache," on him, even though in the past she had made love no matter how she felt. The worst thing was that they had lost that sense of communication, the ability to each know what the other was thinking, to finish sentences for each other. Somehow they were strangers, for the first time in their relationship.

He groaned to himself, "I hope Harry is getting some loving; the rest of the family is striking out."

Still there were no signs of her being interested in anyone else. There were no strange phone calls; she was always at home whenever Vance called or came in; there were no strange expenses, no signs of guilt. They were older, it was true, but she was still a young woman, thirty-four, in her prime. When he suggested that she might like to see a doctor, she became furious, one of the few times she had ever lost her temper with him, telling him that there was nothing wrong with her and if anyone should see a doctor it should be him.

Perhaps it was a mistake to have located his office in their Palos Verdes home. She might have been happier going in to work at an office on an airport. But it was she who had picked the lot, and she had supervised the planning, making sure that there was plenty of space for his office, with a private entrance. He liked it because it positioned him near to North American, Northrop, and Lockheed and still close enough to San Diego to meet any Convair requirements. He could cover jobs in Los Angeles, San Diego, and Edwards Air Force Base in a single day if he flew in his Navion. Seattle meant using the airlines, which was a pleasant relief, having a stewardess attend to you and someone else doing the flying.

The trip to Seattle might settle many things. He hoped that Madeline might agree to go with him, leaving the new house to a caretaker, but he doubted it.

January 24, 1948, Wright-Patterson Air Force Base, Ohio

HARRY HAD NOT believed the recall notice when it arrived. There were thousands of pilots trying desperately to stay in the new and independent Air Force, and suddenly someone found that Harry had to be back in service. It was so totally unfair, and it did not sit well with Anna. He called his father and the mystery was soon resolved.

"You are getting a reputation, Harry, and Al Boyd must have decided that he wants you back in the Air Corps to help him." Like most people, Vance still called the Air Force the Air Corps, by force of habit.

The name was familiar to Harry, for Boyd had brought the world's speed record back to the United States in 1947, flying a Lockheed P-80 at 623 mph. "What does Boyd do?"

"He's at Wright-Pat, but he also runs the test programs out at Edwards. He is a terrific officer; you'll like him."

"Should I try to get out of this, Dad? Anna and I have been looking for a house. . . ."

"Don't you dare even think about not going, Harry. If Al Boyd needs you, you go and go with goodwill. It will only be for a couple of years probably, and you'll get more and better flying than you ever dreamed of. Anna will like Dayton, I'm sure."

To his surprise, Anna took it like a trooper, even though it meant giving up the circle of friends and family she had charmed for all her twenty-two years. Marie protested at first, for she was busily engaged in trying to raise Anna's level of Catholic consciousness. Tom protested, too, not so much because they were leaving but because he wasn't recalled.

Harry and Anna packed their clothes in the huge trunk of his Buick Roadmaster convertible and headed out across the southern United States, stopping like a couple of kids at the tourist traps, rarely passing one of the snake farms on Route 66. The Buick cruised easily at sixty-five miles per hour, and Anna enjoyed teasing him as they drove, kissing his ears, running her hand inside his trousers, and in general preparing him well for a night of lovemaking in one of the roadside motels that they found each evening. The motels ran from squalid to functional, with the worst being the El Hidalgo in Deming, New Mexico, where water from the mildew-laden shower ran across the floor to a drain in the center of the room.

They arrived at Dayton on the fifteenth, rented a furnished apartment on the sixteenth, and moved in on the seventeenth. They spent one day getting the necessities for housekeeping, and Harry reported in, anxious to start working at the Fighter Operations at the Flight Test Division of the Wright Air Development Center.

In his heart Harry realized that he wouldn't have dared to ask for so sweet an assignment after all his bomber experience, and he was truly grateful to be back in fighters after so many years.

The charismatic Boyd was gifted with a dual personality that worked enormously to his advantage. At work he was stern, square jawed, with a commanding air that inspired just the right combination of fear and confidence. A former airmail pilot, he had over time picked up the ability to manage large organizations, and his operation at Wright-Pat, with all its disparate requirements, was noted for its efficiency. Yet off duty he was affable and friendly, able to keep a crowd laughing with the stories of his adventures. Tall, lean, and rangy, he ran a tight ship, sparing with a smile but quick with a scowl. He could not have pulled it off if his pilots, the cream of the Army crop, did not know that he would never ask them to do something that he wouldn't do. More important, they knew that if he chose, he could probably do whatever it was better than they could.

It was Boyd who, after long calculation, ratcheted aviation another notch forward by carefully managing the quest to break the so-called sound barrier, personally selecting Chuck Yeager to fly the Bell XS-1 on the historic October 14, 1947, supersonic flight. Boyd selected Yeager as the test pilot on the same basis that he made all his decisions: who was best for the job. And Boyd knew everything about his test pilots, from the way they flew airplanes to the way they behaved—or misbehaved—at Pancho Barnes's notorious desert hideaway. His greeting to Harry was characteristically abrupt.

"Hello, Shannon. I know your father; he's a good man. Don't think you are going to be a test pilot here, because you're not."

The hopes Harry had harbored about doing just that withered.

"I have better things for you to do than flying hop after hop jotting instrument readings on a knee pad. I need a problem solver, and they tell me you are getting to be as good as your dad. I heard about how you handled that weird Massey airplane. That put them out of business, and they deserved it, coming up with a lash-up like that."

Harry started to say, "What do you want me to do?" but Boyd cut him off at "What do—"

"I've got two main jobs for you. The first one will be fun. Jet airplanes are coming out of the woodwork! We have a whole stable of new planes here that we are running every sort of test on. And every damn one of them has a different cockpit layout, with the instruments all over the place, flap handles that work in different directions, switches that go up in one airplane and down in another. I want you to get checked out in all the fighters and the bombers and figure out what the best arrangement for instruments and controls should be. Then write up a specification we can give to manufacturers to start getting things standardized. We've had more than one guy pull up his wheels when he thought he was putting down his flaps."

Boyd paused to carefully polish his sunglasses, breathing on them and then rubbing them with his silk scarf. "But the real problem we have with fighters and bombers is range. We could whip the hell out of Mexico or Canada, but if we had to fight Russia our fighters don't have the range to get there. We have to do something about aerial refueling for the bombers. I want you to get started on that, but I want you to include fighters. They've got to escort the bombers or Moscow will turn out to be another Schweinfurt."

Schweinfurt was the scene of two costly debacles, both stemming from a lack of long-range escort fighters. The Eighth Air Force had lost sixty airplanes in August 1943 and another sixty in October. After that a decision was made not to fly the bombers deep into Germany unless escort fighters were available.

Without another word, Boyd grabbed his helmet and started out of the room. At the door he turned and said only, "Check in down the hall at Flight Ops; they know you're coming, and they'll get you all the manuals you need, and assign instructor pilots to check you out in all the different airplanes."

While he was digesting Boyd's rapid-fire comments, Harry went down to the Base Operations Officer and got permission to go up in the control tower that was built as a part of the building. Harry paused at the last landing to catch his breath, promising himself he'd get in shape. After climbing the last set of the interminable stairs, he introduced himself to a courteous but very busy team in the control tower, who were directing takeoffs and landings for a continuous stream of traffic.

Harry borrowed a pair of binoculars and began looking up and down the flight line.

Boyd was certainly correct about the airplanes, which crowded the field, lined some taxiways, and were even parked in the open area on the opposite side of the runway. There were plenty of piston engine fighters—Mustangs, Thunderbolts, Lightnings, even two of the new Twin Mustang P-82s, and Harry vowed he'd fly them all if it meant flying every weekend. All the transports were there, from the ubiquitous Beech C-45 and Douglas C-47s to bigger four-engine C-54s and even one of the huge new bug-eyed Douglas C-74 Globemaster transports.

But it was the jet aircraft that interested him. He called them off to himself, "Lockheed P-80, Republic P-84, Lockheed T-33." A grinning staff sergeant in the tower watched him. "You planning to fly them all, sir?"

Harry smiled back, said, "That's the general idea," and went on with his inventory. The strong bond between officer and non-commissioned ranks was one of the American Air Forces' great strengths. They were the only services in which officers were sent in harm's way, tasked with the primary duty of fighting the enemy, and there was not a pilot who did not know that his life depended upon the enlisted personnel who serviced his aircraft. There was a minimum of spit-and-polish discipline, just a nicely tuned atmosphere of mutual self-respect.

A beautiful North American P-86 was parked next to a strange-looking four-jet aircraft. "Sarge, what's the big jet next to the Sabre?"

"That's the North American XB-45; it just came in last week. I don't know if it's going to be here for a while or not. Good-looking airplane, though. Four jets! Imagine that."

After Harry made the long climb downstairs he went into the Flight Operations section, where Master Sergeant Orbin Shackleford ran things with a crisp administrative efficiency. He took Harry to a row of ten-by-twelve offices plastered against the side of the hangar. "Cold in winter, hot in summer, but it's the best we've got, sir."

"Fine with me, Sarge."

"Colonel Boyd told me to fix you up, sir, so I've got your office all set up, all the manuals in place, and a list of instructors for each plane, along with their phone numbers. They all have regular jobs, so you'll have to work out your flight schedule with them. I expect you won't get to fly more than four or five times a week."

They spoke for a while longer and Harry knew he had made the most constructive move of the day, becoming friends with Shackleford, who, like all the top NCOs, really made the Air Force work. It was good to be friends with the Base Commanding Officer and with the chaps at the personnel office, but if you really wanted to get along you made friends with the first sergeants and their like. They would still work with you if you didn't get along, but only to the point that it was correct. But if they liked you, you could count on them to make something happen, no matter how the regulations had to be bent.

That night he took Anna to the Officers Club to celebrate his lucky new assignment. As they walked from the parking lot, Harry, as always, enjoyed the sensation of all eyes being on Anna. It gave him a smug sense of proprietorship, basking in the notion that he not only took this darling woman to dinner, he also took her to bed, and that was what they envied most. Heads turned as Harry and Anna walked through the big reception area and down the hallway toward the dining room, probably the best restaurant in Dayton. Anna pretended to ignore the admiring looks but clearly enjoyed them, the smiles and the nods and the quick greetings never getting old despite her long experience at being beautiful.

When she and Harry had ordered, she reached across the table, pressed his hand, and said, "I don't think I've ever seen you as happy as this, not even at the wedding—not even on the honeymoon, not even on our trip across country."

Suddenly this was clearly dangerous ground, and Harry looked closely in her eyes. Anna could be feisty, and the wrong word here might cause an argument. He was learning. "Honey, I'm just happy to be here with you. It was great to drive across country, but here we are, all settled in like an old married couple, a good dinner here at the club, with all the guys admiring you. And then to top it off, I get to take you home to bed. What could be better than that?"

"Good recovery, but I don't believe a word of it. You are happy because you've got so many airplanes to fly—and if you are happy, then I'm happy, too."

They ate well-done prime rib with enthusiasm, and Anna had another Manhattan with her meal. Harry never drank the day before he flew—his father had taught him that "eight hours between bottle and throttle" was not nearly enough. He would have a beer or two on the weekend, but Anna had grown up in a family where wine was served with every meal, and she enjoyed cocktails every evening.

They had the club dessert specialty, Cherries Jubilee, and she took his hand again, squeezing it, saying, "It's late. You said something about taking someone home to bed?"

The next six weeks flew past in a blur. Harry saw Boyd only twice, and both times Boyd said only, "I see you're making progress." And Harry was, at least on analyzing the instrument problem. Almost all the aircraft had their flight instruments—the airspeed, altimeter, turn and bank, artificial horizon, and, for those that had them, gyro compasses—arranged pretty much in the center of the instrument panel, but beyond that, anything could go anywhere. He had already written draft recommendations about standardizing on instrument size and placement, and he was engaged in correspondence with some psychologists on the West Coast about making the various controls—gear levers, flap levers, throttles—somehow look and feel like their function. It would take time, but with guidance, the manufacturers could begin to get some uniformity into cockpit design. It was more necessary now than ever because things happened so swiftly in a jet. If you made a mistake, you probably wouldn't have time to recover.

He knew intuitively that the range problem was more difficult. Jet engines were getting more sophisticated, but they still gulped fuel voraciously. Each new jet coming down the line was bigger and could carry more fuel, but they also had more powerful engines, which kept their range down to a minimum. The North American P-51 that won the air war in Europe had an extraordinary range for the time, about 1,350 miles. With jets this dropped down immediately. The P-80A's range was only about 540 miles. They were being fitted with wingtip tanks, but even that would only bring the range up to about the same as the P-51. The Air Force's first post-war jet fighter, the sleek-looking Republic P-84A, was supposed to have a range of about 1,300 miles, but the new P-86A's range was only 800 miles, clearly inadequate for combat unless there were plenty of prepared forward bases available. It was almost as bad with bombers. The new Boeing XB-47's range was estimated to be less than that of the B-29.

The irony was that neither Great Britain nor the Soviet Union had an absolute requirement for range. The mission of their air forces was different, primarily aimed at defending against incoming bombers. With less need for onboard fuel, they could use smaller aircraft, interceptors, where a fast rate of climb and speed were more important than range. The USAF had to have bombers with intercontinental range, able to operate directly from U.S. bases against any enemy. And those bombers had to have long-range escort fighters, able to escort them to the targets and back and win air superiority just as the Mustang had done over Germany in 1944.

Harry knew that there were some radical ideas in the works, such as parasite fighters tucked in the bomb bay or attached physically to the end of the wing and flown along like flexible extended wingtips. He had been given some top-secret studies on both programs, and it seemed obvious to him that they failed the practicality test. He called them kamikaze cures because both ideas were too complex, put too much strain on the pilots, and gave the fighter almost no chance of recovery if it engaged in combat—which was the only reason for its existence.

He spent hours reading the manuals on each of the new jet fighters, trying to work out flight profiles that would stretch the range by even a few miles. Then, after a brief checkout, usually no more than a cockpit familiarization, he would fly the flight profiles he had created to see what the results were. By changing the climb speeds, cruising at optimum speed and altitude for the weight, and making rapid descents, he found he could add about 10 percent to the figures in the charts in the manuals. It was something, but not at all what Boyd had in mind. Ten percent of 800 miles for the F-86 gave it an extra 80 miles, almost not enough change to bother about, because other factors—ordnance loads, weather, engine trim—could easily erase the gain.

The days passed all too quickly, and while he had pretty well settled all the issues on the first attempt at standardizing cockpit layout, he had not accomplished much more in the range extension line. His studies had commissioned some wind tunnel tests for new and larger drop tanks, but there had been no significant findings. He did what he and Tom usually did when they were stumped and called his father at his Boeing office in Seattle, getting him on the first try, a rarity.

Tom was not with their father—Marie had some difficulties back in Los Angeles, and although Vance did not elaborate, Harry assumed that it was the sex problems that Tom had only hinted at.

Harry said, "Give them both my love, Dad, and send Anna's, too. I'm not going to tell her anything about this; she can get it straight from Marie." Then he went on, "Dad, your old friend Al Boyd has handed me a tough nut to crack. He's concerned—that's not the right word—he's outraged over the short range of jets, and he's asked me to see what can be done."

Harry went on to tell him about the changes he'd suggested in the flight profile, in fuel management, and so on.

Vance's first response was, as he knew, obvious. "You're considering external tanks, of course?"

"Yeah, but it's strange; they are a big help on piston engine fighters, as we know, but they are marginal on jets. Jets are so clean that the external tanks cause so much drag during the climb to altitude that they don't do much more than pay for themselves."

There was a momentary silence, and Vance came back. "You've put me on the spot, Harry. Boeing is working on some proprietary in-flight refueling ideas, and of course I cannot discuss them with you. They'll be getting to the Air Force with them in time, but right now it's top secret, and it's not as applicable to fighters anyway, not right away. But I tell you what. I'll wire Stanley Hooker in Great

Britain. He's pretty discontented with his work at Rolls-Royce right now, so he may not be in the best of moods. But I'm sure he'll help you if I ask him. They'd done a lot of experimentation with in-flight refueling in Great Britain. A man named Alan Cobham has been doing it for years, and he's got a firm, Flight Refueling Limited. I'm sure Hooker knows him—it's a small community there—and he'll get you an introduction. See if you can get orders to go to England to study the problem. If the Air Force won't send you, see if you can take leave and go. I'll pay for your expenses, charge it off to Aviation Consultants, Incorporated."

They discussed what Vance knew of Cobham's efforts for a few minutes, and Harry rang off, glad that he had used an Air Force phone for the long-distance call.

Harry, ever the student, plunged into a study of everything available on aerial refueling and was pleased to see that it had originated in the United States in 1921, when Wesley May, a wing walker, carrying a five-gallon can of gasoline on his back, stepped from the wing of a Lincoln Standard to the wing of a Curtiss Jenny and poured the fuel into its tank in flight. The Army became interested in 1923 and used a de Havilland DH-4B as a tanker with another DH-4B as a receiver in a series of tests. Some fourteen world records in endurance were set, with the longest flight lasting thirty-seven hours.

Then in 1927, some of the future great Army Air Force leaders set a world record in a Fokker Trimotor. The *Question Mark*, flown by a crew of future generals including Tooey Spaatz and Ira Eaker, essentially proved the value of aerial refueling. The technique it demonstrated was relatively primitive, yet the plane flew for 140 hours before a malfunctioning engine required them to land. Later, because the range of planes such as the Boeing B-17 and B-29 had grown so much, the apparent requirement for in-flight refueling diminished, and little further was done except for some minor experimental work during World War II.

Harry had deferred talking to Colonel Boyd until he was fully prepared, knowing that asking to go to England would look like trying to boondoggle a free trip to Europe. But on the following Monday morning, Harry waylaid Boyd in the hallway. "Colonel, I've got to go to Great Britain to look into what they are doing with in-flight refueling. I'll need about three weeks.—"

Boyd strode past him saying, "Fine. Pick a group and get going. You can use one of our B-29s for the flight; be good training for everybody."

"I'll need contractual authority, probably."

"No problem; have General Carroll pick out somebody from Contracts to go with you. Take a lawyer, too. But get going—you can see we are hurting for range."

The B-29 flight over was uneventful, and even though he gladly took turns flying, Harry had time to read a packet of material Hooker had sent him through the local Royal Air Force representative at Wright-Patterson, Wing Commander Rob Dick. Harry found that Cobham had been experimenting with in-flight refueling for years, making an attempt at a non-stop flight from England to India in 1934 in an Airspeed Courier. He got as far as Malta before an engine malfunction forced him down. Then during the war, he was given a contract to convert six hundred Avro Lancaster bombers into tankers, to enable the Royal Air Force to begin bombing Japan. The war ended before they could go into action. In the post-war years he had done extraordinary work experimenting with refueling aircraft for commercial service, but the advent of the long-range Lockheed Constellations and Boeing Stratocruisers once again snuffed the requirement. Now Cobham was down to a handful of Lancaster tankers and not much of a market. Harry Shannon was confident that they could do business.

His B-29 landed at London Heathrow Airport on March 19, and after a perfunctory run through customs, his team was met by representatives of Flight Refueling Limited. Using two big black Daimlers, they drove him immediately over to their offices in nearby Littlehampton.

Sir Alan Cobham was there himself to greet them, confident, smiling, and with a self-deprecating sense of humor that belied the great successes he had achieved in more than thirty years of flying experience. He was not an aristocrat in the conventional sense, com-

ing from a humble background in London, but he had the aristo-
cratic demeanor of one who has won his spurs in battle.

"Colonel Shannon, we need your business, and we'll do anything we can do legally to get it. I've got two Lancastrians being prepared for a demonstration flight tomorrow, if you'd like to see our
system in operation."

As tired as he was, Harry immediately agreed, and at seven the
next morning he found himself in the back end of a converted Avro
Lancastrian, a transport version of the famous bomber. Unlike the
B-29, the Lancastrian was not pressurized and virtually unheated,
and he was barely able to move in the winter flying gear Cobham
had provided. Paul Russell, Cobham's right-hand man, was similarly
attired and flew with Harry, explaining in detail the length of the
hose, the diameter of the reels, and the cost per refueling. If Cobham's figures were correct, commercial transports could actually
save money using in-flight refueling rather than making intermedi-
ate stops on their transoceanic crossings.

They rendezvoused with the receiver aircraft, another Lancastrian, at 15,000 feet, over the Cotswolds. The two aircraft proceeded
in trail westward, over the ocean. Harry watched as the receiver aircraft let out a long line, weighed down at the end.

Russell nudged him. "Watch out now."

The tanker crewman fired a projectile that streaked out, carrying a light line that crossed the receiver's trailing line, then slid down
and caught on at the end in a device patented by Cobham.

Russell smiled. "Lucky shot—we don't always engage on the
first try."

The receiver crew now began drawing the two lines back toward
the side of their airplane as the tanker climbed. When the airplane
was positioned above the receiver, it began letting out its refueling
hose, which was drawn into the tanker and connected. The fuel
transfer began immediately, with Russell saying proudly, "One hundred gallons per minute."

After five minutes Russell called to the pilot that they were finished. The fuel flow stopped and the refueling hose was drawn in,
leaving the two guidelines still attached. After some brief communi-

cations, the receiver proceeded straight ahead while the tanker turned to the right. The lead lines that linked them together parted company and were jettisoned.

Harry was thoroughly frozen by the time they got back to Littlehampton, but his mind was working furiously. Cobham's primitive system worked, at least for bombers, and it would have to do for now. There had to be something better in the future, something that would work for fighters.

Back in Cobham's office, Harry, wanting to keep a clear head until the business dealings were over, refused the beakers of brandy that were broken out to "thaw them out," as Cobham put it in his non–public school accent.

Harry knew that he was in an extraordinarily favorable position. Each time Cobham had been close to commercial success in the past something had intervened. If Harry chose to be heavy-handed, he could probably force Cobham to the wall and get rock-bottom prices. Yet Harry wanted to get Cobham's system in operation in the United States as soon as possible and also wanted the firm's goodwill in developing a more advanced system. Harry decided to do as his dad probably would have done—be perfectly straightforward and count on Cobham's good sense to see that there was more business in the future.

"That was a brilliant display of in-flight refueling. We are all impressed. Would you be so kind as to tell me what the cost to the United States government would be if you were to provide us with two complete sets of hardware now, that we can take back in the bomb bay of the B-29, and would then manufacture an additional forty sets for later shipment? I'd want to know what the shipping schedule would be, as well."

Harry heard his contracts officer gasp—he was giving the farm away on this deal. But there would be other deals in the future, and he wanted to have Cobham on his side.

Four days later, back in the United States, Harry briefed Colonel Boyd on his mission.

"Looks pretty complicated to me, Shannon."

"It is complicated, the fuel flow rate is too slow, and it won't work for fighters. But we can stick it on our B-29s and get some experience, and perhaps come up with a better system. Let me show you some rough drawings I made on the trip back. They are crude, but they'll give you the idea."

He handed Boyd a sheaf of papers, ashamed at his poor artwork but aware that it told enough of the story to intrigue the colonel.

"See, this is a rigid refueling installation, but it's still flexible because it is flown by an operator, and the refueling tube retracts and extends to make it easier to maintain contact. It means that the refueler and the airplane being fueled will have to fly in close formation, maybe thirty or forty feet apart, but we do that every day."

"How does the operator move this tube—it looks like a crane boom; call it a boom—around?"

"Well, there's plenty of airflow of course, so he could use two little airfoils, about like a Bonanza's tail, fastened on the end of the boom. Should be easy to learn to do."

Boyd nodded his head in agreement. "You talk to your dad about this yet?"

"No, I did not think I should since he's under contract to Boeing and they are looking into in-flight refueling themselves."

"Well, I'm directing you to talk to him. There has to be a better solution than Cobham's—maybe your idea is it. I don't know anybody better than your dad and George Schairer to decide if it is or it isn't, but in any case, they can come up with something better if it's not. I'm not worried about the economics or the competition or the restraint of trade or any other goddamn business problem. I want to have a system where one plane squirts a hell of a lot of gas into another in a hurry. Otherwise there's no damn point in having jets at all."

"I'll give him a call tonight."

Boyd exploded, "You will not! You'll get your ass in an airplane and go up and talk to him in person. This is top-secret material, even if it hasn't been formally classified as such yet. I want you up in Seattle by Monday."

Anna had been delighted to see Harry when he returned, and

he expected her to be upset by his leaving almost immediately for Seattle.

"No, I understand. Business is business. But you can take me out to the O Club for dinner tonight, and maybe stay for a little dancing."

Even though he was dead tired from the round-trip to England, behind work at the office, and needing to prepare for the cross-country trip to Seattle, Harry agreed. He had been neglecting Anna and she needed to be spoiled a bit.

"Have you heard from Marie?"

"Yes, she's having one of her spells. She says she was pregnant and lost the baby, but I doubt it. I suspect she's just looking for sympathy."

Harry was stunned. He had never heard her talk about Marie—or anyone—with such calculated coldness. "Is there some problem? Is there something I ought to be telling Tom?"

"You can tell him that I lived with her for a long time and now it's his turn."

The evening at the Officers Club was much different from their first night. The food was the same, and at first Harry thought it was Anna's comments. Then he realized that his wife was enjoying herself just a little too much with some of the people. It was clear from the quick, casual conversations with passing people, officers alone and couples, that she was not spending lonely nights at home while he was away.

"Anna, you sure as hell seem to have a lot of friends here. Do you come to the club by yourself when I'm gone?"

"Of course I do! What else am I going to do? Knit?"

"Well, you might get a job. We could use the money, and you wouldn't be bored."

"You're right about that. I'm just wasting time during the day. I'll see what I can do; there's always something opening up. But even if I work during the day, I'm not going to spend the nights at home listening to the radio while you are off flying around the world. Don't you trust me?"

He patted her hand. "Of course I trust you. But I'm jealous, too."

She laughed and said, "I'm glad you are." He toyed with the idea of saying something about her having had three Manhattans but decided against it. He had pressed pretty far tonight already.

THE PASSING SCENE

Allies use Airlift to offset Berlin Blockade; Pancho Gonzales becomes men's singles champ. Harry S. Truman wins Presidency in his own right; T. S. Eliot wins Nobel Prize for Literature; Count Folke Bernadotte killed by Jewish terrorists.

CHAPTER NINE

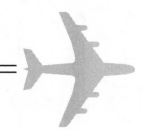

June 30, 1948, Seattle, Washington

*B*oeing always arranged for its minor-league visitors to stay downtown at the Windsor Hotel, an establishment that walked a fine line between being merely seedy and illegal. The rooms were clean, and in the basement the Tiki Bar featured entertainment every night, including a rotating lineup of amateur and professional ladies who were happy to meet visitors from out of town. The food—steaks and a pretty good take on Trader Vic's faux Chinese—was not bad, however, and the Windsor was centrally located and cheap. The scanty per-diem-paid military types covered the hotel bill and one or two meals a day, so even the more fastidious guests didn't complain about the women who wore a shade too much makeup.

Tom had picked Harry up at McChord Field, where he had flown in a T-33, and started back on the long, wet ride from Tacoma to the Windsor.

"Is it always raining like this?"

"Pretty much, but you get used to it, and when it's not, it is so spectacularly beautiful that you won't believe it."

Then they got started on their mutual tales of marital woe.

"I tell you, Harry, I cannot understand it. You remember what a hot little number Marie was before we got married? We damn near had our wedding night on the day we met—and we would have, too, if it hadn't been for the bodyguard of brothers."

"You say she's turned cold?"

"Frigid. But that's not the worst of it. I think she's losing her mind."

"Come on, Tom; not wanting to sleep with you doesn't mean she's crazy."

"Oh, she wants to sleep with me all right; she's like a goddamn octopus at night, asleep, but crawling all over me. But if I lay a hand on her, getting serious, you know, she wakes up and freezes. But that's not it. She's gotten super-religious. Not just being a good Catholic, but praying all the time, and praying in the bathroom, as if it were an altar."

"Run that by me again?"

"Just that. She's got a crucifix rigged up in the bathroom, like in every room of the house, but she goes in there and kneels by the bathtub and prays, for hours. If I say something, call her to dinner, try to get her to go out, she just gets up and locks the door. Then when she comes out, she acts almost normal. You'd never know it, if you happened by after one of her prayer sessions. But they are getting more and more frequent. It's a damn good thing we happened to move into a place with two bathrooms, or I'd be out of luck."

"Wow. I thought I had problems. Have you had her to a doctor?"

"Not yet. She gets furious if I even mention it. I've got to do it, but I don't want her to be hysterical about it."

"Have you talked to her family? Her dad, Lou, needs to know about this."

"Same thing. She says if I complain to her family she'll kill herself. I don't believe she would, but it's clear she has some mental problems. And to tell you the truth, Lou would probably blame me right off the bat. He's a nice guy, but when it comes to his family, you know how rigid he is. But the funny thing is, she keeps saying that she is going to leave me and go back to her family. I ask her why, and she just says, 'That's what Jesus wants me to do.'"

"Well, Lou has to know about this, right away, because if she just shows up on his doorstep, he'll think you drove her out. Worse, she might hurt herself, or you. I'm really sorry to learn about this, Tom, but I did have a hint from Anna. She said that Marie said she was pregnant and lost the baby, but Anna laughed it off, saying Marie was always being dramatic. Is there any chance that she wasn't fibbing?"

"There's no chance that she was pregnant, at least by me."

"I don't know much about having babies or losing them, either."

"And, sad to say, after being married a year, I don't even know anything about making them."

Harry laughed. Tom always exaggerated. "Have you told Dad?"

Tom paused to curse at a trailer-truck spraying water from its eighteen wheels like a fire hose and taking up more than half of the well potholed Route 99, before saying, "Not yet. He's got his own problems with Madeline. She refused to come with him on this trip, even though she loves Seattle. I don't know what their problems are and he sure as hell is not going to tell us, but it looks like you are the only guy in the family with a woman who's not giving him problems."

Harry laughed. "I wish! But I'm not sure I really have a problem. I know Anna is drinking more than I think she should, but I'm a blasted prude as you know. I don't think she'd be unfaithful, but she seems to be awfully popular at the Officers Club."

Tom shook his head. "No, she's been brought up like Marie; she'd never fool around. She's just telling you she doesn't like you being away so much."

"I hope you're right."

They began talking about the prospects of war. A second ring of the Iron Curtain had dropped on June 24, encircling Berlin, already deep within Soviet-occupied Germany. The battered city of 3 million war-torn souls was blockaded by the Soviet Union in an attempt to force the Western Allies—Great Britain, France, and the United States—to leave. The United States, unable to respond on the ground against the thirty Soviet divisions in the area, made a decision to airlift supplies into the beleaguered city. Moscow relished the idea—it had seen the catastrophic failure of the German airlift at

Stalingrad, where only a few hundred thousand troops had to be fed. With the railroads, roads, and canals all shut down, they knew it would be impossible to supply the city by air, and welcomed the chance to have the Allies fail.

"Harry, I know this sounds rotten, but I'm thinking about volunteering to go back in the Marines, or maybe even the Air Force, if I can work a transfer. It's cowardly, but maybe Marie would be better off with her family. I'm obviously the problem, or sex with me is obviously the problem, I don't know which. Going back into the service might help us both. This Berlin Airlift is a worthwhile thing, if it works, but if it doesn't the country is going to be calling for experienced pilots again."

Their father could not get to the Windsor to see them that night—there was an emergency meeting on the B-47 program that he had to attend—but he made arrangements for them both to meet with him at George Schairer's office in the morning.

The next morning they walked through the Boeing plant, escorted by a Boeing security man. Vance said, "It's like a tomb. Four years ago this place was throbbing with B-17s, rolling them out the door, ten, fifteen, or more a day. It's sad to see all this vacant space."

George Schairer met them at the door to his Spartan office. He was a prototypical Boeing executive, always immaculately dressed in a good but not too expensive suit, wearing a white shirt and conservative tie, with shoes highly polished. He was balding, with close-cropped hair, and his eyes gleamed with ferocious intelligence behind his rimless glasses. Like Ed Wells, Bill Allen, and the rest of the top Boeing personnel, Schairer was always the soul of quiet courtesy. So although he was expecting to meet only with Vance Shannon, he showed nothing but pleasure on finding that both Tom and Harry were to attend. His voice had a measured metallic sound, and he talked as if his brain were a slide rule measuring every syllable for exactitude.

"Mr. Schairer, you've met my boy Tom, but I'd like to introduce Harry. He's just been to England to work with Alan Cobham on some aerial refueling ideas, and I wondered if you could spare him half an hour to tell you about it."

Schairer's grin narrowed a bit, and he glanced at his watch and said, "Sure, no problem, let's go in the conference room down the hall here. Anyone else you think ought to be called in?"

Vance Shannon knew he had an opportunity here that might not come again. "How about Wellwood Beale, Ed Wells, Cliff Leisy, and Elliot Merrill?" Beale was the rotund, heavy-drinking chief of engineering, who also happened to be one of the best airplane salesmen in the world. Wells was sedate and retiring but a top engineer who had first brought Boeing to prominence with the 247 transport. Leisy was an all-around engineer who Vance knew had been researching in-flight refueling. Merrill was Boeing's top test pilot since the death of Eddie Allen in 1943.

Schairer snorted. "How about the president, Bill Allen, too? Let's get serious; I call Ed in, and Cliff, but that's it. And I'll give you thirty minutes, because we've got to get back on the B-47 stuff we hashed out last night."

All the Boeing types sat on one side of the table, dressed almost identically and behaving in the normal Boeing way, friendly, correct, but just formal and distant enough to maintain decorum.

One of Sergeant Shackleford's gifts was being a pretty fair artist, and Harry had asked him to sketch out both the British system used by Cobham and the new system he was proposing. Shackleford had used a grease pencil on two-foot-square sheets of paper, drawing in clean, straight lines and even managing a little perspective.

Harry walked them through the Flight Refueling Limited system first, pointing out the strong points—availability and track record. He noted the weak points as well—slow fuel flow, lots of equipment required, and some rather delicate hardware used to engage the lines when they crossed.

"And there is the hazard of equipment and hoses freezing in subzero temperatures at high altitudes. But the system works; they've tested it scores of times, and never had a failure. We are going ahead and ordering forty sets of Cobham's equipment to install on B-29s. We've got to gain some actual in-flight refueling experience, and this is the fastest way to do it. But let me show you a very simplistic idea that I've had drawn up. I don't know how feasible it is, but it seems to me to be a better way to go, because you could use it on both fighters and bombers. The Cobham system will work for bombers only, obviously."

Harry pulled out the second set of drawings, far more sophisticated than the ones he had shown Colonel Boyd. They depicted the rear end of one B-29, fitted with a refueling compartment and an extended boom, equipped with two little wings. Shackleford had outdone himself, and the drawings showed how the receiver aircraft, equipped with a refueling receptacle just behind the cockpit, would move into position, fly formation at a distance, then close the distance, open the refueling receptacle, and have the refueling boom operator steer the boom into the hatch.

Leisy slammed his fist down on the table. "That's it, man; that's it! That will work; we'll get rid of all these damn hoses and reels and throwing lines. This is the way to go, no question about it." He jumped up and looked at the others, waving his arms, saying, "This will save the 377 program; we'll finally make some money on that clunker by turning it into a tanker. This is a godsend." Then, almost confrontational, he turned to Schairer and said, "Well, what about it?," his expression changing as he realized that not only was everyone from Boeing in the room far senior to him, but there were also strangers, before whom such things were never discussed. The 377 was Boeing's Stratoliner, an adaptation of the B-29 into the transport role, using a new fuselage. It was liked by travelers but not by airlines, who found it too expensive to operate, and Boeing was hemorrhaging money on the program.

Ed Wells interrupted, speaking gently. "Sit down, Cliff. It's a good thing we all think you are right. Colonel Shannon, I take it we have your permission to proceed with this? Have you patented the idea?"

Harry was nonplussed. "Patented it? No, sir, it's just something that came to me on Air Force time, and my boss told me to tell you about it. From now on, it's Boeing's baby as far as I'm concerned."

Schairer smiled and said, "How about coming back in the morning? I've got an old friend of yours coming in from Wright-Pat, Pete Wharton. I think all three of you might be interested."

That night at the Windsor, after the flaming pupu tray of appetizers had been pulled away and they were waiting for their steaks, Vance said, "Harry, you probably gave away a few million dollars today."

"No, it would have been the Air Force's money; I worked on it on Air Force time. And the Air Force doesn't care about making money; as Al Boyd said, it's just interested in getting one airplane to squirt a lot of fuel real fast into another."

The steaks were good, and they finished with cognac. Tom had told his tale of wifely woe, and so did Harry.

"Well, it looks like the Shannons are a pretty sorry crew when it comes to women. My woman won't marry me, Tom's may be about to leave him, and the votes aren't in on Harry's. I guess I must have done something wrong when I raised you."

"There's a lot of talent here tonight, Dad." Tom ran his eyes around the room where some of the Windsor regulars as well as some new faces were seated.

"Not on your life, Son, nor on mine."

They were back in Schairer's outer office the next morning, where an old friend, Lieutenant Colonel Wilbur P. "Pete" Wharton, was waiting for them. Wharton ruled bomber development at Wright-Patterson with an iron hand, running it virtually by himself. He worked a three-way street—the Air Force budget, Congress, and the manufacturers—and he kept them all in line, turning out the airplanes, engines, and propellers needed for bombers.

"Pete, how are you? What are you doing here?"

"Going crazy, Harry, trying to keep up with Boeing."

Schairer's secretary opened his door, smiled in the sincerely cordial way that was standard for Boeing office help, and motioned them inside. Schairer's office was as neat as his appearance and his mind, with nothing out of place on his desk and two sets of bookcases totally filled with models of Boeing aircraft, including some interesting projects that had never been built. Vance had worked on many of them and had a fond spot in his heart for some of the most radical—a bulky jet fighter that had a ramjet for power at altitude, a wicked-looking interceptor, with a thin, straight wing and three engines, two jets and a rocket. There was also one that was being developed at the same time as the B-47, a smaller version with two jets and the same bicycle landing gear. It had been dropped because Boeing didn't think there was a sufficient market for it. Shannon always thought it would have made a good aircraft for export sales, but there was no interest at Boeing despite all his work on it. Next to the model case, a huge walnut table was piled with drawings, wind tunnel models, and odd bits of hardware.

Schairer stood like a country schoolmaster beside a large easel. "I know all of you are cleared at least for secret, but oddly enough, everything I'm going to show you except the last sheet is unclassified. I won't show you the last one, although Pete is familiar with it.

"As you gentlemen know, we desperately need to find a way to increase the range of our jet bombers. We need to be able to hit the Soviet Union hard and from high altitude, and the only thing the Air Force has for the job is a few Convair B-36s—basically a 1940s airplane, blown up in size. It's no wonder the Navy is skeptical about spending so much money on it."

Harry had been at Convair the previous August, quite by chance, and seen the XB-36 fly. It was a tremendously impressive airplane, with a 230-foot wingspan and six pusher engines, but it had to be slow—there was no way six piston engines, even the big Pratt & Whitney R-4360s, could push that much metal through the air very fast.

Schairer carefully covered the first chart, then opened the second. The drawings were of the XB-47; a series of photos, taken at every angle, were thumbtacked around the drawings.

"It took a while to convince even me, but this is a terrific airplane, the best bomber in the world. But it is too short ranged of course, and until we get some kind of a tanker fleet, it will be a while before it is really useful. It's fast, though, six hundred mph, and Guy Townsend will tell you that it is also very maneuverable."

Townsend was the Air Force test pilot who had sold the airplane to the Air Force at a time when all the emphasis was on building the B-50, an improved version of the B-29 but still a piston engine bomber.

Schairer went on as if he were lecturing a class, going through the drill of covering the drawings again. It was habit; these drawings had been unclassified, but he couldn't bring himself to leave them open. He opened up the third sheet. "Here's where the problem is, though. I've been working on this devil for two years." He showed a drawing of a huge aircraft with a straight wing, and four enormous turboprop engines. "This is the Boeing Model 464-17. We started out with six engines, but when Wright bumped up the power of their T-35 turboprops to about eighty-nine hundred horsepower we went to four. Less drag, less maintenance, less inventory."

Vance Shannon asked, "What's its gross weight?"

Schairer moaned, "Four hundred thousand pounds and growing. You know the old problem: you need fuel to carry fuel, so you scale up, and then you need extra fuel to carry the extra weight, and then you need extra fuel to carry the extra fuel. It's a vicious circle. We project that the airplane would have a speed over target of about three hundred eighty mph and a combat radius of about three thousand miles. That's way too short, obviously; it's just a little better than the B-36."

Shannon turned to Wharton. "Pete, Pratt & Whitney have some terrific jet engines coming down the pike. You know how I feel about coupled engines and gearboxes—and I feel the same way about turboprops; I just cannot believe they are going have any advantage over a jet engine for a bomber or a fighter. A transport, maybe, but not a first-line combat aircraft."

Wharton responded, "Well, the Russkies wouldn't agree with you. We don't know a hell of a lot about what they are doing, but we do know they are developing some monster turboprop engines, probably based on some German designs. We also know that Tupelov, their big bomber guy, is designing a huge turboprop bomber. Probably looks just like this." Wharton jabbed the drawing of the Boeing turboprop.

The Soviet Union's famed Andrei Tupelov had added another laurel to his crown just after the war, reverse-engineering impounded Boeing B-29s to create the Tupelov Tu-4. The Tu-4 represented a real threat to the United States, for it could reach most of

its major cities on a one-way mission. Almost the entire USAF interceptor force was being concentrated to counter such an attack, but
with the current primitive radar system, there was no doubt that
many of the Soviet bombers could get through.

Wharton flopped down in his seat. "The Soviets scare me. They
inherited a whole mass of German technology, and the stupid Brits
gave away the store by giving them Rolls-Royce engines. But those
will just get them started. They'll bring their own genius to play, and
they'll have airplanes that will be able to hit the U.S. and return.
That's why we'll have to build up Air Defense Command and buy a
whole bunch of interceptors, and build a radar system across the
Arctic. And that's why we have to have something to retaliate with."

The room rocked with the sound of a B-29 taking off on the
factory runway, and they were quiet until the noise was gone.

Schairer rapped gently on the easel and said, "I cannot show all
of you the last chart—it's still top secret, and we haven't done what
we need to do to check your clearances. But Pete here knows what's
there, and I'm going to leave it to Pete to decide how you can help
the program along."

Wharton turned to the Shannons, father and sons. "We have to
do better than we are doing, or we are just going to have to abandon
the heavy bomber program. That will make the Strategic Air Command very unhappy. There are some alternatives—we can base
B-47s overseas and we can accelerate the tanker program—but none
of that is really satisfactory. We need a big bomber we can send from
the heartland of the United States to the heartland of Russia."

He paused for a moment and said, "Harry, I want you to go to
Hartford, to work directly with Pratt & Whitney and get their big jet
engine rolling. Right now they are making plenty of money with
their smaller engines. I want you to convince them to risk a lot of experimental money to get me a new jet engine with at least eight thousand pounds of thrust, no matter what it takes. If you can do that, I'll
switch Boeing off turboprops and get them started on a big jet."

Harry stalled for time. He wasn't ready to be shuffled off to
Hartford, away from the great flying at Wright-Pat. "I don't know
much about engines, and certainly nothing about turboprops."

"I know that, Harry. No one really knows a great deal about jet engines yet, especially turboprops; they are an unknown quantity. But you know people, and I have faith that you can convince them that the Air Force is serious about the big jet engine."

Realizing that he was being reeled in, Harry came back with a fairly weak, not too pertinent question: "What have you learned from the B-47?"

Wharton slapped the desk with his hand. "Good goddamn question! The biggest, most important thing we learned is that the wings don't have to be as thin as they are on the B-47. All the drag calculations on the B-47 were too high, and Boeing's decided it can build the next bomber with a thick wing. It makes for a lighter structure, and means that you can store fuel in the wings, and not have all the tanks in the fuselage like the 47."

"Who'll I talk to up there?" The words were out of his mouth before he realized he'd agreed to accept the assignment without even talking it over with Anna.

"I'll introduce you to Luke Hobbs and Perry Pratt. Luke's been in jet engines since they started, and Pratt is a genius. Good name to have working at Pratt & Whitney, huh? Don't even know if he's related, but he is a powerhouse!"

Schairer looked at his watch again—he checked it about every five minutes—and said, "Come along, Vance; we've got to get down to Ed's office to work the B-47 problem some more."

Tom and Harry left shortly thereafter, picked up Harry's gear at the Windsor, and drove out the rainy highway to McChord.

"Weather doesn't look too bad. Just look out for Mount Rainier after you take off—guys have been known to run right into it."

"No, that's the great thing about jets. I'll be on top at about five thousand feet, and even I am not so dumb as to run into a rock in clear air."

At Base Operations, they shook hands and Harry asked, "Is there anything I can do to help with Marie, Tom? Would it help if Anna came out to visit?"

"That might help, Harry. I'm willing to try anything, but I think time's running out on me. Fly safe!"

Harry carried his gear into the flight planning room, musing on the blistering pace of the last few days and deeply troubled by the red lipstick he had seen on Tom's collar as he got out of the car. He looked vainly for a good explanation for it—maybe Marie had smudged it when Tom was packing. But given the atmosphere at the Windsor, probably not.

July 2, 1948, Boeing Field, Seattle, Washington

"THOSE ARE BRIGHT boys, Vance! I can see why you are proud of them."

"They're good boys, too. Funny, how you always think of them as boys even though they are getting to be thirty!"

Schairer got up and carefully closed his office door.

"Vance, you've been invaluable on the B-47 program, and I have to say that Tom has helped a lot—I'm glad you finagled a way to bring him in on it. But we are making pretty good progress now, and I want to give you a parallel assignment. It will keep you here another six months or more, and I need to know if you have commitments that will prevent you from accepting."

Schairer's tone was as warm and friendly as it got, but Shannon could tell that he was very serious indeed by the way he leaned forward over his desk, his hands grasping a pencil, almost bending it to the breaking point.

"I told Dutch Kindelberger that I'd only be gone for four months. I do have some studies I need to clean up at North American, but I could do that if I commuted down there a couple of days every week or two. How would that work out?"

Schairer stood up and paced back and forth. "I don't know. It's not the amount of time you'd be away; I know you'd work night and day while you were here. But it's the commercial security I'm worried about. If even one word leaks out on what I want you to do, it could cost us millions of dollars, maybe even cost us the company."

Vance's feelings were not hurt by Schairer's concerns. Accidents happen; briefcases get left on trains, all sorts of things. He knew that his friend never exaggerated, nor did he ever understate—he was always clinically precise. This must be something crucially important for Boeing. But why would he want an outside contractor to handle it if it was?

"Look, Vance, here are the facts. Boeing is in economic trouble. We've lost money the last three years, and the only thing that keeps us going is the tax-recovery program, which gives us back some of the wartime taxes we paid, just to help us through this transition process. You heard Leisy talk about the 377 program—he's right; we'll never break even there, not unless we can sell some tankers. And B-50 production will wind down soon. Boeing is coming to a fork in the road. If we pick the right one, we'll survive; if we don't, we'll be out of business in two years, three at the most."

Shannon understood. Douglas had its DC-4s and DC-6 transports coming along, and Lockheed was pumping out Constellations— there was no room for the expensive 377. And both competitors had military contracts as well, with Lockheed producing jets and Douglas building attack planes.

"Then we've got a labor problem. The way the contracts were written during the war, employees have seniority rights. We're down from forty-five thousand people at the end of the war to about fifteen thousand, all senior people, all making good money. The labor force is about to strike for more wages—they want thirty-five cents an hour more across-the-board at a time when we need to slash costs."

"This is quite a buildup, George. You must be setting me up for something big, or something difficult. You never spend this amount of time getting to the point."

Schairer whirled, went to the easel, and tore the cover back. There, beautifully detailed, was a drawing of the most stunning airplane Vance had ever seen, a low-wing jet transport with four jet engines slung in pods as on the B-47.

"This is our jet transport plane. It is based on the B-47, as you see, and it is absolutely top secret. The only chance Boeing has to survive in the future is to build the first jet transport and get it in operation. But we can't get a decision to go ahead because there are too many risks. And here is the biggest one."

He turned the page and revealed another drawing, this one also of a stunningly beautiful jet transport, very different in concept, but with a tail design that told Shannon that it had to be a de Havilland product.

"Wow—where did you get this?"

"There's a term for it, Vance; it's called industrial espionage. I got a call from a man you might know from your Lockheed days, Fritz Obermyer. He's in the United States now, but he passed through England, and a friend got him past de Havilland security and onto the factory floor. He took these pictures." Schairer tossed Vance a packet of eight-by-ten photos, obviously blown up from smaller images, and went on. "Obermyer claimed he worked for Bob Gross before and during the war. I called Bob, and he was embarrassed but confirmed it. Gross said that although all of Obermyer's information had not always been useful, it was almost always correct. Well, this is very useful to us."

Shannon had never heard of Obermyer but remembered Gross talking about foreign information sources that he had. He studied the photos carefully and compared them to the three-view drawing. "Not much sweepback, and broad-chord, thick wings. Good for short-field takeoffs. Putting the engines inside the wing looks good, but I think it would cause a lot of problems."

"So do we. And you can't tell it from the photos, but the airplane is too small for the United States. It looks like about thirty-six passengers would be the maximum. But it could be stretched, or scaled up."

"What are you planning for your airplane to carry?"

"Maybe eighty. We're thrust limited now. We want to use the same engines we're using in the B-47. J47s, they are reliable; we're familiar with them."

"I cannot believe what you are saying, George! We just met yesterday on getting new Pratt & Whitney engines for the big bomber. If you use the same engine on the jet transport you can scale it up to carry maybe one hundred sixty passengers and have a trans-Atlantic range. This is your chance to think big."

Schairer, usually impassive, paled. "You're telling me to go in to the board of directors and tell them that I want to spend twice as much money as we've ever talked about, on a new jet transport, at a time when they are already worried about going broke?"

"Absolutely. If you make an eighty-passenger airplane, you're inviting de Havilland to scale up their plane, to compete. And they've a few years' head start on you." He waved one of the photos and said, "I'd say this airplane will be flying in a year or less. You don't have any time to lose."

Schairer sat at his desk, his slide rule flying. Once he brightened and smiled at Vance. "A bigger airplane would be better as a tanker, too." When he had finished jotting down a whole series of numbers, he said, "Let me sleep on this, Vance. It's just so audacious that I cannot comment now. But I want you to go to Great Britain, and see if you can get a tour of the de Havilland plant. See it with your own eyes, then come back here and report. I want to know if we are right about the size, about de Havilland's marketing plan, and especially about how much testing they are going to do before they put it in service. This airplane might just be a flying prototype for something bigger—you know they are building two gigantic airplanes over there, the Bristol Brabazon and the Saro Princess, a flying boat, of all things. Maybe de Havilland will just use this as a mail plane, and build a bigger one for hauling passengers. If they do, we might have a chance to be first."

"No, George, this is an airliner. They never would have made the fuselage diameter so large, nor would they have stuck these strange square windows in it, if they were just going to fly mail in it. But it's too small and you've got to think big. Mentioning the Bristol Brabazon gives me a point of departure. Stanley Hooker is an old friend, and he's with Bristol, now. I'd have to be up-front and tell him I was looking for information, but he can probably get me a briefing at de Havilland."

"Can you leave in the next few days? If you can get back to me in say three weeks, give or take a week, I'll have time to prepare for the next board of directors meeting. In the meantime, we should hear something from Harry about the new engines from Pratt. They are the key; I wouldn't dream of scaling up this project unless I knew we had the engine problem solved."

August 2, 1948, Hartford, Connecticut

HARRY LIKED BEING treated as visiting royalty. Perry Pratt had been very cordial, telling him, "The first thing you need is background. Pratt & Whitney has a glorious record, but nobody ever thinks about engines; they always think about airframes. You hear all about Thunderbolts and Corsairs and Wildcats and Liberators, but you never hear about the great Pratt & Whitney engines that made them possible. I'm assigning a bright young chap, right out of college, to take you around and show you what's what."

The bright young chap was Harvey Lippincott, and he had an encyclopedic knowledge of not only Pratt & Whitney but any aviation subject. Harvey knew all about Harry's dad and his exploits and questioned him eagerly about flying the Massey Double Quad. But mostly Harvey lectured as they walked up and down the huge factory aisles. Many of them were idle now, with long rows of expensive machine tools, glistening with oil and obviously cared for tenderly, standing silent. Only in one section of the factory was there work going on, and even that section had none of the clangor and bang of a factory under pressure. Still, it was hard to imagine something as big, powerful, and greasy as an aircraft engine being manufactured in an environment as clinically clean as an operating room.

Lippincott knew most of the people on the floor, and about every twenty feet he would introduce Harry to someone else. It wasn't simple schmoozing, either. Harvey knew what they were working on and what they had worked on in the past, and he wove it into a fabric of manufacturing history that dazzled Harry.

"Pratt & Whitney shipped three hundred and sixty-three thousand, three hundred and nineteen engines during the war, with an equivalent horsepower of six hundred and three million, eight hundred and fourteen thousand, seven hundred and twenty-three. They powered fifty-one different kinds of aircraft, including trainers, transports, fighters, and bombers."

After what seemed to Harry to be the fiftieth trip down long rows of expensive machinery, Lippincott came to a halt and said, "But all that is in the past. In the next building, I'm going to show you the future, and it is coming on strong."

They walked another fifty feet to where a guard was obviously waiting for them. As they approached, he flipped a smart salute and opened the doors that held a big "Keep Out" sign.

Lippincott steered Harry to an engine test cell where white-coated technicians were swarming over a long, wasp-waisted jet engine.

"There, Colonel Shannon, is the future. It is the Pratt & Whitney X-176, a twin-spool turbojet. The military will call it the J57, and in commercial aircraft it will be the JT3. It will produce ten-thousand-shaft horsepower dry, and fifteen thousand with an afterburner. You'll see thousands of these engines in the next ten years."

He handed Harry sound-suppressing earmuffs, put on a pair himself, and nodded to the engineering team, who were crouched behind a huge instrument panel that was in turn shielded by a thick glass window. The X-176 engine started with a low roar, shooting a spear of flame out the rear, where it was channeled upward into a chimney that ran to the roof and beyond. The noise grew rapidly. The engine did not vibrate as piston engines did, but as they pushed the throttle forward, increasing its thrust, there was an imposing sense of immense power, carefully controlled. After a ten-minute run, they slowly eased the engine back to idle and then to cutoff. The silence was deafening.

Harry was too moved to comment. This was the engine they needed for Boeing's big bomber. With six or even eight of these, they could create a world-beater that would fly so high and so fast that Soviet interceptors could not counter it.

For the rest of the day, Lippincott continued to make a believer out of him, taking him through the administrative areas, leaving no stone unturned. He didn't see Perry Pratt again until the next morning.

"Well, Colonel, did you learn anything?"

"I learned that you have a great historian giving tours. Harvey Lippincott is remarkable."

"Don't think I'm boasting, but I'll have to correct you. Harvey is a typical Pratt & Whitney employee. Somehow we just attract the best, and that accounts for our success."

"Forgive me for asking, but are you part of the original Pratt founding fathers of the company?"

"Absolutely not, no relation, but I have to say the name has helped me a lot here in Hartford. Luke Hobbs will be here in a minute. You saw the X-176." It was not a question, just a statement.

"Yes, it was impressive."

"Well, I have to tell you that Pratt & Whitney, like every other big wartime manufacturer, has been hit hard by peace. We've lost most of our workforce, and we've even had to sacrifice some really first-rate managers, just because there isn't any work for them. It kills me, because I know they'll be snapped up by rivals."

Luke Hobbs walked in. Lippincott had told Harry how Hobbs had saved the company before the war, throwing out some engine designs that were ready for mass production and insisting on the creation of the R-2800, probably the most successful American piston engine design of the war.

Hobbs came right to the point. "Colonel Shannon, we want to build the X-176 engine, but we cannot do it on faith alone. We have to have a contract that will call for at least one thousand engines before we afford to turn the prototype into an engine fit for service."

"You've put your finger on the problem, Mr. Hobbs. Boeing will build a big jet bomber that could use your X-176s or J57s or whatever their designation is, but they cannot just gamble on you building the engine. I don't know how many airplanes SAC will order for Boeing, but I do know that they've ordered hundreds of B-47s, and are planning to order more."

"Well, we are already working on a turboprop engine for the big Boeing." The tone in Hobbs's voice conveyed his displeasure, for the turboprop's performance continued to be disappointing. Pratt & Whitney regretted that the age of the piston engine was past, and it was entering the jet age uneasily. The turboprop, with the complex dynamics of huge high-speed propellers and the manifest uncertainty of the gearboxes, was even more distasteful to the firm than the pure jet engine.

"You might as well stop work. Boeing cannot get the range or the speed with the turboprop."

Hobbs did not sigh with relief, but there was a visible relaxation of the intensity of his frown. "How many engines are they planning to use on this jet?"

Harry did not know, no one did at that moment, but he said, "Eight."

Pratt turned to Hobbs and said, "If the Air Force just ordered one hundred of the new bomber, that would mean at least eight hundred engines, plus another two hundred spares, and we'd have our thousand. There's a foreign market, too; we could license it if the Air Force would let us."

Harry said, "There is only one way out of this impasse, and that is for you to take the same kind of risk you took when you killed the R-2150 and started the R-2800."

Hobbs smiled for the first time and said to Perry, "You must have given him the Lippincott treatment."

Shannon went on. "What I need from you is a commitment to build the engine. If you do, I'll guarantee that the Air Force will buy at least one hundred big bombers from Boeing."

Hobbs laughed this time. "No disrespect, Colonel, but you really cannot guarantee it. What does Pete Wharton say?"

Harry flushed. Hobbs, a veteran of the game, had nailed him, but he pressed on. "And with equal respect, Mr. Hobbs, you're wrong. I can guarantee it because Pete Wharton told me that I could. There's not a damn thing that happens in Air Force procurement that Wharton doesn't call the shots on."

Hobbs realized he had almost been insulting to Harry and hastened to apologize. "Again, no offense, Colonel, I didn't mean to depreciate your guarantee, and I certainly understand your confidence if Wharton is backing you. I'll tell you what. We have a board meeting coming up a week from today. I'll propose to the board that we proceed on the X-176, and I believe they will go along with me. You go back to Wright-Patterson and tell Pete Wharton that he sent the right man to do his job for him."

Harry did not wait to go back. As soon as he had said good-bye to Pratt and Hobbs and walked to Lippincott's office to thank him, he drove back to his hotel and phoned Wharton.

"Pete, I think they are going to move; Hobbs tells me that he is going to the board to get permission to proceed on the X-176."

"Going to the board is pro forma. They'll do what Hobbs asks. That's great, Harry; I knew you could pull it off. But I want you to promise me that you are not going to tell your dad or Boeing what's happening. I've got a few negotiating irons in the fire with them, and it's better for the Air Force if they don't know the good news until those irons are out and cooling."

Puzzled, Harry said, "OK, if that's the way you want it. I'll just tell Dad that it is still up in the air." He hated to do it and doubted if he could get away with it, for his father still read him like a book.

"Attaboy. He'll understand when the time comes."

It turned out that Wharton's caution was prudent, for the following week, a very dejected Hobbs called him.

"Pete, this is Luke. I've got to renege; I've been outmaneuvered. The Pratt & Whitney board has postponed their meeting until September, and I know why. They don't want to make a decision on the X-176 until the last quarter of the year. There is a possible merger coming up, and they think deciding on the X-176 might affect the deal."

The phone was silent and Hobbs asked, "You still there, Pete?"

"Just thinking, Luke. This might work out best for the Air Force, if you can get me a positive decision by early October. That's when I've asked the Boeing brass to come out and brief on the big turboprop bomber."

"OK, Pete. Thanks for being understanding. I'll get a positive decision by October 15. They have to meet by then, corporate bylaws. If they don't go along with me, I'll tell them I'll quit. I don't use that ploy very often, but when I have to use it, it works."

"Keep me posted."

October 22, 1948, Dayton, Ohio

IT WAS ONE of those perfect fall days in Ohio, when even downtown Dayton looked bright and cheerful and the Van Cleve Hotel seemed the center of the aerial universe. Boeing people always stayed at the Van Cleve, and this time a six-man team of heavy hitters was in town to brief Pete Wharton on the latest developments—none too cheerful—of the turboprop bomber.

Ed Wells headed the team, backed up by George Schairer. While the other four men were specialists, they were also talented in many fields. Maynard Pennell and Art Carlsen were weight experts, able to look at a drawing and estimate what the weight of each component was going to be, usually within ounces of the final figure. Holden "Bob" Withington was a wind tunnel specialist—he and Schairer had advocated the huge wind tunnel that now gave Boeing an advantage over every other manufacturer in the industry. Withington was also an expert on drag estimation. Vance Shannon felt privileged to be in their company. All the men were exhausted, having been working hard on other projects before being subjected to the long cross-country trip from Seattle, some coming by train, some by plane.

The initial meeting was held Friday morning in Wharton's cluttered office in Area A at Wright-Patterson. The Boeing people arrived early, as always, and set up their briefing materials and a brand-new model of the turboprop bomber. They were not very enthusiastic because they didn't have much in the way of good news—they had improved the range only slightly, but the takeoff gross weight had gone up again.

Wharton swept into the room with his usual good humor, apologized for being late, and said, "Gentlemen, thanks for coming, and for setting up early. But here is the big news. The turboprop bomber is canceled. Pratt & Whitney is going to commit its new jet engine, the X-176, to full-scale production. I got word from Luke Hobbs yesterday. What I'd like you to do is go back to the Van Cleve and develop a proposal for a turbojet bomber that can use an engine with these specifications." He handed out the engine specification sheets to the stunned Boeing personnel.

Wells spoke up. "Pete, are you sure about this? If so, it's the best news we've had in weeks."

"If you think you are happy, you ought to have heard Luke Hobbs."

The Boeing engineers wore out room service at the Van Cleve for the next seventy-two hours, working in a frenzy of activity, pooling their accumulated knowledge on a long series of previous projects to create the preliminary drawings and specifications for an eight-jet bomber. All that they had learned from designing, building, and flying the B-47 was poured into the new aircraft. They kept Vance Shannon as a gofer for essentials such as drawing paper, drafting tools, and coffee when he wasn't standing by the telephone to act as intermediary with a variety of Boeing teams in Seattle. There, like a kicked-over anthill, Boeing engineers and executives, dressed in weekend clothes and forgoing the normal suit-and-tie atmosphere, worked round-the-clock to furnish figures to back up the Dayton team's estimates.

Vance would relay questions from the Van Cleve back to every area of the Boeing plant, then get the resulting answers back to the team. In the process he was amazed at the depth of Boeing engineering; virtually nothing came up that had not been discussed before, and almost everything had been tested to some degree. The Seattle people would listen, promise to call back, and usually within thirty minutes have the required data, dug out of an existing file.

On Monday morning, October 25, the bleary-eyed team reassembled in Wharton's office with a thirty-three-page proposal for the Boeing Model 464-49-0. The small packet included an inboard profile, a three-view drawing, all the drag polars, and the weight estimates. The aircraft was huge, with four thousand square feet of wing area, a design gross weight of 330,000 pounds, a high speed of 572 mph, and a range of 8,000 miles with a 10,000-pound bomb load. There had never been anything like it before in the history of aviation.

Ed Wells did the three-view drawings and then helped Schairer and Shannon build a large balsa model of the airplane, painted silver and mounted on a stand so that Wharton could take it back to the Pentagon.

Wharton put the model on his desk, then pawed through the proposal, asking questions but clearly delighted with what he saw.

"This is it, gentlemen. I repeat, the turboprop is officially canceled. I'll go to Pentagon this afternoon, and I'll shepherd this baby through all the congressional hoops. This is exactly what the new head of the Strategic Air Command wants, and he has wanted it since he ran research and development. You can look to building a lot of them."

When the meeting broke up and the fatigued Boeing people went back to their rooms to get a little rest, the first person Vance Shannon called was his son Harry.

"Harry, you rascal, how long have you known about what Pete Wharton was planning?"

There was a pause. "I'm sorry, Dad. Pete specifically asked me not to tell you after my trip up to Hartford. He said he had some negotiating irons in the fire."

"Son, you did the right thing and I'm proud of you. I can't talk about this on the phone, but Boeing and the Air Force and I guess Pratt & Whitney are going to be mighty happy about what happened this weekend. Talk to you more when I get back to Seattle."

December 31, 1948, Palos Verdes, California

VANCE AND MADELINE had long since stopped going out on New Year's Eve, even though they were invited to half a dozen parties all over the state. She was in the kitchen, cleaning up after their simple one-pot dinner. It was chilly for California, and Vance sat in front of his desk, a fire in the fireplace to his left. The desktop was absolutely clean except for a pad of yellow paper, a small ruler, and a few sharpened pencils. Normally the desk was crowded, littered with books, papers, drawings, and the occasional bit of leftover lunch. Tonight it was cleaned off for what had become an annual ritual, an accounting of the way the year had gone, both for his business and for his family. He knew before he made the first entry that the results would be mixed.

His business, Aviation Consultants, Incorporated, was doing very well. The boys had more than earned their keep, and Harry had proved invaluable even after he was recalled into the Air Force. Vance had turned managing both the firm's and the household's money over to Madeline, and she had done her usual remarkable job. The house was run on a very tight budget, and he sometimes had to complain to make her loosen up and spend a bit more on the menu. On the business side, she was very conservative about the stock market but had investments in utilities, railroads, and metals. The only thing he had cautioned her about was investing in the aircraft companies or in airlines. He didn't want there to be the shadow of a doubt about any conflict of interests. Madeline had put most of her effort into buying real estate, small outlying parcels in the San Fernando Valley and well outside the San Diego city limits. He doubted if they would ever appreciate in his lifetime, but the taxes were low and the parcels would undoubtedly become valuable for his sons. As always, she resolutely refused to have her name on any of the investments or property. To counter this, Vance had his lawyers draw up a new will, which divided the estate equally among Madeline and his two sons. When she read the will, she was furious and did not speak to him for two days. It was impossible to understand, and he had to relent, essentially cutting her out of the will. He knew this boded ill for their future but could not make her see what a rebuff it was to him. It was so inconsistent—she was constantly stroking his ego, making him feel good about himself, and then behaved in this abnormal, insulting fashion. Too bad he was such a mouse when it came to dealing with her.

Madeline had also revamped his small workforce, hiring Jill

Abernathy to help her. The two worked together hand in glove, and Madeline seemed to be backing more and more out of anything to do with airplanes and concentrating on the real estate. Jill turned out to be wonderful, a handsome woman of about forty-five, quiet, and able to make decisions on her own. Madeline transferred all the administrative work to her within a period of a couple of months, and Vance never noticed the slightest change in smooth, efficient service. Jill in turn had hired two young women to help her. He hated to see his company's payroll increase so dramatically but knew that it probably took three women to do the work that Madeline had done.

And the workload had grown significantly, with demands on his time from Boeing, North American, Convair, and, more frequently now, Lockheed. Since Harry had been recalled (and Tom might be, too), Vance had hired two young college graduates as trainees. The difficulty was that neither he nor Tom had time to do much training and it might be that he'd have to let them go. The two new men tried hard but seemed to spend as much time talking with the women Jill had hired as doing anything else. Normal but irritating.

Still, financially all was well, and Madeline told him that his net worth had grown to almost a quarter-million dollars, an unbelievable amount for a man who had worked through the depression trying to make enough to cover the rent each month, and not always succeeding.

He took the barest sip of cognac, just wetting his lips and the tip of his tongue. He couldn't drink at night anymore; even one small drink would keep him up. But he loved the flavor, and a bottle of Courvoiser VSOP could last him for six months the way he sipped it. His business had done well because it was in the fastest-growing sector of the aviation industry—jet aircraft and engines. He rocked back in his chair and considered the strides that had been made since 1939, when von Ohain's engine had powered the first jet airplane. Vance thought about Hans at length, for he had rarely met anyone who combined such brilliance with equal degrees of integrity and openness. He decided he'd take a special trip to Wright-Patterson just to talk to Hans, if business did not take him there first. He understood from their mutual friends that von Ohain was doing very well, charming everyone and carving out the prospects for a bright future in America.

The jet had improved rapidly during the war, of course, with the Germans actually getting a first-rate fighter into combat. But after the war, almost everyone assumed that jets were going to be the future—but not immediately. They were wrong. Jet engines had come in at about the same power levels as the piston engines they were going to replace but proved to have a much swifter development time. Fortunately, in the United States a huge engine industry was in place, ready to learn how to design and build jets. Other manufacturers, including General Electric and Westinghouse, applied their past experience in superchargers and turbines to enter the fray. Engine power output had gone up steadily, and Vance was pleased to have a part, however small, in the development of the plane that would use the latest one, the X-176.

Rocket power had been marvelous for experimental work. Everyone applauded when Chuck Yeager broke the sound barrier in a rocket plane, but Shannon didn't believe there was an operational use for rockets, at least not in the atmosphere. When they got into space flight, then rockets were the only thing, but that was a long way into the future, decades probably, maybe more.

In Europe, Great Britain was doing very well. His quick visit to the de Havilland factory confirmed both the fears and hopes of Boeing. The airplane was beautiful, would fly soon, but it was too small for most American airlines to adopt. Vance also had his doubts about the airplane. There was something not quite right, and part of it was the speed with which de Havilland had raced to complete the Comet, as they called their new transport. He had seen Frank Whittle there, and while Frank was still hurt about the way he had been shoved aside by his government, he was tremendously proud that engines stemming from his basic design were used in the Comet.

The de Havilland engineers had briefed Vance at length, insisting that their testing process was thorough, and he could not contradict them, but in his bone he felt that they had gone too far too fast. Boeing, with its vastly greater resources, would never have pushed a project through with the speed de Havilland had done. He hoped he was wrong.

Elsewhere in Europe, France was frantically trying to catch up, using German technology as everyone else did, but building on it with indigenous talent.

It was the Soviet Union that worried Vance most. No one knew where they were developing a nuclear weapon, but they were undoubtedly working on it, and could have it in ten years or so. Soviet security was tight, but they had captured much of the same German equipment and data as had the United States and had benefited from the incredibly stupid sale of fifty-five Rolls-Royce jet engines that Sir Stafford Cripps had engineered. So far there had not been much evidence of any big advances, but Vance was certain they would come.

He turned to a blank page in the tablet, then put the pencil down. This was not the year to record any details about the family. It was just too sad, with both of his boys having marital problems. Marie had left Tom, to return to her family. Tom had expected her father to be furious with him, but Lou was instead apologetic. Apparently they had known of Marie's problems for years and hoped that marriage would somehow bring her out of it. Tom was left bewildered and hurt. He still loved Marie but could not find a way to help her. To help himself, he had plunged into his work, but Vance knew that Tom really wanted to get back into the military. Vance did not blame him. Staying here, with Marie so near, would be difficult. He needed to get away.

Harry's situation was not much better, but there was no talk of divorce. Anna drank too much and would not admit it. Although Harry never alluded to it, Vance knew he suspected her fidelity as well. Again, there was nothing much to be done; they would have to see how it played out.

Ironically, when he could forget the kids' problems, it was the happiest Christmas Vance had spent for years. Madeline was herself again, helpful, cheerful, and more passionate than he could handle. Now she whirled in from the bedroom and knelt down beside him, dressed as usual in her pink cotton robe and nothing else.

"Put down the pencil and come to bed, honey. It's New Year's Eve, and you don't need to be working."

"This is not work, my dear, just some thoughts on paper, and most of them tell me that you are a remarkable woman." He pulled her to him, lifting her up easily to sit her on his lap and running his hand down over her body.

She sat for a while, arms around him, her head inclined upon his shoulder, her feet, as always, busy stroking his legs. Then, without another word, she stood up, took him by the hand, and led him to the bedroom.

It was a good way to end the year.

Communists take over China; North Atlantic Treaty Organization created; Marshall Plan begins; Berlin Blockade ended; Ezzard Charles beats Jersey Joe Walcott; the USSR tests first atomic bomb.

CHAPTER TEN

February 2, 1949, Wright-Patterson
Air Force Base, Ohio

*H*ans von Ohain came to work early, as he invariably did. The office was small, the typical twelve-by-fifteen-foot area allocated civil servants of his rank, but it afforded him tremendous pleasure each day. He liked it because it was private; just closing the door gave him a sense of power. He could work for hours without interruption. Meetings were infrequent, which amazed him, but much of the work being done in the Applied Research Laboratory was unique to the researcher pursuing it. There was an adequate library down the hallway, and it was connected with much more elaborate systems. Von Ohain could get virtually any book, any thesis, that he wanted in a few days, just by jotting the name down on a sheet of paper and handing it to the librarian.

Yet the thing that gave von Ohain the most pleasure was that he was working for a good cause. The United States was a fantastic country, welcoming him and his colleagues with open arms, even though they had fought for Germany. From the start, in 1937, he had never reconciled himself to the idea of working on projects that would benefit the Nazi government. His time at Heinkel was a mixed blessing. He had been given the opportunity to explore entirely new areas of propulsion, but it always bothered him that ultimately his work was for an unworthy cause.

Not so at Wright-Pat, as he had learned to call it. He relished the informality of life in the United States, where colleagues soon assumed a first-name basis. It contrasted with the stiff formality of life in Germany, where your race, your education, and your position decided exactly how you were to be addressed and the perks you would receive and, for the most part, where you would end up in life. There was a blessed egalitarianism here that fostered cooperation and made research a pleasure.

The phone rang and he jumped as he always did. In Germany, a call on the phone not only often presaged bad news, but you were constantly aware that the calls were monitored and that some chance comment could bring the authorities down on you. Knowing that it was not so in America, von Ohain breathed a sigh of relief as he picked up the phone, saying, "Hello, von Ohain here."

"Greetings, Herr Doktor von Ohain. I am an old friend. Do you recognize my voice?" The caller spoke in English, with a heavy German accent, but his tone was cheerful, expectant, as if he was certain that von Ohain would be delighted to hear from him.

Von Ohain rapidly went through the list of scientists he had known who had been brought to the United States under Operation Paperclip and then assigned elsewhere, to Huntsville, perhaps, or to Los Alamos. Nothing registered. Typically unwilling to offend, von Ohain replied, "Forgive me, perhaps the telephone is disguising your voice, but I must ask who you are."

"Ah, let me give you a hint. Do you remember '*Von Ohain fliegt schneller, ohne Propeller*'?" Then quite unnecessarily, the caller said in singsong English, "Von Ohain flies faster, without a propeller."

His knees buckling, von Ohain sat down at the table. It was Fritz Obermyer, the Nazi hoodlum who had used rhyming jokes to conceal his rough nature. He had blackmailed his way to becoming a close associate of an unwilling Ernst Heinkel and often wrote poems that joked about von Ohain's work. What in the world could Obermyer want? Then the thought shot through von Ohain—was he sure the phones were not tapped? Was anyone listening?

Voice cracking, he asked, "Herr Obermyer?"

"Please call me Fritz! We are in America now; we should be like Americans, use first names and always speak English!"

Von Ohain was relieved. If his lines were tapped, he did not wish to be speaking to Obermyer in German. English was bad enough.

"Yes, Fritz, how are you? What can I do for you?"

"Ah, Hans—I would never have dared call you Hans in the old country—it's not what you can do for me, but what I can do for you. I have the opportunity of a lifetime for you."

Von Ohain's hands trembled so badly that he had to hold the phone to his ear with both hands. "And what is that, please?"

"Hans"—Obermyer seemed to roll the name over his lips, as if savoring the pleasure of being on a first-name basis with so distinguished a scientist—"Hans, you remember the Volkswagen, the People's Car? It was such a promise to so many, and it is being built again. In a few years they are going to start shipping them to sell in America. If you are interested, I can see to it that you obtain a dealership, at no cost to you."

As distressed as he was, von Ohain could not restrain himself from a nervous laugh—it was a preposterous idea. "But Fritz, the Americans will not want the Volkswagen." Von Ohain thought of the used Chrysler sedan he had just purchased, a powerful car, comfortable. You could almost fit a Volkswagen in its trunk. "They would never drive such a small car; it is too slow, too uncomfortable. I don't want to insult you, but I think you are too optimistic."

Obermyer laughed jovially in response. "I know it sounds crazy—I am driving a Mercury myself, a fine car, big V-8 engine—but believe me, the Volkswagen is coming to the United States and it will be a great success. There is a lot of money behind this idea. And, even though it is small, the Volkswagen is a very good car."

"That may be so, but why would you give me such an opportunity?"

"When the time comes, there will be huge advertising campaigns. Your name is not so well-known to the public, but it is to the engineering world. You would give the Volkswagen credibility at the highest levels. And in return, I could see that you obtained the rights to the first Volkswagen dealership in Dayton."

"Well, thank you for your thoughtfulness, Herr Obermyer—"

"Fritz."

"Yes, well, thank you, Fritz, but I am completely absorbed in my work here. I would have no idea about a dealership, or selling cars."

"You forget Max Hahn!"

Max had been the mechanic who had done so much to turn von Ohain's ideas into hardware in creating the prototype engine.

"No, I don't forget him, but what about him?"

"He could run your dealership for you; you would both become wealthy."

"No, thank you so much; it is just impossible. I have commitments here, and I'm not a businessman. I think you know that."

"Well, Hans, think about it. Nothing is going to happen for two years or more, and then we will start small. But if you need to get in touch with me, I'm with Hoffman Importing in New York City. And now that we are in contact, I'll be sure to stay in touch with you. *Auf Weidersehen!* Ach, I meant, good-bye!"

"Good-bye."

Von Ohain hung up the phone, physically ill. He wanted nothing to do with Obermyer or with any of the Nazi past. Von Ohain hated everything about it then, and he certainly would not deal with any of them now. He wondered if he should report the call, then reluctantly decided against it. There was nothing to report. If Obermyer was in this country, he must have been cleared at some point. And just being a Nazi was not a crime, not anymore. If he knew Obermyer at all, he was no longer a Nazi, anyway—there was no longer a profit in it. But to think that there would be profits in the Volkswagen. What an idea. Obermyer must have had something else in mind. Everyone at the Heinkel plant knew that he was corrupt, but no one knew exactly how.

Nervous, von Ohain spoke to himself aloud: "What can he want? What do I have that he would need?" The answer was obvious. Obermyer presumed von Ohain was working on highly classified projects, and he wanted information.

Von Ohain's office suddenly seemed less secure, less private. With a shudder, he finally sat down to resume his work, his eyes continually returning to the—he hoped—untapped phone.

March 15, 1949, San Diego, California

TOM SHANNON HAD faced the ultimate embarrassment of an annulment with Marie's help. She had testified quite willingly, almost with pride, that their marriage had not been consummated and that she was still a virgin. The whole matter had been arranged discreetly, with the complete cooperation of the Capestro family. Lou Capestro, famous for his fiery temper and his fierce protectiveness, had been apologetic to Tom.

"Son, do not feel that there is any blame on your part. We are really at fault. In our love for her, we helped conceal the fact that Marie was not the person she seemed to be, because we hoped that marriage would help her. I am glad that we can use the annulment process and avoid a divorce."

"Lou, I still love her. It hurts me that she is not well. I'm not a doctor, but I believe that she is torn between her fear of making love to me and her shame at disappointing me by being cold."

His language was obviously too candid for Lou. "Let's not talk about that. You are doing the right thing here, and we'll get her medical attention. You have a life to live, I know. We will keep you informed on how she is doing."

Tom looked at him, knowing that Lou was lying, that he would never do anything that might revive the marriage. He seemed content that his baby was back at home, where he could take care of her. It was clear that he did not dislike Tom, but it was equally clear that Tom had served his purpose. He had been allowed to try to help Marie; he had failed; the experiment was over; he was no longer necessary. In Lou's view Tom was now an impediment to Marie's well-being.

Talking with Lou about the annulment had been easier than talking to his dad or to Harry. It was humiliating to admit to them or to anyone that he lived for almost two years with Marie without possessing her, nor could he mitigate things by saying at times she would accommodate him with her hands. He absolutely could not tell them that he had, for the last year, maintained a torrid affair with another woman, one they both knew, for she worked with Jill Abernathy in the family business. Jill had hired two girls to assist her, with one, Nancy Strother, mostly doing public relations. He and Nancy had hit it off almost immediately and soon became lovers. Tom believed they had deceived everyone but Madeline, who looked on with equanimity, neither approving nor disapproving, just accepting.

Not surprisingly, Nancy was very different in appearance and personality from Marie, being taller, blonder, and far more athletic. She surfed and snorkeled, and much of their time together was spent on Mexican beaches, far away from anyone who might recognize Tom. The long drives down Route 101, crossing the border at San Ysidro and then having a drink at the "Long Bar" in Tiajuana, were a magic preparation for their long nights of intensive, inventive sex.

Both Harry and his father had reacted to the news of the annulment admirably. Both were stoic, expressed their sympathy, wished Marie well, and urged Tom to get on with his life.

For Tom, getting on with his life meant getting back into the service, where he could do some real flying. Nancy seemed to understand this. She had been pleased at the news of the annulment but careful not to presume that they were now going to wed—at least right away. Tom felt that they had an understanding. She was not sure but accepted the situation, willing to let him have some time to recover from his years with Marie.

Tom had made many friends during his tour flying foreign fighters at Eglin, and one who owed him a great deal was Lieutenant Colonel Ralph Mahoney, now commander of the 4th Fighter-Interceptor Wing at New Castle County Airport, Wilmington, Delaware. The 4th was assigned to the Eastern Air Defense Force, and its mission was to stop any incoming Soviet bombers.

The memories of their last flight at Eglin raced through Tom's mind. Ralph was flying a clunky British carrier plane, the two-seat Fairey Firefly, with Tom on his wing in a P-51. The Firefly's Rolls-

Royce Griffon engine let go with a catastrophic malfunction that blew the cowling off its front attachments, heaving it up like a dive brake as the canopy was drenched with oil. Mahoney called a Mayday and began letting down. Tom told him to bail out, but Mahoney refused, saying he could make it back to the field even though he had no forward visibility.

Mahoney next lost all communications, and a trail of smoke began curling from underneath the cockpit area. The excess drag from the blown cowling kept pulling the Firefly down. About six miles out from Eglin's main runway, and too low to bail out, it was apparent that Mahoney was going in. Tom pulled up on his wing. When Mahoney glanced to the side, Tom indicated he would fly him in to a forced landing.

The two planes descended rapidly, as Tom led Mahoney to the only cleared acreage for miles around, a fairly short strip, not wide enough for both airplanes, bounded on all sides by tall pine trees. They were a little too close and Tom S-turned, to kill off altitude, with Mahoney matching him inch for inch. Finally, at the last second, Tom pulled up to avoid the trees and Mahoney put the Firefly down, gear up, at the very edge of the strip. In the meantime, Tom was on the radio, guiding the fire trucks and ambulances out to the field where Mahoney now stood on the Firefly's wing, waving his jacket in thanks.

So when Tom called Mahoney, explained his situation, and asked for a flying job in the Air Force, he got a response in two weeks—report to Nellis Air Force Base in Las Vegas for requalification training and then to New Castle to fly with the 4th. The only downside was Tom's rank; they bumped him down to captain, despite the fact that he was a nine-victory ace with the rank of lieutenant colonel. An earnest young lieutenant had called from the Air Force personnel office in San Antonio and explained the situation to him, but it still didn't make any sense. In the end, he didn't care; he was just glad to be back doing some real flying.

The six weeks training at Nellis went well, and Mahoney was waiting for Tom the day he reported in at New Castle.

June 1, 1949, Wilmington, Delaware

"TOM, I'VE HAD them get your flying gear all set. You and I are going out and do a little rat racing, to show you how we do it in the Fourth."

A moist spring had turned the countryside into a riot of color. Long used to California's burnt hills, Tom found the rivers, lakes, and green farmlands of Delaware enchanting. The day was warm enough for heat waves to send mirages that sheathed the runway distance markers in a shimmering haze. Tom was already soaked with sweat by the time Mahoney turned on to the runway and was cleared for takeoff.

They rendezvoused after takeoff in the climb, with Tom getting in trail with Mahoney, who leveled off at 25,000 feet and called, "Tom, just follow me through; try to stay with me."

Things started conventionally, with Mahoney making fairly tight turns to the left and right. He gradually tightened them up so that they were pulling four g's, before beginning a series of sharp reversals. Tom stayed with him as he reversed, then counterreversed, and they wound up in a spiraling dive, canopy to canopy, noses pointed straight down until the approaching ground had them break off and fly back to land.

In the briefing room Mahoney had laughed, saying, "Tom, you looked like a blasted decal on my mirror; no matter what I did, you didn't move out of position. I'll get you some flights tomorrow with some of the other guys."

Tom slept better that night than he had in months, more at home on the flat springs of a narrow Army cot than he had been for years back in his double bed in California.

July 27, 1949, Hatfield Aerodrome, Hertfordshire, England

IT WAS LATE in the evening. They had enjoyed a few drinks and a barely acceptable meal at the White Horse and were contentedly reliving the day's events.

"Stanley, I cannot thank you enough for inviting me to be here, of all days. What a treat Cunningham gave us!"

Hooker, still tall but bent over a bit from his years of scanning drafting tables and production lines, smiled jovially. "Well, you are most welcome, but no one was more surprised than I when John took off."

A few hours earlier, thirty-year-old John Cunningham had celebrated his birthday by making the first flight ever in the new de Havilland D.H. 106 Comet, a passenger jet that surpassed all previous transports. Tall and blond, the affable "Cats Eyes" Cunningham was Great Britain's premier night-fighter pilot in World War II, with more than twenty kills, sixteen in a Beaufighter and four in a de Havilland Mosquito. Dressed in shockingly dirty white coveralls, Cunningham had spent the afternoon in taxi tests and in short "hops" where he lifted off the runway and touched down immediately, braking. Then, unexpectedly, he had the aircraft refueled, called his four-man crew aboard, and made a takeoff that left the few hundred de Havilland employees on hand gasping.

Shannon and Hooker had stood with them as the truly beautiful aircraft taxied slowly down the taxiway and moved into position on the relatively short runway. There was a roar as the four engines were brought to full power and held there. Shannon knew what Cunningham and his crew were doing, checking every instrument, making sure that nothing was overlooked. Then the brakes were released and the Comet moved forward, slowly, majestically at first, its wheels running along a runway that had launched so many previous de Havilland designs, from the tiny Tiger Moth to the swift, deadly Vampire. The Comet gathered speed and broke ground so quickly that both Hooker and Shannon let out involuntary cheers. With its big wing area and huge flaps, the Comet took off more swiftly than many smaller piston engine aircraft.

Cunningham climbed to 10,000 feet, flew around at different airspeeds for thirty minutes, then made one low-altitude, high-speed pass over the runway to the roar of an elated crowd. They knew what they were watching—Great Britain had just seized the initiative in the airliner race—and they knew, too, that no one else was within years of competing with them. Cunningham was not just flying a gorgeous jet airliner; he was flying national prestige, thousands of jobs, and millions of pounds in sales. Only the British press would take exception, for the flight was made without prior notice. The de Havilland public relations people were disappointed, but Cunningham did not care, for more than five years of intense development had obviously paid off with a first-class aircraft.

Stanley Hooker asked, "One more whiskey?" and, against his better judgment, Shannon nodded yes. Hooker ordered two large whiskeys at the bar, brought them back, and said, "To John Cunningham."

They sipped their drinks, and Vance said, "We need at least two more toasts, so let's stretch this drink out. First of all, we must toast Frank Whittle, because while the Comet's engines may have Rolls-Royce's name stamped on them, they wouldn't exist without Frank's work and sacrifice."

"To Frank Whittle."

Shannon lifted his glass again; there was a half finger of whiskey remaining and he said, "To Geoffrey de Havilland," and Hooker responded, "And his sons."

They drained their glasses and were silent, each man thinking of his own family in the light of the de Havilland tragedies. Geoffrey de Havilland had lost one son, John, in 1943, in a mid-air collision of Mosquito fighters. Then in 1946, a second son, Geoffrey, was killed testing their experimental D.H. 108, a tailless, swept wing jet designed to gain information for the Comet and for supersonic flight. He had been preparing to break the world's speed record when the airplane broke up on a high-speed run over the Thames Estuary. Vance was glad that his own two sons had survived their flying so far, but he knew that all aviation was built on sacrifice and that his sons accepted the dangers. He had put them at risk in their youth with his own flying. There were dozens of times when he might have been killed, sometimes on the first flight of an advanced aircraft, sometimes in a routine test hop when things suddenly went wrong, sometimes when testing some individual's ill-advised private design.

Shannon and Hooker looked up and smiled, coming out of their mutual reveries. Hooker brought them back to the real world when he leaned forward and said, "Forgive my asking, but what do you think today's flight means to Boeing?" It was a not so gentle reminder that Hooker had invited him to Hatfield Aerodrome as a matter of their mutual business concerns.

"Well, for one thing, it means they'll have to get someone high up in the chain of command over here to see the airplane. They'll be glad to have my report, but you can bet that Ed Wells or Bill Allen will be over in England before the year is out, looking for themselves. But from my point of view, it means that Boeing has got to get cracking on a jet transport right now, without losing a moment, or it will be left at the starting gate. This is the start of the second revolution in jet aviation. The only chance Boeing would have to catch up is if something happens to the Comet during testing, or when it finally starts carrying passengers."

"I don't think that likely. They've been testing the airplane pretty extensively, and de Havilland has a world of experience."

"That's true, Stanley, but look at the record for new transports. The Germans lost their Focke-Wulf FW 200 prototype before the war, ran it out of gasoline in Manila Bay in November 1938 as I recall. Then the next year, Boeing lost a prototype 307—the first pressurized airliner—on one of its early flights. Lockheed had a devil of a time with its Constellations when they started out—electrical fires and crashes. They were grounded for months in 1946. The same thing happened to the Douglas DC-6—in-flight fires caused some crashes and they were grounded. I think a jet transport faces bigger hazards—they fly faster, higher, over longer routes. They'll be making more cycles, more takeoffs and landings, and they'll have to be heavily used, because they are so expensive."

"What's your advice to Boeing going to be?" Hooker was interested because a Boeing jet opened up another market for jet engines and that was his reason for living, designing, building, and selling them.

"I guess 'make haste slowly.' They'll have to rush to catch up to de Havilland, but they've got to spend a lot of money to do enough testing so they get it right the first time. When the first jet passenger plane crashes, it is going to make worldwide headlines, and sales will suffer. And a jet passenger plane will crash; it is inevitable."

"You are right, of course; when lots of jet transports are flying, jet transports will crash. But I don't see a special risk for de Havilland with the Comet. They have worked it over very thoroughly."

Vance nodded yes, to be agreeable, but there was something wrong with the Comet; he felt it in his fingertips. Placing the engines inside the wing roots was undoubtedly beneficial aerodynamically, but what happened if there was a fire? He knew all too well that jet engine fires were far from uncommon—that's why they had so many fire-warning light sensors on them. And those square windows. They just didn't make sense to him, not in a pressurized aircraft. Still both the Connie and the DC-6 had square windows, so perhaps it was OK. De Havilland had led the world with the Mosquito; perhaps it would lead the world with the Comet.

August 6, 1949, Palos Verdes, California

THE CAB DROPPED Vance Shannon off in front of his low-slung ranch house, and he had to carry his luggage up the curving concrete steps. At the top he was breathing heavily, as much from his anger and concern as from exertion. The trip back from England had been exhausting, for he had to first fly to Seattle to brief Ed Wells and George Schairer on the Comet, then spend the night at the dreary Windsor Hotel, where some hookers down the hall were partying until three o'clock in the morning. He'd been up at five to catch an early plane south to Los Angeles. The night before, he had called Madeline and she sounded delighted to hear his voice and promised to pick him up at the airport. When he got in, she was not there, and she had not answered his calls at home. Jill Abernathy was out of town, and he didn't feel he knew Nancy Strother well enough to ask her to come to the airport to get him on a Saturday afternoon.

He put down his bags, looked for his keys in all his pockets, then remembered he had them in his briefcase. When he finally got the front door opened he bellowed, "Madeline," but the house was silent.

Vance carried his luggage through the house to their bedroom, a prescient fear mounting in his heart. He dumped his two bags the minute he saw the envelope on the bed. It was addressed simply to "Vance." He knew what it was even before he tore it open. It read:

Darling Vance,

Thank you for giving me a wonderful life. I loved you and I love you, but I must go now. Don't worry about me; I will be fine. Tell the boys I am sorry I never measured up to their expectations.

Don't hate me. Just love me and forget me.

Madeline

There it was. A twelve-year love affair done up in four lines.

He slumped at the edge of the bed, then went to her closet. It was apparently filled with her clothes; she had not taken much with her. He went to her jewelry box. He had never bought her lavish presents, a few nice pieces, an Omega watch, an engagement ring she wouldn't accept or wear but that he induced her to keep. They were all in the box.

He sped from room to room, checking for her presence as much as for her absence. It was the same. She had left taking little more than the clothes on her back.

Then he wondered about their finances, hated himself for doubting her, but ran down to his office, where he opened the safe. Another envelope, attached to one of the brown expandable accordion files.

This time the note said:

Vance,

All your financial papers are in this packet. Everything is in good shape; you've become quite wealthy, and I am happy for you. I know you wouldn't think that I would take anything, and you'll see that I did not.

Madeline

Ashamed of himself for his suspicions, he just glanced at the tally sheet. Somehow he was worth almost a half-million dollars, and he would have given twenty times that amount to have Madeline back for just one hour.

Vance went back in their bedroom, lay down on the bed, and willed himself not to cry. Exhausted, he drifted off to sleep, dreamed that the doorbell rang, that Madeline had come back, and woke up to find the house still eerily empty.

He stumbled into the kitchen, eyes bleary from fatigue and holding back tears, and put some ice cubes in a glass, taking a couple to rub on his eyes. Filling the glass with Old Grandad bourbon, he went to their library, a cherry-paneled, book-laden sanctuary that had been their favorite room. As he walked through the house he admired the way it was decorated. Madeline was really not interested in such things, but she had had the house decorated expertly and fairly expensively, then let it be. He couldn't recall a single adjustment she had made from the time the decorators left.

He could not call anyone yet, not even his sons. But he did have to locate Jill. She must have known something was up; she might know where Madeline had gone. It didn't matter where. He wouldn't follow her; she was too strong willed for that. But he had to know. He called Nancy Strother, to see if she knew where Jill was staying on her trip.

To his surprise, Tom answered.

"What are you doing at Nancy's, Son?"

There was no way for Tom to dissemble. "I'm seeing Nancy now, Dad. I hope you don't object. How was your trip?"

The words didn't mean anything to Vance. "Tom, ask Nancy if she knows where Jill is staying, if she has a number for her."

There was a pause, and Tom came back on. "Dad, she says that she doesn't know but that Madeline must. Can you ask her?"

"No, Son, I can't." He hung up, leaving Tom embarrassed and puzzled.

Vance went back into the library and sat in the big leather chair. The pain was deep. He truly loved Madeline, wanted her to be with him always, but he always knew that she had intended to leave someday. That's why she refused to marry him and refused to own any property with him. He wondered if she knew about Tom and Nancy, and how long that had been going on. As if he gave a damn. Tom was entitled to any happiness he could get out of life, and Vance hoped that Nancy would give him as good a twelve years as Madeline had given him.

"No one should ask for more." The words did not soothe him, but they did make a kind of cosmic sense to him. He had been lucky beyond belief for twelve years; now it was over.

He knew she would be OK. He wondered if it was another man. Probably so, probably someone fairly wealthy, able to buy her anything she needed. No, that wasn't right. She never cared about money. Someone interesting perhaps—it would not be difficult to find someone more interesting than him. An artist, perhaps, or a writer. Or maybe he was French, and she would return to France with him. That would be the best, for them both. A chance encounter would be difficult; it would be well if there was an ocean between them.

He put the Old Grandad down untasted on the table beside him. There was only one antidote for his pain, not whiskey, not sedatives, just work, and he had plenty of that to do in his briefcase. Boeing's big bomber was gaining steam, Bob Gross was asking him to come down to Lockheed to look at an unpiloted missile project, and North American was clamoring for his services. The one job that he really wanted, working with Jack Northrop on his jet flying-wing bomber, had never come about. Well, maybe he should give Jack a call and see if there was something he could do. Maybe he could get back more to test flying. There were a lot of new airplanes coming out, smaller jobs like the Johnson Rocket and the Globe Swift. It would be good to have a challenge, something to force him to concentrate.

He slapped the side of the leather chair with his hand. "My God, I miss her so." The phrase would become his mantra of pain, said over and over, usually under his breath, but not always. Occasionally he caught himself doing it at work and saw the fleeting expressions of sympathy on the faces of those who heard him.

THE PASSING SCENE

North Korea invades South Korea; MacArthur strikes back at In-chon; MiG-15 fighters appear; 1.5 million television sets sold in the United States; Einstein presents "General Field Theory"; Senator McCarthy hunts for Communists in government; Dr. Ralph Bunche wins Nobel Peace Prize.

CHAPTER ELEVEN

June 27, 1950, Palos Verdes, California

Vance pressed his finger gently to Jill Abernathy's lips, stopping her in mid-sentence. "Sorry, honey, listen to the radio."

They lay in each other's arms, transfixed by the news of the rapid progress of North Korea's invasion of South Korea. U.S. forces were already involved, and the United Nations had passed a resolution to provide assistance to South Korea.

"Do you think this could start another world war?"

"I hate to think so, but it might. After the Soviets quit blockading Berlin, I thought we had called their bluff. North Korea has to be backed by the Russians, and the Chinese, too. They never would have dared do this on their own."

With familiar conjugal accord, they kissed quickly and turned to dress. Jill had been in love with Vance almost from the day Madeline hired her. Six months after Madeline disappeared, Vance recognized Jill's affection and responded to it. By now his pain at Madeline's departure had eased to the point that he could accept the dreadful irony of Madeline selecting Jill as her replacement, for it was done as Madeline had done everything but leaving him—with good heart. For her part, Jill joked about it, calling herself a pinch-hitter.

Neither of them had a bad word to say about Madeline. They credited her for her good points, her business sense, and especially the way she had taken care of Vance and the house. Vance did not arrogate to Jill the financial responsibility he had given Madeline, not because he didn't trust her but because he knew it was outside of her interests.

In long conversations, deep in the night, they agreed that Madeline was somehow possessed by another calling and that she had known all along that her time with Vance would be limited. Both blessed her for being farsighted enough to bring Jill into the picture. Jill was delighted with the way things had worked out and worried only that Madeline might someday return. Neither of them believed she would, but as a safeguard, Vance asked Jill to marry him, and they had set the date as November 1. Both Tom and Harry were grateful for the turn of events, for their father had been desperately unhappy after Madeline's departure. They worried that his judgment might be affected so much that he would be dangerous flying.

Their own marital affairs were still in disorder. It was now clear to Harry that when he was away, as he was so much, Anna drank too much and probably fooled around when she did. He had no hard evidence as yet. If he did find out for certain that she was unfaithful, he was determined to divorce her. In considering it, he recognized in a clinical way that he could not in good conscience desert her if she had a drinking problem, but infidelity would be a justifiable cause. He knew this was a cynical view, for the two problems were intertwined. Still, he had a life to lead, and if she did not agree to some kind of psychiatric counseling, he felt he could divorce her in good conscience.

Tom was happy with Nancy, but the problems with Marie had spooked him and he was not eager to marry again. He was sorry that he was now flying on the opposite coast, but Nancy said she was willing to wait—at least for a while—until he felt comfortable with the idea.

As Vance and Jill dressed, he wondered what effect the war in Korea would have on his sons, both on active duty in the Air Force. Harry, a full colonel, was still all wrapped up in pushing aerial refueling and was preparing a flight of single-engine, single-seat Republic F-84s across the Atlantic. He was somewhat frustrated that the experiment was not using Boeing's new "flying boom" aerial refueling technique but instead a variation of Flight Refueling's hose system. Precious few bombers and only a handful of specially equipped fighters were equipped for boom refueling, but it was clearly the path to the future. Tom was still a captain, to his chagrin, but was happy flying as a flight leader in the 4th Fighter-Interceptor Wing.

Jill called Vance in to his usual bacon and egg breakfast, asking, "What will the boys do?" She had adopted the term "the boys" from Harry, although she was only ten years older than they were.

"They'll both volunteer for combat; that's certain. Tom says he has developed some new tactics for the F-86 he wants to try. As for Harry, I don't know. He'll try to get into F-86s, too, probably, but he might well wind up back in B-29s, because that's the airplane that will be doing the bulk of the bombing and he's an experienced bomber pilot."

"What about you?"

"You mean 'what about us'! We'll have a hell of a lot more business, of course. It's hard to believe how short the Air Force and the Navy are on airplanes, equipment, everything. We had huge air forces at the end of World War II, and have thrown them all away in just five years. Everything will have to be built back up, and it will take a couple of years to get going. There will be a big buying spree, just like the early 1940s. Then when the war's over, we'll junk everything again. It's a crazy world."

"How long will this war last?"

"The way it's going right now, it looks like they are going to throw us off the Korean peninsula, back to Japan. That will mean a long war, and we might have to use nuclear weapons. The Russians and the Chinese have so much manpower that we can never match them on the ground, division for division. The only hope is that they recognize the fact that we would be forced to use nuclear weapons, and back off."

He paused to look at her, wondering how Madeline could have got it so right. Jill was almost as tall as he but slender, with a volup-

tuous bosom that she covered decorously in the office but managed
to reveal when she worked around the house. But beyond her sensual
appeal, Jill exuded a sweetness that soothed Vance and everyone else.
A furious contractor could call on the phone, demanding some impossible results, and within minutes Jill would have him calmed
down, reasonable, and eating out of her hand. She was instinctively,
intuitively kind, in every instance, no matter the provocation. Once,
when a bank had charged her twenty-five dollars for a bounced
check, Vance had commented wryly on the bloodthirsty mercenari-
ness of banks. Jill immediately came back with a stout defense of the
banks, saying they had expenses, that people were careless, automatically bringing her inherent kindness into play.

She was not as efficient as Madeline. They both knew this, accepted it, and never mentioned it. Jill needed Nancy to complement
her, and they worked so well together that they decided not to replace the secretary Madeline had hired. She had left for a better job,
as did the two young engineering trainees, because Vance never had
time to train them and he didn't like having them hanging around
the office when Jill and Nancy were there.

September 22, 1950, over Labrador

THERE WERE FEW things worse than being an extra crewman on an
overcrowded bomber, high over the North Atlantic, hoping that an
experiment about which you had mixed emotions would succeed.

Cramped, cold, and hungry, his circulation cut off by the chest-
pack parachute harness, Colonel Harry Shannon sat in the rear end
of a Boeing YKB-29T tanker, waiting for two Republic F-84 Thunderjet fighters to appear from the mists that seemingly covered the
entire ocean.

The lead Thunderjet was flown by the legendary Colonel David
Schilling, once again the commander of the Wolf Pack, the 56th
Fighter Wing. Leading the same outfit in World War II, flying Republic P-47 Thunderbolts, Schilling had shot down twenty-two and
one-half German aircraft and destroyed ten and one-half on the

ground. Forceful, charismatic, and a leader who led by doing, he was now somewhere over the lonely Atlantic in a single-engine jet, accompanied by his wingman, Lieutenant Colonel William D. Ritchie.

The two men were engineering rivals to Harry Shannon, for both had pushed for the probe-and-drogue refueling system, and Schilling had even worked with Flight Refueling Limited to create a special refueling hose. Schilling had devised a means by which a hydraulic valve in the refueling hose was closed at all times except when a fighter's wing- or nose-mounted probe entered it and the receiver pilot triggered a switch on his control stick to open it.

Harry had nothing against probe-and-drogue refueling except that it represented a dead end to him. Boeing was making tremendous progress with their flying boom. It now had a delivery rate of 700 gallons per minute, three times the amount that could be passed through a hose. But his boss, Al Boyd, had assigned him to the YKB-29 to watch the operation and see what conclusions could be drawn.

Schilling and his wingman had departed RAF Manston, near the Dover Strait, some nine hours before. They had already refueled twice by civil Flight Refueling Limited aircraft. The first, a Lancaster, refueled them near Prestwick, Scotland, while the second, an Avro Lincoln, the Lancaster's successor, had met them over Iceland. According to radio reports, both refuelings had gone off smoothly.

With the Korean crisis building, the mass transfer of fighters was essential, and if it could be done with aerial refueling it might tip the balance. Things were different from World War II days. There was no time to build up forces and there were not enough fighters to go around, not enough cargo ships to put them on, and not enough bases to prepare them for combat. With in-flight refueling they could be flown to the combat area ready to enter combat when they arrived.

Schilling was a go-getter, and while he saw advantages to the flying boom in the long run, he knew that a probe-and-drogue system could be fitted sooner to more fighters—if it worked at high altitudes and at the speeds the jets flew.

Harry and Schilling had planned the mission for days. There

were no arguments, Schilling understood Harry's point of view on the flying boom, and he understood Schilling's desire to get more equipment sooner. Both men realized that it was dangerous enough to fly a single-engine jet across the Atlantic, where chances for survival after an ejection were virtually nil. To do so with a fairly fragile probe-and-drogue refueling system upped the hazard. Fatigue would be a big factor, because flying a jet for eleven hours, much of it on instruments, and doing three in-flight refuelings in the process was exhausting. Yet the payoff would be enormous if it succeeded, and that is what Schilling sought—a quick payoff that would translate into use in the Korean War.

The refueling equipment operator nudged him, then pointed to the stiletto-slim lines of two F-84s emerging from a bank of cirrus clouds, each one fitted with a probe on its left wing.

Harry had his own checklist and he followed the process, mentally monitoring each step in the procedure. The two F-84s slowed to the tanker speed and pulled in position behind it, Schilling in the lead, Ritchie to his left and rear.

The refueling hose streamed out, led by the feathery-looking drogue, an aerodynamic basket that stabilized the hose and held Schilling's new hydraulic shutoff valve. The refueling operator declared the system ready and Schilling moved in, inserting the probe in the drogue on his first attempt. He pressed the switch on his stick and the valve opened, with fuel flow beginning immediately. Harry could see the skill Schilling was using, flying formation so perfectly that there was no loss of time or motion. When his tanks were topped off, Schilling broke away, and the hydraulic valve automatically shut off the flow of fuel.

It was Ritchie's turn. He moved in with the same precision Schilling had used, but when he depressed the control button on his stick, the valve did not open. Ritchie backed off and came in again, twice.

In a very calm voice, Ritchie called, "That's it, gang. I'm out of ideas. I'll climb with the fuel I have left, and glide toward Goose Bay for as long as I can, then eject. Please see if you can get some rescue aircraft out to me. So long."

The tanker's aircraft commander came back, "Roger, good luck, we'll get them out ASAP."

Inside the Thunderjet, Ritchie began a careful climb, trying to trade his fuel for as much altitude as possible. As he rose toward 36,000 feet, he adjusted his parachute harness and made sure his helmet straps were tight. When his engine flamed out from lack of fuel he called, "Flameout. I'm starting my glide west." There was a faint "Roger" in his headset, from either the YKB-29 or, he hoped, the Goose Bay rescue people.

The overcast began at 34,000 feet, and as the F-84 slipped earthward Ritchie began the procedures that would take him as far as possible. In the incredible silence, he quickly checked that the throttle was closed, the fuel tank selector was off, and the landing flaps and speed brakes were up.

Ritchie wiped his eyes. The rush of moisture over the canopy seemed to blur his vision, but when he focused on the instrument panel, dimly but adequately lit, he knew it was an illusion.

He hit the switch jettisoning his tip tanks and was glad to see them both depart—the last thing he needed now was a hung tank. The aircraft was eerily quiet as he trimmed it to its best glide speed of 220 mph. He knew he could glide for about thirteen miles for every 5,000 feet of altitude. He was passing 30,000 feet now, so he was good for about eighty miles before he would have to eject. That would put him eighty miles closer to Goose Bay and eighty miles farther away from the cold, dark waters of the North Atlantic.

Ritchie hoped that he had a good battery to keep his electric-powered instruments and radio operational. He focused on the instruments, continuing to ignore the continuous rush of gray moisture that sloshed over his canopy like water from a hose. After that last faint "Roger" there had been no responses to his radio calls, or if there had been he had not heard it. It didn't matter; he could only glide smoothly down to 3,000 feet, then pray that his ejection seat worked. En route he worked out a sequential prayer process. If the ejection seat worked, he could pray that his parachute opened; if the parachute opened, he could pray he was over land; if he was over water, he could pray his poopy suit, the massive rubber survival suit required for over-water flights, would work and not upend him, head down in the cold, dark sea. And most of all, he would pray that the rescue teams could find him.

At 3,000 feet, still in the soup, he ejected, the red bang of the ejection seat pyrotechnic lighting up the sky beneath him, hurling him up and out of the cockpit with a spine-compressing jolt that disoriented him momentarily. His helmet and oxygen mask were torn off in the rush of wind, but he separated easily from the seat, pulled his ripcord, and started his third set of prayers. So far all had worked and when he looked down between his legs he saw a welcome snowy landmass below.

The touchdown was hard, and the wind caught his chute, pulling him along like a sled until he managed to hit the quick-release button and separate from the canopy. Then, cold, alone in the middle of nowhere in Labrador, he said a final thank-you prayer.

Ritchie went through all the survival routines, gathered in his chute, dug a little cave in the snow, dried off his equipment, and began what he knew could be a long and perhaps terminal wait.

Two hours later he heard his rescuers calling using his name. He had made it to within nineteen miles of the huge base at Goose Bay, and radar had tracked his airplane down to 3,000 feet. He was grateful that they had wasted no time.

Harry's KB-29 was still en route back to its base when the news came that Schilling had landed successfully at Limestone and that Ritchie had been picked up, alive and well. The first single-engine jet had flown non-stop across the Atlantic, thanks to aerial refueling. Harry snuggled down in a stack of parachutes and began to think about the logistics of moving an entire wing of aircraft, not just across the Atlantic but across the Pacific. It would be a monumental effort, but the time and money it would save would be incredible. A capability like that would have the effect of multiplying the Air Force by three or four times, with only a relatively minor increase in the number of tanker aircraft. The plans were forming in his head when he drifted off to sleep.

December 1, 1950, Suwon Air Base, Korea

ON THE PRECEDING November 11, Mahoney stopped Tom Shannon as he walked toward the operations section, saying, "Tom, mandatory pilot meeting at ten o'clock. See you there."

He waited in the big briefing room with about fifty others from the First when the familiar call to attention—"Ten-shun"—rang out, and there was tension aplenty as Mahoney strode down the aisle. Tom knew this was serious business from the expression on his face.

"Men, this is it. We are departing tomorrow at one AM for Korea. Our planes will be flown to the coast and ferried over on a carrier. We will go as a group to Travis Air Force Base, and be flown over in Military Airlift Command airplanes. Pack everything you need, because I understand we'll be living under pretty primitive conditions for a while."

When the buzz died down, Mahoney went on. "As you know, the Chinese and the Soviet Union are backing the North Koreans. They are using a brand-new Soviet fighter, the MiG-15. It's about the same size and performance as the F-86, and it's better than anything we have in Korea or in Japan now. They are shooting the hell out of our B-29s, and we're going to stop them."

The trip over was the usual amalgam of hurry up and wait, made easier by the continuous poker games played in the air and on the ground. It was November 23 when they finally reached Japan, and Tom was three hundred dollars poorer than when they had left. Word came that it would be another two weeks before their airplanes arrived and a week after that before they would be ready to fly. Word was wrong; the F-86s had been placed on carrier decks and suffered badly from corrosion. Magnesium had been used in the construction of the wings, elevators, and rudders of the F-86 to save weight, but wherever it was riveted to aluminum, the dissimilar metals reacted to the salt spray and corroded. Of the seventy-five Sabres shipped over, only thirty-two would be airworthy when they arrived. This meant a lot of Sabre pilots would be milling around, waiting for the repairs.

Tom was on his way to the mess hall when he heard his name being called over the base loudspeaker system. As he stopped to listen, a tall, bandy-legged pilot grabbed his arm. He was a major or a lieutenant colonel; his flying suit insignia was so dirty, Tom couldn't tell.

"Are you Captain Tom Shannon?"

"Yes, sir. What can I do for you?"

"Captain Shannon, I'm Lieutenant Colonel Howard Fisher. I've got amended orders for you right here in my hand. You are now a member of the 7th Fighter Squadron, 49th Fighter Group. Grab your bags and meet me at Flight Ops; we are going directly to Korea."

Tom looked at the orders, checking the serial number to see if there was a mistake. There wasn't. He saluted, turned, and trotted into his barracks. Mahoney wasn't around, so Tom left a note on his bunk explaining what had happened and asking him to recall him as soon as the airplanes were ready. Forty-five minutes later he was sitting on a cold steel bucket seat in the back end of a grimy C-47.

Fisher showed up at the last minute and slid into the seat beside him, carefully placing his chest-pack parachute on the floor at his feet. He grinned at Tom and said, "Just like the Royal Navy, eh, the way they used to impress sailors. I picked up five pilots today, and we need every one of them."

Tom looked around—they were the only pilots in the back of the C-47; the rest of the people were enlisted personnel, mechanics, judging by their toolboxes.

Fisher saw the look and said, "I've sent them on ahead, this morning. Yours was the first name on my list, but I couldn't find you anywhere. I had the loudspeaker going, but I guess you didn't hear me."

Fisher put his legs out in the aisle, shoved a ditty bag behind his head, closed his eyes, and fell asleep. He didn't wake up until the C-47 made the first of its four bounces landing at K-13, Suwon Air Base, South Korea.

Yawning, Fisher unsnapped his safety belt, said, "I needed that," and asked, "How much time do you have in the F-80?"

"F-80" still sounded unusual to Tom; they had changed the designations of fighters from "P" to "F" in June 1948, but he still thought of it as the P-80.

Tom thought for a moment. "Maybe three or four hours. Not much."

"Well, you must have had some time in the T-bird?"

"About the same."

"Well, don't worry; I'll give you two hours in the F-80 before we go on a mission. It's a piece of cake after flying the F-86."

A wet wind accelerated the biting cold, and Tom was grateful when a helpful sergeant directed him to his new home, a bunk in a twelve-person squad tent, canvas on wooden frames, with wooden doors. A tiny coal-burning stove flickered, trying vainly to make up its mind whether it was there to warm or asphyxiate the pilots. He stored his few possessions in an ammunition box that stood on end by the bunk. Fisher came in and took him to dinner at the mess hall—two Quonset huts joined together.

Fisher smiled at him. "The food's pretty bad, but you'll get used to it. Breakfast is the best meal of the day; for some reason they are able to get real eggs here, not the powdered kind. We usually have sandwiches brought down to the flight line while we are refueling and rearming, and then if things cool down a bit, get a late supper. By then we're so hungry it doesn't matter how bad it is."

Tom nodded and kept silent, wolfing down a helping of stew that Dinty Moore would have refused, knowing that he shouldn't inquire about the source of the few pieces of stringy meat.

At 0700 the next morning, Tom ruefully checked his equipment. He'd been issued a brain bucket, a helmet so old that it had adhesive tape stretched over the cracks and rubber pads torn from some insulating material as cushions.

Fisher put him in the cockpit of an F-80, showed him where the various switches were and how to start the engine, then got down and ran to his own waiting airplane. They took off in formation, and Fisher took him for a quick tour of the local area, then signaled that they would go back in and land.

"You can handle it OK. Let's go do an hour on the gunnery range, and I'll put you down for this afternoon's missions."

Tom swallowed and remembered one of the things his dad used to tell him and Harry. It was, "If you are in a new organization, keep your mouth shut and your eyes open for at least three months. Listen to everything your boss says, and don't volunteer any ideas unless they ask you specifically for them. After three months, you'll be one of the boys, and you'll get along."

The gunnery session went well—Tom had always been an expert at gunnery, especially deflection shooting, and when they came back from the range Fisher complimented him. "You did good, Shannon. Just remember tomorrow you'll be a lot heavier than we are today, so don't get frisky too soon."

They ate sandwiches—pink Spam, white bread, and yellow mustard—as Fisher briefed him on the first mission.

"Good mission coming up. The North Koreans have a column of Russian T-34 tanks moving up to the line. The only way we can hurt them is to concentrate on the turret—if you do it just right, you can open it up with the six .50-caliber guns. If you don't, maybe the next guy will. Don't bother to shoot at their tracks or try to hit their fuel tanks or anything. Just chip the turret open, and the slugs going inside ricochet around enough to kill the crew and start a fire."

"We can do that with fifties? The Germans had a hell of a time working on the T-34s with 37mm cannon."

"Yeah, and I wish we did, too, but what we've got is six fifties, and if you use 'em like I said, you'll be surprised. They put out a lot of lead, and the turret top is the only weak point for us. Try it; you'll see."

The first mission, a flight of four, took off at one o'clock. Fisher, in Red One, led the way directly to the map coordinates where the T-34s were supposed to be on the move. Even though heavily loaded, the F-80 was a pleasure to fly, especially when Tom remembered his days in the Grumman Wildcat.

Fisher rocked his wings and Tom saw the tanks at once, eleven big, lumbering T-34s with infantrymen crowded on top and with clouds of dust spraying out from the tracks. They were well spaced out, with perhaps two hundred yards between them, but the narrow road ran between steep hills, leaving the tanks nowhere to go except forward or in reverse.

Fisher set up a firing pattern and called, "We'll attack in elements of two. Red One will take the lead tank; Red Two takes the last tank; Red Three and Four work over the tanks in the middle as we come back for another pass."

Tom was Red Two and he lagged behind Fisher a bit to let him make his attack. He followed Fisher down, picked up the turret of the last tank, a mud gray and green monster, carrying a circled red star insignia. The infantry spilled away like a broken necklace losing beads, diving for cover in the shallow ditches beside the road.

Tom's first slugs hit the turret, popping it off like a beer-bottle cap. He flew past the tank, then climbed back to pattern altitude. As he turned he could see that Fisher had stopped his tank, too. It was billowing smoke and as Tom leveled out to set up the next pattern he saw it blow up. The other nine tanks were trapped. The damn fifties worked!

Fisher led him out wide, assessing the damage that Red Three and Four were doing. Another one of the tanks was smoking, and the rest moved to find whatever cover they could. Two T-34s drove into houses by the side of the road. The structures collapsed around them, giving no concealment but perhaps making the tankers feel better. In the meantime the infantry were flat on their backs firing their rifles and machine guns, setting up the wall of lead through which they would fly in the next minute.

"Red Two, I'll take the tanks at the far end; you work the rear again."

Tom double-clicked his mike button to acknowledge and rolled in. This time his guns seemed to have no effect—he was battering the turret, but nothing happened—and he pulled up, looking back in time to see Jim Miller in Red Three fly directly into a tank, disappearing in a boiling ball of black smoke and red flame.

Fisher said, "They've got a 20mm flak battery set up at about the middle of the run. I'm going after it; you work the tanks over again. This will be our last pass; we're getting short on fuel."

The flak battery disappeared in the hail of Fisher's six .50-caliber guns, and Tom torched another tank. Red Four joined up with them and they flew back to Suwon in silence.

After they had debriefed, Fisher said, "Well, Tom, what do you think about your first mission?"

"I'm sorry we lost Miller; I'm not sure exchanging a pilot and an F-80 for four or five T-34s is good business."

"It's not, Tom, except that it's the only business that is keeping the North Koreans out of Pusan. If we don't stop them, they'll push the South Koreans and the Americans into the sea."

"That's true, I know. But there has to be a better way. This is no different than World War II, and not much different than World War I. It doesn't make sense to fight an attrition war against countries that don't care if their people are killed."

The missions assumed a regular tempo over the next few days, and not all of them were so costly. They were operating off pierced-steel plank runways. When the armament load included either one-thousand-pound bombs or napalm, the ordnance would sometimes scrape against the steel runway, sending a shower of sparks back. When heavily loaded, the F-80s could have used another thousand feet of runway for safety. Instead, the runway led to a riverbed, usually dry, but quite wide after heavy rains. Beyond the riverbed was a sheer drop of about eighty feet and on another half mile was the beginning of the ridgeline that looked like a barricade when Tom was sitting on the end of the runway, running up full power and waiting for clearance to go. He picked out a little dip in the ridge that lined up pretty well with the departure heading. Sometimes, if the weather warmed just a little, he'd find himself flying right through the dip, unable to coax any more altitude out of the F-80's wheezing jet engine. There were lots of accidents. In February the USAF announced that it had lost 221 planes in Korea—but only 10 of them in combat. The rest were accidents because flying went on whatever the weather or the experience of the pilots.

The 7th Squadron operated on a simple premise: if you were past the front lines, you shot at anything that moved. Sometimes they would catch a convoy of trucks in the open, and just shoot the hell out of them. If Tom was lucky, some of the trucks would be carrying ammunition or fuel and set off secondary explosions. All too often, though, the trucks would be a setup for a flak trap and the

Chinese would throw everything at them, 20mm, 37mm, and 57mm, all in a furious barrage that seemed impenetrable but which in fact rarely hit anyone.

What finally hit him was considerably smaller. Tom came back from a mission dying from thirst, his mouth cottony from the tension. Drenched in sweat that he could feel freezing on him, he jogged toward the operations shack where they would debrief. En route he diverted a hundred feet to get to the mess hall, where he knew they kept a jug of purified drinking water. It always tasted of chlorine, but they kept it cold, and he had just finished one glass and started on another when a cook ran out and yelled, "Stop—we haven't purified that water yet."

It was too late. From late that afternoon on, Tom wished he'd been shot or had some other relatively pleasant accident as the diarrhea took hold. Eighteen days later and weighing thirty-two pounds less, he was sent back to Japan to recuperate. Score: Korean E. Coli 1, Tom Shannon 0.

Red Chinese retake Seoul; Seoul recaptured; General MacArthur relieved of command; peace treaty signed with Japan; Albert Schweitzer wins Nobel Peace Prize; Julius and Ethel Rosenberg sentenced to death; Jersey Joe Walcott knocks out Ezzard Charles.

CHAPTER TWELVE

October 23, 1951, Korea

*H*arry's seemingly endless flight from Wright-Pat to Kadena Air Base, Okinawa, was Kafkaesque with its interminable delays, cancellations, sudden departures, and catalog of maintenance problems. There was only one way to react without going crazy, and that was passive acceptance, using the downtime to read his B-29 manuals, and when the incessant WARNING, CAUTION, and EMERGENCY notices began to bore him, he would switch to the pack of paperback Kenneth Roberts novels he carried with him. When he was not reading, Colonel Harry Shannon thoughtfully considered the Korean War and his contributions to it, which, to date, could only be called not much. While Tom had covered himself with glory flying F-80s, Harry had been stuck with non-combat jobs that he hated even though he knew intellectually that they were important.

Harry had irritated his boss, Al Boyd, with constant requests for combat duty, and he volunteered for F-84s, F-86s, and B-29s. Each time his request had been turned down. Now he was on his way to combat at last—assigned as an observer, in a B-29 that had been pulled out of storage, refurbished, and manned by a crew of reservists who vastly resented being called back to war. Fortunately, the 307th Bomb Wing commander was an old friend and, instead of making Harry fly in a jump seat, checked him out as a copilot. The 307th was shorthanded, and with Harry's long experience in bombers, it made sense, even though it contravened at least twenty Strategic Air Command directives.

His job was straightforward enough; he was to fly with B-29s out of Kadena and assess the threat of MiG-15 attacks when the bombers were escorted by fighters. Unescorted bombers no longer could operate in the regions where the MiG-15 appeared, and whether the F-80s, F-84s, and relatively few F-86s could defend against them was uncertain.

The MiG-15 had come as a tremendous surprise to the USAF, though it should not have, for the Soviet Union had proudly debuted the airplane at Moscow's Tushino Airdrome air show in 1948. What was even more surprising was the massive numbers of the airplane in the theater, an estimated 450 all told, compared to fewer than seventy operational F-86s. The nature of the war and the geography gave the MiGs an almost unassailable advantage, for they could operate out of Soviet and Chinese territory with impunity, while the U.S. aircraft had to be careful not to intrude across the North Korean borders.

There was a mystery about who was actually doing the fighting. All of the MiG-15s were manufactured in the Soviet Union, and they were allegedly furnished to the North Koreans by the Red Chinese. But many of the aircraft encountered in combat still bore the markings of operational Soviet units. Rumor had it that most of the airplanes were flown by Soviet pilots, for the intercepted radio transmissions were generally in Russian. There was also a report, possibly apocryphal, of a MiG-15 pilot ejecting close enough to be observed by the F-86 pilot who had shot him down. In the story, the MiG pilot had long flowing blond hair.

The initial attack on June 25, 1950, had carried North Korean forces to the Pusan Perimeter, where they were halted by a tough defense, a lack of supplies, and the interdiction of their supply lines by the American Far Eastern Air Force. In September, General of the Army Douglas MacArthur had launched his brilliant but risky invasion at Inchon. The overextended North Korean Forces had fallen back past the Thirty-eighth Parallel, streaming toward the border with China. The People's Republic of China announced that if the pursuit was continued, it would intervene. General MacArthur discounted this, and the UN forces were totally surprised when hundreds of thousands of Red Chinese soldiers swept across the Yalu and once again drove the UN forces back down the peninsula, threatening to throw them into the sea. Airpower, ruthlessly applied, saved the day. The front was stabilized, and the UN forces advanced again under the cover of airpower, to a point almost coincident with the Thirty-eighth Parallel.

The air war was just like the ground war—an up and down battle—but while the ground war eventually bogged down after several massive military defeats had been inflicted on the Red Chinese forces, the air war continued at a hectic pace. Now the ground war was heating up again, as the Red forces massed for another attack intended to drive the UN forces into the sea. The Red Chinese army, far from being an undisciplined horde, fought according to Soviet tactics, employing artillery and manpower en masse and ignoring casualties. The only means to stop them was airpower, choking off their supplies and rendering them incapable of a sustained offensive.

The B-29s bore the brunt of the long-range bombing, with Douglas B-26 Invaders handling the night interdiction. But the November 1950 introduction of the MiG-15 fighter spelled the end of American air dominance. The guns of the B-29 were not capable of tracking the swift 600 mph MiGs, and casualties were growing. Neither the F-80 nor the F-84 was useful as an escort fighter, and only one tactic would serve, bottling up the MiGs with enough F-86s to keep them in place. The problem was that the B-29s had to keep bombing even though there were still not enough F-86s on hand to do the job.

Shannon did not like being a copilot, not after years in the left seat of a B-17, but his pilot, Carl Chance, was capable and friendly. The rest of the crew accepted Harry, because of his experience with B-17s. For the first time in months, his conscience was letting up on him. He was in combat where he was needed, and he was being depended upon not only to do the copilot's duties but also to make a perceptive analysis of an unacceptable situation: American air inferiority.

Today's mission was eleven hours round-trip to strike the Namsi Airfield, where a buildup of both jet fighters and piston engine attack aircraft had been seen. Eight B-29s were tasked with the mission, flying in two flights—Able and Baker—of four. Shannon was in the lead ship of Able Flight. On paper their escort looked formidable, with thirty-four F-86s ranging out in front and fifty-five F-84 fighter-bombers joining in the mission.

Based on his World War II experience, Shannon approved of the tactics, developed by the ace Hub Zemke in World War II. Using what was called the Zemke Fan, the F-86s would stay out in front of the B-29s so that they could disrupt any MiG attack on the B-29s before it began.

Even though the B-29 was pressurized and possessed what was laughingly called a heating system, the cold was piercing at 25,000 feet, and Shannon pounded his hands together to try to keep feeling in them. Chance waved to get his attention and pointed up to the two o'clock position. A positive wall of MiG-15s, at least one hundred, maybe more, was falling out of the sky, between the F-86s and the B-29s, cutting the Sabres off and isolating the bombers and the F-84s.

Chance's distinctive southern voice came through the intercom: "OK, we're at the Initial Point. We'll be straight and level until bombs away, so you-all keep a sharp lookout; this looks like a setup."

There had been the brief flurry of intercom clicks to tell him he'd been heard when Shannon saw the trap sprung. Forty eight MiG-15s, in twelve flights of four, were cascading out of the sun straight for their formation—six MiGs for every B-29.

Shannon expected a head-on attack. Instead the MiGs formed a ring around the slow-moving formation of B-29s, F-80s, and F-84s, reminding him of the old Western films where the Indians circled the wagons. They made only one circuit before boring in, their 37mm cannon stuttering in the odd, almost comical way they had, the shells visible as a phosphorous blob arcing in, the 23mm cannon rattling faster.

The MiG attack came just at bombs away; to his right, Harry

saw a B-29 drop its bombs, start a slow turn, and blow up. Now the MiGs began a seesaw attack climbing to altitude, diving through the formation, and climbing back for another attack. The F-84s responded vigorously but lacked the speed to engage the MiGs, which brushed them aside almost contemptuously as they fired into the turning formation of bombers.

The B-29 gunners threw out an enormous amount of lead. He heard one claim a victory, but if it was true, it was an accident; the MiG had simply flown into the barrage of .50-caliber shells. As they neared the coast, a Baker Flight B-29 nosed out of the formation, heading for the sea, two engines burning, two engines turning. Shannon said a hurried prayer for them, his Catholic instructions suddenly welling up.

Then suddenly it was over; the MiGs departed and the skies were clear of enemy aircraft.

Harry had plenty of time to think on the long flight back to Okinawa and through the endless debriefing. The B-29 gunners claimed three MiGs and an F-84 pilot claimed another one, but Shannon doubted all of the claims. The B-29 gunners had put more slugs in the B-29s accompanying them than in enemy fighters, and the F-84s were simply outclassed.

He realized that it would have taken at least 150, perhaps 200 F-86s to fight off that many MiGs and there still would have been losses. The B-29s were clearly obsolete and would have to be relegated to night bombing to survive.

The irony was severe. The poorest major power in the world, China, had put as many as a thousand MiG-15 jet fighters, one of the best in the world, into the theater, with half that many ready for combat on any given day. The richest country in the world, the United States, had fewer than seventy-five F86s in the theater, and of these, only about half were ever operational at one time. Shannon guessed that Headquarters, USAF, thought that the threat of Russian bombers was greater than the threat from the MiGs. They might have been right, but that was no answer. The richest country in the world should be able to afford enough jet fighters for both jobs.

May 20, 1951, Suwon Air Base, Korea

TOM SHANNON BELIEVED that patience pays. He had flown fifty missions in F-80s, and while he never grew to love the aircraft the way he felt about the F-86, he respected it for the job it did. Now he was collecting his reward, back flying Sabres with the 4th Fighter-Interceptor Wing out of Suwon.

It's not that the missions were easy. The F-86s always had to fly up the length of the Korean peninsula to where the MiG-15s wanted to play. MiG Alley was a parallelogram of some sixty-five hundred square miles that stretched from the Korea Bay in the west to Hui-chon and from the Yalu River in the north to Sinanju. Up to five hundred MiGs operated out of several bases, with the principal complex of airfields centered around Antung, in Red China. The geography and the rules of engagement gave the MiGs a tremendous advantage, for they could take off and climb to altitude in Red China, where they were immune to attack. Then, at a time and place of their choosing, they could make a diving attack on a formation of F-86s and slice back across the Yalu to their sanctuary again.

Today the 4th was flying a standard fighter sweep over Sinuiju. Tom was at 27,000 feet, leading the second of four six-ship flights, a maximum effort for the F-86s. He hoped that the MiGs would attack; often they did not, making just a feint attack to force the F-86s to drop their auxiliary tanks.

Shannon felt an incredible sense of well-being. Unlike flying the F-80, where his mission was to take munitions to where they were most needed by the ground forces, here the mission was to kill MiGs, nothing more, nothing less. There was an adrenaline rush from knowing that he was flying the best fighter in the world, that he had six .50-caliber machine guns at his command, and that there was no enemy pilot who would survive an engagement with him. In short, he was feeling like a fighter pilot should feel.

As they started their second pattern of turns, Lieutenant Colonel Ben Emmett, leading the first flight, commanded, "Drop Tanks."

Elated at the coming combat, Tom hit the jettison switch, but only the left tank came off, spiraling away, while the right one stayed tight on his wing. He hit the switch again, but nothing happened.

The standing procedure was to depart combat, with your wingman, immediately, if a tank failed to jettison. The aircraft was suddenly far less maneuverable and the asymmetric weight and drag condition could cause real problems as you pulled high g-forces. Tom muttered, "Screw it," and continued turning, straight into the oncoming MiGs, firing as soon as they were in range. Miraculously, the two formations passed through each other without a mid-air collision, and Tom's wingman called, "Break, MiG at your six o'clock." Tom pulled the F-86 into a tight a turn as he could, given the tank he still retained, slid behind a MiG-15, and hosed it with all six of his guns. Parts flew off the MiG, the canopy departed, and the aircraft half-rolled into a dive straight toward the ground. He repressed a momentary urge to follow the plane down and make sure of it, but when he looked up he saw the remaining twenty-two Sabres mixing it up with at least fifty MiGs.

Leading his wingman to the extreme edge of the battle, Tom found six MiGs forming up for a dive on the encircled Sabres below. He burst right through their flight, turned, caught the lead MiG in his sights, and once again fired a five-second burst, sending about thirty-nine pounds of lead smashing into the enemy. The MiG blew up, and Tom moved to the next aircraft. They were lower and slower now, and as he began to fire, the MiG pilot ejected in panic.

Suddenly Tom was alone in the sky. His wingman had disappeared, so had the MiGs, and what Tom hoped was the rest of his unit was streaking away south. One look at his fuel gauges and he knew why. He started a climb to his optimum altitude, probably about thirty-two thousand feet, knowing he had just enough to get back to the base at Suwon if he flew conservatively, if the winds were favorable, and if no one had crashed on the runway. God, it felt good! Three MiGs down. That gave him twelve victories, counting the nine from World War II. He was no Rickenbacker or Jabara, but he was getting there. He had passed through 9,000 feet when he saw the MiG-15 letting down, heading for the Yalu River. Tom watched the "Ivan" gliding away, wings straight and level, probably thinking about his "*stogramoy,*" the one hundred grams of vodka he would knock back when he landed at Antung.

Tom glanced at the fuel gauge, winced, and glanced at the MiG again. This was how he liked it, no maneuvering, just slip in behind the airplane and kill it. Advancing power, he dove under the unsuspecting MiG and maneuvered behind him. He fired his remaining .50-caliber rounds into the MiG, in one ferocious sixty pounds of lead lump that tore the plane apart in a violent red and black explosion. Ivan probably never knew what hit him.

Another glance at the fuel gauge and it showed him down to five hundred pounds—roughly eighty gallons. Tom started a nervous climb, and when he got to 16,000 feet, he called in to the K-13 weather officer. He knew a knot of pilots would be gathered there, hanging around to listen to the fights, trying to visualize events from the rapid-fire radio calls that streamed in, determining from the pitch of the friends' voices how scared or how elated they were.

Somewhat to his surprise, Gordon Maxson, a friend from his days at Nellis came on saying, "Don't shoot them all down, Tom; leave some for us."

"Gordon, I'm low on fuel, and I need to know what the winds are. If there's much of a headwind, I can't make it back."

"Stand by one."

There was a minute's wait; Tom could imagine Maxson riffling through the weather data, checking for any pilot reports. He came back on, "Doesn't look good, Tom; you've got about a fifty-five-knot wind, quartering from the east. No help, a lotta hurt."

"Roger, thank you, Gordon. I'm not going to make it back to Kimpo, so I'll turn west, and try to land on the beach at Pen Yang Do."

Pen Yang Do was an island twenty-five miles out in the Sea of Japan. The "Dumbo" rescue aircraft, a Grumman SA-16 Albatross, usually orbited there.

Maxson came back, "Roger, Pen Yang Do."

Tom looked at his fuel gauge again, bumping toward empty. "That may be too far for me. Ask them to come in closer to the shoreline; I think I'll have to leave this bird pretty soon."

"OK. Stay on this frequency and let us know how things are going."

A few minutes later, at 11,000 feet, the engine flamed out. He kept the airspeed at 220 knots and flew as precisely as possible, trying to stretch the glide as far as possible. At 3,000 feet he called Maxson again.

"Gordon, I've cleared the coast; I'm about three thousand feet and I've got the Albatross in sight. I'm going to eject pretty soon."

"One second, Tom; there's a few guys here with something to say to you."

Ed Chalkley came on the horn and said, "Tom, you cheap bastard, you're just trying to get out of paying me the five bucks you owe me. You get your ass safe back home here!"

Another three or four guys came on with similar rough sentiments and Tom felt pretty good.

"Adios, you guys, I'm leaving now."

He reached down, unfastened his safety belt so that the windblast would rip the seat away, and pulled the ejection seat handle. The next instant was filled with pain and confusion as the canopy blew off and the ejection seat fired, compressing him down as he shot out of the aircraft, no longer a pilot but a projectile. Numb from the shock of the ejection, hoping he hadn't collapsed his spine, he kicked clear of the seat, deployed his parachute, and hit the water within a minute.

The icy water sent chills down him, but he got rid of his parachute canopy, inflated his dinghy, and crawled in.

The Dumbo had followed him down and was already taxing over to him. A rope line was fired from a big hatch in the rear fuselage, and Tom grabbed it, pulling himself close enough to the plane for two crewmen to help him up into the opening. As soon as he was aboard, the SA-16 started moving forward. His mind went back to the Catalina that had rescued him off Guadalcanal, and the image was heightened as a North Korean shore battery began lobbing shells out toward the Grumman. He turned to the grinning airman and said, "Two wars, two bailouts, two rescues. Not a bad average."

The whole 4th Fighter-Interceptor Wing had been monitoring

his radio calls and there was a huge celebration going on when the Albatross put down its wheels and landed at Suwon.

Tom's heart sank when he saw the wing commander, Colonel John Meyer, waiting for him. Meyer was tough; he had twenty-four victories in World War II against the Germans and had shot down two MiG-15s in Korea. He was a disciplinarian who demanded that rules be followed, and he obviously had heard from others about Shannon engaging in combat when his tip tank wouldn't jettison.

"Captain Shannon, you know what the rules are about a hung tank, don't you?"

Tom mumbled, "Yes, sir," and Meyer was into a five-minute tirade about discipline, rules, safety, and ego. His face grew red and his neck veins bulged as he leaned into Tom, his finger jabbing him in the chest. Then, abruptly, he finished with, "But seeing that you got four confirmed kills, I'm not going to court-martial you; I'm putting you in for a Distinguished Flying Cross. You are dismissed."

Tom saluted and turned to head for the bar, thinking, *That makes thirteen. Boy, this is really going to burn Harry up.* He got about twenty feet before the medics reached him to take him off for X-rays, standard procedure after an ejection.

April 15, 1952, Boeing Field, Seattle

CONSTRUCTION OF THE XB-52 and YB-52 had taken place in a restricted area of the Boeing plant, where the workers were all veterans with top security clearances. The two planes were virtually identical, the difference in their designation coming only as a funding ploy that allowed $10 million in production funds to be spent on the prototypes.

Superficially similar in appearance to the B-47, the prototype B-52s were much larger, with a 185-foot wingspan, eight Pratt & Whitney YJ57-P-3s, placed in four nacelles of two engines each, and a strange-looking undercarriage, four trucks of two wheels each. The wings had a thickened wing root that both decreased weight and increased fuel capacity. The cockpit used tandem seating, as in the B-47, but General LeMay had insisted that a conventional side-by-side cockpit be used and the production aircraft were already re-designed to accommodate his wishes.

The airplane would have flown in 1951, but in November of that year the XB-52's pneumatic system had suffered a massive fail-ure, blowing out the entire rear section of the wing. The incident had forced Boeing to put in a hurry-up call to Vance Shannon to come in and advise on the redesign that was incorporated in the YB-52 and subsequent aircraft.

The super-secret security surrounding the airplane disappeared the week prior to April 15, as Boeing public relations gave newspa-pers advance notice of the first flight. The hillside east of Boeing Field and all the perimeter streets were jammed with spectators, anxious to see what the future held for Boeing and Seattle. To them the aircraft represented jobs, careers, new cars, and house payments—and also the defense of the United States.

Shannon was in the privileged group watching the first-flight crew, Tex Johnston and Lieutenant Colonel Guy Townsend, go through their methodical preparations. Johnston's career had fol-lowed Shannon's by about ten years but had closely paralleled it in many ways. The amiable but sometimes tempestuous Johnston had made many first flights and also flown racers at Cleveland, winning the Thompson Trophy race in 1946. Townsend had been vital in the B-47 program and was credited with selling the airplane to the top brass of the Air Force.

Everyone who had participated in the famous 1948 Dayton "weekend at the Van Cleve" when the proposal for the B-52 had been created was on hand. Vance's job was done, and he asked Vaughn Blu-menthal, the aerodynamicist, how he thought things would go.

"Vance, there's only one thing I'm worried about, and I think we took care of it. The ailerons are so big, I was afraid that they might overbalance and perhaps flutter at higher airspeeds. So we've rigged the control forces to be very high, and set the pickup point for the spoilers at about forty-five degrees of control movement."

"That should avoid the problem, all right, but won't it make it tough to handle?"

"That's what Johnston gets paid for, handling. I get paid for making sure it doesn't come apart in flight."

All the conversation dwindled as the YB-52 moved down toward the end of the runway, moving its nose from left to right, as if it were a ludicrously huge hound dog sniffing the wind, as Johnston checked the crosswind landing gear. After the check, he caused a collective gasp from the spectators by allowing the aircraft to move sideways down the taxiway, compensating for the slight crosswind. Lightly loaded at 225,000 pounds, the wingtip outriggers were well above the ground. Shannon had seen fully loaded taxi tests when the wings drooped so that the wheels rolled along the ground, keeping them from touching it.

The takeoff began with a ground-shaking run up to 100 percent power on all eight of the 9,000-pounds-of-thrust engines, with black smoke pouring out behind in a torrent. Then Johnston released the brakes, and the YB-52 jumped forward, accelerated rapidly, lifting off at 11:08 AM to begin its climb for the flight to Larson Air Force Base at Moses Lake, Washington, where additional testing would be done.

Shannon turned to George Schairer, who stood watching the aircraft, still visible from its trailing plumes of black smoke. "Well, George, you are off to a good start. How many of these things do you think you'll build?"

"Well, we're building lots of B-47s and they'll be around for a while. I figure we'll build a couple of hundred B-52s, at least. They should stay in the inventory for ten years, maybe fifteen, so we'll have a good aftermarket for modifications and parts."

That night Vance heard the story about Johnston's landing at Moses Lake. The YB-52 had flown for three hours and eight minutes, probably a record for a first flight, with Johnston and Townsend checking every system in the aircraft before making a first landing attempt at Larson. They were well down on final when a scramble of Air Defense Command interceptors forced a go-around. On the second attempt they landed smoothly, Townsend deployed the brake parachute, and the aircraft came to a halt before a crowd of awestruck military leaders and plant officials.

In the debriefing room, the Boeing and Air Force engineers were surprised to find that the enthusiasm of both Johnston and Townsend was guarded. After most first flights, the test pilots are exuberant, and it's rare that the airplane is not called the best they had ever flown. But both Johnston and Townsend seemed fatigued. One of the engineers, Paul Demchak, asked Johnston, "Well, what do you think is needed?"

Johnston, deadpan, replied, "New flight suits."

Nonplussed, Demchak asked, "New flight suits? I thought you had new flight suits."

And Johnston shot back, "If we are going to have to manhandle this son of a bitch around, we're going to have arms bigger than our legs, and we'll need new flight suits."

Demchak took the point, passed the word to Blumenthal, and the aircraft was rerigged before its next flight.

Shannon knew how Johnston felt—and how Demchak felt, too.

September 3, 1952, Kimpo Air Base, Korea

THEY CALLED IT K-14, and as Major Tom Shannon stepped out from the C-54 transport and looked around, he could see very little improvement over his last base, K-13, some twenty-five miles due south. But it was soon evident that the American penchant for comfort had been working hard. The offices all seemed well equipped, the supply officer had a complete array of flight equipment, and there was even an Officers Club, just varnished plywood interior, decked out with photos and models, but still a cut above anything he'd experienced at Suwon.

The big difference, of course, was on the flight line, where gleaming new F-86Es had begun to replace the war-weary F-86As. There were now 127 F-86s operating in Korea. About half were here and the rest were with the 51st Fighter-Interceptor Wing based at his former base, Suwon. The Communists had perhaps five times that number of MiG-15s in the theater. Unaccountably, they had not sought air superiority, being content to engage the Sabres on favorable terms over MiG Alley. Still the threat was always there, and the Chinese continually built new airfields in Korea into which a formidable air force could be flown on an instant's notice. If the Reds seized air superiority and used airpower to back up their massive infantry and artillery, the UN troops would probably be rolled back down to Pusan—and maybe all the way into the sea.

As he stretched to rid himself of the cramped muscles from the flight, he thought, *I wonder what's wrong with me*. He had finished his last tour in Korea in January, returned to the United States, and married Nancy in February. He took her with him to Nellis and then to Williams Air Force Base near Phoenix, where he had instructed in gunnery. She had been completely happy until he told her he had volunteered for a third tour in Korea.

That evening would play forever in his mind, for although he had felt like a jackass many times before, the evening brought him to a new height—or depth—in the realm of jackasses. They were getting ready for dinner, and Nancy had prepared London broil, one of his favorites, on the little charcoal grill he'd bought. She was standing next to him, the platter of London broil hot off the grill in her right hand and an open bottle of Paul Masson Emerald Dry Riesling, her current favorite wine, in the left.

"Honey, I hope you'll understand, but I've got a chance to go back to Korea. It's my chance to command a squadron."

She hesitated for half a beat and said, "You are kidding, of course?"

"No. I hate to leave you, but I can't pass up this opportunity."

The grace that stood her so well on the dance floor now paid off in the swift movement of her hands, as the right dumped the London broil in his lap, her left deftly pouring the wine over his head.

Jumping up, he knocked the table over and, rebounding, fell backward over his chair. From the floor he pleaded, "Jesus, Nancy, there's no need for that."

"There's no need for anything, obviously, especially me. Well, I've got two little surprises for you. One is, I'm leaving, tonight. The other is that I'm pregnant, due in seven months." She stormed from the room, pausing at the door to say, "Marie had it right all along. I never should have slept with you, either."

For the next thirty minutes, sincerely contrite and utterly humble, he had been on his knees, pleading with her through the locked bedroom door, promising to get the orders canceled, begging her to stay. The door didn't open until the horn of a taxi sounded and she left, suitcase in hand. Her parting words were, "Well, you're some big ace; you've shot down thirteen planes and two wives."

Since then he had heard of her only through Jill, who told him that Nancy never opened any of his letters or telegrams, and threw out his flowers and presents without looking at them. Jill told him frankly that he was the biggest jerk in history, and so did his father, who sided entirely with Nancy. Even Harry, who normally supported him no matter what he did, now took Nancy's side and told him so.

Harry told him, "Dad feels like I do. You had a terrible experience with Marie, and now you are treating Nancy badly. She's pregnant, and just when she needs you most, you run away to play soldier again."

Tom knew that they were all correct, that he had acted badly, and that his was a sad and stupid case. But as he stood surveying the familiar scenery, the busy mechanics working on the jets, aircraft in the traffic pattern, and the unforgettable weird mixture of Korean farm odors and the scent of hot jet engine exhaust, he knew something else. He knew he had to be here, that this was his job, and sad and stupid as he might be, he was going to do it.

It was like coming home to be back with the 4th Fighter-Interceptor Wing, even though most of the people he had known before had rotated out. Where there were once mostly veterans of World War II, the 4th now had a large component of new pilots, fresh out of flying school, and compared to them, Tom felt he was an old man at thirty-four.

But he was an old man with experience and within the first week, even before he had flown his first combat mission, he had identified three major problems. The first he could not do much about—there were simply too few F-86s in the theater. The second was more worrisome, however, because even the low in-commission rate sapped the Sabre strength even more. Parts were in short supply, and the logistics train was endless. Requests for parts had to go through the chain of command, through Japan, Hawaii, and then back to the United States, where the depots, working as hard as they could, would try to fill the request and get it shipped back over. The problem was that requests were lost and others took four months or more. In the meantime, the worst thing for maintenance and morale went on—cannibalization of parts from one airplane to another. The third was the way the flights were flown. Too much time and, worse, too much fuel were used in assembly and cruise, making the few F-86s that were available to patrol MiG Alley even less effective.

Still, he was the new guy, and despite his four kills on his last tour and his thirteen total, he'd have to prove himself again. It was always that way—you came in as a new guy and were treated with formal respect and deference until it came to the flight assignments; then you were under suspicion until you proved yourself.

After his first three combat missions, he identified a fourth problem. His flight commander, Greg Frey, an affable major, didn't seem to be able to find his way into the fights they listened to on the radios. Tom heard the reports of engagement coming in, they all did, and Frey would lead them in one direction and then another, never quite finding where the combat was going on. When they got back to base, they'd hear the other squadrons talking over their fights and their kills, and Tom vowed that when he commanded a flight—and it would be soon, given his record—he would mix it up on every engagement. No more milling around, but straight to the sound of the guns—or at least to the sounds of the radio calls.

Two weeks later, Frey was rotated home after one hundred missions—and no kills. Since everyone, from the wing commander down, was satisfied with Tom's performance, he became fight commander and, like all good leaders, called a meeting of his flight immediately.

"Gents, we're changing tactics. So far, from what I've seen, we've been flying defensively. From now on it's going to be pure offensive flying. Instead of being spread out, like we've been doing, I want everybody closed up, with the wingmen close enough to read the itty-bitty numbers on the lead's tail. The flight leader—that's me—and the element leader, that's you, Mellinger, are going to be the shooters."

Captain George Mellinger looked pleased; he'd been a wing-man for twenty-six missions; now he was going to be a shooter. Tom continued, talking in short bursts, moving his hands to show what he meant, inoculating the other three with his enthusiasm.

"Greenberg, you are going to fly on my wing. We'll go out this afternoon and do some rat-racing and I'll show you what I mean." Marty Greenberg, a second lieutenant fresh out of Nellis, smiled, almost stunned with pleasure after getting the best job for a new guy in the squadron.

"And, last but far from least, Sam, I'd like you to fly George's wing."

Lieutenant Sam Norton snapped an informal salute, said, "Roger that; George has no worries now."

Pleased with their reactions, Tom went on. "We're going to try some new tactics as well. I want us to practice these before I ask per-mission to use them—I'm afraid I'll get turned down as some crazy new guy reinventing the wheel. If they work out, we'll have the data, and then try to persuade the CO to go along."

Tom wouldn't have dared to try this in most outfits, but the 4th FIW was commanded by Colonel Birch Matthews, a twenty-two-victory ace in World War II and one of the most respected airmen in the theater. Matthews's easygoing personality permitted him to al-low innovations even as he kept discipline fine-tuned for combat.

The first change Tom introduced was simple. In the past, the F-86s had joined formation over the field, then climbed as a unit to about 43,000 feet, then slowed to about Mach .84 until they were in the combat area. Tom had them take off and immediately begin clawing for altitude, forming up in the climb. Then, when they reached 43,000 feet, they flew at Mach .90. The difference was sub-tle but effective; they reached altitude with twenty minutes more fuel for combat, and when they reached the MiG Alley they were al-ready at speed, ready for combat.

Within two weeks, all four members of the flight had scored victories, with Greenberg's at the very end of a mission when they had run into one of the "Honchos," the experienced MiG pilots who knew how to fly and fight.

Shannon had led that attack, and the MiG had turned in to them, beginning a long duel that carried them down from 40,000 feet, turning in a spiral descent that brought them ever closer to the Yalu. All through the fight, Greenberg had, as usual, stayed glued to Shannon's wing. When the MiG broke to the left for a final run to the Yalu, Shannon called, "Marty, this one's yours. You do the shooting and I'll cover your tail."

"Roger, moving in."

Greenberg moved farther to the left, lined up the fleeing MiG in his sights, and fired a long burst that cut the fuselage in half right at the cockpit.

Shannon called, "You can stop firing now, Marty; congratulations. Let's go home."

The victory came long after the time when they formerly would have had to have left MiG Alley, using the old tactics. When Tom briefed Matthews on his new procedures, showing him the increased mission times, the CO adopted them for the entire wing.

The parts problem was not as easy to solve. Tom asked for and got additional duty as maintenance officer, and he pored over the requisitions, seeing how certain key parts—generators, thermocouples, IFF (identification, friend or foe) boxes, radios, slats, and other hard-used items, went on the requisition lists—and stayed there for weeks and months. Even ridiculously routine items, such as washers, nuts, and bolts, were scarce. Every once in a while, a C-54 would drop out of the sky from Japan and off-load a seemingly random selection of parts, never enough to bump up the in-commission rate, which was down to a miserable 68 percent of the F-86s in commission on average. If the figure fell to 50 percent or below, the war in MiG Alley would be over—there wouldn't be enough Sabres to do battle.

Over the next week, even the combination of dedicated mechanics and the marvelous technical representatives—tech reps—

from North American, working night and day, began to lose the battle, and the in-commission rate dropped down to 57 percent.

Shannon called in John Henderson, the hardworking North American tech rep, and asked him what he thought.

"It's just red tape, Tom. North American has all the parts we need boxed ready and ready to go. The problem is in the supply chain. They are computing replacement requirements on a peacetime basis, instead of using the figures we send them about combat. So stuff is backing up at our end."

Tom looked at his six pages of closely written notes, which listed all current parts deficiencies of the 4th. "What if I offer to buy these out of my own pocket, and pay the shipping costs? Would North American send them?"

Henderson laughed. "Good one, Tom. There's about fourteen million dollars there. If North American garnishees your wages for the next two thousand years, we might come out even."

"I'm not kidding, John. The Air Force would pay for them eventually; you know that. It would just be us, you and me, putting our necks on the line. But what if we ordered them, and North American chartered an airplane to deliver them here. How long would it take?"

"Well, it would take more than one airplane, that's for sure, three for sure, four maybe. But if we ordered today . . ."—he stopped to think, factoring in the cruising speed of the DC-4s that would be used, the stops that would be made—". . . maybe six or seven days. But you know this is totally illegal; you don't have the authority to buy the parts, and I don't have the authority to say ship them."

"A perfect fit. We can be cellmates at Leavenworth. But the 4th will have the parts."

"Well, if we are going to do it, let's do it right. The mechanics are short on tools; let me gin up a list of wrenches, screwdrivers, pliers, and what have you, enough for you and the 51st as well."

"Let's double the parts order. The 51st must need the same stuff we do; we'll ship half of it down there. What do the Brits say, 'In for penny, in for a pound'?"

Henderson grinned, shook his head, and said, "Well, we'll prob-ably be in for twenty years and that pound will be a chunk out of our asses. Let me send the list in. I'll tell John Casey what I'm doing, and he'll back us up, for sure." Casey was the top North American guy in the theater, a square-shooting take-action type. Shannon knew he'd not only approve; he'd facilitate the action.

"Tom, are you going to tell your boss, Matthews?"

"No, if I did he'd either have to agree and put his own neck on the line or overrule me. I don't want to put him in that position."

"We could go to jail for this, for real."

"Hell, that would just make my wife happy! But I'm going to cover myself. When you tell me that North American is shipping the stuff, I'm going to send a message to the Air Force Chief of Staff, General Vandenberg, telling him what I've done. And I'll copy everyone in the chain of command, all the way down to Matthews."

"Tom, you have balls, no question about it. I just hope the Air Force lets you keep them."

Still shaking his head, Henderson took the lists and walked down to the tent where North American kept its communication gear. An hour later the order was back at North American, being filled. Two hours later, Shannon was standing at a brace in Matthews's tent, watching his boss explode as he waved Tom's mes-sage around.

"Are you out of your mind? Messaging the Chief of Staff? Don't you think he's got a few other things on his mind? Why didn't you come to me?"

"I didn't want you going to jail, Colonel."

"Well, that's for sure where you are going. And we're starting with confining you to your quarters except to fly."

For the next four days, the in-commission rate continued to drop, and grounded F-86s were idle, spotted in their pits around the field. On the fifth day, the rate hit 50 percent, and one of the three scheduled missions was canceled, the first time ever for the 4th. There just were not enough airplanes to fly.

On the sixth day, C-54s began landing at Kimpo, off-loading supplies. By that evening, the in-commission rate had jumped back to 75 percent, and Matthews called Shannon into his office.

"Tom, that was either the dumbest or the greatest trick I've ever seen. Right now, looking at these in-commission figures, I think it was the greatest. Forget about the court-martial; forget about being confined to quarters. I can't get you a medal for violating procedures, but I'll do better than that. I want you to lead the whole 4th Fighter-Interceptor Wing tomorrow, every plane that can fly! I'll fly your wing, and we'll get us some MiGs."

King George VI dies; Eisenhower elected President; Mau Mau killings in Kenya; Rocky Marciano defeats Walcott; Stalin dies; Queen Elizabeth crowned; U.S price controls lifted; peace talks continue in Korea.

CHAPTER THIRTEEN

May 3, 1953, Palos Verdes, California

*I*t was a mini-gathering of the clan, and for the first time in years, laughter was rocking the walls of their Malaga Cove house. Vance, on his way to get ice, was happier than he had ever been since Madeline had left him. The irony was that the happiness was almost all Madeline's doing. He was convinced that she had deliberately chosen Jill as a substitute for herself, and Jill turned out to be the most wonderful wife any man could have wanted.

As smart as Madeline had been, Vance now realized that she lacked what Jill had in abundance, an ability to love unconditionally. Jill constantly exerted herself for others, and it was the combination of her pushing and Tom's begging that had finally persuaded Nancy to try again. Now the three of them were in the backyard, laughing and talking as if there had never been a problem, all three of them convinced that the baby in the crib, Vance Robert Shannon, was the cutest, most brilliant child in history. Born on Groundhog Day, February 2, 1953, Vance Robert was named for his two grandfathers, and they were already calling him V.R.

Tom had come home from Korea in January, resigned his commission, and thrown himself on Nancy's mercy. She was so glad to see him and to have him there when the baby was born that they reconciled immediately.

Harry and Anna were in the backyard as well, joining in the laughter, but with an obvious constraint. After a long, steady decline that accelerated every time Harry was sent somewhere on temporary duty, Anna had at last faced her problem and agreed to go to Alcoholics Anonymous. The Shannons had never been big drinkers, and all of the backyard laughter came not from alcohol but from goodwill and soft drinks. Anna was perfectly open about her problem, as she had to be, and the whole family was trying to help. She spoke sadly of Maria, now in a mental hospital in San Diego.

Harry had come to Vance earlier, asking, "Dad, I think Tom has done absolutely the right thing, and I wonder if I shouldn't follow his example?"

"You mean give up your commission and leave the Air Force?"

"Yes. Anna needs me, and I've been gone too often."

"Well, Harry, I could certainly use you in the business here. It would be like we originally planned, back when the big war ended, the three of us working together. The big thing, though, is Anna's health. I don't think you have much choice; you've got to stick with her."

The bag of ice cubes had frozen solid in the big Deepfreeze where Jill kept enough food to supply an Army division. Vance threw it into the sink and began pounding on it with a wooden mallet, considering how life tended to even things out. Both of his sons had been blessed with extraordinary good fortune in their health, their intelligence, and their careers. Both had more than their share of marital problems, but at least Tom's seemed to be smoothing out. In contrast, Vance had enjoyed a wonderful life with Margaret, twelve good years with Madeline, punctuated by six months of intense despondency when she left him without any explanation. Now he was incredibly happy with Jill. He wondered why he should have been so lucky when his boys had to endure so much.

The phone rang in the study. "Damn, people shouldn't be calling on Sunday." He yelled out the window, "Harry, would you pick up this ice, please?" and ran down the hallway. Madeline had had the house decorated once in all the years she'd lived there. Jill had already redone the house twice and was talking about a third go at it. It was a matter of supreme indifference to Vance, but if it made her happy, he wanted her to do it.

He answered the phone and George Schairer's voice came through, not calm and collected as usual but brimming with tightly controlled excitement.

"Vance, did you hear the news? A Comet crashed yesterday after takeoff from Calcutta."

"Jesus! Was it the same as the last one?" The previous March, a Comet had lifted its nose too high and run off the end of the runway at Karachi—something that had happened before, at Rome.

"No, they tell me this one exploded in mid-air. They don't know whether it was a bomb or what. Forty-three people killed."

"What do you think, George? Sabotage?"

"Our guys think it might be a massive explosive decompression, caused by metal fatigue."

"With all due respect, George, I doubt it. I saw the test results, and they were thorough. De Havilland believed the airplane was good for eighteen thousand flights before fatigue would be a problem. Anybody know how many cycles this one had?"

"We've been tracking the Comets pretty well, Vance, and this airplane couldn't have had more than six or seven hundred flights."

"There you are. How about turbulence? Maybe it just broke up in a storm?"

"That's a possibility, but we doubt it from what we know now. But we'd like you to come up here tomorrow, Vance, if you can, and let us brief you on all we know. De Havilland has requested that you be brought on board their inspection team." He paused, shaking his head, then went on. "They woke me up in the middle of the night, and asked me if we could send a team over to check their figures. They asked specifically for you to be on the team. This tells me they are worried about pressurization, too. They begged me to keep it a secret, of course; they've got a lot going on this. I said I would, and you'll have to, too, of course."

"Can I take Jill?"

"No reason not to, George, but we want you to be at de Havilland's by the end of the week, if at all possible. Perhaps she could join you if she cannot make the trip with you."

Vance knew that would never do and hastened to set the trip up. Jill had never been abroad before and was enchanted with everything from their flight across the country to the wonderful trans-Atlantic service on a Pan Am Constellation. On whim, Vance had booked them into the Basil Hotel and found that it had changed very little from his wartime visits. Even the food had not improved, and he and Jill were much impressed with the ceremony by which stone-cold toast was brought to them with their "full English breakfast" in the morning. He left Jill in London to shop while he went up to Hatfield Aerodrome, to spend time with the de Havilland people.

The de Havilland factory was plunged into gloom. This was the third incident for the Comet since October 1952. The first accident, on takeoff from Rome, had been caused by the pilot rotating too soon. The increased drag from the nose-up attitude planted him on the runway until he ran off the end. Fortunately, none of the forty-three people on board—seven crew and thirty-six passengers—had been injured.

The crash at Karachi on March 2, 1953, had been a repeat of the first, with the pilot raising the nose too soon and allowing the aircraft to tear off the end of the runway. This time the airplane exploded, killing the crew of five and six de Havilland support personnel.

When Vance walked into the de Havilland offices, he found he had stepped into the middle of an internal company fight. One faction, headed by Sir Geoffrey de Havilland himself, was convinced that the aircraft had been sabotaged and resented any implication of a possible structural defect. A much smaller, less powerful, but still forceful faction, headed by Ronald Davies, was more open-minded, demanding that a full investigation be made of the structural integrity of the aircraft.

Davies was hosting him. He was small, well-spoken, with glasses that seemed about to catapult from his prominent nose. He had been with de Havilland since 1939. His concern was obvious. As with most de Havilland employees, he was both depressed and defensive, but strangely defiant.

"Three accidents in seven months. This could sink us, Mr. Shannon. We've got to get to the bottom of the cause, and do it now. One more accident and you can write the Comet off."

"I hope that's not the case, Mr. Davies. The first two accidents were clearly pilot error, and you've taken the necessary steps to avoid similar accidents in the future. And this one may have been sabotage."

"It sounds insane to say so, but I hope it is sabotage. We can deal with that; we can watch who our passengers are, inspect our cargo, and so on. But has Mr. Schairer told you what we fear?"

"Explosive decompression due to metal fatigue? Yes, he told me, and that's a real possibility. But you'll be able to tell that, will you not, when you recover the wreckage?"

"I can only hope so. We have nineteen aircraft flying, and thirty more on order. If we don't find the cause now, I don't think de Havilland can survive."

Shannon spent the next ten days immersed in data. They showed him everything he asked for and gave him all the staff support he needed. It was less like an American firm than an old-fashioned English insurance organization, with clerks wearing green visors and sleeve protectors. But they were very competent, anticipating his requests and never failing to come up with a requested document.

He could not come up with an answer. It was impossible to examine all of the years of data, but each time he took a sample of the figures and analyzed them, they made sense. These were professionals, serious people who had sought to make a great advance, realized the risks involved, and taken every possible step to build a safe airplane.

Still, there had been a pell-mell rush to production. He looked at the dates. The decision to go ahead with the basic design was made on September 27, 1946—ironically, the same day that Geoffrey de Havilland's son was killed in the D.H. 108. No connection, of course, but somehow unsettling. The Comet flew thirty-three months later—an incredibly fast process for so large and so advanced an aircraft. Production was authorized even though only sixteen aircraft had been ordered.

Shannon was troubled and he could not articulate the reason. Intuitively, he felt that placing the engines in the wing was wrong, and he could not avoid focusing in on the square windows in a pressurized cabin. He could tell de Havilland of his feelings, but he could not point to any data to back them up. Even when he reported to Boeing he would have to be careful not to appear unscientific.

Vance arranged it so that he could go to London to see Jill three or four times in the interval, taking her to the theater each time he did. Other than beginning to be a bit bored by English cooking, she was having a glorious time people-watching at pubs, on the underground, and on the street. She made friends by the carload, and oftentimes he would find that she had invited another couple to dinner with them, and they were always interesting people. The idea that the Brits were staid was totally wrong—Jill always found a way to break the ice and get conversations rolling, and it was their guests who sometimes got a little ribald in their conversations, using expressions that Vance would never have allowed at home.

On his last day at the de Havilland plant, Davies cornered him. "Well, Mr. Shannon, what do you think? Did we do our homework?"

Shannon had carefully reviewed the testing process de Havilland had used. Pressurized sections of the fuselage had been placed in an altitude chamber and taken up to a simulated 70,000 feet with temperatures of minus seventy degrees centigrade. They had built a huge water chamber into which a fuselage could be submerged, and pressure-checked it there at up to sixteen and one-half pounds per square inch. Everything seemed eminently reasonable.

"Mr. Davies, I find no failings at all in your test procedures, in their rigor, or in the conclusions drawn from them. Based on them, I think your estimate of sixteen-thousand flights, or cycles, is conservative. But . . ."

His voice trailed off and Davies bristled. "But what?" His tone was at once insistent and pleading.

"May I speak off-the-record?"

"Certainly."

"Intuitively, I think that the problem is metal fatigue and that the proper course for de Havilland would be to ground all the Comets and redo the entire pressurization test program. Somehow there is an element missing in the test program that is encountered in actual operations. It might be that there is more stress induced by repetitive pressurizations and depressurizations in flight than in your test program. It might be the combination of the stresses of flights, landings, and pressurization. In that case, the storm might have triggered the violent explosion in the last accident. But somewhere in the mix is a fatal flaw."

Davies exploded, "What are you talking about? That is absolutely absurd. You are supposed to be an engineer, not a bloody fortune-teller! You and Boeing would like nothing better than to see de Havilland ground the Comet and leave the field open to you!"

Yet even as he spoke, Vance could tell that Davies believed him.

"I don't want to offend you, Mr. Davies, and I certainly have no malice toward de Havilland, a company I greatly admire. You asked me to speak, off-the-record, and I did. My remarks will not be in my formal report, but I feel I've discharged my duties to you by telling you what I really think. Believe me, Boeing is competitive, but they would never wish aircraft disasters on you or on anyone."

Davies turned and walked away, obviously shaken.

Both Vance and Jill were glad to climb aboard the Pan Am Connie for the flight home. "What's the matter, Vance? You've been gloomy ever since you got back from de Havilland."

"Well, I figure I ruined the possibility of doing any future work for de Havilland by telling them what I thought. And I cannot decide how to put this to Boeing. If I don't do it just right, they will think that I gave de Havilland a whitewash. Especially since I really have to tell them what I think, so that they don't get into the same trouble as de Havilland did."

He was quiet for a moment and went on. "Don't get me wrong, they are going to try to outsell the Comet as soon as they get a jet on the market, but they would never want to see a string of accidents ground the Comets. They want people to have faith in jet airliners, and nothing could be worse for Boeing than having the first jet airliner prove to be a disaster."

He waited for a moment more and said, "I wish I had been quick thinking enough to tell that to Davies."

September 18, 1953, Seattle, Washington

VANCE HUNG UP the phone. Harry had called, and Anna was in trouble once again. She had been acting strange, and when he flopped down on the couch, his hip had hit a vodka bottle tucked into the cushions. Vance and Harry had chatted a few minutes more on what effect the end of the war in Korea would have on business, but both of them were preoccupied with Anna. There seemed no way to help her. She would stick by AA rules for a while, then slip back somehow into drinking.

Vance glanced at the wall clock—it was almost ten, and he had an appointment with Schairer at 10:30. Boeing was always miserly with their office space, and for a consultant like Vance getting a room with a desk, a clock, a telephone, and a couple of filing cabinets was a coup. Secretarial help was hard to come by officially, but the Boeing administrative staff was so accommodating that Vance got by without a private secretary. He would just take his drafts, pencil-written on yellow legal-size tablets, and Schairer's wonderfully efficient and quite beautiful secretary Dorothy McCain, would either do them or have them done within the hour.

Vance had been continually corresponding with de Havilland, usually with Ron Davies, who turned out to be a most accommodating friend. Davies had recovered all of his natural British charm and aplomb after the company's investigators concluded that the breakup of the Comet flying out of Calcutta had been solely due to turbulence and that there was no need to consider grounding the fleet. He was particularly pleased—as close to bubbling over as a proper English gentleman could get—by the increase in sales. Thirty-five of the Comet 2s with Rolls-Royce Avon engines had been sold to British Overseas Airways Corporation and seven other major foreign airlines. Eleven of the even more advanced Comet 3s, which would have trans-Atlantic range, were already spoken for, five by BOAC and, ominously, three by Pan American.

Vance shook his head. This was exactly what Boeing feared— Pan American getting on board with de Havilland! But the sales figures were not as impressive as the performance figures. By the end of April, the BOAC Comets had flown almost ten thousand hours, carrying twenty-eight thousand passengers. It was making money, hand over fist, early in its first year of operations. But what struck Shannon most was the load factor—the Comet was operating with 80 percent of its seats filled, all the time. This was what was generating the profits, for fuel costs were double that of a piston engine airliner. And it meant that people liked flying in it. Of course; why should they not? It was faster, quieter, and more comfortable than anything else in the air. Boeing had its work cut out for it to beat the Comet.

All of his data had gone into the final report. He was about ready to sign the cover letter when Dorothy McCain popped her pretty head in the door and said, "Can you come see Mr. Schairer?"

"Right away, thanks, Dorothy." He clipped his cover letter to the report and walked down the hall to Schairer's office. George, uncharacteristically did rise to greet him but said instead, "Vance, this is Ted Higgins. He heads up our security. I think we have a problem."

The tone of Schairer's voice spoke volumes and Shannon knew that somehow he was in trouble. It surprised him to see three models of Boeing experimental aircraft that he had worked on placed on the conference table at the side of the room. There were photos beside them, but he could not make out what they were.

"What is it, George? Can I help?"

"Vance, I hope so. Mr. Higgins, will you show Mr. Shannon the photos, please."

Higgins, balding and of medium height, his hair combed over, was obviously ill at ease as he motioned Vance over to the table. In front of each of the Boeing experimental models was a photo of an aircraft with French markings. The aircraft were identical to the models.

"This is the Sud-Ouest Trident, the Sud-Ouest Vatour, and the Sud-Est Baroudeur. They are all new aircraft, making their appearance within the last year." Then somewhat redundantly, Higgins added, "They are all French."

Shannon had seen the Vatour in *Aviation Week*, noting its resemblance at the time to the Boeing project and to the B-47, but he had not seen the other two aircraft anywhere. One, the Trident, had, like its Boeing predecessor, two jet engines on the wingtips. The Baroudeur was a small interceptor that had dispensed with a landing gear—it was catapulted into the air and landed on a skid. But the shocking truth was that all three were similar to the earlier Boeing experimental designs that he had worked on.

Schairer spoke. "Vance, these are not just coincidental look-alikes. We've had the full-scale aircraft analyzed, and they are identical dimensionally to our experimental studies. They have the same airfoils; they are powered by engines of about the same power. There is no question that they derived anywhere but from our studies."

Shannon looked at him. "I worked on all of these projects, George; you know that. You don't think I sold them to the French, do you?" As he spoke it began to dawn on him.

"You didn't, George, but Madeline did. She didn't sell them. She was an intelligence agent for the French government from the day she met you. She still is. We've confirmed this; we're not guessing. Madeline was a spy and we think you must have been careless with security."

Emotion choked, Shannon waved his hands and sat down in the chair by the table. Schairer, almost as affected as Shannon, brought him a glass of water, spilling it in his anxiety. He wiped the water up with his own handkerchief and went back to the silver decanter to refill the glass.

Vance was slumped in the chair, the enormity of the deceit crushing him. He mumbled to himself, "So that was it. Twelve years of lying, twelve years of sex, all wrapped into this debacle. How could she have done this to me?"

Schairer heard him, knew it was an involuntary cry for help, and didn't answer. Then he said, "Vance, we are keeping this quiet, for now at least. I don't think any real harm has been done. These aircraft are either dead ends or already obsolescent. And France is nominally a friend. I just hope to God that no Soviet prototypes show up with a Boeing background."

Shannon had never before felt so weak and helpless. No matter what the problem, there had always been a way out, over the side with a parachute, if necessary, but some way. He had been sandbagged.

"I hate to do this, Vance, but we've got to sever our relationship. I know you didn't know anything about this, but I have to hold you responsible for Madeline getting this material. I just hope this is it, that nothing else crawls out of the woodwork. And, we have to report this to the Air Force. I don't think they will prosecute you, but you can be damn sure they'll be asking you some embarrassing questions."

Shannon nodded.

"Vance, are you in any shape to tell me how you think this happened? We can go over it tomorrow, if we have to, but Bill Allen knows about this, and he'll be calling me any minute. It would be better if we could at least explain how it happened."

Vance waited a moment to be sure he had his voice under control. "There's only one way it could have happened, George. I took material home to work on, but I always kept it locked up. If she was smart enough to fool me for twelve years, she was smart enough to figure out the locks. She could have had access at night, after I'd gone to sleep, or even sometimes over a weekend, if I was off on another job. The material was never top secret—rarely secret. I think most of the information on these planes was not even classified by the government. But it was proprietary, of course."

Schairer was nodding his head. "Vance, we had a pretty complete inventory done. You had checked out all the material you had, and you are right—none of it was classified; it was all proprietary. But that's bad enough. It's incredible; we've relied on you for your judgment for what, twenty years now—and you made this fundamental miscalculation. I'm really sorry, Vance. You know that."

Vance nodded, his throat too dry to speak.

"Now this is important, Vance. Do you have anything else from Boeing in your files at the present?"

He croaked, "Nothing but backup material on this de Havilland project. Nothing classified, nothing proprietary."

"You won't mind if our people take a look?"

"Of course not, George."

The next three weeks passed in a nightmare of interviews and what amounted to cross-examinations by Boeing and Air Force Office of Special Investigation personnel. Vance kept expecting the FBI to show up, but they never did. The worst of it was that he was sworn to secrecy. He could not tell Jill or his boys or anyone else. He made up excuses to stay in Seattle that did not fool Jill for a moment. Then Vance had astounded her when he came in without any notice on the morning of September 23, with Higgins and a young, polite OSI man from the Air Force. He showed them into his office, opened up all the locked files and the safe, and went out to Jill, hugging her.

"Vance, you're in trouble. What is it, income tax? You can tell me."

The sorrow in her voice broke what was left of his heart. "Honey, I'll tell you as soon as I can. This should be over pretty soon, and I'll be home—for good, probably. I'll tell you all about it as soon as I can. Right now I can't." He gestured into the office where the two men were working quietly and efficiently, going through one file after another.

Trying to joke, she said, "It's not another woman, is it?" Then real fear gripped her and she said, "Is it Madeline? Has she come back?"

He wanted to say, "Yes, she's come back, but not as you think." Instead he had to be abrupt, saying, "Stop it. Get off my back. I'll tell you about it when I get home for good. I can't tell you now."

The rest of the time passed slowly in Seattle. The Windsor Hotel, in an unaccustomed fit of largesse, had recently installed television sets in most of its rooms. Vance would watch for hours, drifting off to sleep late at night, and the next day could not recall a single thing he had seen.

The nightmare ended on October 9. He had filled out his thousandth form, signed his thousandth statement, and was given his final check from Boeing. Typically, they had paid him at his full rate through the ninth. There was no final meeting with his friends at Boeing. George Schairer had called him at the Windsor the night before.

"Vance, you understand, we won't be saying good-bye formally."

"No going-away party, eh, George? I understand."

"It has been wonderful working with you, Vance, and I'm sorry this happened. If I have anything to say about it, we'll work together again. This will blow over; it was really sort of a tempest in a teapot, but security is so tight now that there was nothing we could do."

"I don't blame anyone but myself, George. It was my fault, and I'll take the fall with no complaints. Thanks for all your help in the past, and good luck in the future."

Vance spent the last night as usual, wondering what Madeline could have been thinking of to betray him so shamefully. It was almost two o'clock in the morning when he realized that Madeline must have thought that she was being totally consistent. She was honest with him in all ways, except for her fulfilling her duties to her government. He had been her cover, and she had treated him well. She had done what she thought was right, from setting up the Capestro girls for Tom and Harry to running Vance's finances, to hiring Jill, to being a spy and stealing secrets from his safe. As for their sex life, she probably enjoyed it as he did—she couldn't have been so enthusiastic, so innovative, if she had not. But that, too, had been part of her job, and she had done it well, as she did all things well.

The most ironic element was the communication. He had always felt that much of their attraction for each other was the way they communicated, by voice, gesture, word, and deed. Now he realized, it had been a one-way street—he was communicating with her, but she had not communicated with him.

Oddly enough, it was going to be easy to explain everything to Jill. She would respond happily to anything that ensured Madeline would never enter their lives again. It would be difficult with the boys, for a number of reasons. It would revive their old animosity for Madeline, and when the news got out, as it undoubtedly already had, it would destroy his business. Maybe Tom and Harry could form their own firm and subcontract to him.

The truth, and he knew it, was that he had probably ruined Tom and Harry's business careers as well. As large as the businesses had grown in volume, the aviation community was relatively small, and gossip circulated with the speed of light. Within weeks, there would not be anyone in the business who would not know that he had been fired from Boeing on a security lapse. That would carry over and tarnish his sons as well.

Yet in Vance's innermost being, at his most fundamental level, he knew that he did not hate Madeline. He no longer loved her—she had done too much harm. But he could not hate her. In a way she retained an essential purity of purpose that he admired when he thought she was applying it to their common interests. Now he saw that her purpose was pure, all right, but that it was in the service of her country.

Nasser seizes power in Egypt; U.S. Supreme Court rules against seg-regation in schools; **On the Waterfront** *wins Academy Award;* **Tolkien's The Lord of the Rings** *published.*

CHAPTER FOURTEEN

December 25, 1953, Palos Verdes, California

Strangely enough, in the nightmare of the business being destroyed, several financial bright spots had emerged. Tom and Harry had never sold the La Jolla house, renting it to a succession of Convair executives over the years, men who needed a comfortable place to stay while their own homes were being built in the constantly expanding San Diego suburbs. Its value had quadrupled and it was free and clear. They hated to sell it now, but if that was necessary, it would bring in a huge sum.

Madeline's other real-estate investments had done almost equally well, although it was impossible to beat the returns that the La Jolla location generated. The stock portfolios had gained a little, not much, but there was enough money available from selling off some of the smaller, less desirable real-estate parcels that Vance was able to live comfortably and continue to pay Harry and Tom the salaries they had agreed upon. But as far as Aviation Consultants, Incorporated, went, business was kaput. The boys picked up an occasional test-flying job, usually with some local outfit that had all of its money tied up in a prototype that was never going anywhere. It was fun, slightly dangerous, but had no real long-term potential. Without business from major companies, Aviation Consultants was dead in the water.

All three men were driven by a desire to work, not for the financial return but for the sheer pleasure of achieving new goals—and of course for the pleasure of flying. Despite the hard evidence that new aircraft, whether would-be Piper Cubs or would-be DC-3s, were almost impossible to certify and promote, all three dreamed of designing and manufacturing their own aircraft.

They explored a range of possibilities, but Tom had come up with the most provocative suggestion at one of their stand-up lunches in the kitchen, where Jill would put out a spread of goodies—Parma ham, thin sliced roast beef, provolone, onions, roast peppers, sardines, tomatoes, the works—and they would make big, wet dripping sandwiches that they ate over the sink. The impromptu lunches were among the few times that Vance rose up out of his depression to joke a bit.

"Come on, Tom, swallow; don't talk with your mouth full. I've been telling you that for thirty years now." Vance's voice was slightly less dispirited than usual, and his sons took it as a good sign, shooting each other a quick glance.

Tom chewed, swallowed, took a drink of his Coke, and said, "What is the one thing missing in the airplane market today?"

Harry answered, "An inexpensive new plane?"

"Come on; be serious. We've got little Cessnas, bigger Beeches, and a whole raft of military conversions, Lodestars, B-25s, what have you. They are all piston engine airplanes, and this is the jet age. Why don't we design and build a jet transport for executives? Something about the size of the Twin Bonanza, or the Cessna 310, but maybe a little bigger, carry two pilots and maybe four to six passengers."

Neither Harry nor Vance responded at once, meaning they accepted it as a serious suggestion, worth an answer instead of the usual put-down wisecrack.

Vance said, "What engine would you use? That's the key, getting an engine that will deliver the performance but not be so expensive that you can't afford to fly it."

Harry said, "I've been following the various companies. You know that little stint I had up with Pratt & Whitney, back in the old days, sort of intrigued me with engines. Problem is, everybody keeps building bigger engines; not much market out there for a little one."

Tom came back swiftly. "Except General Electric. I know a man there, Jack Parker, and he's heading up what he calls the 'Small Aircraft Engine Department.' Catchy name, eh? But he's talking about building an engine for an Air Force decoy, the Quail."

"What's a decoy?"

"I think the bombers are supposed to carry them; they drop them when they get near the anti-aircraft belts, and the decoy flies ahead of them to confuse the radar. Anyway, the engine he's developing will have about twenty-five hundred pounds of thrust at the start. That will build over time, of course."

"Remember Nate Price's old equation? That means about twenty-five hundred horsepower when it is at cruise—that's pretty powerful stuff. And you need two engines, for safety.'"

Vance spoke, his voice vibrant, sounding like himself. "We'd have to keep it small, under twelve thousand, five hundred pounds, so that the government will certify it for single-pilot operation."

Harry chimed in, "This would have to be a luxury item, the best interiors, sleek paint jobs, something that would appeal to the movie stars."

Vance nodded. "There's a long tradition of that—Wallace Beery always had an airplane, and Robert Taylor, Bob Cummings, and a bunch of them fly. I'll bet we could get one of them to come in, not so much for finances, but as a name to hang it on."

Tom walked over and put his arm around Vance's shoulder, his sandwich dripping on his shirt, and kissed him on the forehead. "Dad, we're going to name this airplane after the best damn pilot, engineer, and father in the business. This is going to be the Shannon Jet, and you are going to be the front man. We don't need a movie star; we've got you."

They moved from the kitchen into the office, where Vance shoved aside papers that had not been touched for weeks. He put down a clean sheet of drafting paper, sat down, and began a freehand pencil sketch of a needle-nosed twin jet, with swept wings and tail.

"Looks good, Dad, but you've got the engines on the wings—on a plane that size they'd be scraping the ground, sucking up every rock in a quarter-mile area." Reaching down, Harry rubbed out the low-slung engines, hung much as those on the Messerschmitt 262 had been. Then with a few pencil strokes, not so neatly or as accurately as his father, Harry put the engines on little pylons on top of the wing. "There—you see—they'll be up where they won't get any foreign object damage."

Tom laughed and said, "All wrong, brother dear, all wrong. You'll deafen the passengers with the engines there, and ruin their view, too. Here's where the engines go." He rubbed out Harry's poorly drawn examples and then very neatly attached the engines on the fuselage, high and to the rear. "Voilà! Mount them here, they are behind the pressure cabin, the wing is clean, you don't have much noise, and you don't get the stuff from the tarmac sucked into them."

Vance was excited now. "Yeah, and it looks good, too. Nothing like it on the market. Never thought pusher engines would come back, but there they are!"

Vance looked at his two sons, saw their expressions, and knew what they had done—conspired together to snap him out of his malaise, to give him a project he could sink his teeth in. Well, they'd done it.

"OK, boys, let's think about this a bit. I know we don't have anyway near the capital to swing this by ourselves, and I don't want to get a partner so big that he'll tell us what to do. Maybe we can sell some stock, but I hate to do that, because this will be one risky project."

Tom said, "Here's what I think. Let's go on like we're doing, trying to build Aviation Consultants back up, bit by bit, and keep working on this idea. We can look around for a factory site, maybe pick up a few guys with ability that might want to invest with us. The main thing is to keep it small."

Vance nodded agreement. "There is still a whole raft of work to do, on the engineering side and the business side. We've got to figure out what airfoil to use, how the airplane sizes out, what it weighs, and so on. Then we have to figure out its operating economics. I think we can find a place to build it, when we are ready to go, and we'll have no problem hiring people."

Half an hour later, the two boys left, walking down the curving steps that led to their cars.

"Well, that worked pretty well, Tom. Good idea."

"Sure. Even if it is totally impractical, and I'm sure it is, it will get him fired up until a real project comes along. He just needs something to apply all his knowledge in a positive way."

Inside the house, Jill was cleaning up, moaning about the messy floor. "I thought you were going to eat your sandwiches over the sink. Don't make those wet sandwiches and then walk around—we've got a table and chairs, you know."

Vance picked up a towel and began doing his own mopping up. "They're really something, aren't they? Trying to cheer me up, feeding me this pie-in-the sky idea about a private jet airliner. God love them, they mean well, trying to get their old man back on track."

He stood looking out their kitchen window over the immaculate backyard, idly rubbing the counter with the towel.

"Still, a private jet airliner would really be something, wouldn't it? And they wanted to call it the Shannon Jet! That's pretty good. I'd like that."

February 2, 1954, Palos Verdes, California

IT WAS V.R.'S first birthday, and Jill had decorated the house to celebrate. Though she had never had any children herself, she was the quintessential grandmother to young Vance Robert, babysitting at every opportunity.

Everyone was coming to dinner, everyone except Anna, who was at yet another clinic, still trying—or appearing to try—to shed the ravaging burden of alcohol that had consumed her beauty even as it consumed Harry's life.

Vance came in from the garage, where he had had spent the

morning changing the oil in his old De Soto, their second car. "What are we having? Turkey, roast beef?"

Jill looked at him sadly and put her arm around his neck. Vance's question was pro forma. His appetite was gone; he no longer exercised and spent most of his time in his office, supposedly reading, but most often staring at the wall. Changing the oil was the most positive thing he had done in weeks.

"It's your favorite, beef Stroganoff. And you had a call while you were in the garage. I didn't want to disturb you just when you were draining the oil, so I took the number."

"Who was it?"

"He said he was an old friend of yours, Bill Lear. Sounded like a real nice person, laughing and kidding."

"Well, if it's the Bill Lear I think it is, he is a son of a bitch, a no-good bastard. We were at a party over at North American about twenty years ago and he made a pass at Margaret! I decked him, just belted him without thinking, knocked him ass-backward over a table. He's a big guy, too."

"You actually hit him?"

"Well, I'd had a couple of drinks, and that was not usual for me. But he was always romancing everybody. There was actually a round of applause when I slugged him."

Jill laughed and kissed him. "Always a knight in shining armor! I hope you'd do the same for me."

He kissed her back and said, "But he is one smart guy as well. He's the guy who invented the first practical car radio, plus a lot of stuff for aviation—direction-finding gear, autopilots, and so on. Won the Collier Trophy one year, 1947, I think, and that's really something. Right now he's in the modification business, taking old clunker Lodestars and cleaning them up so that they are fast, long-ranged executive aircraft. Calls them Learstars."

"Well, go ahead and call him."

"I'll go into the office, where it's quiet."

"The hell you will! I want to hear this."

Smiling, Vance dialed the number she gave him. A big booming voice answered, "Lear here."

"Bill, this is Vance Shannon. You called me?"

"Absolutely, Vance, and thanks for calling back. I need your help. Can you spare me a few months of your time?"

Vance would have liked to have said, "Not on your life, you fanny-patting bastard." But economics intervened, and he said, "Maybe; what's it all about?"

Lear went into a lengthy explanation. He was taking war surplus Lockheed Lodestars and putting them through a modification process that included bigger engines, new instruments, ultra-deluxe passenger cabins, and so on, but the whole enterprise depended on increased speed for sales.

"Vance, here it is in a nutshell. My guys have slicked this buggy up as much as they know how, and we are still twenty miles per hour below our guaranteed top speed and fifteen below our economy cruise speed. If we don't get that fixed, I'll lose a sale of about twenty airplanes to an importer in South America. I want you to come in and see if you can squeeze a lot more speed out of it. I'd like to exceed the specs, if I could, but I need to at least meet them."

Shannon felt reborn, just as he used to feel as a kid after Confession when he had said the usual five Hail Marys and five Our Fathers for penance. This was perhaps a way back into the industry. It was a start, anyway.

"I can't pay you what the big outfits do, Vance, but I can make it interesting. What do you say?"

"When do I start?"

"Come on up to my office in Santa Monica on Monday. We'll have a contract for you to sign, and we'll get started."

Shannon said good-bye, put down the phone, and moved over to the window. His eyes were misting. It was sort of humiliating, going to work for Bill Lear, polishing up piston engine leftovers from World War II, but by God, it was a start.

Jill didn't say anything. She saw the emotions flashing across Vance's face, knew that it was good, that whatever Bill and he had agreed on was helping him. There was no need to kiss him or congratulate him. She let him soak it up from the inside.

On Monday, Lear greeted him like a long-lost father. As Vance walked through the immaculately clean plant, he enjoyed the badinage between Lear and the workers. The man clearly was the boss, and the people liked him. That was promising.

Lear led him to the end of the hangar where no fewer than seven airplanes were completed.

"These Learstars are all ready to roll—but they haven't passed our acceptance tests because they are too slow. We cannot figure it out."

"They look mighty slick, Bill."

And they did. On this casual inspection, it looked like everything that could be done was done. The finish was beautiful. Lear's experts had filled in every crevice with body putty and sanded it down before painting, so it gleamed from end to end with none of the usual plates sticking up, fasteners exposed, and so on. The cowling was long and beautiful, and the propellers were enclosed in a deep spinner that seemed almost anteater-like in appearance. The cowl flaps were like articulated wings, perfectly matched when open or closed.

"Can we fly one, Bill?"

"Damn right, I'll fly you myself." He began shouting orders, and one of the Learstars, finished in an immaculate deep emerald green, was rolled out. Lear climbed into the left seat, motioned Vance into the right seat, and quickly, expertly, went through the checklist. Behind them stood Lloyd Carr, an experienced instructor pilot, carefully following the process. Lear nodded to him, saying, "I never fly without another qualified pilot on board. Getting too damn old, I forget things."

Vance had flown Lockheed Hudsons during the war and the Lodestar was just an enlarged version, but the Learstar had far more instrumentation and was much more comfortable. They climbed to altitude heading out toward the ocean, and Lear leveled off at 6,000 feet, saying, "You got it."

Shannon flew the airplane carefully, moving it through a series of ever steeper banks. Then he did a few speed runs, on which the airplane topped out at about 240 mph. Before he turned to go back to Santa Monica, he did some stalls. The airplane paid off rapidly and rolled to the right, far sharper than Vance liked. "This could be tough for a novice, Bill. That's a wicked stall."

"Yeah, I know, but we can't do much about it. It's just built into the airplane—the Hudson and the Lodestar did the same thing."

When they got back to the field, Lear made a perfect wheels landing, and they taxied in without speaking. After he had shut the airplane down, carefully going through the checklist, he turned to Vance, saying, "What do you think?"

"Well, it's a hell of an improvement over the Lodestar, obviously. And you really have a slick interior. The stall worries me, though, and I don't see any obvious way to boost the speed. Let me think about it, and I'll come back to you tomorrow."

"What about your contract? It's up on my desk."

"Let's see if I can do you any good first, and we'll talk about the contract later."

All the way home from the plant, all during dinner, and until late at night, Shannon analyzed the airplane. He hadn't said anything to Lear, but to him there was an obvious connection between the sharpness of the stall and the inability to reach higher speeds.

Shannon spent the next five days crawling over the Learstar, examining it in every configuration, flaps up, flaps down, gear up, gear down, flaps up, gear down, flaps down, gear up. Sometimes he flew his own Navion in formation with a test pilot flying the Learstar, giving him instructions on what to do. There had been a little resistance to Vance's being there at first, but Lear had quickly ended that by announcing that whatever Shannon wanted he would get. By the end of the first day, everyone was cooperating.

On the following Monday, Vance went into Lear's office with a memo and a couple of sketches. Lear was noted for not wishing to read any more than he had to. "Tell me what you said, Vance. I don't have the time to wade through long reports."

"OK Bill, a question for you. Did you ever run the prop spinners through a wind tunnel test?"

"No, we did the earlier ones. They were sort of snub-nosed and we figured these would be even lower drag."

"Well, here's what I want to try. It won't cost much, and your guys can probably do it in a day. First of all, let's pull off the prop spinners entirely. Leave a bare hub, for tests anyway. Then I want you to have about sixty of these made. We'll fasten thirty of them to the wing on each side, where I say they should go."

He handed Lear a little drawing of a small airfoil, about two inches high, with a plate on the bottom that could be riveted to the wing. There was a little hole at the top of each airfoil.

"What the hell are they? They look like little turbine blades."

"They are vortex generators, Bill. I think you are getting a flow over the engine cowling that moves out onto the wing, and creates a lot of drag. It also causes the ultra-sharp stall. I think if we put these in the right spots, we can smooth out that airflow, pick up the airspeed, and smooth out the stall."

"What's this little hole for?"

"We can tie a cotton tuft there and see how the airflow behaves. Just like using smoke in a wind tunnel."

Lear looked doubtful, but he carried the drawing out to the machine shop himself. They told him they'd have sixty made by the next morning.

In the meantime, Vance had a ladder thrown up to the wing. He crawled out and, using a drawing he had created, marked the exact spot for each airfoil on the wing surface.

"Bill, we can check this in a wind tunnel later if you want, and maybe improve its efficiency. I'm always leery about wind tunnel results on very small surfaces, though. Sometimes an empirical approach is best. We'll put tufts on these and take some film when we fly it—could give us some more ideas."

It took longer to install the vortex generators than Vance had estimated, and it was not until Friday that he and Lear suited up once again for a flight in the emerald Learstar. Carr had two assistants standing in the rear, equipped with motion picture cameras to film the cotton tufts attached to the vortex generators.

This time Lear did not relinquish the controls to Vance at any point. Lear took the Learstar up quickly to 6,000 feet and put it in a speed run that saw the airplane reach 265 mph, five better than required.

"Damn, that's amazing, Vance. Do you think we can squeeze any more out of her?"

"Maybe. We'll look at the film and see if we should move the vortex generators around a bit, or add a few to the layout. Might put some right on the cowling itself, but we'll see. Why don't you see how she stalls now?"

Lear was a careful pilot. He did two ninety-degree clearing turns, racking the Learstar up on its wing to be sure there was no one in the area, then did a series of stalls, gear up and gear down. The airplane entered the stall just as before, but instead of the sudden snap, it just shuddered and fell nose-first forward until airspeed had built up.

"Stalling like a Convair 240 now, just easy-greasy."

"You really did it, Vance. No wonder they call you Mr. Fix-It."

"Bill, this was just a cut-and-try setup. We can improve this a lot with some wind tunnel time, or if you don't want to pay for that, just let me play with moving the vortex generators around, and we'll see if we can't squeeze another five or ten miles an hour out of it. You've got plenty of power there, and if you up your cruise speed a bit, it will do wonders for your range."

"Sure, Vance, you do what you want—we'll experiment as long as you wish—but the twenty planes for South America are going to get the fix just like this. I can't wait to improve on it."

At a celebratory party that night Lear called his engineers together and told them they were going to do a massive retrofit. "We are going to fit these things to every Learstar in the field, at no cost to the owners. And every new Learstar will get them from the start. Shannon here calls them vortex generators, but from now on they are Learspeed generators, and don't you forget it."

Before the party broke up, Lear called Shannon into his private office, where he poured three fingers of Jim Beam into crystal tumblers. "Vance, we've had our problems in the past, and I apologize for those. You gave me a good shot, and I thought maybe someday

I'd get a chance to pay you back. All that is just water over the dam. You've made a hell of a difference here, and I want you to go on retainer for me, four thousand a month for a maximum of ten hours a week. More than that, and I'll bump the ante. What do you say?"

"That's great; I'll be pleased to sign a contract for that. Maybe you could find some test work for my boys, too."

"Sure I can do that; be glad to have them. But we don't need a contract, just a handshake. And do you have any other ideas? I've been thinking about maybe buying up some Catalinas, fitting them with four engines, for the really wealthy sportsman."

"Bill, I do have an idea, but it's proprietary with me and my boys. I'll show it to you, but we'd have to have a majority interest."

"Well, maybe we can work something like that out. What have you got?"

Vance reached into his battered old leather briefcase and brought out a portfolio of drawings of the Shannon Jet. "I think this is a sure thing, Bill, but it will take a lot of capital to develop. The idea is to create a small jet transport for executives to use to really make better use of their time."

Lear looked at the drawings and said, "Executives, hell. This is an airplane that I'll have people like Sinatra and Elizabeth Taylor lining up to buy! It will be expensive—we can't do it overnight—but we'll do it, by God!"

March 15, 1954, Wright-Patterson Air Force Base, Ohio

LIFE WAS SWEET and getting sweeter for Hans von Ohain. No longer just a five-thousand-dollar-per-year contract employee, he was a U.S. civil servant, eligible for promotions and pay raises. He had brought his parents and his brother over from Germany, and they were adjusting as well as he had to life in Ohio. Since 1949, Hans had been a legal immigrant, and he was soon going to apply for citizenship. Best of all, he was married to a beautiful girl, Hanny Shukat, and they had three children—Steven, child from Hanny's previous marriage, and two of their own, Chris and Cathy.

In company with all this domestic bliss, Hans's work was increasingly challenging, as the Air Force moved from plumbing his knowledge about jet engines to applying his abilities to new and ever more exotic projects at the Aeronautical Research Laboratory. Projects on thermo-mechanics, hypersonic speed, and even an electro-fluid dynamic generator passed his desk, and he could participate as he wished. He had fifteen scientists working for him, something he never would have believed possible when he left Germany.

He was especially proud of the electro-fluid dynamic generator and knew that his guest today, Anselm Franz, would be helpful with a problem he was having. Von Ohain fussed around the office, polishing the chair that Franz would sit in with his handkerchief and arranging and rearranging his desk to look neat yet still busy.

Franz had always been more daring than he. During the war, Franz had brought the Junkers Jumo 004 engine from nothing to mass production with daring innovations. Then, in 1951, he left contract work with the Air Force for a position at Avco Lycoming, where he was now developing gas turbines for ground equipment and helicopters. Von Ohain was happy that Franz, brilliant man and always pleasant, was doing so well.

There was a knock at the door, and von Ohain literally ran to admit Franz. They talked first of their families, then of their old friends in Germany, and finally of the reason for Franz's visit, taking care to speak only in English.

Franz said, "I wish you would think about joining us at Avco, Hans. We need you. There are certain fluid flow problems with the turbines that I have not been able to solve, nor have any of my people. I know how you work: you visualize the problem; you see the currents and the eddies."

Von Ohain jested, "You must be thinking of Kármán; that is his specialty."

Franz laughed and said, "Yes, he could do it as well. But you are the man for Avco. What do you think? I don't have to tell you that commercial companies are much more generous with their salaries than the government."

"Dr. Franz, my friend, I'll gladly try to help you, but from here.

Let me show you what they have asked me to work on, and I think you will see why I couldn't leave."

The two men spent more than an hour immersed in the reports and documents on von Ohain's desk. Occasionally von Ohain would pick up the phone and ask someone to come in to explain a particular point. Franz's remarks were confined for the most part to, "Fascinating," with an occasional *"ach du lieber"* slipping out.

At last Franz leaned back in his chair and said, "I hate to say it, but I understand why you want to stay. This is like an engineering toy store for you!" He glanced at his watch, saying, "I'm sorry, but I have to go. It has been wonderful seeing you."

Visibly distressed, von Ohain said, "Are you not going to come home to dinner with me? Hanni will be so disappointed."

"No, but before I leave, I have a compliment to pay you. From Sir Frank Whittle."

Perplexed but smiling, von Ohain stood there, waiting.

"Frank was knighted, as you know. Now his primary work is advising the Shell Group. It is not very much to his liking; he'd rather be doing what you are doing, or what I am doing. But when I saw him in London earlier this year, he inquired about you. When he learned that I would probably see you in the next few months he said . . ."

Franz stopped to pull a folded piece of paper from his pocket. Smiling, he said, "I wrote this down to be sure I say it exactly as he said it." He looked at it for a moment, then declaimed, "Sir Frank said, 'Dr. Franz, just as you and I were, Dr. von Ohain was a true pioneer in jet engines. But I have been following his work in the United States, and I believe he has gone beyond all of us. Like a good jet engine, he has grown in strength, and I salute him for it.'"

Von Ohain was speechless, his eyes tearing. Franz bowed, saying, "You deserve that, Hans! And I agree with Sir Frank."

Franz pressed the paper into von Ohain's left hand, shook his right hand, and quickly left the room. Von Ohain reread the message and went back to his desk, pleased beyond measure and wondering how he could tell Hanni about it without appearing boastful. Forty minutes later he was still sitting there, Whittle's paper in his hand, staring out the window, thinking of the days back in the Heinkel plant, working on the first engine.

The phone rang, jarring him out of his reverie.

"This is Sergeant Lutz at the Main Gate, Dr. von Ohain. You have another visitor here, and he's driving the funniest little car I've ever seen. He says his name is Max Hahn and that he is an old friend. Can I send him in to see you?"

"Of course. Thank you, Sergeant Lutz. Will you give him directions, please?"

"If he'll let me ride in his funny car, I'll ride over with him in person, sir."

Von Ohain was thinking how odd that he should see both Franz and Hahn on the same day when the door sprang open and in walked Fritz Obermyer.

"Hello, Hans. Sorry about using Max's name, but I wasn't sure that you would see me."

"Herr Obermyer—"

"Fritz, please, Hans, we are in America, after all. Come with me; I want to show you the Volkswagen. Once you see it you'll reconsider my idea about a dealership."

Numb with a sickening combination of annoyance and fear, von Ohain allowed Obermyer to lead him down the highly polished brown asphalt tile hallway to the entrance door. Right in front in a clearly marked "No Parking or Stopping" zone sat a black Volkswagen.

"Sergeant Lutz is standing by the car, just so no one will complain about where we parked it."

Obermyer opened the door to the black Volkswagen and motioned for von Ohain to get in. He ran around to the other side and quickly sat beside him, "Go ahead; start it up."

"No, no, I don't want to drive it. I have enough trouble with my car."

It was true; von Ohain was always preoccupied with his engineering challenges as he drove, and he had more than his share of minor accidents.

"Hans, we are going to sell more than six thousand Volkswagens in the United States this year. Next year, we are planning on selling five times that number. You really must think about taking the Dayton dealership."

"Why don't you take it, Fritz? You would be a fine car salesman; you know all about it."

"I cannot. I've been given a dealership in Los Angeles! I'm on my way there now, driving across country in this wonderful car."

The two men climbed out of the car and von Ohain extended his hand. "I wish you the best of luck. But it's out of the question for me. I hope you sell a million cars someday."

"We'll sell many more than a million, and there will be a day when you'll say, 'If only I had listened to my old friend Fritz!' But now, can we go back in your office and talk?"

Von Ohain flushed with annoyance. He had already wasted too much time with this man. "I've an appointment in a few minutes. Can we talk here?"

"No, the office would be better. Sergeant Lutz, will you watch over the car for a few minutes?" He threw him the keys, saying, "Take it for a short spin, and tell me how you like it."

Once settled in von Ohain's office, Obermyer came right to the point. "Hans, you are a fool if you do not take my offer. All I want in return is the mention of your name at automobile shows. And perhaps, other bits of information."

Von Ohain stood up. "You want me to be a spy for you? You want me to betray the United States for a miserable car dealership? You must be crazy."

"No, I'm not crazy, Dr. von Ohain. You might be if you don't listen to me. You have a nice position here; I did a little investigation; you have a nice home and family. You'd like to keep all that, I'm sure."

Von Ohain gripped the edge of the desk. "Are you threatening me?"

"Yes, I am. Not with bodily harm, but there are certain stories that I can provide that would be uncomfortable for you, to say the least. For example, you will recall that we manufactured Heinkel He 162s, the *Volksjaeger*, at Nordhausen, using slave labor."

Sputtering, von Ohain said, "I had nothing to do with that! You know that I did not."

"I know it and you know it, but who can say who might testify otherwise? Your whole career here could go up in smoke."

"Just like the people that worked at Nordhausen, eh? Get out of here, Herr Obermyer, and never come back. Do whatever you wish, tell whoever you wish, I will never work with you on anything."

Obermyer stood up saying only, "You'll regret this, Dr. von Ohain."

Von Ohain slumped at his desk for almost fifteen minutes, regaining his composure. Then he picked up the phone and asked for an appointment with the judge advocate general. He had to get this conversation on-the-record, no matter what the consequences.

May 1, 1954, Seattle, Washington

THE OLYMPIC HOTEL was a far cry from the Windsor, and Vance was as grateful to Boeing for putting him up there as he had been surprised by George Schairer's call the previous Tuesday morning. Schairer's haggard voice had shocked Shannon—he was sure that trouble had surfaced with Madeline again.

"Vance, can you come to Seattle on short notice?"

"Sure, George, but when? Is it the Comet thing?"

A Comet 1, G-ALYP, had taken off from the airport at Rome at 9:31 on January 10 and only minutes later rained down in pieces into the sea near the island of Elba. Thirty-five people had died, and the Comet fleet was grounded again.

The wreckage was more than six-hundred-feet down, and before it was recovered, de Havilland had made more than sixty precautionary modifications that convinced the British government to reinstate it in service. Then on April 8, another Comet, also taking off from Rome, exploded in the air, coming down into the sea near Naples.

"Yes, and we have to keep this confidential. Try to get in late Friday night, and go right to the Olympic Hotel. I'll have a suite for you there. And I'll come see you on Saturday morning. Sorry about the secrecy, but I guess you understand."

"What I don't understand is why you are calling on me?"

"Vance, you know more about the Comet than any other American, and you have Ron Davies's implicit trust. He called me and said he was having a complete package of the latest data couriered to me, and he specified that you be on the team. And I want you, as well. The package will be here by the twenty-ninth at the latest."

Shannon had hung up, pleased and furious at the same time. The work at Lear was at the point where he could leave it for a week or two, and he was glad to have more work. It upset him, though, that Boeing felt it had to keep him out of sight from the public. As he thought about it, his indignation had grown, and he almost called Schairer back and refused to come. But the feeling passed, and he realized that this was, maybe, a better way back into the business than working with Lear.

Schairer came in, looking positively delighted to see Vance again; he introduced two engineers he'd brought along, Henry Myers and Ray McAteer. Both men professed their admiration for Vance's previous work on the Comet, and it was clear from their remarks that they had studied it carefully.

The suite had a large coffee table, and they quickly spread out the documents that Davies had sent over. The wreckage of the Comet that crashed near Elba had been dredged up from six hundred feet of water, and by April 15 the engines, wing center section, and many parts of the splintered fuselage had been flown to Great Britain to the de Havilland plant. A rush pressurization test had been repeated on the entire cabin of a complete Comet, and after a total of about three thousand simulated flights, the cabin structure failed—at the corner of a cabin window.

"George, how many flights did this plane have on it?"

"Just under thirteen hundred. The last one to crash had only about nine hundred. Apparently there's a wide band where the failure can occur. Look, Davies and his crew have exactly the same material you have. They want us, with you leading, to evaluate the material and come up with a recommendation. They'll compare that to their own findings, and decide what they have to do."

"How long have we got?"

"Ten days, George, and it's absolutely critical for Boeing."

"How so?"

"We are going to roll out the Dash 80, our new jet transport, on May 14, and we don't want to have it on the same day that newspapers are saying that jet airliners are inherently dangerous. If you or if de Havilland comes up with something we haven't considered, we need to be prepared. We can't delay the rollout. Too many people are invited—including you."

Vance found that both McAteer and Myers were very able, and they had teams of engineers at their disposal. The three men worked twelve hours a day for six days, checking figures but, more important, checking the rationale of the de Havilland investigators.

At the end of the week, Vance called Schairer.

"George, there's no question about it; the Comet's structure is susceptible to fatigue cracks that propagate far more rapidly than anyone could have predicted. Every Comet is an accident waiting to happen. They have to keep them grounded, no matter what the cost is. I cannot see how they can come up with an engineering Band-Aid that will ever permit them to fly passengers. They might do enough patchwork to convert them to military use, but that would be it."

"You are saying that they need to do a complete redesign of the fuselage?"

"Absolutely, and doing that will force a major redesign of the wings and tail as well."

There was silence, and Vance asked, "How does this square with de Havilland's findings?"

"I'm glad to say that you and Davies are on the same frequency. They will have to scrap the Comets they've made and go back to the drawing board. I just hope to God that we don't run into something like this with the Dash 80."

Vance was packed and ready to go when the desk clerk called and said a Boeing car was waiting, ready to take him out to the airport. He checked out of the hotel and was surprised to find Schairer sitting in the back of the big Cadillac limousine.

"Thanks for coming up on short notice, Vance. I just got a phone call from Bill Lear telling me that I had to get you back down to Santa Monica; I guess he needs you there."

"Bill's a funny guy, but he's smart."

"Well, we were not very smart here, Vance, when we let you go. We have some tough projects coming up, and we want you to come back on contract with us. Hell, we'd prefer you to come up and work for us, but I know you've got other irons in the fire. Anyway, come on up on July 15; bring Jill and your sons. We're going to do the first flight of the Dash 80, and you ought to be a witness."

"We'll do it—and thanks, George, one more time."

The last time he had flown from Seattle to Los Angeles, Vance's heart had been heavy with Madeline's betrayal and his own sense of failure. The flight this time was much less stressful.

July 15, 1954, Seattle, Washington

HARRY AND TOM had wanted to stay at the Windsor, for old time's sake, but decency and common sense prevailed, and Vance put everybody up at the Olympic. Everyone had come up to Seattle, including Anna, doing better this past year, and V.R., doing well as always. More than anything else, everyone was pleased by Vance's evident delight at having Boeing as a client once more.

Now they were all in the VIP stands that Boeing had put up at Boeing Field as the beautiful 367-80 was towed out of its hangar, gleaming in the usual Boeing copper brown and cream yellow colors. The very top Boeing brass—Bill Allen, Ed Wells, George Schairer, and the various members of Boeing's board—were seated in the row in front of them, and Schairer had been thoughtful enough to have Vance's family positioned immediately behind him, so that they could talk. There would be some ceremonies, a few short speeches, as the Dash 80 was preparing for its scheduled 2:15 PM takeoff, but the two men had a lot of catching up to do.

Schairer moved his chair around and said, "Did you ever think you'd see the day when there would be a Boeing jet transport, Vance?"

"I knew there would be—I was just doubtful about me being here to see it."

"That's all in the past, and we'll say no more about it." He paused and looked around, saying, "Nice crowd."

Vance nodded and said "Too bad that Sir Frank couldn't come, nor Hans von Ohain. They really should be here."

"You're right it's a shame. Jet aviation has grown so much that we tend to lose contact with the pioneers. What a world of difference there is between now and when those two geniuses started out!" Schairer looked sober and said, "There's a lot of other people who ought to be here, too, Vance, including some of the old-timers."

Shannon nodded. He knew Schairer was referring to the people who had lost their lives testing airplanes in the past.

Tex Johnston suddenly appeared and walked directly over to Bill Allen, Boeing's chairman. Vance could not hear what was said, but it was evident that Allen was worried and Johnston was trying to reassure him.

"Bill's worried. He's got sixteen million dollar's worth of Boeing's future riding on this flight."

Tex and Dix Loesh climbed aboard the Dash 80, as everyone called it, and soon the beautiful airplane was moving down toward the end of the runway. Vance felt Jill's hand creep into his. He glanced at his sons, both staring raptly at the airplane. Anna and Nancy were fussing over V.R., ignoring the moment.

There was a roar and a blast of black smoke as Johnston first gave the Dash 80 full throttle, then released the brakes. The aircraft leaped forward and twenty-one hundred feet later was airborne. The crowd was on its feet, some yelling, some crying, a few, especially Bill Allen, probably praying.

The Dash 80, followed by a company chase plane, a leased T-33, climbed away toward Mount Rainier and the crowd began to thin out. Schairer was occupied with his company people, but he said, "Stick around, Vance. Tex is going to fly about an hour and a half, if all goes well, then come back and land. It will be worth waiting for."

Vance took his family over to the shade of a hangar. After an hour of waiting, V.R. was crying and Nancy asked if Tom could take her back to the hotel. Anna and Jill decided to go along, so Harry left as well. Vance said he'd get a ride or a cab back.

Schairer came over to say good-bye to them and when they were gone turned and asked, "Well, Vance, what are you going to do next?"

"I'm sixty, you know, George, probably going to have to be put away in some home for old pilots. Actually, I'm thinking about taking Jill on a cruise, maybe turn the business mostly over to the boys."

"That's a little hard for me to believe, Vance. I understand you and Bill Lear are working on a jet of your own."

"What an industry! Nobody can keep a secret. Yeah, we're playing with an idea for an executive jet. It's hard to figure out what the market will be, but Bill's intrigued, and he's a guy who can make things happen. But the truth is, I'm going to be spending a lot of time over at Lockheed for the next couple of years. Kelly Johnson has some projects cooking there that are just unbelievable. And . . ."—a little ruefully,—"they are good at keeping them secret, God bless them, a lot better than I am."

"Well, keep a little time on your clock for us; we've got a few things in the mill as well."

They heard the roar of four jet engines coming, and they turned to watch Tex Johnston make a flawless approach and landing in the Dash 80. He taxied in, and Bill Allen, visibly relieved, was the first man to greet Tex when he bounded out of the Dash 80's entrance.

"Bill, you've got yourself a good airplane. That sixteen million was well spent."

Vance Shannon watched Bill Allen blossom as the weight soared from his shoulders. He seemed to grow an inch in height as he stood there, slapping big Tex Johnston on the back.

Then Vance felt Schairer's elbow prodding him.

"It's a winner; I can tell by the smile on Johnston's face. He never kids around."

Shannon nodded, smiling as everyone else was doing. He walked around the big Dash 80, not so pristine now, a little oil visible on the engine cowlings, creaking as it cooled. It was one magnificent machine. He thought about Harry's briefing back at Wright Field, when he had shown the drawing of the first jet, the Heinkel 178. This was where that little single-engine airplane, a test vehicle, pure and simple, had led. Jet aviation had progressed rapidly, despite the turbulent world into which it had been born. All over the world men and women had advanced the science despite the ravages of war, the uncertainty of peace, and the new and blinding threat of nuclear combat. No matter what was happening, wherever there were pilots and engineers, new and better jet planes emerged, each one seeking to stretch the bounds of human endeavor. Sadly, so far the greatest advances had come in military weapons.

Shannon walked on the hot Boeing tarmac a distance away from the gleaming transport and surveyed it at a distance. It was clearly a turning point, and he wondered where the Dash 80 would lead in the next phase of the jet age.